THE GENTLEMAN SHOPKEEPER

*To my oldest chum MOREEN
with love from the author!*
    D.V. Haines
    18 Sept 2017

(Happy birthday!)

THE GENTLEMAN SHOPKEEPER

A mystery novel

D. V. HAINES

Copyright © 2017 D.V. Haines

The moral right of the author has been asserted.

Apart from any fair dealing for the purposes of research or private study, or criticism or review, as permitted under the Copyright, Designs and Patents Act 1988, this publication may only be reproduced, stored or transmitted, in any form or by any means, with the prior permission in writing of the publishers, or in the case of reprographic reproduction in accordance with the terms of licences issued by the Copyright Licensing Agency. Enquiries concerning reproduction outside those terms should be sent to the publishers.

This is a work of fiction. Names, characters, businesses, places, events and incidents are either the products of the author's imagination or used in a fictitious manner. Any resemblance to actual persons, living or dead, or actual events is purely coincidental.

Matador
9 Priory Business Park,
Wistow Road, Kibworth Beauchamp,
Leicestershire. LE8 0RX
Tel: 0116 279 2299
Email: books@troubador.co.uk
Web: www.troubador.co.uk/matador
Twitter: @matadorbooks

ISBN 978 1788036 733

British Library Cataloguing in Publication Data.
A catalogue record for this book is available from the British Library.

Printed and bound by CPI Group (UK) Ltd, Croydon, CR0 4YY
Typeset in 11pt Adobe Garamond Pro by Troubador Publishing Ltd, Leicester, UK

Front-cover design: Pauline Crouch

Matador is an imprint of Troubador Publishing Ltd

MIX
Paper from
responsible sources
FSC   FSC® C013604

To Keith Sykes
who would have so relished performing
this character in audio.

CONTENTS

CHAPTER	PAGE
1. Hitherto Unaccused	1
2. In the Hottest of Hot Water	32
3. Curiouser and Curiouser	57
4. More Little Surprises	89
5. Hoping to Hoodwink Miss Holland	118
6. Miss Holland Turns Detective	139
7. Oh Dear, is She Starting to Suspect Me?	160
8. Left in the Lurch	177
9. A Further Spot of Bother	195
10. Just a Little Local Difficulty	212
11. Closing Ranks	252

THE GENTLEMAN SHOPKEEPER

ONE

Hitherto Unaccused

I

No gentleman talks about his private life, but I must break this rule.

How else can I tell you about being accused of killing a wheel-clamper?

I shall take you through the events in the same order as they happened. I shall stick the same facts under your nose which fate stuck under mine.

Would you have been able to cope with these rather mysterious events better than I?

We shall see. Be on your mettle from this moment on – intellectually, I mean. But this I need to reveal in advance. I am no intellectual myself. I was quite the wrong sort of person for these experiences.

And not only that.

I am probably the wrong person for describing them. Certain ladies in my story will complain that I'm a man of limited perception. They are probably right. But who else is there?

Do I live in the modern age? Of course I do. It's simply that I can't accept computers and things of that sort. I just smile and nod when I hear of 'facebook' or 'twitter' or, for that matter, Mr Microsoft and Mr Google.

Am I, therefore, just an old buffer? Far from it. I only pretend to be an old buffer. I do so because I have always been fascinated by old buffers. From my earliest youth, I sort of collected them. I vary the act, but my favourite is my old-colonel act. It is still my ambition, when I reach retirement, to become a champion among old English buffers.

My other reason for the act, of course, is that it amuses my young and pretty wife. She gets a bit exasperated with it from time to time, but our two little girls are still my best audience. Nevertheless, under the surface, I am still very much fly to what 's what. You can't start and run a shop like mine if you're a complete idiot.

So please don't regard me as a silly ass on a sticky wicket. A lot of people have made that mistake. May I quote my old headmaster? Of Beagley College, no less?

"For all we know," he wrote on the school-leaver report, "this boy is gifted with an exceptional intelligence. We cannot be altogether sure. Even if he has a modicum of brilliance, we can only say that he appears to be unable to make use of it. This is perhaps due to a failure to concentrate. He is an enthusiastic cricketer, for example, but is never able to connect the bat with the ball. Let us hope this does not become a metaphor in coping with his future problems. Although the possibility cannot be entirely ruled out, he does not appear to be innately stupid."

There you have it. Not a total condemnation.

Nowadays, I suppose, a headmaster wouldn't be allowed to write like that. I'm not complaining, but even the old Buzzard of Beagley (as we used to call him) got one thing wrong. He had not remembered that I once made three runs. Almost a boundary. (Startled applause but applause.)

More than just a lucky hit, I would say. Certain people reading this account of mine, may I just add, need to keep this in mind.

II

I say again, no gentleman talks about his private life.
I am quoting my nice old father. He was a real colonel (in the Royal Army Ordnance Corps) and in no way an old buffer. Because of being at Beagley, I never saw much of him. But he leaves me reluctant to tell you about my Saturday breakfast.

Yet everything – everything! – stems from that banal domestic moment when, having finished, I got up from the kitchen-table (to go to work).

"Say goodbye to the kids for me," I said, neither one of our two little girls being at the table with us. "Why haven't they come down?"

"Now don't rush off," said my young and pretty wife. "You've forgotten, haven't you? Me and the other mums are taking all the kids to the zoo. Coach goes at half-past eight."

"Madam," I said, "I am the one forking out for this binge. Of course I've not forgotten. I'm merely asking why the kids are still upstairs."

"Because they're getting ready. We have to be outside the church at quarter past. Please be helpful. Make the beds and tidy up while we get ready – then come and see us go. Is that really too much to ask?"

"No, madam, it is not. But I have a business to run. I can't hang around making beds. I need to nab a good place to park before everyone else beats me to it. I, madam, am a very wily dog."

"Then park in the nice new multi-storey. Plenty of spaces there – even on a Saturday. You need to try it."

"Madam, I will have nothing to do with that foul monstrosity."

"But darling, it's nice and near the shop."

"Expediency, madam, is no excuse for bad taste. It has ruined the entire character of the town-centre. Furthermore, the charges are exorbitant. I can park in Willow Tree Lane for nothing."

"But that's much further away from the shop. Just for once,

darling, do as I suggest. It's only for this one Saturday. Be a nice man. Stop being so nasty. Stay and see us off."

"Time, madam, is already running out. I'll be in hot water if I'm late."

"But darling, you're the boss. Put your foot down. You can be as late as you like."

"Try telling that to Miss Holland," I said, and with feeling. "Detain me not," and I had to hurry out from the cottage to the garage after only the quickest of kisses.

Hardly had I driven a few yards down our little driveway when Stephanie – the young and pretty wife – came dashing out of the cottage.

"You silly old fool," she boisterously yelled, "you've forgotten your new brief-case."

Old? I had only just turned forty-seven.

She was displaying it ceremoniously, but there was no roll of drums or any other signal to commemorate this moment. To commemorate it, I mean, as a moment for me to curse for ever.

I jumped out of my smart and much-loved Honda Civic. I stuffed the fatal brief-case behind my driver-seat, then dragged open our front-garden gate and left it for Stephanie to shut after I had gone.

She blew a raspberry after I had gone. I know she did. It was a habit of hers. But do not ponder the inner meaning of this form of farewell. She was in no way to blame for any of the troubles soon to beset me. Stephanie was no plotter. Exclude her from the evidence you are keenly gathering. As for me, I loved my young and pretty wife. I loved our two girls. I loved the village where we lived – Kind Maiden Green. You won't find a sweeter name or place in all England. I also loved Dackley, the historic country-town where I had my shop. More about the shop later (which I also loved).

Am I going to burden you with the exact geography of this paradise? I am not. A vague grasp of it is all you'll need. Dackley is just six miles from Kind Maiden Green. Always a nice journey in fair weather – and as soothing to the heart as Stephanie's smile.

The town-river was sparkling with charm as I drove alongside it on the esplanade road. Those municipal river-gardens are always beautiful, but were particularly so on that Saturday morning. Early April it was, fresh and sunny. Lots of town daffodils.

"Ha," said I to myself, checking my watch. (The exclamation 'ha' is always an exclamation of triumph when it comes from my particular lips.)

As usual, it had only taken thirteen minutes to get into town. Traffic was still light at just eight o'clock; it would stiffen up by half-past. I had bags of time, both to park and to have a nice healthy walk (along by the town-river) to my shop. Turning right into Mill Street, I only had to turn left – off Mill Street – to be in Willow Tree Lane.

A fateful location if ever there was one. But was it in any way sinister at the time? Certainly not. It has always been an attractive but inconspicuous location. To me – and to other local businessmen in the know – it was safe and above all free from the Council's growing mania for parking restrictions.

But you couldn't park in Willow Tree Lane itself. This is an important point. Remember it. You had to drive down the lane – past back-garden walls on your right and a plank-fence on your left. A high fence. You would then come to a time-honoured gap in this high fence. Once through this gap, you would be on waste-ground, the former site of a demolished brewery. Plenty of hard standing.

"Ha," I said again, after pulling up in much my usual spot. "Beaten them all to it!"

I took it to be a triumph, you see, in being the very first motorist to park there on that particular morning. This was a rare accomplishment. Especially for a Saturday.

All cock-a-hoop, I got out and locked up. Off I went for my brisk walk along the river – along the esplanade with all those daffodils. Hat and suit only. (Bowler-hat.) No top-coat.

Have you guessed what I had forgotten? Of course you have. I remembered it myself only a little way into my brisk and healthy walk.

I very nearly didn't bother to go back to my much-loved Honda Civic. Crime in those days had not yet affected Dackley as badly as elsewhere. I would have had no great worries about the brief-case. I was sure I could leave it where it was – behind the driver-seat. But I was also remembering Miss Holland's figures. They were in a folder inside the wretched brief-case. Miss Holland's figures, let me tell you, were not figures to be ignored. Thinking I might be questioned about them at the shop, I made the decision. I went back. I re-crossed the esplanade road (traffic still not stiffening all that much) and walked back down Willow Tree Lane.

Once through the gap in the fence, I saw that no other vehicles had yet been parked on the waste-ground.

Except for a certain yellow van.

"Where on earth," I said to myself, "has that sprung from? What's going on?"

This yellow van bore no mark of its trade and was disgustingly dirty all over. It was parked close to my Honda Civic. My much loved Honda Civic. An oafish-looking young man was on his knees and attaching a wheel-clamp to one of my sacred wheels.

Strange as you may think it today, I had never before seen a wheel-clamp. I had certainly never heard of anyone in Dackley falling victim to it. The fellow rose as I approached.

"Excuse me," I politely said, "but would you very much mind telling me what's going on? What have you been doing to my motor-car?"

The fellow replied in a coarse but quite matter-of-fact sort of way, as if what he had done was a perfectly natural act.

"You have parked here illegal, mate. You has to pay me a release-fee. Thirty pound for release here and now. But that's only whiles I'm on duty. Once I'm gorn, it's fifty pound for a call-out. That's me leaflet under yer wiper. You've been lucky. I could have been gorn. Pay me now and I'll release yer. Thirty pound."

"But I've been parking here for years!"

"Not any more you can't. You needs to park somewheres proper – like in the multi-storey."

"Look here," I said, in all sincerity, "you seem to be a nice enough chap. Not nearly so oafish as I first thought. Tell me, please. Why do I appear to be the only one to know of this unexpected prohibition?"

He looked puzzled. "I don't know, mate. I only know I has to do as I'm bloody told."

In no little bewilderment myself, I said: "This entire spot would normally start to fill up by now. Normally, by quarter to nine, it will be choc-a-bloc."

The man's face cleared and he looked well-pleased. "Christ, is that a fact? Thanks for the tip, mate. I reckon I'll 'ang around."

He peered in a short-sighted fashion at the vegetation surrounding the site. "I could hide myself up in them bushes, couldn't I?"

"I suppose you could, yes. But look here, old chap. Are you genuinely working-class?"

He looked puzzled again. He frowned and said: "What if I bloody am? It makes no bloody difference. What's it to be? Thirty pound now or fifty if you calls me out."

"As a genuinely working-class man," I tried telling him, "you are suffering as much as we all are from the Recession. Mrs Thatcher is doing her very best to get us all through it. Thirty pounds is too excessive in these difficult times. I don't even have that much on me."

"I can't do no concessions. Got a cheque book on yer? Or in the car?"

"I have, yes."

"Then, mister, you write me a cheque. Make it out to me

7

personal. Leo Rivinni. That's me name. Thirty quid. Got a bank-card? I won't accept no cheque without no guarantee-card."

I must now tell you something very frankly. In my life to this point, I had never been threatened by anyone from what my mother used to call the lower orders. Perhaps I had been lucky. But I had grown up leaning more towards my idealistic father. He was much older than my mother and had long been dead and gone by this date. He used to say: "Such people, old son, are the salt of the earth. They are the real people. It's they who have won us two world wars."

I loved my father and mother, but their discussions about The Workers had often become horribly heated. Could this have left me with an inner conflict? Something which tended to make me indecisive?

Whether due to that or not, I was in two minds about this fellow Rivinni. Although he was an odd mixture of the utter dolt and what my mother called a sharp pleb – even having a bank account – he did not seem physically threatening. I had no fear of him. He, in fact, was the one looking apprehensive. Furtively nervous, perhaps, might best sum him up. It was because of this that I said: "Don't worry, old sport. Do please excuse me a moment."

I unlocked my driver-door. Leaving it wide open, I picked up the brief-case from behind the seat and slid into position at the wheel. For a second, I misconstrued the clamp. Thought I could drive off when Rivinni wasn't looking. With the brief-case on my lap, all I could do next was to sit there feeling helpless. How on earth could I now extricate myself from this situation? Playing for time, I opened the brief-case. Began groping in it. All I had was a determination to pay nothing. Apart from being hard up (£30 was a lot of money in those days,) I was beginning to think I could be dealing with a fraudster.

Looking more relaxed, Rivinni leaned his backside against the wing of my Honda Civic and began rolling himself a cigarette.

"Just make it out to me personal," he happily repeated; and he loudly spelt out his surname, hardly bothering to see what I was doing. "And it's still thirty quid," he added.

He must have assumed I was groping in the brief-case for my cheque-book and bank-card. He was wrong. My bank-card was in my wallet in the inside-pocket of my jacket. With it was just one blank cheque for real emergencies. My cheque-book was locked away in my bureau at home.

Suddenly, I decided. I would get out of the Honda and appeal more firmly to his roots – as my nice old father would have done. But I had attended a 'posh' boarding-school, had I not? It had its ugly quota of 'posh' boys. They would kick you in the you-know-where if you displeased them. Despite my father's faith in the salt of the earth, I felt a need to be ready for a similar form of attack. (Mother's advice: "Don't always believe Daddy, dear.") I therefore re-buckled the brief-case. Next, I gently unlocked and detached the lock-bar.

May I dwell for just a moment on this second possession of mine? It was destined to become rather significant.

"Sweetie-pie," Stephanie had said, some three years before, "all this talk of England becoming a European republic will mean more foreigners. That will mean even more crime. You don't want our Honda stolen, do you? Go and buy a good strong lock-bar. Fix it to the steering-wheel every time after you park."

Modern motorists might not know, but a lock-bar in those days was no light-weight thief-deterrent. Mine was neatly designed for hooking around one of the floor-pedals (in conjunction with the steering-wheel rim); as an oaf-deterrent, it could come in very handy I now imagined. Just a little tap on one side of his knee – enough to fend him off – was all I intended if this Rivinni were to turn nasty.

He didn't notice the lock-bar when I got out of the Honda. Holding it in one hand, I was concealing its long slim length behind my trouser-leg. In my other hand, of course, I was holding my brief-case – and in the necessary covering-position.

"You," I told him, "are among all those who are the backbone of the nation. Without the working-class, two world wars could never have been won. We who have never been deprived of education and opportunity, as you so obviously have, must never forget that."

His face began to contort. It began to resemble in itself the very picture of a clenched fist.

"Be true to your roots," I ended by saying. "The endurance and honesty shown by the British working-class must always be the inspiration for a better world. Do not betray your roots. Remove that contraption from my wheel and I'll gladly shake your hand."

Amazingly, I only felt a slight crackle in my nose as his very real fist shot out and hit me. It didn't seem all that serious a blow. It was enough to make me drop the brief-case and stagger a little. Nothing more.

His other fist was coming at me in the very next split-second. This time I was ready for it. I was able to dodge. I was also able to give the side of his knee a neatly quick little tap. (I hadn't let go of the lock-bar.)

Raising his knee and clutching it with both hands, he let out a howl of pain and began hopping around on his other leg. He almost spun round, perhaps I should say. He then crashed down on the surface of the former dray-yard – granite setts.

And never moved again. Not a twitch.

At first, I didn't realise I'd killed him. I was full of bonhomie towards him. Looking down at him, I said: "Come along, old sport. Let's get that clamp-thing off, shall we?"

I stooped to look at him more closely. It was then that I realised I had a strange talent for diagnosing death. I assure you I am in no way a medical man. But I knew he was dead. In trying to imagine what might have happened – in view of further developments – please don't imagine I was wrong. This fellow was never going to get up and walk away. I can only tell you I knew him to be dead. I tell you this despite the fact that he had no sign of any visible blow to the head – nothing of that sort. He was just lay there on one side with his head slightly twisted. Both eyes open.

May I tell you what really upset me? He had a plug of cotton-wool in one ear. I feebly said: "Touch of ear-ache, old chap?"

No reply, of course. But that one detail made him seem so human and real. It was at this dreadful point that I found my nose to be dripping blood everywhere. I had to back away hastily. It wouldn't be too clever, I quickly realised, to drip my own blood all over him. Also, I realised I needed to stay calm. I was remembering a lovely old aunt of mine – Aunt Bartle.

"To be calm at all times," she used to tell me, "is to be strong at all times."

I was very fond of Aunt Bartle, but (may I say) to be calm and strong is no great advantage if you fail to concentrate. Things don't get done which should be done. But I did at least do one thing well. Fearing that other motorists would soon be coming through that gap in the fence, I snuffled back as much nose-blood as I could and got my driving-gloves on. (Mustn't leave fingerprints.) I was able to remove the clamp with no trouble at all. (Rivinni had left the key in position.) Calmly and strongly, I was able to toss the clamp into the back of his van (the door was wide open) as easily as if it were an old tennis shoe. He had a lot of clamps in there, I noticed. He had obviously expected to have a field-day.

Against all my well-known principles, I decided to make for the multi-storey car-park. My luck, it seemed, was in. I met not one single motor-car as I drove off up Willow Tree Lane. How amazing, I was thinking, that so much of such dire importance could happen in so short a time!

With my blood-soaked handkerchief still at my nose, I was on the drive-in to the multi-storey within minutes. I could hardly believe it. Just four minutes after half-past eight! Thinking far more time had passed, I quite thought my watch had stopped.

The loathsome edifice was not automated in those days. You had to buy a ticket from a clerk who sat in a transparent cubicle.

"Why," he jovially said, "if it ain't old Jim! Nice to see yer. Changed yer mind about us, Jim?"

"We all have to move with the times," and I forked out the exorbitant fee without demur.

"Blimey, Jim," he said, staring, "is you 'aving a nose-bleed? It's all darnyer."

"Nothing serious, my good man. Just a silly stumble. And please don't call me Jim. It's not a name I accept. The name is James."

"Sorry, James."

"And I don't accept James either – not from those I regard as family and friends. They call me Jay. You, too, may do so."

Humbly pleased, he said: "I didn't know you was called Jay. I'm sorry, sir. Thank you, Jay. Nice of you to let me in on it. Try dropping a cold key darn yer neck. But on a piece of string. It will stop the bleed."

"And why the string?"

"So as you can pull the key up, sir, and stop it dropping too far darn yer back."

"You've been most helpful," and I drove on up to the topmost (and almost empty) floor.

I was surprised to find myself instinctively making friends with a potential Crown witness. I'd never known I had such criminal depths. But don't misunderstand me. I really do have a soft spot for the working-classes. Never think I mock them. Strange, though, how a servile 'sir' slips out of them from time to time.

I had no need to make use of their key-and-string method. The nose bleed stopped as soon as I had parked. I only had to remove my blood-stained tie and tidy myself up with the kids' moisture-wipes. But I was now beginning to have bad thoughts. What if my victim had a wife and kids himself? And what a nasty shock for anyone coming across his body on such a lovely day! Trying hard to ignore these things, I could only hope his body had been found by now and reported by someone not too easily rattled. Why on earth had I not made use of the van? I should have lugged the body into it, shouldn't I? Quite apart from saving someone from a bad surprise, this could have given me more time to muddy the trail – if you know what I mean. Discovery of the body could have been delayed for many days. Who would have given any immediate attention to a dirty old yellow van?

I was about to get out of the car when, of course, I was horrified by something more.

The brief-case – and my lock-bar! Where were they? Left behind at the scene of the crime, that's where.

"Golly gum-drops," I cried, using one of my young wife's expressions. "I'm done for!"

I remembered letting go of the brief-case but, for the life of me, I couldn't remember when I lost contact with the lock-bar. I could only suppose I had laid it aside before so cleverly attending to the wheel-clamp.

Slowly, I got out of my beloved and faithful Honda Civic. No other motorists were around. The silence of their respectably parked motor-cars was all part of that foul building's total indifference to my fate.

It was at this point that I thought of going to the cops. After all, I hadn't directly killed the chap. But, no matter how you look at it, death is death. I felt guilty. The police-station was only a terribly short distance away from the multi-storey. I looked at my watch. My young and pretty wife, with our two girls, were by now well on their way to the zoo. What if I were to be arrested? How soon would I see them again? How soon, indeed, would it be before I could once more drive my Honda Civic? How innocent it looked!

I was at the point of locking up the innocent Honda Civic and plodding off to my possible doom. But a folded slip of paper caught my eye. It had been tucked under my windscreen-wiper. Rivinni, you may recall, had mentioned it as a leaflet. I had driven away without even noticing it.

I unfolded it and read as follows: "You have parked your vehicle illegally and have therefore been wheel-clamped. You must phone our Depot to agree a time for declamping. The release-fee is £50. Warning: do not try to remove the wheel-clamp yourself. By order, Dackley Wheel-Clamping Services," and it ended with a local phone-number, given in offensively big red figures.

It was the two words 'by order' which aroused my worst instincts.

"By God," I heard myself savagely muttering, "what crust. I'll give them by order," and I shoved the leaflet into my trouser-pocket.

I got back into my Honda and made for the multi-storey exit. Never before had I known myself to be possessed by such coldly determined but total fury.

"I should have smashed his skull to a pulp," I growlingly declared. "I dealt with him too lightly. Far too lightly."

I was heading back to Willow Tree Lane. Emboldened by the cold fury, I was already concocting a subtle plan. My mind was working at incredible speed (another novelty).

The dead body, I reasoned, would by this time have been discovered. The police would now be in busy attendance. I would mingle with any gawpers. At an opportune moment, I would approach a constable who looked the most youthful and inexperienced.

I would say: "Excuse me, officer. I parked here earlier this morning without knowing of any restriction. I was wheel-clamped. I paid up, of course, and drove off to the multi-storey, as advised. But I had stupidly put my brief-case on the roof of my car while I was paying. I drove away without remembering it — until I got to the multi-storey. It must have slid off almost immediately. Have you found it, by any chance? You still handle lost-property, do you?"

I had no intention of mentioning the missing lock-bar. As soon as I had bamboozled the inexperienced constable, I would buy an exact replacement. I completely forgot that my fingerprints would be on the original. I admit that to you frankly. One can't think of everything, can one? You understand me perfectly.

But where were the police-cars with their flashing lights? Where were the gawpers? Where were the ribbon-cordons for holding them back?

Having driven down Willow Tree Lane and through the gap in the fence, I found no sign whatsoever of any such excitement.

That good spot of waste-ground was now filled, in its old familiar way, with silently parked motor-cars. No motorist present except myself. All spaces bagged.

I managed to squeeze-park into just one tiny space on the far side, but it could only be temporary – while I had a look around – because I would be blocking in two other motorists.

I could see no yellow van.

I examined where it had been parked. The space was now occupied by a contented-looking Ford Escort. I bent down and peered underneath it. No sign of my brief-case and lock-bar.

No sign of a body either – or even the self-rolled cigarette, which I now recalled being thrown away just before the punch.

My cold fury had now abated, but I wasn't getting the jitters (I was surprised to find); but I was certainly starting to feel uneasily confused. Could it be that police-officers and a mortuary-vehicle had come and gone? Surely not? In so short a time?

"Most extraordinary," was all I could keep repeating.

Without knowing why, I carefully searched the margin of sickly trees and undergrowth, which partly surrounded the place. Nothing had been disturbed there for years, if at all. My only reward for this futile act was to have my left shoe filled with stinking wet mud. (This was from a shallow stream I tried to step across.)

After taking my shoe off and wringing out my wet sock, I drove back to the multi-storey. The same entry-clerk greeted me.

"Sorry, Jay, me old fruit. This ticket you bought ain't got no more useability."

"Then just give me another, you abominable peasant. I'll fork out yet again."

Giggling in all his fat, the abominable peasant issued the ticket. As I knew he would, he added: "Jay, I seed you drive out. Jay, why did you come in and drive out again so quick?"

"Because I suddenly discovered I'd lost my brief-case at the place where I was wheel-clamped. Must have slid off the roof. Know anything about wheel-clamping, do you? In Willow Tree Lane?"

He looked very shocked. "Wheel-clamping? In Dackley? It's the first time I've 'eard of it."

"And I've still to find my brief-case. I'm beginning to think your fellow-peasant made off with it," and I drove through the portal to re-park.

"Honest, sir," he shouted after me, "I don't know nothing about it."

In walking from the multi-storey to my shop – and in a slightly squelching left shoe – I regretted having to deceive that splendid fellow. But, once again, a natural instinct had come to the fore. He would be spreading his gossip as soon as he could. I was as well-known in the town-centre as he. To influence the testimony of future witnesses could only be beneficial as a tactic, could it not?

Miss Holland, however, was a different kettle of fish.

My stride faltered. Trepidation affected me. I was now indeed getting the jitters. I feared that woman's cross-examination skills more than those of any possible barrister at the Old Bailey (or wherever).

Even on previous days when I hadn't killed anyone at all, I always approached my shop of a morning with this strange fear of Miss Holland. I was at an absolute loss to account for it. After all, I was her employer – her superior officer, as it were. She was only my managing-assistant, nothing more. She knew the trade, of course, and I loved what we both sold: high-quality home-ware accessories. (Not fancy-goods, as some people carelessly describe them.)

I had employed additional shop-assistants in the past. Not now. She was therefore alone behind the counter when I entered. She was serving a couple of well-heeled old trouts – our usual type of much-valued customer.

"Good morning, Miss Holland," I said, taking off my hat to her (as I always did). "Everything all right? Anything you need to report?"

"You, James, are guilty of a crime."

Horribly startled: "Crime? What crime?"

"Repeated unpunctuality, James. That's twice in one week. You are beyond the pale."

She was quick to spot that I was without the brief-case. Accordingly, in tones akin to those of a nursery-governess, she asked: "Have you studied the figures I gave you yesterday? Or is that too much to expect of you?"

Looking me up and down in total disdain, she also asked: "Has someone been dragging you through a hedge backwards?"

"I will explain everything a little later on," I humbly said, "if you would be so kind as to reserve your judgement. I have certain confusing matters to sort out. Please will you excuse me," and I made off up the stairs (to escape to my little office).

Those stairs, you need to know, were not palatial, but they descended in a projecting staircase at the back of the shop – a lovely Regency curve. As soon as I got to the landing, I hid just around the corner instead of going along the landing to my office. Miss Holland had jumbled my thoughts like confetti in an old paper bag. I wanted to know what she might be saying to those two tittering old ladies. (I shouldn't have referred to them as old trouts. Bad form. Forget that bit.)

"Was that the proprietor?" one of them titteringly asked.

"It was," said Miss Holland, and she added: "A man totally incapable of foresight."

But don't imagine that she was some sort of battleaxe. Far from it. Peeping around that corner, I was surprised to find myself thinking: "Gosh, she would be quite good-looking if she were not so snotty," and she was certainly looking particularly elegant that day.

"What a wonderfully English voice he has," the other old lady said. "I do like to hear a voice like that. So different from the coarseness and lack of clarity being encouraged these days – even by the BBC."

I was not flattered. I had been brought up not to comment on the way other people speak – except when their language is foul. As for sounding wonderfully English, I had always wanted to speak like a Scotsman. I love the Scottish accent, but I have no talent for imitating it. I have tried many times. I'm no actor. My Harry Lauder party-piece – inspired by an old gramophone-record I still had in my possession – had always been a flop.

Remembering all those Harry Lauder flops as I stole along to my little office, I told myself sternly: "Face it. You're a bad actor. You'll soon need to tell far better lies than you've told so far. And that, my boy, means becoming a far better actor. Get to it."

In other words, I had firmly decided to solve this whole weird business all on my own.

III

You need to know this. (Don't think I'm rambling.) My little office was not, in fact, little. It was a nicely-sized room, over the shop and with no less than two good windows. They overlooked Dackley's genuinely ancient high street.

It was my holy of holies. Please never forget that. All my best thinking (about life as well as business) had been done in that room.

After a spluttering cold wash in my little wash-room (which really was little), I dashed back into the office itself like a whirlwind.

Inside of three minutes, I would say, I was in an alternative suit of clothes and socks and shoes. (I had a clothes-cupboard in the office, naturally. Certain times of day need certain changes. Tweed for the afternoon, for instance.)

I was sitting at my handsome old desk and studying the wheel-clamping leaflet. (You will remember that I had crumpled it up and shoved it into the pocket of my other pair of trousers.) I was using a big magnifying-glass, just like Sherlock Holmes. Those stories, in fact, were in a nearby bookcase, along with other favourites from my youth.

And my nose felt fine. No longer any sign whatsoever of any swelling.

Suddenly and intrusively, the squawk-box on my desk burst into life. It gave me quite a fright, more than was normal. (My nerves, it would seem, had not yet settled down.)

"James," squawked Miss Holland, "come down here at once. We have seven customers in the shop. You've had ample time to make yourself presentable. I need your help, such as it is," she very nastily added.

"Just a few more moments, Miss Holland," I said. "You have no need to panic."

I switched off the receive-key and did a bit of brow-mopping. (Sweat had broken out.)

"Jay," I had to tell myself, in the kindly tones of Aunt Bartle, "you are at a special testing-time in your life. Never forget. To be calm at all times is to be strong at all times. You need to find where this so-called depot is situated. You must investigate immediately. Time spent in reconnaissance is never wasted."

She was quoting an old Army maxim which all my childhood-family often jokingly quoted. It now had to be taken really seriously.

No address on the leaflet. All it yielded was the phone-number you were supposed to ring. As for that name Dackley Wheel-Clamping Services, it was nowhere to be found in the directory. I leafed to-and-fro, calmly but strongly trying to find it.

Inspiration! The wheel-clamper's name – what was it? Leo something – Rivinni!

Could his name be in the directory, rather than the name of his business?

It was. And did it correspond with the number printed on the leaflet? It did. But the address! This was another big shock for me that day.

"Orchard Ash Road," I heard myself feebly croaking. "How can this be even remotely possible? A wheel-clamping depot? In Orchard Ash Road?"

It just so happened that Orchard Ash Road was the most swagger road in all Dackley. Respectable as you may think my background, I had no friends or even acquaintances who lived there. Untouched by the Recession, the residents were said to own similar fairy-tale properties abroad. My parents (and particularly my mother who, let's face it, was a bit of a snob) had never moved in such circles. Even the servants of these grandees were as remote to us as courtiers in Buckingham Palace. As far as I knew, no one from Orchard Ash Road had ever set foot in my shop.

Yet this was where Rivinni lived! Or HAD lived, I should perhaps say. (I'm striving for accuracy in these memoirs.)

Galvanised into action (not only by the intellectual challenge but by Miss Holland's effrontery), I began by dialling the wheel-clamper's number. I had no idea of what I might say. As all expert liars probably do, I was instinctively relying upon the spur of the moment.

No reply. I replaced the receiver at 9.42, took up my hat, brushed it and left my little office. I had recovered my proprietorial confidence. Descending the curving staircase, I sang out: "Miss Holland, I have to absent myself. Sorry to leave you in the lurch. Shut the shop any time you need a break. I'll be back as soon as I can."

I was now in an iron-grey pin-stripe suit (from Savile Row, no less) and yes, the Beagley Old Scholars' Reunion-Tie. The suit had cost me all of £9 from the discreet charity-shop further up the street. I looked a dish, if I may say so. But it was only the old ladies who responded. All turned and smilingly watched my descent.

"Ladies," I announced, in an even more expansive tone, "I have to confess. I have committed a terrible crime – something far worse than unpunctuality. I fully expect to be boiled in low-grade cooking-oil for at least seventeen hours. I have gone and lost my nice new brief-case. It was a birthday present from my wife. She saved and scrimped to buy it. I have lost it within the space of less than one week."

Miss Holland, let it be said, had no comparable need for the charity-shop. She was stinging me for a good salary and was worth every penny. She had all the appearance of knowing it as she paused in serving our usual Saturday influx.

"James, just tell me this. Was my financial report still in your brief-case when you stupidly lost it?"

"Miss Holland, I'm afraid it was. And for that I beg your forgiveness."

"Did you actually spend any part of yesterday evening in looking at my figures?"

"Well, no – not really. But I promise you, in front of these our customers, that I will study them far into the night as soon as I get my brief-case back. I now need to search all the places where I might have lost it. I must also pop into the police-station. So do please excuse me. I can't delay. I have a terrible fate to avoid."

Nodding gallantly to the titteringly sympathetic ladies, I donned my hat and strode away from the shop. I had a feeling that Miss Holland came to the door to watch my departure, but I didn't dare to look round to see. My fear of her had only been temporarily suspended. I imagined her standing with menacingly folded arms and a long-distance stare.

I was heading for the local police-station for two reasons. First, to validate my public lie about my 'lost' brief-case. Secondly, to check on an even more delicate matter. For all their absence from

Willow Tree Lane, what if the police had somehow got wind of my deed? Bounding up the steps into that Victorian building, I vaguely imagined a trap. ("Gotcha," I could imagine detectives shouting as they pounced.)

May I just mention something at this stage which may surprise you?

This was my first-ever visit to any police-station, which certainly included Dackley's. Unlike a few traders in other parts of the town, I had never been burgled, never been shop-lifted, never had a window broken. Unusual? Perhaps, but a fact.

Far from being confronted by any lurking detectives, I found the place to be as quiet and as self-absorbed as the local museum. I had to rap the counter in an empty waiting-room.

A middle-aged constable emerged from some faraway interior. No vocal greeting. He simply jerked his chin up to denote his tardy presence. (He may have emitted a tiny grunt.)

"Officer," I said. "I have a question. Is it unlawful to park one's motor-car on the waste-ground in Willow Tree Lane?"

I had never seen this constable before. (These were the days when you could see such constables on the beat in Dackley. I knew several by sight.) This constable seemed to be one of Mrs Thatcher's worst bargains.

"Anyone can park there, sir."

"But only this morning I've had to pay some fellow £30 to have a wheel-clamp taken off my Honda Civic."

The constable looked as if he wanted to yawn. Instead, he used his breath to say: "I reckon you shouldn't have paid. I has heard of it going on in other parts of the country. It's a racket what's come over from America. It's something the police can't do nothing about. Not until there's a law brought in."

"But this is outrageous!"

"Well, sir, I can only tell you I'm fair surprised. I didn't know it had come to Dackley." The yawn almost came. "Is there anything else, sir? Anything in the nature of a real police matter?"

For an insanely tempting moment, I felt like snapping: "Yes there jolly well is. I'm lying to you. I paid no money. We had a short altercation. The fellow died. I left, but I went back. Both man and van has disappeared."

Instead, of course, I said: "Yes there jolly well is. I've lost my brief-case. You do still deal with lost property, do you?"

"Yes, sir," he said, and with a sigh he opened a sort of paperback ledger. "Where did you lose it, sir?"

"In Willow Tree Lane," I loudly said.

To make doubly sure of no eavesdropping detectives, I decided to repeat the ominous name loudly enough for the more distant parts.

"Did you get that," I said to the constable, and then I absolutely bellowed: "WILLOW TREE LANE."

Detectives still didn't appear and I felt nicely contented, but the constable did not. He reprovingly said: "No need to shout, sir. I do know the place. Are you sure the brief-case was lost? Not stolen?"

"All I know, officer, is that I paid the chap you are saying I shouldn't have paid. Before doing so, I had temporarily put the brief-case on the roof of the car."

"There's many as do something as daft as that, sir."

"Quite."

"You then forgot all about it, sir, and then drove off."

"Officer, you have painted the complete picture. You obviously know what's what."

"No, sir. It's not complete. Not by a long chalk. You probably think your property slid off the roof immediately, especially if you made an immediate turn. But it could have stayed on the roof all the way up the lane."

"I went back to Willow Tree Lane, officer, after re-parking in the multi-storey and finding the brief-case gone. There was no sign of my brief-case anywhere. And no sign, either of the wheel-clamping man or his yellow van. That's all I know."

"Anything of value in the brief-case?"

"Little more than a financial report, which I'm sure my assistant can duplicate."

"But you wouldn't want to lose a nice bit of leather, sir, would you? That's what you mean, sir, isn't it?"

"My thoughts exactly."

"Well, sir, don't you worry. Even these days, the public can be more honest than you might think. Stuff does get handed in."

"Splendid. Thank you, officer."

"Anything else, sir?"

I hesitated. For all of two seconds, I would say, I considered whether or not to hand in that leaflet (the one I had transferred to the pocket of my fresh pair of trousers). It would have added weight to my story, would it not? But what if it over-stimulated a team of smart-alec detectives? They might well get to Rivinni's people before I did. Forensic evidence, as it is called, might then have been found on my brief-case and, worst of all, on the lock-bar. For that reason, I therefore decided not to present the leaflet.

"Nothing else, officer, thank you."

After saying those words, I perhaps made for the door a little too hurriedly. I had Phase Two of my battle-plan up my sleeve. I was anxious to move on.

"Hey," shouted the constable, as sharply as a drill-sergeant. "Just a minute!"

I nearly had a split-second heart-attack, but all he wanted was my name and address.

If I have dwelt too long upon this interview, it is for two momentous reasons. First, in airily descending those old police-station steps in Providence Square, I was secretly conscious of having just crossed a Rubicon. For the first time in my life, I had lied to a policeman.

Secondly, I was conscious of something which, frankly, worried me a lot more.

I was instantly sure I was being watched. But by whom?

Not by the police – of that I was convinced after glancing back at their windows. All sturdily blank. (The police-station was the quietest bit of the whole complex.) I had nothing to substantiate my instinctively strong feeling. As for Providence Square itself, it was still only sparsely busy and with traffic which looked totally impartial.

I crossed the road, which encircled the public open-space. I then crossed the grass by way of one of the diagonal paths. The feeling was getting stronger. Most people were still too busy shopping in Bell-Market Street to make use of the benches in the centre of the space. There were just two push-chair mums on one of the benches. Both exhausted. Both dragging on their fags. I looked them both over as I passed. Both took as little interest in me as they did in their two grizzling children, despite my raising my hat. Yet it was here that a feeling of being watched was at its strongest.

Was a mate of Rivinni's up one of the few trees around those benches? With a shot-gun, perhaps? I went quickly from tree to tree, but saw nothing suspicious hiding behind them or, indeed, up in the branches.

Could it be Miss Holland who was on my tracks? Definitely not. I phoned her from a phone-booth on the far side of the square (to ask if she were still in the shop).

"Of course I'm still in the shop. James, I want you back here as soon as possible," and she rang off like the Empress of Russia.

I replaced the receiver and hurried to execute some of the manoeuvres we learn from spy-films. I went in at one door of Debenhams in King William Street and out through one at the back. I nipped along an alley or two. This really did result in an ebbing away of the feeling. This put me in a calmer frame of mind for executing Phase Two – the purchase of a new lock-bar.

In the motor-accessories shop in Bell-Market Street, I asked the assistant: "Do you have a lock-bar in stock? I gather that it helps to deter thieves. The brand I've been recommended is manufactured in Germany. Hard steel, but painted dark green."

I had bought the previous lock-bar in this shop, but the assistant was new and had no interest in his job. I had to reject several inferior brands before he found the right replacement. He would soon forget me even if he survived being sacked.

"Thank you, young man. Wrap it for me, please. And give me an emery-pad."

I hurried to the multi-storey with my surreptitious purchases. Avoiding the eye of the abominable peasant in his sweaty cubicle, I had some initial difficulty in finding the floor where I had parked. This puzzle did, I must admit, frustrate and annoy me. It took me damn near twenty minutes – up and down in those smelly lifts – before I found the Honda. (I was beginning to think it, too, had been spirited away.) But I was well able to heed Aunt Bartle as soon as I found it. I was as calm as anything as I set about faking the new lock-bar. Standing at the back of the Honda, with the boot-hatch raised to aid concealment, I abraded the new lock-bar most artistically (if I may say so). Within moments, it was looking cleverly similar to the more used-looking original. It fully deserved one of my exclamations of triumph.

"Ha!"

Who would ever suspect it as a replacement if (as I could only hope), the original were never to turn up? After closing the boot I went to a nearby litter-bin and deposited the wrapping-paper and the emery-pad. I put the new key on my key-ring. I tossed the old key out of the open casement.

Only then, as I was about to slide behind my steering-wheel, did I see what I saw.

"By God," I heard myself roar without restraint, "what further effrontery is this?"

Tucked under the windscreen-wiper, in exactly the same place where the leaflet had been left, was a tightly folded piece of paper. Worse still, on unfolding this paper, I found it to be a sheet taken from Miss Holland's impeccably-typed financial report.

On the back of this sheet, which she had left blank, someone had clumsily written some strange capital letters in red Biro.

DND NUXMO.

What on earth was Nuxmo? Some revolting form of vegetarian sausage-meat? Further down on the sheet and encircled as if they were part of a signature, were the words TLI SU.

Could this be a signature in Chinese? Could it be the signature of an oriental master-criminal – someone like Fu Manchu? My mind went right back. My housemaster, Mr Bishop, used to read those stories to us in the dormitory when we were juniors. But don't worry. I won't bore you with all the lurid theories, which went through my mind. You will, I'm sure, agree with my more scientific deductions. The message, or whatever it was meant to be, was clearly in some sort of code. Since it was clearly intended for me, it must surely have related to my homicidal adventure.

I have never been good at deciphering codes. Beagley College was not Bletchley Park. I almost tore up the desecrated page, but, remembering Aunt Bartle's dictum, I clung to my calm. I carefully re-folded the thing and stored it in the glove-compartment. At the very least, if I eventually had to call in the police, it might yield fingerprints.

"James," I said, as I started my engine, "keep one thing in mind above all else. In spite of the crudity of that lettering, you are dealing with people of high intelligence. They were able to find your car in this horrible place a damn sight quicker than you."

I tooted my horn at the exit-portal. The abominable peasant was in the line of sight and I wanted him to notice me. He stood up, craned his neck and waved merrily. A lovely guy, as the Yanks say.

Phase Three of my battle-plan was now in progress, but, in heading for Upper Dackley and Orchard Ash Road, I was no longer enraged. That spasm had passed. I was bent only upon outwitting any threat.

"James," I said, as I swung into Orchard Ash Road and pulled up, "solve this mystery and you can solve anything. You will achieve intellectual parity with Miss Holland. Her financial reports will become instantly understandable. You'll even be in a position to point out their flaws – if flaws there be."

I attached my brand-new but well-faked lock-bar to the steering-wheel plus pedal. I got out and locked up. I began searching for the Rivinni residence.

The road was on the magnificently wooded outskirts of Dackley. It was deserted. Not a soul in sight, nor any vehicle – neither parked nor moving. A well-heeled hush prevailed.

The address I was seeking, as yielded by the directory, was number four. But this was one of those roads, it would seem, where helpfully visible numbers were thought to lower its prestige. I had to hesitate at several carriage-gated drives – all of them encouraging no further view beyond a well-shaded bend. I finally arrived at a judgement. The surface of one drive was unlike the others in being rather unkempt. This surely had to be the most probable?

I opened the unlocked side-gate to this unkempt drive (the carriage-gate to it was heavily padlock-chained). Venturing through, I found I was right. Around the first corner of the first bend there stood a copper-beech (not yet in leaf). On it's poor suffering trunk was daubed a figure four – in pink emulsion-paint, with dribbles.

What was my plan? Would it have been yours? See what you think and then decide.

My plan was this. I would take a quick look at the residence – from a safe distance – before retreating. I would then call on the nearest of the fellow's neighbours. I would pretend to have called at the door but to have had no answer. I would then extract what details I could before planning my next move.

Carefully, I peeped out from behind that suffering trunk of the once-splendid beech. I was a bit frightened, I must admit, but also must honestly say I felt more excited than frightened. I was starting to feel a boyish stirring of a lust for adventure.

Everything quiet. Nothing moving.

And what a slum!

Built in the early twenties (as I was far later to learn), a former luxury-bungalow was to be seen on the far side of a huge lawn. The lawn had once been a grand oval with a drive sweeping around it. The oval was now little better than a rubbish-dump. Various crates and items from the building-trade nestled amid the overgrowing grass and flowers. There was even that most ugly of sights – an old car with its doors torn right off. As for the bungalow itself, it looked uncared-for even from a distance.

Thinking it would improve my story, I decided to see what the front door actually looked like. Did it have a knocker, a bell-push or a bell-pull? The door was in shadow, under a porch, and I couldn't distinguish these details.

I delicately moved forward to get a better view. I had moved but two yards, I would say, between those stacks of rubbish on the oval.

I heard a rustle behind me. I turned.

A whacking great dog with a frightening hump to its back was coming at me in a crawling rush. Its teeth fastened on my leg, just above the ankle. I was pulled over. I was dragged along the ground.

"Let go," I shouted, "you loathsomely foul animal. Do as you're damn well told."

Had those awful teeth got me by the flesh? Not really. (I'm striving for accuracy in these memoirs, as I've told you before.) It was really only Savile Row tailoring that suffered. The teeth were gripping me by the trouser-leg rather than the leg itself. Almost half a leg of trouser ripped open all the way along the seam. (It's always the stitching in posh old suits, which tends to be the weakest element. I once had one which fell to pieces.)

Although being dragged flat along the ground, I managed to wrest myself into a sitting-up position. At much the same time, I was able to snatch up an edging-tile from an indistinct flower-bed. A heavy tile, but I hardly noticed the weight. I gave the dog a really good clout in the face with it.

He let go of the Savile Row trouser, and, for a fleeting moment, had a look of quite human surprise on his face. In that one moment of respite, I need to tell you, he looked more like an affectionately puzzled old Bruin that a guard-dog. He even sneezed once or twice in a quite human sort of way.

I didn't linger very much over this more favourable impression. I grabbed up my hat – which had tumbled off – and made a dash in the direction of the gate.

Or rather, in what I thought was the direction. Instead, I was alarmed to find my nice old beech-tree – which I was looking for as I would a dear friend – had utterly vanished. I found myself madly dashing down a fork in the drive which led past a decayed garage. I then found myself thrashing and trampling around in an absolute wilderness. The dog had snarlingly recovered. My only protection from him was the vegetation between us.

"Will someone very kindly call off this dog," I angrily yelled, but a fat lot of good that did.

Clutching my hat to my head like an old lady in a thunderstorm, I found myself panting along a neglected pergola-walk. The dog broke through the side-trellis, making a splintering crash like a burst of machine-gun fire.

This gingered me up considerably. Finding myself at the rear of the bungalow, I made for a long terrace, which came into view. It had a set of French windows, all of them looking inhospitably shut as if for all eternity. Leaping up the steps to this desolate terrace, I seized upon a wicker-work chair. With this as my only shield, I stood at bay.

"Sit," I shouted at the dog. "Sit!"

The dog replied by fastening his teeth on one leg of the chair.

He began chewing it up as easily as a stick of celery. Groping behind me with my other hand, I tried to open one of the French windows. Any port in a storm. But no go. The door, as I had already guessed, was locked.

And looked like remaining so. By the time the chair was all but in tatters, I was more or less praying for a miracle. It was then that I heard the French window behind me being unlocked.

I managed a desperate glance over my shoulder.

A woman stuck her head out. Quite a mop of hair. The dog instantly squatted and went as still as stone.

"Madam," I breathlessly complained, adopting the best of my pompous old-buffer acts, "I came here on legitimate business. This dog has attacked me. I have literally been dragged along the ground. See this trouser-leg of mine? Ripped all the way up. Who is in charge here? I shall sue for damages. This suit was from Savile Row no less."

Looking more closely at the woman who had appeared, I nearly fainted.

"Good God," I weakly said.

The last time I had spoken to her was on her death-bed. And that had been more than sixteen years before all this unpleasantness.

She was now smiling at me in the kind and golden-haired way I had known so well.

"Aunt Bartle," I managed to say, "how is this possible? What on earth are you doing in a place like this?"

I took off my hat in astonished reverence and was having to struggle with my feelings.

"Auntie," I said, in a voice turning into a reedy squeak, "I'm so happy to see you again, but, frankly, I'm at a complete loss. And how long have you had this whacking great dog?"

TWO

In the Hottest of Hot Water

She opened the French-window door but didn't emerge.

She was beaming in a way, which I took to be welcoming. I don't exaggerate. This was exactly the way Aunt Bartle had always opened her front door to me. That smile had always made me think of ripened corn gently swaying in a slight breeze – on, of course, a perfect summer's day. It did so now.

In a voice far coarser than Aunt Bartle's, this apparition said: "What's your game, mister? Why was you poking around in my garden?"

Gloomily but quickly, I realised that I had just experienced an inexplicable moment of insanity. How else could it be described? This golden-haired lookalike, be it noted, was not Aunt Bartle. And she isn't going to turn out to be her long-lost twin-sister – no drivel of that kind. A complete delusion. Pure insanity.

"Madam," I said, sternly replacing my bowler, "I can only apologise for my initial confusion. I do, however, have a serious complaint. I am looking for one Leo Rivinni. I understand he lives here. Am I correct?"

Still beaming like Aunt Bartle, the woman said: "You a mate of his?"

"A mate? Certainly not. I am here on a matter relating directly to the loss of my brief-case in Willow Tree Lane."

Still beaming: "Mister, I ain't so sure I believes you. What's your real game? I'll repeat myself. Why was you poking around in my garden?"

"I got lost, that's all, in trying to find my way up the drive."

She not only beamed a whole lot more but fluttered her eyelids in what seemed to be amusement. And just like Aunt Bartle's pretty eyelid-fluttering, but, as I did realise, the amusement looked dangerous. She said: "You're telling lies, mister. You was up to no good. That's why my dog Masher ripped yer."

"The dog, madam, attacked me without any provocation whatsoever. What's your position here? Who's in charge?"

"Masher don't make no mistakes, mister. He don't go for no one as stays on the path. Can't you bloody read? The notice by the gate says keep to the path. You was poking around our stuff. That's why you was ripped."

"Madam, I saw no such notice. Does that fellow Rivinni live here or not? If so, I wish to speak to him."

"You'll see him, mister, when he gets back. I'm waiting for him myself, believe me. I'll then find out what the two of you has been up to. Come indoors," and this beaming delusion of mine opened the French-window door more widely.

I hesitated, and Masher (a well-chosen name, I'd say) stood up and hackled. I decided to obey. Removing my hat, I stepped inside.

Masher followed me in, as silently as a ghost. The woman then locked the French-window door. She then shot home its two bolts (both top and bottom) in a smart manner I can't altogether describe as welcoming.

"Come into me office," she commanded, leading the way between stacked-up cardboard boxes, "and don't bloody touch nuffink."

But I kept my eyes watchful. This first example of a room was darkened by partly-drawn curtains. They were of a most beautiful royal blue – and velvet at that. I was obviously passing through a drawing-room of previous elegance. It was now empty of anything other than the scruffy boxes. As a possible escape-route, however, it seemed promising. This surely very strange woman had left the key to the French-window in the lock – just as Rivinni had left the key in his wheel-clamp.

Who was it who said I was incapable of foresight? Miss Holland, that's who.

Following my captor (with Masher behind me), I found myself passing through a darkened but huge hall (lots more boxes) and into a former dining-room.

"Sit down," said my captor, cocking her thumb at a solitary dining-room chair of undoubted quality. (A remnant of a once-fine room?) It stood on the bare brown lino at a short distance from a grey tin-type desk and a swivel desk-chair draped in a shawl. Again, this was a room with partly drawn but magnificent curtains. However, not much air. Musty smell, even rather sooty. Again, lots of stacked-up boxes. I obeyed. I sat down.

Masher squatted in the open doorway to the hall. A fairly solid obstacle to my faintly-formulated escape-plan. Very worrying.

"Madam," I tried saying, "might I just point out that you are keeping me here against my will?"

"Shut your gob," she said, "and don't disturb me no more. We waits for Leo. Masher and me will then sort out the both of yer."

She resumed tap-tapping on a computer-keyboard, the activity which my visit had evidently interrupted. The sight of someone so like my aunt at a computer became, for me, totally fascinating. Did many people know about computers in those days? Not in Dackley, I was sure. Even the elegant and efficient Miss Holland didn't own one (as far as I knew).

What on earth, I began to wonder, was my Auntie Lookalike actually computing? Her fingers were moving about as busily as a swarm of bees. The screen was no clue. My view of it was too oblique. All I could see of it was how its glaring light changed her golden face to the pallor of the witch in the The Wizard of Oz.

I had never liked that witch, not even as a grown-up. (It had always had the power to frighten me.) But, witch or not, two matters about this woman were reassuring me. First, it was now obvious that no one had told her of Rivinni's death. Secondly, my fear of any of his accomplices being on these premises was unfounded. There could be no one else around.

I began to relax a little. I began to think I might be able to charm her, as I used to charm the real Aunt Bartle when I misbehaved. I judged it wise, however, not to speak until spoken to by this weird substitute. After no less than half an hour (I sneakily timed it), she suddenly stopped computing. She swivelled round in her chair and spoke. No longer beaming.

"Where is my Leo?"

"I've no idea," I said (if ever there was one, a grisly half-truth). Inventively but ingratiatingly, I asked: "Would he have stopped off somewhere for a spot of lunch?"

"He wouldn't bloody dare," she said.

"Actually," I went on, in what I hoped was a helpful tone, "I could do with a spot of lunch myself. May I suggest that I leave now and come back a little later? Frankly, my greatest anxiety concerns my lost brief-case. I'm happy to overlook your dog's behaviour."

My hat was on my lap. Holding it, I rose from the chair.

"You was to sit down, Mr Lah-de-Dah. I won't tell you again. Sit down and don't you move one inch off that bloody chair."

I sat down and she went on: "When did you last see the stupid sod?"

"If you're referring to Mr Rivinni," I said, trying to be more formal, "I last saw him when I went back to my car for my brief-case. I had parked in Willow Tree Lane but, after I had walked a little way along the river, I realised I'd forgotten it. I found Mr Rivinni fixing a clamp to my wheel."

"What time was this?"

"A little after ten past eight or so. No other cars had yet parked there. Only his yellow van. He told me he would take off the clamp if I paid him thirty pounds."

"And that's what you paid 'im?"

"Yes, madam. I then drove off, as he advised, and re-parked in the multi-storey."

"You're a liar, Mr Lah-de-Dah. You didn't pay 'im nuffink."

I turned a little hoity-toity. "Madam, you were not present at that sordid transaction. You can't possibly know if I paid him or not. He said the release-fee was thirty pounds."

"That's right. That's the fee for release if 'e's still on site. Thirty pound, in cash or by cheque. But you didn't bloody pay neither way. So tell me the truth."

"Listen, darling," she drawlingly said (actually calling me darling – ugh!) "I gave Leo the clearest orders. He was told to phone me after every single payout. He was to phone me on his mobile. It's why I bought it for this new job I've put him on, starting today."

She paused. Two new things now puzzled me. First, her use of the word 'mobile'. In those days, the only 'mobile' I had ever heard of was the arty dingle-dangle, which had been a middle-class craze. It was designed for suspending from the ceiling. Miss Holland had thrown the last of them out about two years before this strange encounter.

"Oh," I said, trying to be decently chatty, "you must mean a portable telephone. I don't think I know of anyone who owns one. The device is still too expensive and, I understand, quite cumbersome. It's also unreliable."

The second thing that puzzled me was a sudden change in this awful woman's speech. She had abruptly stopped dropping her aitches. Her voice was no longer coarse. Her tone and accent were far more top-drawer than mine. No doubt about it!

"You see, my dear man," she scornfully went on to say, "Leo would have phoned me if you had paid him. He wouldn't have dared not to. He should, in fact, be back here long before now – with beef-curry for the two of us. So tell me the truth. What really happened in Willow Tree Lane?"

"Before we continue with that fruitless line of enquiry," I primly said, "might I just ask if you are the author of this leaflet which Mr Rivinni left under my wiper? I didn't actually read it until after I first went and parked in the multi-storey. I had clean forgotten that he'd stuck it under the wiper."

I took the leaflet from my trouser-pocket and uncrumpled it with care. Reaching forward but remaining warily seated, I held it out.

This strange woman stood up to take it from me, then sat down and promptly re-crumpled it into a tight little ball. She tossed it towards Masher in the doorway. He scooped it up and swallowed it as if it were a tit-bit.

"Madam," I said, "that's not likely to agree with his digestive system. Also, there were aspects of that leaflet that I wished to discuss."

"Don't worry about it, my dear fellow," she sneered. "I printed off quite a few. Leo has them in the van. You can ask him for a new one if and when he turns up. But yes, I am the author. Alone I did it, as I do everything."

Slowly swivelling this way and that in her office-chair, she began eating biscuits from a packet. Her eyes were fixed strongly and suspiciously upon me. Yet my hope of an escape seemed more feasible. She had just made a tactical error, had she not? Masher was no longer watching me but HER.

I decided to talk her off her guard, then, if possible, seize any advantage, which might present itself. I would shut both of them in the room. I would somehow wedge the door. I would make a dash for that French-window in the former drawing-room.

"Madam, as soon as I read your leaflet, I should have known. It could not possibly have been composed by your Mr Rivinni."

She took another biscuit from the packet, broke off a portion and tossed it to Masher. A salivating crunch ensued, which I didn't much like the sound of. She herself chewingly said: "I have been doing my best to teach Leo how to read and write. He would get a really good thump if he got anything too stupidly wrong. Will I ever be able to thump him again? I'm beginning to doubt it. What did you do? Kill him? In a fit of rage? Smashed his skull in? With a half a brick, perhaps?"

Because I had succumbed to rage – after the event – and had indeed expressed regret at NOT having smashed Rivinni's skull in, I felt as guilty as if I HAD smashed it in.

"Of course I didn't do any such thing," I said, but I knew my whole manner to be unconvincing.

Quaveringly, I tried to divert her horribly half-accurate intuition.

"Madam, let us return to the matter of the leaflet. It has shown you to be a well-educated lady," and I added (hoping to flatter her), "I am also beginning to believe that you're from a level of society higher than my own."

"Far higher," she said, without scorn and with something of a faraway expression. Then, with very real scorn, she said: "Why do you wear that stupid tie? It's nothing to be proud of. Beagley was always de trop," and she pronounced that last phrase with off-hand contempt.

She was right about Beagley but one must stick up for the old place. Not entirely without sincerity, I riposted strongly.

"And you, madam, have nothing to be proud of either. To pose as working-class when you are not is shameful. It's an insult to many generations affected by poverty and cultural deprivation. I knew there was something false about your act. Not quite right, was it? Like my Harry Lauder piece, it didn't quite ring true. Why have you adopted this disguise I begin to ask myself. What or who are you in hiding from? Having gone through so much today, I'm entitled to a full, frank and honest answer."

I stood up in fervour, my hat in one hand and held aloft, and with my other hand on my hip. A dramatic but harmless pose.

I was instantly bitten in the leg.

Well, not the leg as such. (I'm striving to accuracy in these memoirs.) Masher had come up behind me. He had bitten me in the bit of leg just above my left heel. Done quietly.

"God Almighty," I roared.

I collapsed back on the chair in a pain I can't describe. I had never in my life been bitten by any dog. Perhaps the shock of a new experience affected me more than it should? I can only say the bite was like red-hot needles for teeth – the sort of bite you might expect from the giant rat of Sumatra.

"Madam," I savagely said, applying my breast-pocket handkerchief, "I have already been to the police once today. I'm willing to go a second time – to insist this dog be destroyed."

"It's only a nip," she had the smoothly colossal cheek to pretend. "You were told to stay on the chair. I let you off after your first disobedience. Another and you'll do worse."

Masher had already gone back to his on-guard position in the doorway. He was tossed a whole rewarding biscuit. The words 'pretty boy' went with it as if he were a well-behaved parrot. To mix these comparisons a little, I would say he caught the biscuit as expertly as a seal catches a fish. The sight not only made me think of my wife and two children at the zoo – with the keeper tossing fish from a bucket. It made me think of Aunt Bartle. She had taken me to the zoo to see that same performance. Same zoo.

How on earth could I ever have imagined this ghastly female to be like Aunt Bartle?

"This impostor," I resolved (in a fury, I admit it), "must be dealt with a lot more firmly. I shall not weaken."

"And now for the truth," said the impostor, continuing her slow munching and chair-swivelling. "When did you first meet my Leo?"

"Today," I snarled, "in Willow Tree Lane."

"That's a lie. And don't think I can't prove it. I know a conspiracy when I smell it. What made you quarrel with him? What made you kill him?"

"I tell you, madam, that I never met him before today!"

"Met him in the Market, did you? When?"

"I have NEVER met him in the Market!"

"That's where you first met him, isn't it? In the Market. At my Leo's pitch – the stall."

"Dackley Market," I roared, "holds no attractions for me whatsoever. I don't even know what you sell there."

"I'll show you want we sell," and, in a gleaming-eye sort of way, this woman got up and scuttled across the room.

She burrowed in a series of cardboard-boxes and dragged out, finally, a frying-pan.

"I sell all sorts of things," she said, "but this is good quality at a low price," and she came over and displayed it to me. "Isn't this something you wouldn't mind buying?"

"Not today, thank you," I was frigidly foolish enough to say.

I never saw it coming – the blow from this frying-pan. Wielding it like a tennis-racket, she brought it smashing down on top of my head – exactly as clowns do in a circus.

Again, I can't describe what this new experience was like. I think I might have had a loss of consciousness for a moment or two. All I was really aware of was a feeling of being like a small empty boat, which, for one reason or another, had slipped its mooring. It was being swept away in a rushing current.

"Are you now ready," I heard someone saying, "to tell me the truth?"

It was she – back in her office-chair. The frying-pan was on the desk. She was shaking out the packet of biscuits into it. These she resumed sharing with Masher. Again, she was tossing the biscuits to him. Again, he was catching them expertly – and without moving from the doorway.

How, I was thinking, could I ever hope to get past Masher? My hope of an escape-route to the drawing-room (and that potential French-window) was fading fast.

"I expect to be told the truth," the woman said, "by the time every biscuit has left this frying-pan," and she tossed Masher another two in quick succession.

"I can only repeat," I said, and rather feebly, "that I have never met Rivinni before this morning. You claim you can prove me wrong. I'd like to hear your proof."

"You gave yourself away when I found you on the terrace. You spoke his name. That means you already knew him."

"Well of course I knew his name," I had enough strength to say testily. "He gave me his name because he thought I might prefer to write a cheque."

"That," the woman said, tossing another biscuit, "has to be a lie. Leo was under strict orders not to give out his name on this particular job. Besides, you've said you paid in cash. It's a lie, but that's what you've said. Your story is inconsistent. Full of holes."

"Madam, Rivinni told me his name – and even spelt it out – so that I could make out a cheque to him personally. I didn't write him a cheque. But he thought, you see, that I was doing so. It was all a bit of a muddle. To that I will agree. Nevertheless, that's the history. It's how I learnt his name."

In possibly her nastiest voice so far, the woman said: "That can only be another lie. Leo doesn't have a bank account. Cheques are to be made out to Dackley Parking Services – not to him."

"You appear, madam, to be labouring under a misconception. For the umpteenth time, I repeat. He gave me his name – and for the reason stated. It's how I was able to trace where he lives. The name of your dubious firm is not in the directory. His name, however, is very definitely in the directory. And listed as a resident of this illustrious road. That, if I may say so, seems to me very odd. May one enquire as to the reasons for it?"

"One may not," she said, and her eyes, I have to say, actually darkened.

Never before had I seen such a change of colouring in the eyes of a human being. They became like the colour and even the shape of school prunes. Had her real eyes, perhaps, flooded with bile? It didn't last very long, but I thought it didn't bode well for my own future. As a phenomenon, it scared me stiff.

Another biscuit was tossed to Masher. Another salivating crunch. She had lost interest in eating them herself.

"Why," she said, in a trance-like sort of way, "didn't you phone? You had my leaflet. Why did you call and start poking around?"

"But madam," I said, trying to sound conciliatory, "I did try phoning. I phoned from my shop after I had re-parked in the multi-storey. I especially noted the time – 9.42. I could get no reply whatsoever. My lost brief-case, I must tell you, is a matter of urgent concern. Getting no reply, therefore, I decided to pop out and report my loss to the police – and then to call here," I added, in the tones of Uriah Heep, "to see if your chappie had picked it up. As I mentioned to the police, I think it must have slipped off the roof."

I was talking too much. I knew it, but couldn't have stopped had she not interrupted.

"Cut the cackle," she sharply said. "This bit could be partly true. I had to go to the fezzy at that time – to vomit."

Always the gentleman, I mechanically said: "Sorry to hear that. Feeling better?"

"I am, yes. It's why I want my lunch – my dinner, as Leo calls it. Why did I vomit? Tell me the reason. I heard the phone go but couldn't answer it. It was the only time it rang all of the morning. So why did I vomit?"

"Madam," I said, "how can I possibly be expected to answer a question of that sort?"

"It's not like me to have any form of stomach-trouble. Both at home and all the schools I was ever sent to, it was said that I could digest bricks."

"Ah," was all I could say to this.

"Did you get Leo to put something in my coffee-tin?"

"Madam," I said, in the most tactful way I could, "that really is a preposterous suggestion. I must ask you not to pursue it."

"I need to know the truth. You've said he's got his own bank account. That means you helped him to set it up. He couldn't have done that himself. Too stupid."

Nothing can be more annoying to a liar, I was now discovering, than to be accused of telling lies when he is not. This annoyance, I was also interested to discover, was giving me some much-needed energy. Alertness was re-possessing me despite an increasing headache.

"I always have my cup of coffee," the woman glitteringly said, "at quarter to nine. Leo must have told you that. You got him to poison me. I don't blame him as much as I blame you. What was the poison? It acted almost immediately. And pick up your silly stupid hat," she contemptuously added.

I was unable to remember letting go of my much-valued hat, but I'd obviously done so when Masher was biting the back of my ankle. It was at a short distance from me, on the lino. I wouldn't describe it as looking silly, but, uppermost and forlornly empty-looking, it did strike me as a bit sad. Why do I like hats? I like hats because they can always be raised to the ladies – and that's still appreciated even in this day and age.

"I can't quite reach it," I thought it wise to say, "without moving from this chair. Do I have your express permission to get up and retrieve my bowler-hat?"

"Just do as you're told," she snapped, "and you'll be all right. Pick it up. Who wants your silly hats cluttering up the place? Pick it up, you vile skunk."

I got to my feet and picked it up. At the same time, this highly irrational woman tossed another biscuit to Masher.

A bit distracted, I suppose, she was rather careless this time. The throw was no longer accurate. The biscuit flew well over Masher's head and into the darkened hall behind him. He instantly turned to root for it where it fell.

Who is it who says I'm not a man of action? Just as instantly, I threw my hat aside and made for the door. I slammed it shut.

"Ha," I said (my exclamation of triumph).

Luck favours the bold. There, in the keyhole, was a key. I was able to turn it and utter, "Ha!" yet again. I had triumphantly shut Masher out.

I put the key into the pocket of my ruined trousers. I strode towards the tin-plate desk. Not quite the plan I had in mind, but I felt I was doing rather well. I felt in command. The Bartle Doppelganger made far too belated a grab for the frying-pan. I got to it first. I flung it across the room, the last biscuits in it sent flying. The utensil itself landed in the grand fireplace.

"How dare you," she quietly and staringly said. "You'll pay for this. Give me that key. It's mine. You've stolen it."

"The question of who pays," I sweetly said, "may need to be settled by the police and then in a court of law if you don't co-operate," and I began inspecting her modern telephone-contraption. "How does this phone of yours work? Why doesn't it have a dial? Which of these ridiculous little buttons do I need to press?"

For a moment or two, she sat in her office-chair like an ancient priestess in a Rider Haggard story. She began nodding as if nodding assent to a human sacrifice. But I felt no fear of her. If anything, I wanted her to see me as an old chum. I wanted to console her for the chap whose death I was at least partly responsible for.

"Look here," I said, "do you by any chance happen to have a couple of aspirins I could take? I've a bit if a headache."

These words were hardly out of my mouth when she sprang from her chair like a fiendish acrobat. I dropped the receiver for a reason I blush to mention.

"Give me back my key," she said, and she stuck her hand in my trouser-pocket and began feeling for the key very rudely.

The trouser-pockets of that particular Savile Row suit were narrow-cut but deep. She couldn't get her fingers on the key and I was determined to prevent her. We twisted this way and that for perhaps a second or two. She then not only stamped on my foot but put her other hand and arm around my neck. She dragged my head down to her mouth (I'm fairly tall) and screamed with all her might – right into my ear.

This, again, was an experience I cannot fully describe. I can only tell you that we both fell on the floor in a struggling heap. My only advantage, if you like to name it thus, was that I was more-or-less on top. She panted for a few moments and suddenly relaxed. My first feeling, may I say, was one of huge embarrassment. I scrambled up clutching my ear and feeling badly done by, but, basically, the feeling was one of embarrassment.

Hovering over her, I said: "I really am terrible sorry about all this. But I do have to say that your behaviour has been very peculiar. I honestly don't know what to make of it. May I help you back to your chair?"

She didn't respond, but I wasn't immediately worried. Unlike Rivinni, her eyes were screwed shut and I thought she was simply out of breath and – well, simply resting. Expecting her to spring up and attack me after she had recovered, I tried to be as sincere as I could.

"Madam, I don't go around supposing everybody I meet to be abnormal. I wasn't prepared for all this. Can't we now discuss our differences amicably? In a more normal sort of manner? Do please let me help you up."

Still no response, but I did think I saw slight movement. This encouraged me to go on (hastily): "It does of course mean accepting that tragic accidents can happen. They can happen without any evil intention."

Still no response. I began to expect her to open her eyes and say "Boo!"

It really is odd how one's mind can go back to one's childhood memories in a time of crisis. Aunt Bartle used to play at being dead when my sister and I were children. A strange form of play, I suppose, but it was what grown-ups used to do. Aunt Bartle couldn't keep it up for long. We used to tickle her until she opened her eyes and gave in.

In no way did I tickle this woman, but I did go down on one knee for a closer persuasive talk. It was at this point that I became aware of something very strange indeed.

It was like the sound of rising wind on a winter's night – the sort of sound you hear in movies where people are marooned in an old dark house. But rather worse than that. At first, I thought it could be due to the after-effect of the scream. (My ear had not yet recovered.) No, this was additional. It was like a hideously mournful east wind blowing through the sharpest of thorns.

"By God," I gasped, jumping up, "that's a cry for the dead. It's Masher! Her soul-mate."

I don't mind telling you, I felt terribly upset. How could this possibly have happened twice in one day? My ability to diagnose death (as in Rivinni's case) had not aided me. This death was a total surprise, but I now needed no proof of it. Masher was supplying all the proof I needed.

Suddenly, he stopped that awful howling and began banging on the door with all the force of a recurring cannon-ball. (I could only imagine he managed this by retreating for a few yards and then hurling himself at the door full tilt.) Although stout, the door shuddered in its frame at each blow. I could only thank my stars that I had been able to lock the door. The ordinary catch-lock could never have held, the more so as Masher frequently broke off his cannon ball attack and began twisting the door-knob with the aid of his teeth. The slobbering growl, which went with this effort, was the worst growl I had ever heard from any dog.

I was becoming quite hypnotised by the sight of the inside-knob twisting this way and that. I had to speak to myself sternly.

"James," I said (I always address myself as James if I have to address myself sternly,) "you need a new plan. Examine the windows. Look slippy. You must escape from this amazingly awful situation IMMEDIATELY. That's an order."

There were eight large windows in that once-splendid dining-room. Presumably, they had commanded an impressive view of the estate. The vegetation outside was now crowding out both sight and light. All the glass was so filthy on the outside as to be opaque. But I now discovered something far worse. These big windows were all metal-framed and latticed. All had brass lever-handles for opening them as wide as any escapee could wish. But ...

"Foiled," I cried, after trying each of the lever-handles. "Locked!"

Not one single key had been conveniently left in any one of those particular key-holes. I felt as imprisoned as if I were already in Wormwood Scrubs. Had the windows been wood –framed, I could have used the punishment-chair for smashing my way through. Metal frames and metal lattice-work made that impossible.

On guilty tip-toe, I skirted around that dreadful body on the brown lino and nervously inspected the serving-hatch. It was shut and immovable. But it could have been a risky escape-route, so I didn't much mind. (Masher could have cut me off in the servery.)

What, then, could I do?

The answer came to me in a flash of inspiration – a whole plan, cut and dried in the space of little more than a second!

I quoted one of my father's favourite sayings: "The problem, when solved, is simple."

It was inspired by the new fact that Masher suddenly went as quiet as a mouse. Quieter, I would say. Putting my ear to the door, I could hear neither squeak nor rustle.

"Congratulations, James," I whispered. "This is a jolly nasty situation. But you're in control. No need to waver."

All I needed to do, I reasoned (in a flash, as I've said) would be to unlock the door gently. I would leave it fractionally but temptingly ajar. Masher would thus feel encouraged to nose it open. He would then hurtle straight to the horrible inert body of his owner. I, being concealed behind the door, could then skip around it and lock him in. You wouldn't believe (and neither would Miss Holland) the sheer speed of my thinking. It was so far-reaching that I could see myself safely leaving the bungalow and tidying myself up in my unobtrusively parked Honda. I would pin my torn trouser-leg with safety-pins from the first-aid box. I would then call on one of the woman's neighbours. (It would be bad form to leave Masher locked in for too long.)

"Excuse me," I would say, "but I've just tried to call on your neighbour at number four. I could get no reply at the front door. I had to leave. I was worried, however, by sounds of a hullabaloo from within. I suggest you call the police."

So confident did I feel after having solved the problem so brilliantly (and in so brilliant a flash of time) that I felt wonderfully and genuinely calm. Foresight, too, enhanced my mind.

"James," I said, "I'm not criticising. But remember what Robbie Burns tells you. The best-laid schemes of mice and men gang aft agley. Find something to arm yourself with before you unlock the door. You're dealing with something very similar to the Hound of the Baskervilles. You might be attacked."

I didn't have enough foresight (I admit it frankly) to realise that I was leaving my fingerprints all over the place. Who can think of everything? I should have kept my driving-gloves on even before I entered the gate. But I didn't and that's that.

"James," I said, as I began hunting among and in the many cardboard boxes, "just look for something reasonably prong-like. Something to fend him off with, that's all."

What I had in mind was something very like an ornamental toasting-fork of the very kind I sold myself. But all I could find, at first, were things like toy tomahawks (made of bendy rubber) and hundreds of tubes of unbranded toothpaste. Not a lot of use against a dog who, be it noted, suddenly re-started his twisting of the door-knob. Nevertheless, I remained wonderfully calm. Within but a few more moments, I was able to exclaim softly: "Ha, this looks promising!"

I had come across a very old wooden box with rope-handles. On the lid was scrawled 'Lot 264' in faint white chalk. It looked familiar to me, being like the elongated army-box used by my father (merely for gardening-tools). No padlock. Just the hasp. I raised the lid, expecting little more than a hand-fork for use in a green-house.

"By God," I exclaimed again, this time in greater satisfaction. "Ha!"

Hardly noticing that Masher had again gone inexplicably silent, I found the box to contain a jumble of historic but real-life pistols and revolvers.

I went on to exclaim: "Now wouldn't my nice old dad have just loved to get his hands on all this!"

You may not know it, but avid collectors of old firearms build up their secret museums from job-lots of just this sort. But please get this right. I was never a collector myself, nor all that much of an expert. All I had done, in my boyhood and youth, was to help my father to clean and arrange (or rather re-arrange) his treasures.

That's the only reason why it was easy for me to recognise some of these weapons. I found, for example, an Enfield revolver, a Webley-Fosbery and a Borchardt-Leuger. But, although some were still partly loaded, all these weapons were too badly damaged – as well as coated in mud as hard as cement – to be fired. Only one pistol seemed to be undamaged, although dirty. It was a type I have never before seen. The foreign markings completely baffled me. It was heavy, about ten inches long and looked like a mischievously large water-pistol. It was unloaded, as far as I could judge, and I had no knowledge of its appropriate ammunition.

"Well, James," I told myself, "it looks like some sort of automatic. See if you can find any ammo that fits the magazine-thing."

I managed to force-load it with one of the several grimy rounds from the bottom of the box. A dangerous thing to do. I admit this fully. I had not loaded or fired a gun of any sort for upwards of thirty-two years. My father had let me fire one of his pistols, for the first and last time, when I was fifteen. On my birthday, I only narrowly missed him. He afterwards advised me to stick to my cap-gun.)

But you understand, don't you? Of course you do. I was hoping I wouldn't have to fire. It was just a precaution. I still had confidence in my original plan. All the same, I decided upon an additional precaution. The grubby shawl which had been draping the office-chair (remember that detail, do you?) had fallen to the floor. Fearing a scorching recoil if I did have to fire, I used this shawl to envelop my trigger-hand and the entire pistol. (Scorching recoil? Let me say: a badly-loaded gun can explode like a grenade.) All that was now visible of this pistol was an inch of muzzle – poking through one of the lacework holes in the shawl.

"Masher," I said, raising my voice, "is going to think twice before he turns on me – now that he knows I've got a gun. He's no fool. He knows what a gun is, doesn't he? He knows which side his bread is buttered. No doubt about it. Hear that, Masher?"

Unlocking the door with all the tact and delicacy of a brain-surgeon, I then turned the knob and imperceptibly pulled the door ajar.

There now followed a silence so profound that all I could hear was the sound of breathing. For one spooky moment, I thought it was coming from the dead woman, but it was my own breathing. (It was being made more audible for coming through one constricted nostril – a legacy from friend Rivinni. I had to stop breathing for a second or two before I was sure.)

"You stupid animal," I suddenly heard myself shouting. "Go to your master why don't you? Your mistress I mean."

Masher had shouldered his way around the door and was leaping up at me, at my throat I could only presume.

I can't actually remember squeezing the trigger. I must have done, because the recoil was so powerful that I thought the pistol had exploded – like a grenade, as I've already mentioned. I either dropped the bundled-up pistol or it flew out of my hand. Either way, Masher was killed. It was so messy a sight that I couldn't stand it. I bolted.

Ignoring my pre-planned route through the French window in the drawing-room, I went out by way of the front door. It had a spring-lock and was easy to pull open – and to pull shut behind me. I was half-way down the drive before I realised the implication of a gentle breeze ... Oh, so cooling to the head! I stopped. I yelled at myself: "James, where in the name of all your gods is your stupid hat?"

I had left it behind me, had I not? You remember, do you, how I had thrown it aside when I first out-manoeuvred Masher?

I hurried back up the drive. All the world knows what Sherlock Holmes had deduced from an abandoned hat (in the story about the blue carbuncle). The police would also know that story. Retrieval was imperative. Immediate retrieval, however, was impossible. That front door was shut fast, and so was each back and side door to the whole beastly bungalow. (I had to thrash all through the surrounding vegetation to make my inspection.)

"You utter imbecile," I said, "Miss Holland is right about you. Total lack of foresight. Why on earth couldn't you have made your exit through the French window as you planned? Now look at what you've done! It's not just your tell-tale hat you've left behind – but your fingerprints," I roaringly added, having belatedly realised the implication. "You've GOT to get back in."

I feebly picked up a bit of rock (with a view to smashing the panes of the French window – to get at the inside key and bolts), but I nearly went berserk with myself over that idea.

"How DARE you be so stupid! What's the point of leaving a trail for the police to find? What are you expecting from them? A vote of thanks? Think again, imbecile."

I did think again, and again, it all came to me in a flash. The pantry window! Wonderfully calm again, I thrashed my way back to where I had seen it (but had passed it by because of the bars grouted into the sill). It was a large enough window for me to squeeze through if only I could remove the bars. The window itself, behind the bars, had been left inwardly ajar.

"Hacksaw," I said. "You've got one in the Honda Civic. Go and get it. You only need to saw the bars off neatly and level with the stonework. It will then look as if no bars were ever there. Jump to it, James."

Unfortunately, I found the hacksaw was no longer on board when I got to the Honda Civic.

I had to drive all the way to Kind Maiden Green – where I knew it had to be. But it was nowhere in the garage, neither on my work-bench or under it.

Can you imagine where I found it? Up in the loft, of all places. Damn near two hours to find.

"Who the hell," I shouted, "left it HERE? Why can't people put things back where they belong? Don't bother to answer that, James. I know you only too well, you utter idiot."

I drove back to Orchard Ash Road and parked in much the same place as before. Although still dishevelled and feeling naked without my hat, I was once again calm after the ticking off I had given myself. Everything seemed quietly the same, except that I was now keeping my driving-gloves on.

What did I find on this second visit?

Walking up that drive boldly, I first of all had my eyes bulgingly drawn to the front door.

You remember that I had left it immovably shut?

Of course you do. Well, it was open. Slightly open, but open. There was no mistaking that shadowy oblong. Enticingly open, would you have thought – like the jaws of a trap?

Quite apart from being left with a superfluous plan for the pantry window – and with the hacksaw under my arm (folded in with the Daily Telegraph) – I was now in a complete funk.

Could a bunch of crooks be within, awaiting my arrival and eager to pounce?

I pushed the bell-button. Hearing no sound either near or distant, I rapped on the door. It swung open a little wider.

I sang out: "Anyone at home? Is everything all right? Shall I come in or not? Answer me, please, if you can. I am here to be of service."

No reply, which, at first, I thought of as horribly reassuring. Ugh! Venturing into the box-encumbered gloom of the hall, I continued to chant: "Anyone in need of assistance? A gentleman is on these premises – ready to be of service."

This chanting, of course, was not only for bluffing any waiting crooks but any detectives who might just as cunningly have set the same trap. But everything seemed as quiet as – well, as quiet as the grave. (No better description.)

I reached the wide-open door of the former dining room and the scene of my previous deeds.

I now found that my auntie-lookalike had disappeared. She had vanished as completely as that fellow Rivinni in Willow Tree Lane.

Were you expecting this development? I daresay you were. But imagine, please, the effect upon someone less brainy – myself, for instance. It was like being winded at rugger.

And were you also expecting old Masher to vanish? All that was left of him was a faint vestige of swab-marks on the brown lino.

Other missing items? Both the pistol and the shawl I had used (for enveloping it) had gone.

And my beloved bowler-hat … also gone.

The room itself was left neat and tidy (well, as neat and tidy as you could expect such a degraded dining-room to be.) The computer-machine had been switched off and the frying-pan had been put back in the very box it had been taken from. Not one single biscuit (either whole, broken or crumbled) lay on the lino. The lid of the old-style military-box (which I had left open) was now closed. Even the silly modern telephone, which I was sure I had left dangling, had been put back in place.

I tell you this frankly. I was so stunned that I completely forgot the fingerprints, which I had intended to wipe away. The damp face-flannel in my hand remained unapplied. I interfered with the new scene in no way at all, except to pull shut the front door behind me (again!) after I crept out. (I hardly knew I was doing it.)

Emerging from the driveway into Orchard Ash Road, I was so hot and confused that I was jolly glad to have Stephanie's face-flannel with me. A cooling influence. But, dabbing my face, I was only able to exercise a very small amount of comprehension. For instance, I was able to note the cobwebby condition of the carriage-gate hinges (and, indeed, the padlock and chain. In the same way as I had entered the driveway, I still had to use the side-gate). Like a schoolboy pretending to be Sherlock Holmes, I huskily croaked: "Whoever these corpse-removers are, my dear Watson, they could not have made an exit through this gate in any kind of vehicle. This main gate has not been opened for months."

Dazedly speculating upon this (were the corpse-removers flesh-eating zombies from outer space?) I shuffled along the road. I then found myself lingering at the carriage-gate to the next-door driveway. I was wondering whether or not I should resort to my earlier plan – namely, to call upon the nearest neighbour and pretend to have called at the Rivinni residence without success. I might then be able to extract useful information. Frankly, I was exhausted. I hadn't eaten since breakfast. It was now well past four o'clock. (I apologise for these personal details concerning my stomach.)

Realising that I still had the heavy-duty hacksaw under my arm (although still hidden in the folds of the newspaper), I was about to return to the Honda (to stow it in the boot) when I was interrupted.

"You there," said a woman's cheerful voice, from the other side of the gate to this better-kept drive. "Just open the gate for me, will you?"

A small motor-car had appeared from around the bend in the drive. It had come to rest at an adequate distance from the gate. Engine left running. The voice came from a head stuck out from the car-window. "Be quick, please. I'm in a hurry."

I'm ashamed to say I could only stand and stare. She had a mature but pretty face and was wearing a pretty headscarf. (I took her to be, perhaps, the eldest daughter of the house.) Impatiently switching off the engine, she jumped out of the car and opened the gate herself.

In a not unkindly tone, she said: "Whatever's the matter with you?"

I couldn't reply. She went back to her car, got in and drove through. Getting out to close the gate, she paused to look me up and down.

I wouldn't have thought I looked all that bad. A bit dishevelled, yes. But I had used two safety-pins from my first-aid box to pin together my torn trouser-leg.

"Listen, old boy," she said. "Don't call at the front door. You'll be in hot water if you do. Go down the service-lane. The entrance to it is further down the road. Go down it until you get to the trade-door, then ring the bell. People like you are always welcome to bread and cheese and half a tomato. But not at the front door. The Bannerfield-Frishleys won't stand for that. And you must eat in the lane."

Doing my best to speak haughtily, I said: "Who and what are the Bannerfield-Frishleys?"

"The very nice people who live here. I'm their housekeeper. But they're not here at the moment. Due back tomorrow – from abroad. I'm not on duty. I'm going off, in fact. But Vanessa is still on. She's the maid. She'll hand you out the usual. Includes a mug of tea. Don't you go thinking I'm sending you away. I'm just warning you not to call at the front door. We must have rules."

Something unfortunate happened at this point. The hacksaw, inside the folded newspaper, was still under my arm. But the hacksaw was quite a weighty object, having a strong metal frame. Because of this and my growing enfeeblement, the hacksaw slipped from the folded newspaper.

It fell with a clatter at this housekeeper's dainty feet.

"My goodness me," she said, jumping back, "whatever is that for?"

I was unable to answer, so she added (and severely): "Mister, I think you'd better pick up that thing and move on. Do as you're told, please. Pick it up. Move on."

I did as I was told and she stood watching me go, but I came back to where I had parked the Honda as soon as she was out of sight.

I was thinking: 'Why only half a tomato? Why not a whole one, for heaven's sake?'

This question totally preoccupied me all the way back to Kind Maiden Green, which, actually, would normally have been a fairly short journey from Upper Dackley and Orchard Ash Road. But that would have meant going through the village of Swerton, where my unmarried sister still lived – in our childhood home. So I took the long way round. I couldn't risk being seen in Swerton by my sister. She would have waved me to a stop. She would have resumed nagging, trying to make me buy two donkeys for the paddock. Her heart was set upon them.

I had too much on my mind (wouldn't you agree?) to bother with the subject of two donkeys.

And, of course, I was so hungry. Once back in the cottage, I dished myself up bread and cheese – not with just half a tomato.

A whole one, a big one and a juicy one.

THREE

Curiouser and Curiouser

The next day, Sunday, tired me more. I tell you frankly. Fearing that my wife and children could be attacked while I was at work, I had to move heaven and earth to evacuate them to Swerton. You haven't forgotten that name, I hope? I have already mentioned that village. My childhood home. My old sister was living there on her own.

I won't bore you with the domestic arguments I had to deploy, except to say they included my falsehoods about the bedroom ceilings.

"I've been up in the loft," I more or less had to yell at Stephanie, "and the situation is dangerous. The ceilings are sagging. They could fall in on all of us as we sleep. I, of course, shall stay here – and sleep on the sofa. I shall have to get a man in first thing Monday morning."

Knowing that Stephanie hated spiders and imagined them to be running riot in the loft, I added: "But you can judge for yourself. Come up with me and I'll show you," and, as I knew she would, she shiveringly declined.

At last she agreed to the evacuation and we drove over to Swerton, but not without my having to agree, with my sister, that I would pay for those two donkeys.

"It has to be the two," she insisted, "because they are inseparable. But it's a price worth paying, you mean old swine. The children will love them."

Donkeys notwithstanding, don't you think this manoeuvre a smart one? Having my brief-case in their possession, a gang of oriental blackmailers (my worst fear) could so easily trace my home address to Kind Maiden Green. (Wife Stephanie had inked a return-to-this-address-if-found notice inside the flap.) Swerton, I reasoned, would not be so easy for foreigners to trace.

As for Monday, I felt fastidious about the death I had caused in Willow Tree Lane. So I avoided parking there. I parked in the multi-storey car-park. This being so much nearer my shop, I entered the shop (my own property) only twenty minutes late. Did I get any credit for this degree of punctuality?

None whatsoever.

"Good morning," I cried, in my usual way and raising my hat (a mere trilby, of course different from the hat I'd lost). "Another lovely day, don't you think? Everything all right? Anything to report?"

The shop was empty of customers, as it always was so early on a Monday morning. Miss Holland had nothing to do behind the counter except prime the till. Surely she must have had some idea of how I was feeling? Yet all she could find in her heart to say was: "James, I'm not going to say this many more times. We would do much better, as a business, if you were to become habitually punctual."

Re-donning the mere trilby, I turned and went off up the stairs. I tell you frankly, had she extended just one slither of sympathy I would have told her everything. I was so upset at having had to lie to Stephanie and the two girls. I was longing to pour out my troubles to Miss Holland, the more so as she looked so attractive in her Paris blouse and her close-fitting sheath of a skirt. My inexplicable fear of her had not vanished. Be in no doubt about that. But it had become temporarily suspended – lulled as you might say. The word 'Nuxmo' was still bothering me. You can be as sure as I was that Miss Holland – a woman who spent every lunch-hour in her back room doing the Times crossword so speedily – could have twigged the meaning of 'Nuxmo' within seconds.

I had reached the half-landing when she called after me: "And where is your brief-case? Did you manage – during your long and unexplained absence on Saturday – to find any clue to its whereabouts?"

I froze to the spot. All my fear of her returned in full measure. It was the word 'clue' which upset me. Would she find more clues and unleash a juggernaut of a police-investigation?

"Madam," I managed to croak, "there is no heed for anyone to make a fuss. The police are attending to its recovery. I would, however, be grateful if you wouldn't mention the brief-case to Stephanie if she rings up. We've already had a bit of a tiff."

"I only ask," said Miss Holland, closing the till-drawer with quite a slam, "because you and I have a meeting at the Bank on Thursday at half-past ten. I need to know if I have to go to the copy-shop to reproduce my figures."

"Coffee-shop, did you say?"

"Copy-shop," she snapped, almost stamping her foot. "We don't yet have our own photo-copier, an omission you consistently fail to grasp."

"Miss Holland, I do beg your pardon. I'm in no fit state to think ahead of myself. Please cancel the Bank meeting. I'm in a spot of trouble."

For a moment, she stood intensively still before coming out from behind the counter. Advancing to the foot of the staircase, she stared up at me and said: "What sort of trouble, James? Anything really serious?"

The craving to confide in her almost overcame me, but she too eagerly added: "I can always come with you to your solicitors. Even if it's something very nasty, I can help to clarify your admissions. I've done a bit of law. I considered taking it up. There might well be psychiatric reasons for leniency. Come down, James, and come into my room. We can shut the shop. You can tell me all about it."

Even from the half-landing, I didn't like the glint which I could see at the back of her eyes. This and her remarks had stiffened me.

"Thank you, Miss Holland. I have, however, done nothing nasty. I'm not that sort of a person. I was merely referring to the fact that I've had to evacuate my little family to Swerton. We have bedroom-ceilings in danger of imminent collapse. Stephanie and my sister do not get on, I regret to say. In addition to that, madam, my sister is a moral blackmailer. I've had to agree to all manner of totally absurd eccentricities. Negotiations were prolonged throughout all Sunday. No day of rest for me I can tell you."

Miss Holland was quick to say: "That, James, only accounts for Sunday. What of Saturday? Where were you all of Saturday? During the one silly phone-call you made, I told you to return here. You failed me. May I now have an explanation?"

I decided to adopt the army-officer voice, which my father had taught me (for intimidating bullies at my school). Never before had I used it on Miss Holland.

"Very well," I barked at her, and I descended the staircase. She was certainly surprised and backed away (but only slightly).

"It just so happens, madam, that I had my car wheel-clamped in Willow Tree Lane only a short time after parking there. I had to pay thirty pounds before the oaf of a wheel-clamper would take the clamp off. Thirty pounds!"

"Oh dear," said Miss Holland, suddenly becoming facetious. "As much as that?"

"Yes, madam. As much as that! What's more, before driving off to re-park in the multi-storey which blights the town-centre, I absent-mindedly left my brief-case on the roof of the car. I only discovered this, of course, after I had re-parked after forking out yet more money."

"Oh, dear," she repeated. "Although I don't drive, I've heard of cars being wheel-clamped in other towns. I didn't know it had come to backward old Dackley."

"Neither did the police," I barked. "The man, it seems, was unofficial. A fraudster. I intend to get my money back. It was for that reason I traced his address and went there. I was also hoping, of course, to recover the brief-case. I had a strong feeling that it must have slid off the roof – very possibly in Willow Tree Lane itself. I was sure he would have picked it up. My expedition, however, turned out to be unsuccessful in every particular way. I very nearly came to a very sticky end."

Miss Holland was starting to splutter with laughter, which she was scarcely bothering to conceal. For one insane moment, I nearly burst out: "You can start laughing on the other side of your face. I have caused two separate deaths – three, in fact, if we include Masher."

Instead, I just as instantly saw the advantage of encouraging Miss Holland's disloyal sense of humour. Knowing how she would soon be gleefully promulgating the details, I decided to spin her a brand-new lie.

"Listen carefully, Miss Holland. I was unable to call at the man's address because, when approaching his dilapidated place of residence, I was chased away by a simply huge dog. I never even got as far as the front door. I was obliged to run for my life. I actually had to climb a tree to get away from that dog. I was stuck up that tree for hours. Eventually, the dog either tired of waiting or was called off by someone I never saw. Only then was I able to climb down the tree and make my way back to my car."

Miss Holland uttered a muffled shriek and dashed into her little back room. (This was really our major store-room, which she had partly annexed as a cosy office of her own.)

I followed her in. "Madam, can you now comprehend more clearly the reasons for my delayed return to work?"

She was standing with a cushion pressed into her face, perhaps because she didn't want me to see her loss of control. Her shoulders were heaving. I had never before seen her so completely helpless.

"Not only that," I went on to say, "but I was bitten in the leg during the chase – just here, behind my leg and just above the ankle. You can see the marks even now. Look!"

She emerged from behind the cushion with tears of mirth running down her face. Ignoring my wound and hugging the cushion, she collapsed into her arm-chair. Recovering with an effort, she said: "I don't understand myself. Why am I still working for this half-wit?"

Within only a few more seconds, she recovered completely. She stood up and briskly said: "James, whereabouts did you have this misadventure?"

A picture of that housekeeper flashed into my mind – the one who told me to move on after I dropped the hacksaw at her feet. What if Miss Holland and she were to get together and compare notes? (A good liar must always think ahead to possibilities of that sort.) So, in the army-officer voice at its sternest, I said: "Lesser details of my misadventure as you call it need not concern you. Resume your duties."

I turned and left her room to go up the stairs. She followed me, saying: "James, I see no reason to cancel our meeting with the Bank on Thursday. I need you to mind the shop while I get my figures re-copied. I'll go and get them done now."

"Madam, you will cancel the meeting."

"James, we need to discuss larger percentages. There is no other way to off-set the stock-turn rate. The only other way is to sell items of lower value. As the Bank-manager will tell you, this should be evident even to the most stupid of shop-keepers."

She was getting ratty. I ignored her. I went on up to my office. I heard a nondescript voice down in the shop say: "Excuse me, marm …" but I paid no attention. I assumed the voice to belong to a first customer, in from the street. (Our shop-door was always wide open from nine onwards.)

I began opening the morning's post which Miss Holland had pointedly arranged on my desk. All were from suppliers expecting to be paid within the next seven days. I felt too pleased with myself to be irritated. Had I not just engineered a master-stroke of a lie? I had neatly established that I had never been inside that bungalow. Also, lest anyone had noticed, I had accounted for the length of time my Honda Civic had been parked in the road. Miss Holland had not only swallowed this whopper of whoppers – a separate triumph in itself – but it meant that she would henceforth be unwittingly supporting my alibi. I had a far-reaching instinct about her disloyal sense of humour. For her, it would be for the sake of amusing other people at my expense; for me, it would be a valuable influence upon local witnesses if I were to be arrested.

"Ha," I cried, and after that triumphant cry I swept all those demanding letters into the WPB.

Taking out the Nuxmo-message, which I had with me in my inside-pocket, I began studying it with a brilliant feeling that I could now solve it.

I was immediately impeded by the memory of a rhyme from my days at Beagley College. It was taught to the new boys, on their arrival, by the more worldly senior boys.

> *"Never complain*
> *And never explain,*
> *And kindly refrain*
> *From straining the brain."*

In later years, it was explained to me as having only a satirical meaning, but I took it seriously. Indeed, it seemed to match my natural inclinations. I spent most of my time in class in day-dreaming about playing cricket for England; the only positive ambition I had was that one day I would like to own, and run, a shop. Although I had achieved that ambition, I was now aware that a grammar school (which we were taught to regard as socially inferior) would have done me a lot more good. Even that awful woman at the wretched bungalow had been right. Schools like Beagley were an unnecessary stumbling-block. They were, as she had said, 'de trop'.

Gloomily thinking that I was pretty well 'de trop' myself, I found myself still incapable of solving that Nuxmo-message. It had been, if I may remind you, written on the back of a page torn from Miss Holland's impeccably-typed financial report.

At this precise moment of increased stupefaction, I was startled by the squawk-box on my desk.

"James!"

As guiltily as if Miss Holland could see her desecrated page, I stuffed it back into my inside-pocket before pressing down the receive-key. But I managed to keep up the army-officer voice. "Yes? What is it? There had better be an important reason for this interruption."

"James, a lady has called. She is asking to speak to you specifically – and on an extremely important matter. Come down at once. I strongly recommend that you don't keep her waiting," and Miss Holland, having rendered me petrified, snapped off her speak-key.

I released my own lever-key and arose with terrified difficulty. That housekeeper from the residence next door to the beastly bungalow! Had she put two-and-two together? Had she traced me in some smart-alec way? Had she called to raise the subject of the hacksaw which had nearly fallen on her toes? Had she, in fact, already conferred upon it with Miss Holland? I descended the stairs fully expecting Miss Holland to say: "James why were you hanging around in Orchard Ash Road with a hacksaw? What other burglary-tools did you take there? We both want to know."

A woman was indeed in the shop, standing beside the sphinx-like Miss Holland, but, without wishing to cause offence to the politically-correct brigade, I would say she was clearly no lady. Nor was she the housekeeper, but this, for me, was no relief. Could it be the scullery-maid whom the housekeeper had mentioned? The one who was to have doled me out bread-and-cheese and half a tomato? What was her name? Vanessa?

"That's it," I barked. "You're Vanessa! Why half a tomato? I've been wondering. What happens to the other half for heaven's sake?"

This small and rather dumpy woman, I now realised, was far more frightened of me than I was of her. As plaintively as an orphan-child in a melodrama, she looked up at Miss Holland (the taller by quite a bit) and whiningly said: "Please, marm, I ain't no Vanessa. What's he mean?"

"I haven't the faintest idea," sais Miss Holland, beginning to show signs of a smirk (a totally unprecedented smirk, let me say). "But he is, I do assure you, the much-esteemed proprietor of this high-class shop. You've said you wish to speak to him. Well, I've now produced him. Here he is, the great man himself. State your case, Mrs Tridwell. You have the floor."

The woman became tongue-tied, opening and shutting her mouth while staring at me.

How can I best describe her? I can only say I can see her now – as on that day when she entered my life. She wasn't ugly. I cannot say anything so ungallant about any woman, not even that woman whose death I felt strongly responsible for. But this younger woman, I do have to say, was quite the plainest woman I had ever seen.

"Come along, Mrs Tridwell," said Miss Holland. "Speak up. As far as any of us know, he's relatively harmless."

The woman remained tongue-tied, quite desperately so it seemed to me. The army-officer voice did tend to have an effect upon people, but not to this extent. I looked her up and down as encouragingly as I could, feeling a bit sorry for her. She really was such a pathetic sight. She had on a grubby summer dress and over that a skimpy and scruffy denim jacket – unbuttoned. On her slightly turned-in feet were those ghastly articles of footwear I couldn't loathe more – trainers, with one lace undone. Her hair was the colour of post-office string. Her skin was sallow. No make-up of any sort. Her age could have been anything between twenty-two and just under forty.

Miss Holland now took it upon herself to introduce her in slightly more detail.

"Mrs Tridwell is a local amateur potter. She wants to speak to you about her many works of art. Local talent, as I'm sure you will agree, is always of the utmost importance. She is hoping you will help her to sell her range of pots and little dishes. Don't be shy, Mrs Tridwell. Show the gentleman your samples. Like me, I'm sure he will be most impressed."

The woman so-named had two or three straw shopping-baskets about her, clutched to her as if her life depended upon never letting go. Looking as if beaten into doing it, she began to fumble in the largest of her bags. From it, she withdrew a simply terrible example of a pot. She put it on the counter, following it with two smaller but equally similar monstrosities. She stood back, hanging her head – as well she might, I inwardly fumed. The bigger of the pots, which I presumed to be her masterpiece, was a crudely coiled mass of clay only very roughly resembling a beaker-jug. Totally and utterly hideous.

I glared at Miss Holland. What the devil was she playing at? Local amateur artists of all kinds often used to come in and try to get us to retail their rubbish. Never would they get past Miss Holland. Never until now had she troubled me about them. But here she was – with me in the midst of all my troubles – standing there with a look of mischievous expectancy on her face.

"Very well," I inwardly snarled (and through clenched teeth as it were), "two can play at this sort of joke."

Aloud, I no longer used the army-officer voice and smoothly said: "Mrs Tridwell, I'm glad our Miss Holland has drawn your work to my attention. It reveals talent of a very high order. I would be interested to learn more of your entire range. You must come up to my office. Miss Holland," I said, turning to that treacherous female, "accept my congratulations. Your taste, as always, is beyond reproach. I suggest you clear a space in the window immediately. We shall fix the prices for these first three specimens after Mrs Tridwell and I have come to terms. Bring up coffee and biscuits, will you? This way, Mrs Tridwell."

Miss Holland, I was pleased to note, was starting to frown. I paused to relish the sight of her frustration. She had clearly been hoping to see me in a dither – forced into dealing with this woman for myself and making a mess of it. Our Miss Holland had failed to anticipate that I could be willing to lose a few pounds in calling her bluff.

And she was very surprised indeed – as I must say I was myself – by a feeling of tender sincerity, which suddenly affected me concerning this unknown woman.

"My dear Mrs Tridwell," I found myself saying, "there's nothing for you to be upset about or frightened by."

I had spotted a whacking great tear-drop sliding down her cheek. She really did look like a child who is miserably perplexed by a tiff between its parents. Instantly, I became genuinely determined to promote her ridiculously bad pots. I even bent down to her grubby trainers to say: "My dear young lady, never walk around with your laces undone. You could trip up and hurt yourself," and I tied her trailing lace in as neat a bow as I could manage. Rising, I patted her on the shoulder and added: "Let's go upstairs and sort things out, shall we? It won't take long. I'm decisive but fair."

I don't think Miss Holland had seen the tear-drop which had inspired my whole-heartedness. She was both struck dumb and saucer-eyed. In watching my gentle shepherding on the stairs, she was only able to recover her ironic style of speech by the time the pair of us had reached the very top.

"James, what else did you stupidly lose on Saturday – in addition to your brief-case? Could it have been your hat? I did notice, you see, that you came to work in a different hat today. I always understood your previous hat to be the one you favoured most. At what point on Saturday afternoon did you lose your more favoured bowler? You were wearing it when you arrived on Saturday morning, James, and you were wearing it when you set off for the police-station. So was it your hat you also lost? It suited you much better than the one you arrived in this morning."

I was transfixed by this seemingly innocuous speech as soon as Miss Holland began it. How dangerously intuitive she was! All I had as a defence, as I now fully realised, was my instinct.

"Madam," I managed to bark over the top-landing banister, "am I unable to exercise a choice of hat without being microscopically cross-examined? You've had your instructions. Obey them."

It was a poor reply, but it served to shut her up for the time being. She was left to gaze with folded arms at the three pots on the counter while I got our unexpected visitor along to my office. Yet strangely, it was the unexpected visitor who was the more affected by Miss Holland's seemingly innocuous speech.

"Mister," she gasped, as soon as I was alone with her, "I reckon you didn't ought to be so nasty-like to that lady. She could make a lot of trouble. Pardon me as says it, but she's got brains and you ain't."

I blinked at this last remark, but I was still feeling too charitably sentimental to be offended. Going grandly behind my desk, I said: "Poor girl, poor sweet pleb. Don't worry. Miss Holland can't possibly harm you. I'm sure she wouldn't want to. Do sit down. All you're trying to do is to earn a few extra pennies. I fully understand you, but I do need to discuss how best to help you. Sit!"

She collapsed rather than sat down (on one of the two visitor-chairs facing my desk). She clutched her floppy shopping-baskets even closer to her. Sitting down myself, I waggishly added: "You've certainly no need to be afraid of me. As Miss Holland told you, I'm relatively harmless."

"Pardon me as says it," she further gaspingly said, "but I'm a lot more frightened of that lady than I am of you. She shivers my spine. All brainy women frighten me. I'm only frightened of you because you're barmy. All barmy people frighten me, but you ain't all that barmy. More daft than barmy, I reckon. But time will tell."

I blinked rather more at this and still more after she added: "You're a bit like my dad. He wore more daft than barmy. He hardly ever frightened me at all. Can I have a drink of water, sir?"

"Water? Just water? Wouldn't you prefer a nice cup of coffee? And biscuits if you're peckish?"

"I don't need coffee, sir. I just want water."

Hurriedly fetching her a glass of water from my wash-room, I stood in amazement as she sat gulping it down. Between each successive gulp, she gargled – head thrown well back – before completing the gulp. Long and loud gargles.

"Thank you, sir," she said, and put the empty glass on my desk. "It's me throat. It gets that painful when I try to speak hextra nice to people like you and that lady. Coffee and tea don't do it no good. Has to be water."

"Would you like another swig or two?"

"No thank you, sir," she said, with a politeness of tone that touched me to the core.

I sat down at my desk again and reached over to the squawk-box. "Miss Holland, have you begun making the coffee?"

"I most certainly have not," she squawked back, "and I don't intend to. Stop your games, James. I need you down here. Three customers."

"I'll be down in due course, Miss Holland, and not before. I'm simply notifying you that coffee will not now be needed. Mrs Tridwell only required water," and I snapped off and sat back.

I couldn't help sighing. I was thinking of my father. How he would have loved to chat with this Mrs Tridwell! It had been his life-long hobby to study the speech of what my mother called the lower orders. He had even compiled a dictionary of the dialect around Swerton and had it privately printed. I had a copy of it on the homely bookshelves in my very office. I can't claim to have studied it, but I had at least learnt something from that hobby of his – just as I had learnt something about hand-guns.

And something began to puzzle me about this Mrs Tridwell's accent. It was genuine enough, I was sure, but it wasn't local. Yet Miss Holland had introduced her as a local amateur potter!

She was fingering her throat and seemed to be quite placid, as if she had now accepted Miss Holland's description of me as relatively harmless.

"Mrs Tridwell," I said (tactfully, of course), "might I ask where you make your pots?"

She didn't say anything for a moment and continued to finger and stroke her throat. Her eyes were on the squawk-box. Her hands, I then noted, were far from dainty. They were big and strong-looking. Her fingernails were as black and as splintered as those of an old village cobbler.

Abruptly and harshly, she whispered: "Can that lady downstairs hear what we talk about? Through that box of yourn?"

"Certainly not," I smilingly said. "It has no eavesdropping function. It's purely for two-way communication. You see, this little red light would need to go on – "

Before I could even begin my explanation, this Mrs Tridwell had leapt to her feet. Her big strong fist came crashing down on the box – which was, in fact, not just a box but an elegant little mahogany cabinet – and smashed it to smithereens.

"Mrs Tridwell," I had difficulty in saying, "I can hardly believe what you've just done. It's outrageous. Sheer vandalism."

She was shivering from head to toe. "Believe me, mister, we don't want that lady hearing our business. She's already putting two and two together I can betcha. If she ain't, she soon will."

"Madam," I said, slumped in my chair with real shock, "this apparatus only needed to be unplugged if you were suspicious of it. What a strange young woman you must be! Even if Miss

Holland could hear us, the subject of your pots is hardly likely to excite her. I tell you that frankly."

She sat back down on her chair and said: "Excuse me, sir, but I ain't made no pot in all me life."

More real shock. "You haven't? Mrs Tridwell, whatever are you saying?"

"I ain't no Mrs Tridwell neither. That's just a pretend. Them pots too. Bought them down the road. From a charity-shop this morning, open early. Didn't hardly cost me nothing."

I stood up to say: "Madam, are you in league with Miss Holland?"

"Blimey, no."

"Both of you trying to make a fool of me?"

"Honest, sir, I didn't hardly speak to your lady. All I did was to come in to pretend I'd got them pots to sell. She's the one who goes and tells you I made them myself."

"Outrageous behaviour on her part. I'll be dealing with her later," and I began pacing about the room in bewildered anger. "Why this hoax? Why all these lies? Lies!"

The wretched woman cringed on her chair as if about to be smacked. "All I wore trying to do, sir, was to get in and see you private-like. All I asked your lady was permission to see the chief."

"But why those unbearably hideous pots?"

"Seeing as how you has tea-sets in the window, sir, I thought them pots might be a way of getting us together. It wore only an idea. I wore there sitting in the coffee-shop across the road waiting for you, sir. Waiting for you to turn up. I sees your lady come. I didn't want to speak to her, but I had to – after creeping-in like. You was having words. I didn't mean to upset you, sir. Can I have another glass of water now? Me throat feels bad again."

Automatically the gentleman: "Certainly, madam."

Having handed her the re-filled glass, I stood and watched this woman giving a repeat-performance – of the long and loud gargles. Not exactly a social grace. But, in spite of my anger, I was touched anew. Her effort to enunciate as clearly as she could had exhausted her throat again. Surely this effort on her part was a form of good manners? Tolerably mollified, I sat down at my desk and gave her throat three whole minutes to recover.

"Madam," I said, after checking my watch, "since you no longer appear to be Mrs Tridwell, may I now ask you to clarify your identity?"

Her reply: "What do you mean?"

Accurately as I am trying to write these memoirs, I cannot reproduce that reply exactly. To do that, I would need the international phonetic alphabet, which my father (in vain) had tried to teach me. (For me, trying to learn it was as tough as learning Greek at Beagley.) I have given you only a civilised translation. Her reply "what do you mean" was more like "warrior mane."

And even that is only an approximation of the horrible sound she emitted. But here are two points, which you need to grasp. First, she was henceforth to make no great effort at speaking clearly. Secondly (and this is a weirder development), I was to find myself understanding her perfectly! What can be the meaning of that? Can anyone tell me? After a bit, she was even able to understand my own speech equally perfectly.

"Let me put it this way," I said, unscrewing my fountain-pen. "Who is Mrs Tridwell if she isn't you?"

"Wait on, mister, she said, for the first time speaking sharply, "don't you go writing nothing down till I tells you." ("tiller telsh yer.")

I suspended my pen and spoke sharply myself. "At least tell me who you are personally."

"I ain't Mrs Tridwell. That's because she's dead. Very old she wore. Used to run a sweet-shop when I wore a kid. I just loaned her name off her, that's all. Can't use me real name, can I? I'm here on secret business."

"Madam, am I allowed to know your real name?"

"As long as you keep quiet about it, yes. My first name is Asti. Me other name is Glertish. So now you know. I am Asti Glertish."

"My goodness me," I said, trying to restore my good humour, "what an extraordinary name! I've never heard of anyone called Asti. I've heard of Asti Spumante – you know, the drink. My wife likes it."

"So did my real mum," said this now re-named woman. "That's why she called me Asti. Me, sir, I doesn't like any kind of booze. It's muck."

"Are you, in fact, a married woman?"

"Blimey, no. I'm me and no one's else. I am Asti Glertish and that's that."

"Tell me," I said, trying to be delicate in my pursuit of information, "is your name a name I should regard as being of any importance?"

"Yes, mister," she said, steadily but with no hint of menace, "I reckon you should."

"Do you live locally?"

"Blimey, no. Don't hardly know this town. Ain't hardly been here two week. Got a stay-place in a road behind the station."

"Where, then, are you from?"

"London, south of the river." ("Lunnen, sarfer der river.")

"I don't often go to London," I said, chattily but uneasily. "Might I ask why you've come all this way? Is it just to see me?"

"Not at first, no." Miss Asti Glertish, as I must perforce now call her, was beginning to look restless. "Didn't even know you existed."

"How long do you intend to stay in Dackley?"

"Until our secret business is done."

"And what," I said, with my heart beginning to thump, "is the nature of the business?"

"For the moment," she said, getting up and tip-toeing around, "never you mind." ("nivia moind.")

Although, as I've said, there was no hint of menace in her tone, I nevertheless feared she could be an emissary of the oriental blackmailers. After staring through the windows and into the high street, she drew the curtains slightly and said: "You got a clean envelope in that desk of yourn?"

"Yes, Miss Glertish."

"Then get it out, please, and write on it your name and address. And put a stamp on."

"As you please, Miss Glertish."

"Does that lady downstairs read your letters?"

"The ones that come to the shop, yes."

"Does you ever live or stay over this shop?"

"Of course not, Miss Glertish. I live with my wife and family outside of the town."

"Then put down that address, mister. Don't want that boss-lady in on all this," and she stood over me until I capped my fountain-pen. "I want to stay in touch after I get back to London. Now, please, you read that out."

"Read out my name and address? Do you wear glasses? Is that it? Forgotten them, have you?"

"I don't wear glasses. I just can't read and write too good."

"In this day and age? You can't read or write?"

"A bit, yes, but not too good. Like I say, please read out what you just put," and she looked so impatient with me that I hastily complied.

I began reading, carefully and like a good tutor (pointing with my fingertip) word by word.

"James Crackery, Rose Cottage, Kind Maiden Green – "

She interrupted with the most repulsive snort you could possibly imagine, presumably of amusement. Snatching the envelope from me, she almost danced around the room with it as she gabbled: "Ho yes! Ho yes! What a name! Mr Crackers! If my name's a queer one, then yourns even more queer I reckon! Mr Crackers! Certainly suits you, don't it?"

"The name," I tried to tell her, "is Crackery. Let me advise you that I've heard all the jokes. I'm tired of them."

"That's all right by me, Mr Crackers."

Becoming abruptly serious again, she sat down and put the envelope away in her scruffy shoulder-bag. And not only serious but more self-confident.

"Mr Crackers, let's get down to brass tacks. You deaded Leo. I sees you do it. Killed him."

After about a hundred years (actually all of five seconds), I chokingly said: "You could not possibly have seen me. There was no one else there."

"No one's else but me," she smartly said. "I wore over in the bushes. You didn't see me, Mr Crackers, but I could see you plenty OK."

"Over in the bushes," I weakly repeated. "Whatever were you doing in the bushes?"

"Doing a wee-wee, sir."

This really was a brow-clutching moment.

"I do beg your pardon," I bleated. "I didn't mean to be intrusive. I – er …"

For the first time in my life, I lost my voice. It was like having it pulled out of me by a magician and thrown away to the four winds. I have to admit I stared blankly. All I could do. I was only aware of my own stupidity as never before. How could I have not twigged that she had somehow seen me? And not twigged why she had tracked me down? It had to be blackmail. There could be no other explanation.

My glumly swivelling eyes watched her as she got up and went to the door. Opening it slightly, she cocked an ear at the gap before closing it and returning on tip-toe to her chair. She said: "That boss-lady's being kept busy down there, thank Gord. Don't want her barging in on us, do we?"

I could only give a trembling nod, but I was beginning to realise that her words 'doing a wee-wee' had not been spoken with a sinister connotation. They had been a simple statement of realistic fact. In much the same obligingly informative tone, she went on to say: "I didn't see you actual arrive. That's because I has to go fair deep into them bushes. I didn't want that stupid Leo peeping at me, did I? Not me! But, after I done, I makes me way back. By that time, you and him wore talking. I had a listen. The two of you was having yer words about the multi-storey and that. That's as how I come to see everything you then duzz."

My voice huskily returned. I was able to say: "Miss Glertish, I am at a loss in trying to grasp the situation you describe. Why were you in the vicinity at all?"

"Because that stupid Leo calls early in the morning – at my stay-place. Hardly gives me time to finish me bought and paid-for breakfast. He wore that keen to take me in the van to see him start wheel-clamping. He wore that full of hisself. All week he wore boasting as how he could deal easy with the mugs – people like you who was parked up in that lane-place. That's why I wore real sick of him. It's why I kept quiet in them bushes. I wanted to see someone give him what for. I didn't expect to see him killed though."

Very huskily: "What happened, of course, was very much an accident. Extremely regrettable. Might I ask, Miss Glertish, if you had been his girl-friend?"

"Him? That common bloke? Not likely. I chums up to him for strictly private reasons. I only let him know what I wants him to know. Same as with you, Mr Crackers. The less you knows, the better. Let's get down to business." ("lits geddarner busy-nurse.")

To find that I had not killed a much-loved boy-friend was a relief. But only a slight relief. And it was made no slighter by what this amazing woman did next. Reaching down to one of her floppy shopping-baskets (beside her chair), she withdrew two separate objects – and they were not pots.

She plonked them down on my snow-white desk-blotter.

One was the wheel-clamper's highly recognisable tobacco-tin, with a rubber-band securing the lid. Under the rubber-band was tucked a Rizla fag-paper packet. The other object was the then modern device – which I had not previously seen – but which I knew only be a 'mobile' telephone.

"There you are," said Asti Glertish, sitting as still as a rock, "do them things prove what I tells you?" ("warra telsh yer.")

I stared down at these two unwholesome reminders of my deed in Willow Tree Lane. Again I couldn't speak.

Again, her words had been a simple statement of realistic fact; but, shocking as it may be to public morality, all I could think of next was my missing brief-case.

"My brief-case," I managed to gasp, "did you by any chance find my brief-case?"

"That leather bag of yourn? Of course I did. I couldn't bring that here, could I? Too big. But don't worry. It's at my stay-place, safe and sound." ("stye-plice, siphon-sarned.")

"Oh, thank goodness for that! Miss Glertish, you are a remarkably resourceful young woman. You really are. Might I just ask, however? When can I expect to get it back?

She looked at me steadily but with a frown. "Mr Crackery, pardon me as says it. But you ain't bright. You still needs to pretend, sir. You has been to the police-station about that bag. You has reported it as being lost hasn't yer?"

"Good heavens, Miss Glertish! How on earth did you know what I said at the police-station?"

"Because I followed you there. I wore sitting on one of them seats in the middle outside. It wore as clear as daylight you'd gone in to tell a lie. You wouldn't have been out so quick if you's been in there telling the truth. They would have kept you in, wouldn't they just. But not for lost property, eh?"

Light began to dawn upon me. "You were one of those two women on the bench in that square?"

"Of course I wore."

"But they had babies! Two pushchairs!"

Patiently, Miss Glertish said: "There was two women there, yes. I joined 'em. One of 'em went off across to them toilets, leaving me to have a nice smoke and a natter with her mate. You then come out and down them steps. You walks right by me, but you looks right in my face. You thinks nothing of me. You walks on, I catches up with you a bit later, but not close enough to speak to in private."

Partly out of aversion to the two objects befouling my desk, I stood up and moved away.

"Not so clever, were you," I said, feebly trying to assert myself. "I knew someone was following me. Instinct. And I know a thing or two about tracking! I soon shook you off, didn't I?"

"No, sir," she said, again sitting as still as a rock. "It wore me what gives up on you. I has other things to do. I lets you go."

"Well anyway," I said, feeling a bit stung, "you're missing the point. When do I get my brief-case back? It was a present from my wife."

"Pardon me as says it, sir, but you is the one missing the point. You has told the police about your lost bag. That means you has to keep up the pretend. You has to let the police return it. Don't look so sick, sir. I can easy get it handed in all proper-like."

"I need to be consistent, you mean?"

"That could be the word, sir, I'm sure."

"I apologise, madam. You're right and I'm wrong. You really are outstandingly intelligent for someone so badly educated."

This compliment, like the others I had made, didn't seem to affect her in any way at all. She simply sat there like a monumentally unwanted guest at a dinner-party. Although she was not threatening in her manner, I couldn't avoid feeling that dark forces were in control of her. Since she now seemed to be sunk in thought, I prowled about a bit more before trying to fish for more information.

"Madam, can I take it that you were instrumental in – er – removing the remains?"

"That's right, sir. I took it away in the van. The body. The dead body is what it's called."

"Entirely on your own?"

"That's right, Mr Crackers. On me own."

"But good heavens! Surely it was a hefty thing to do? I couldn't have shifted him myself I frankly have to admit."

"I am used to shifting heavy stuff, mister. I'm in the motor-mend business. I'm a tyre-fitter." ("oima tar-fidda.")

Trying to lighten these details, I said: "Dear me, I thought it was only in Russia that ladies did that sort of work!"

"I don't know nothing about Russia," she said, and in a vigorous tone that left me very uneasy, "but I do know I won't be doing no more motor-mend. From now on, it's going to be a better life. A much better life. More swank."

It was hardly a favourable way of changing the subject, but, in a state of complete funk, I helplessly asked: "Where did you go? I mean, how did you dispose of the – er – problem?"

"Never you mind." ("nivia moind.")

"Madam, I feel I need to know."

"Knowing won't do you no good," and this incredible female now astounded me further.

Delving into another of her three floppy baskets, she produced something wrapped in tissue-paper. A bulky but light-weight object, about the size (I guessed) of a hat.

She stood up to present me with this new surprise. I unwrapped it and indeed found it to be a hat. It was the very bowler-hat I had stupidly left behind in that bungalow.

"By Jove," I cried, reverting instantly to one of the old-time expressions of a true gentleman. "Miss Glertish, I cannot thank you enough. Why, it looks as good as new!"

"I gives it a good brush-up at my stay-place," she quietly said. "It wore that dusty."

"One of my best-ever hats," and I put it on for one or two delighted moments, preening a bit in the mirror (the mirror over my office fireplace). "As Miss Holland has pithily remarked, it suits me a lot better than the trilby."

I hung this better hat of mine on my office hat-stand. Beside the trilby (the only other to be occupying a peg), it really was superior (and, in fact, had cost me a lot more). Only then did a serious and nasty thought occur to me more strongly. That ghastly bungalow!

"Miss Glertish, might I ask how you came to be in possession of my bowler-hat?"

Not replying, she continued to look at me steadfastly for a few seconds. (I remember her look so clearly.) Then, abruptly, she sat down and reached into one of her floppy baskets. From it she withdrew a transparent plastic bag. I couldn't quite see what was in it, but it looked rather heavy. I saw more clearly after she leaned forward and plonked the bag on my already sullied blotter.

"Ah," I exclaimed. "Hmm …"

It was, of course, the exploded residue of the pistol I had used for killing Masher. Along with the tobacco-tin and the 'mobile' phone, it could not have emphasised my unspoken bond with this woman more strongly.

"Quite a collection," I quavered. "What am I supposed to do with it?"

"Well, sir, I has already done my part. It's only fair that you do yourn. In other words, sir, you can be the one to get rid of them things. Let's see if you has the brains to know what to do."

"Is this what my meant by your use of the word business?"

"More or less, yes." ("moara luss, yuss.")

It was at this tricky moment in my relationship with Miss Asti Glertish that both she and I froze in terror.

There came a simply thunderous hammering at my office door. It was the sort of noise any suspected person can expect to hear when the police make a dawn raid.

Asti Glertish was the first of us to react. In a flash, she scooped up the grisly items into a basket and fled (with the other two baskets) into my wash-room.

Alone, I felt stronger. How dare the police invade my holy of holies unannounced! I strode to the door. This time I used not the army-officer voice but the voice of my old headmaster (when entering an offending classroom).

"What's all this noise?"

Having yanked open the door, I was amazed to see the true culprit. It was, as anyone but I would have known, the meddlesome Miss Holland. She faced me coolly. In her hand was the brass owl (a paperweight from her own office) which she had been using for banging on my door.

"James, you've taken this game too far. We've no more customers for the moment, but once again you have failed to pick up your end of the log. Today is the last straw."

She sweepingly began to go back down to the shop, but she stopped. She turned to say: "What exactly has been going on up here? Have you been indulging in any form of improper behaviour?"

I knew this to be a deliberately preposterous insult, but it knocked me askew. I brimmed over with an urge to tell the truth and began to burble it.

"It's all a bit complicated, you see. There are one or two little mysteries I need to sort out. Then I'll know what's what."

"Mysteries? What sort of mysteries? Do they involve Mrs Tridwell?"

I managed to rescue my presence of mind by resorting to a new and hurriedly concocted lie.

"Well, yes. She doesn't hope we'll sell her pots and do nothing more for her. She seems to want a job here. I fully admit to being sorry for her. Despite things being as they are, I did think we could help her out."

"Mr Crackery, I have a contract. It clearly states that I must be consulted about the appointment of staff."

"Yes, Miss Holland. But I thought we could use her for shifting all the junk out of the attics. As you've so often said, we could use that space."

Miss Holland smiled in lofty surprise and said: "Why, James, that's actually a quite intelligent suggestion! But what are the mysteries you hint at?"

"More conundrums, really, than mysteries. I'm rather worried that she might not be strong enough to carry heavy weights. She's only a young woman. A bit on the delicate side, I would say."

"Rubbish. She's obviously as strong as a horse. If not stronger," and Miss Holland pushed her way past me into my office. "I will speak to her myself. You go down and mind the shop. But where on earth is she? James, what have you done with Mrs Tridwell?"

"She's in my wash-room," I said, whispering in a tone of humane concern. "As I understand it, something she had for breakfast didn't agree with her. She has a sick-headache."

Miss Holland, showing genuine concern, gently knocked on the wash-room door. "Are you feeling a bit better, Mrs Tridwell? I have indigestion-mixture in our first-aid cupboard downstairs. Would you like some?"

No reply. Giving up, Miss Holland said: "I must go down to the shop. You stay up here. Bring her down as soon as she recovers. You've handled this matter badly, but as least you've had one good idea today. A few more good ideas might persuade me to alter my opinion of your abilities. My God!"

On the point of leaving the room, she had spotted the smashed-up squawk-box. Pointing in real and dramatic amazement, she almost shrieked: "No wonder I couldn't get through! Has it come to this? You smash up your antique intercom in a fit of psychotic rage? Just because I request you to help with your very own customers?"

This accusation stiffened me. "That's not what happened, Miss Holland."

"Then what did?"

"It got pushed off the desk quite by accident. Clumsily, I admit, I happened to tread on it after it had fallen to the floor. No great harm done. It can be mended."

"But how on earth did it get pushed off the desk? What were you doing with Mrs Tridwell? Wrestling with her? On top of the desk?"

"I was simply re-arranging things on the desk so that she could set out some of her smaller samples – little dishes which she had in one of her baskets. Return to your duties, Miss Holland. I don't like your tone."

It was now that the doubting Miss Holland spotted my hat – the restored bowler which, like as ass, I had left on open view on the hat-stand. (Why couldn't I have put it in the cupboard?)

"So," said Miss Holland, "your well-favoured hat has now reappeared! Now that, Mr Crackery, is either a mystery, which needs to be explained or proof that you are mentally extremely confused. Which is it, Mr Crackery?"

Also, she now spotted the letters which (you may remember) I had consigned to the WPB.

Without another word, she retrieved them and placed them in open order on my desk. She then walked out and down the stairs, leaving me to close the door. Feeling like a hot and bothered flunkey, I closed it – and then found the wretched Glertish at my elbow.

She, I can only say, was in a far worse state than I.

"For the sake of all the saints in heaven," she said, "get me out of here! Don't let her get near me I beg of yer."

I was already anxious enough, but her pitiful terror of Miss Holland raised my own anxiety to much the same level. In an effort to calm myself, I defiantly put on my controversial hat. Opening the door, I stole along the landing to look over the banisters and down into the shop. Miss Holland was standing there, arms folded. Preoccupied, but she was obviously awaiting our descent. Incredibly, fate intervened (on my side for once). The shop was luckily still without customers, and the phone rang – in her office!

"Quick," I whispered and beckoned to the hesitating Glertish, "she's gone into the back room to answer the phone."

We stole down the stairs, me with heart in my mouth and the Glertish with her three baskets and with her knees as weak as water. I had to support her with my arm around her – most embarrassing. We were crossing the floor and were almost at the threshold. Miss Holland had her back to us, but she suddenly turned, the phone still at her ear. She saw us – through her wide-open door!

"James, where are you taking that woman? I've questions to ask her. I want to see what else she has in her baskets."

Once outside, the Glertish and I scampered off up the High Street as if our backsides were on fire. We didn't pause for breath until we were around the corner into King William Street and the Memorial Gardens. For all her strength, the Glertish was as breathless as I. We sank down on an empty bench and she offered me a cigarette. I politely declined and she lit up draggingly. She said: "Blimey, that wore close. Daft of me ever to have come into yer shop. I know brains when I sees 'em. Never again. Like I say, she real scares me."

Trying to sound light-hearted, I said: "I'm a little scared of her myself, I must admit. I can't think why."

"Oh, come off it! The reason is as plain as the nose on yer face. You is in love with her. What you is scared of is love – real love."

I nearly fell off the bench. "You're being completely ridiculous. I have a wife and two children. In love with Miss Holland? It can't be true."

"Of course it's true. You're as daft about being in love as my dad. He wore so daft he got his heart broke. You going back to the shop now?"

Struggling under this big revelation, I said: "I don't think I can. I don't feel up to it …"

"Then what are you going to do next?"

"I think, Miss Glertish, that I need to take your advice – about being consistent. I need to go home. I told my wife – and Miss Holland as well – that our ceilings were in danger of collapse."

"Yes, Mr Crackers, I heard you say so after I crept into the shop. Was it a lie?"

"Of course it was. And I need to keep up the pretence. I need to go home, as I now realise, and phone for a builder's man. I can pretend to be reassured and my wife and children can then come home. Good morning, Miss Glertish," and I tried to stand up.

She restrained me with a grip on my wrist, which really was like a vice. (I can feel that grip to this day.) "Pardon me as says it, Mr Crackers, but what you done strikes me as complete bonkers. What wore the point of telling a lie about them ceilings?"

"It was just a ruse. I needed to get my wife and children out of harm's way. I thought a gang might be hanging around who might attack my little cottage."

"Gang? What gang?"

"A criminal gang, Miss Glertish, with Chinese connections."

She was so surprised by this that she released my wrist and threw away her cigarette. Moving away from me slightly, along the bench: "You is real barmy, mister. A real mad nut."

"Oh I am, am I?" I reached into my inside-pocket. "Then kindly explain this message, madam," and I forcefully dangled the desecrated page in front of her face. "Explain why I found it under my windscreen-wiper in the multi-storey car-park. This signature," I said, indicating the encircled words TLI SU, "would appear to any reasonable man as being that of a Chinaman."

"I ain't no Chinaman, Mr Crackers, but I do be the one who left you that message. Forget it. It don't mean nothing now because you ignored it."

"I have spent hours – hours! – in trying to decipher this illiterate scrawl. What threat were you trying to convey?"

"It wore just a message, that's all."

"Meaning what, damn you?"

The wretched Glertish lit another of her foul cigarettes and said: "Don't do nothing more till I sees you."

Her pronunciation was not as I have must represented it, as I'm hoping you will by this time be able to appreciate. The sentence came out of her mouth a bit like this: "Dunda nuffinmer tilla seizure."

Imitate the same pronunciation but with fewer consonants. You might then emit the same hideous sound. The words on Miss Holland's sheet of paper, if I may remind you, were DND NUXMO – with an apparently encircled signature TLI SU. For me, of course, this was a moment of utter chagrin. I had made a total ass of myself. I remembered, all in a flash, one of my mother's girls from the village (Swerton). Like Asti Glertish, she had been almost illiterate. After breaking some piece of crockery or other, she would leave behind her an apologetic note. The wording would always consist of capitals, truncated and spaced out in the same ridiculous way. When not knowing the right letter for a spoken sound, she would put an 'X' – just as the Glertish had done (for the T and the H the word 'nothing').

Although dialect varies, this form of writing is presumably the same for all Britain's illiterates. I don't really know. But one thing annoyed me about the Glertish sample.

"Why on earth," I demanded of her, "did you encircle the last bit of your so-called message? Extremely misleading. It's what made me think you were a member of a Chinese gang."

"Them last words," she said, "was real important. Till I sees you means you was to wait. I wasn't to know, was I, that you ain't bright. I made them words as clear as I could. That's why I put a circle all around 'em. But you takes no notice and that's that."

Dropping my voice (for there were a number of saunterers criss-crossing those town-centre gardens), I said: "At risk of seeming even more obtuse, might I ask if you are, in fact, a part of any criminal gang?"

Recklessly loud: "A gang? Me? Of course I ain't. I keeps myself to myself. I'm me and no one's else. I ain't no criminal neither."

"Do please keep your voice down, Miss Glertish. Are you saying that I've paid for two moth-eaten old donkeys for nothing?"

Even more loudly: "Mr Crackery, I don't know nothing about no donkeys."

"At least tell me this, madam, and speak more softly. How did you manage to find my car in that complicated multi-storey? To put this message of yours under my wiper? That's something which really baffles me."

She threw away her cigarette again – a gesture, it would seem, of despairing disgust with my intellect. "Mr Crackery, you must be even more stupider than Leo if you doesn't know the answer to something so simple. And you give me that," she added, snatching the desecrated page from my hand. "It ain't got no meaning now," and she used her lighter, right there on the bench, for publicly burning it.

Uneasily looking around, I could only hope anyone who saw this action wouldn't think she was burning a love-letter from me. (You know how people talk.) I was worried, too, by the lighter itself. It was an old storm-lighter, the sort used by sea-captains and engine-drivers. It was Rivinni's. I had seen him using it. (Might become a clue?)

She stood up. I stood up too (always the gentleman). I said: "At least tell me, madam, at what time you left your message under my wiper."

"The answer to that, Mr Crackery, is something else plain simple. It wore afore you altered all my plans by going off and killing that evil old witch – up at that bungalow-place of hern."

I sat back down again, collapsed in fact. Why couldn't this wretched Glertish keep her voice down? Feebly, I said: "Her unfortunate death was wholly accidental."

"Mister, I doesn't care either way. She's dead and that's that. You doesn't have to tell me nothing. I sees you do it. I wore there. I sees and I hears yer."

"You couldn't have seen me," I gasped, "not unless you were invisible. There was absolutely no one else there."

"No one else's but me, Mr Crackery," and she dumped one of her floppy baskets on my lap. "Go home, sir. And on your way get rid of these things of Leo's. You're a local. You must have enough brain to know of a nice deep pond. And get rid of this while you're about it," and she slipped the storm-lighter into the basket. "I has one or two things to do before I goes back to London. See you later."

The words 'see you later' were spoken, you might be interested to hear, without the inclusion of one single consonant. No educated person, I would imagine, could possibly reproduce such a sound. To speak as badly as Asti Glertish in saying 'see you later' can only be a linguistic gift.

Frantic as well as fascinated, I jumped up in a confused attempt to detain her. I all but bellowed: "But you couldn't have seen me! How could it even be remotely possible?"

She halted to whisper: "You needs to keep your voice down, sir. Ask yourself. Who's else could have cleared up after yer?"

"You couldn't have seen me! This time there can be no possible explanation."

"Try working it out for yourself, sir. Put a wet towel around your head, like my silly dad used to do when he had a problem. But don't strain yerself wilya?"

Off she went, leaving me clutching the basket in one hand and with the other clumsily raising my hat – my much-loved bowler.

FOUR

More Little Surprises

I awoke on Tuesday morning at half-past seven. The birds were singing their guts out. They sang as if they and everyone else in the world – including me – had no troubles at all.

I ate my lonely breakfast gloomily and made no effort (as advised) to strain myself. To put it more analytically, I decided not to theorise upon what I didn't yet know. The mysterious Glertish was not bent upon blackmail. That, at least, I could assume.

Why, then, had she gone to such grisly lengths to protect me? How could she even bring herself to do such things? Removing bodies? Ugh!

"James," I said, scraping out the last of the marmalade (for my toast), "the answer can only be in those words of hers about that frightful fellow. Don't ponder upon them. The answer will come in time from she herself. You only need to remember Aunt Bartle and stay calm."

I reminded myself of the words ("I chummed up to him for strictly private reasons") and I hurried out into the garden. Other things the Glertish had said (need I remind you?) were too disturbing to me. I couldn't even bring myself to phone my young and pretty wife at Swerton, to say nothing of my carping sister. It was only the children I wanted to speak to but couldn't. (It was only they I was missing.)

I was therefore paying maximum attention to refreshing the incinerator at the bottom of the garden. (I had started it up, with paraffin, before going to bed.) This helped to keep me calm, although I felt a bit like Dr Crippen.

"What are you burning?" ("worra yer boynin?")

These words seemed to come out of the air, as if in a nasty dream. This end of the garden, may I tell you, was no dump. It was my fruit-and-vegetable garden, reached through a well-trimmed arch in the hedge (with a wicket-gate). A private place. Yet there she was, the Glertish – standing right behind me in the same old clothes as the day before.

"I think it wise," I said, "to burn every item of apparel which could possibly connect me with certain recent events. Even my nice new driving-gloves."

"You is being too fussy, sir. I clears up after you real good."

"And for that, Miss Glertish, I am truly grateful. Thank you very much for everything you've done for me. I shall never forget you."

"Excuse me, sir," she said, politely and even humbly, "but you needs to get one thing straight. What I done was done for me – not for you. I would never have done a thing if there wasn't nothing in it for me."

"I see," I said, feeling (heaven knows why) a little hurt.

Uninvited, she sat down on the old garden-seat which fronted the side of my shed – my private garden-shed, and she began to light up a cigarette.

"No smoking," I sharply said.

"What, not even in the open air?"

Knowing I had been stupidly churlish, I hastily said: "I was about to invite you indoors for a cup of tea. Or water, if that's what you would prefer."

She sprang up like a happy child and said, "Ooo, tea would be nice," and she followed me back to the cottage like a lamb following its mother.

Her first act, at the kitchen table, was to drink her tea from the saucer instead of the cup. (I hadn't seen that done since I last visited a long-retired village carpenter.) Her second action was far more outlandish. She began it by saying: "Mr Crackery, did you get rid of them things yesterday?"

"Yes, Miss Glertish. In the Bilsington reservoir. Very deep. More like an abandoned lake now. Said to be toxic."

"And has you phoned the builders? About coming to look at your bedroom ceilings?"

"Not yet, no. I shall phone them today."

She put down her cup and saucer and said: "Mind if I looks at them ceilings?"

With a shrug of surprise, I said: "If you wish, certainly ..."

I led the way upstairs and let her look in at the matrimonial bedroom. She gave it but a glance. Leaving me in the doorway and as quick as a monkey, she was up on a chair on the landing and had gone through the hatch into the loft.

A moment later, I was startled by her trainer-clad foot coming through the plaster – above my particular bed, open and still unmade. More plaster came down as she widened the hole, stamping about with her foot.

After descending from the loft and rejoining me, she said: "There now – that makes the pretend a lot better. And keeps your wife and kids away a bit longer."

"It just so happens," I said, more than a little frostily, "that I want them back as soon as possible. Today, preferably."

"Don't be daft, sir. Always start as you means to go on. You still has other things to do. Come with me, sir – out to the van."

I yelled in alarm: "The van? You surely haven't got that wretched yellow van parked outside?"

"How else would you expect me to get here, Mr Crackers? It's a good van. The old witch didn't buy rubbish when she got that van."

"But nothing could be more conspicuous!"

"Don't you worry, sir. I'm on my way to London in it. You won't never see it again," and the Glertish led the way to my own gate, ushering me through it with perfect courtesy.

At first, out in the road and with the sun in my eyes, I could see no sign of the wretched van. Only did I see it as she led the way to where it was parked – on the wide verge opposite the gate and under the trees.

It was no longer yellow. It was now a very dark blue.

"Resprays it yesterday," the Glertish explained, unlocking the back door. "Does it in the street after dark. Done rough, but OK enough until I gets back to London."

There was nothing in the not too clean back of the van except an inelegant Dick Whittington bundle (her more personal belongings) and two items of far more handsome luggage. One, a steamer-trunk; the other, smaller but nevertheless large. I can only describe it as a huge Gladstone bag.

"This here," said this amazing woman, reaching for the huge Gladstone, "is for you to deal with – as you think fit. I'll help you indoors with it, but I can't stay long. I has to get back to London. I'm relying on you, Mr Crackery, to make sure you hide this bag somewhere real good. I am also relying on you to be real clever in getting rid of what's inside."

She closed the van door, locked it and began humping the weighty bag up my front-garden path. Over her shoulder, she added: "You can't hide it in the loft, not even for a little while – not with having the builders in. So where's a good place for it whiles you think things out?"

I was following her in horror. "Wait, Miss Glertish! Wait!"

She stopped. "What's the matter?"

"Miss Glertish, please don't tell me what's in that steamer-trunk. Please just leave and take that bag with you."

She put the bag down and stared at me in disappointed wonder.

"Mr Crackery, it really does puzzle me as to how someone who talks as nice as you can be so stupid. What is it you thinks I has got in this here bag?" ("this ear barg.")

"From what you've said, madam, it clearly contains the sad remains of that woman's dog. I can't go along with any more of this. I really can't. I really must beg you to excuse me. It's all too much."

She bent down, unlatched the bag and pulled it wide open. "Have a look inside, Mr Crackery."

Amid all the birdsong and under that morning-blue sky, I found myself looking down into a bag containing dozens of small plastic packets. They appeared to be – and, in fact, were – transparent freezer-bags. Inside each plastic bag was a juicily fat roll of bank-notes. Each roll had a rubber-band for keeping the roll in shape. Sticking one of these rolls under my nose, Miss Glertish said: "This and all the others is for you, sir. You is now quite a rich man."

"Am I really?" I could hardly breathe. "How jolly nice of you …what about yourself?"

"Oh, I done plenty all right! All you has is the dregs as you might say."

"Dregs? You call this dregs?"

"The place wore stuffed with money under them boards. Plenty to divide up real clever."

She spoke those words unexcitedly, then re-packaged the fat little roll and returned it to the bag. Picking up the bag, she added: "Fancy you thinking I has a dead dog in here! Cor lummy. Got it now? For the time being, sir, you has to hide this bag some place safe. So where's it to be? Blimey, sir – hold up!"

Reluctant as I am to admit it, my knees were buckling and I very nearly fainted. A rich man, did she say?

Never in my life before had I fainted, as far as I can recall. In the same way as I had supported Miss Glertish – in getting her out of the shop – she now had to support me in getting me back to the cottage. She was holding that whacking great bag in one hand with her other hand under my armpit.

"Take me through to the sitting-room," I had to tell her. "I need a brandy."

She spoke in a slightly annoyed tone: "You got heart-trouble or something?" ("art-trubbla sunnick?")

I was only able to reply after she had got me to the sofa: "Only slight. Enough to reject me for an army-career and to put my damn car-insurance up. Sideboard! No soda."

After sniffing the stoppers, she handed me a brandy and said: "I hopes you don't die like my dad did. And I hopes you ain't on the booze like him neither. I needs you, sir, to keep an eye on that bungalow-place whiles I be in London. Daft as you is, sir, you've got to do." ("you gorra do.")

I was recovering with a speed that surprised me. I sat up like a jack-rabbit, my eyes automatically gluing themselves to the bag. (Miss Glertish had dumped it on the floor as casually as if it meant nothing.) Although still rather dazed, I could already see myself paying off my debts in a grand manner.

"How much, madam, is in that bag?"

"Not as much as I've got in the trunk, I can tell you that. I've even given you a bag of them gold coins called Krugers. That's to bring you luck. I didn't have no time to count. The old witch had such a lot hidden up. She couldn't fool me, though. She fooled everyone else. Not me, though – NOT ME."

She spoke those two last words with a vigour and a gesture, which I was soon to see as characteristic. The gesture was a prod into her own bosom – with a self-pointing forefinger.

"Not me," she repeated, in quite a yell.

I was to remember this not-me gesture all my life. Meanwhile, it worried me no end.

"Miss Glertish, this is all very kind of you. But I have to say that certain matters are puzzlingly mysterious. I – "

She interrupted me, not rudely but firmly. "I ain't being kind to you, sir. The money in that bag pays you to keep our secret. Also, it's a big payment for not asking me too many questions. I shall take it quite hangry if you keeps on at me."

I became a little irritated. "Madam, some questions are vital if

I am to understand – and indeed guard against – any unforeseen consequences. Miss Holland is always saying I'm not a man of foresight. She's wrong. I have bags of foresight. But how can I exercise foresight – on both your behalf and mine – if you're going to stay clammed up?"

Miss Glertish instantly went into a sulk. She actually kicked that bag – kicked it savagely – before flinging herself into the armchair facing me.

"All right," she said, for the first time looking as if she despised me, "waste more of my time. There's nothing you couldn't work out for yourself if you used the brains you ain't got. But some things won't do you no good to know, not ever. You remember that, Mr Crackers."

Perhaps it was the blow on the head from that frying-pan – at the bungalow – or perhaps I had been going steadily mad beforehand. But that huge Gladstone bag, on the carpet by the door, seemed to be getting bigger. At the same time, I could feel myself drooling. I had to keep using the back of my hand on each corner of my mouth. Drooling. No other word for it.

Anxious to keep in favour with this amazing benefactress, I began to say: "Miss Glertish, if we are to be partners in stealing this money, I think we – "

She interrupted harshly. "How do you like being called a murderer?"

"But I'm not a murderer," I feebly said. "What happened on both occasions, I do assure you, was entirely accidental."

"And I'm no more a thief neither. So get that straight, Mr Crackery."

"But the contents of that bag," I tried to insist, "obviously amount to stolen money. We have to call a spade a spade. We both need to keep our grasp on reality."

"It's my money. Mr Crackery. All mine. Everything what belonged to that old witch is now all mine. She's dead and so it's mine."

"Might I just ask how you manage to arrive at that conclusion?"

"Because I, Mr Crackery, is a relation. A close relation. Very close. She wore married to my dad. I can prove it. I has got the marriage certificate." ("the marge sir-stifficate.")

At this new shock, I have to admit, I really did crumple up. "Oh, how dreadful! Are you saying I killed your mother?"

Impatiently: "Don't be so daft. She wore my step-mum. My real mum ran off with a fancy-man when I wore six year old. Never sees her since."

"So it was definitely your step-mother I inadvertently killed?"

"Very definitely. She used to thrash me black and blue. Bought a cane she special-tested."

"Oh, how awful! Did your father do nothing to protect you?"

"Him? Too much in love," she spat. "I puts up with it until I wore old enough to pay out to be a lodger – with Mrs Tridwell."

"Ah! The old sweet-shop lady?"

"And she wore more of a mum to me than any real mum," and Miss Glertish began to shed tears. "Now she's dead too. I be all I got."

Wrenching my eyes away from the treasure-trove bag (where they constantly strayed to), I applied sympathy by rising and patting her on her shoulder. "No blubbing, Miss Glertish," and she desisted, although giving me the nastiest look so far. "Do tell me, Miss Glertish. How long did this terrible marriage last?"

"Up to the day my dad dies from too much booze – two year ago. Dies in the pub. But the old witch knowed nothing about it. She never knowed."

"How certain can you be of that?"

"Total certain. Why else d'you think she put her address in Leo's stupid name? She wore tormentifying my dad – making it hard for him to find her. She wore always going away without notice, then coming back without notice. Broke his heart. Always playing tricks on him. Real cruel tricks. She does one to you, doesn't she? Screams darn yer ear-roll. You won't forget that in a hurry, Mr Crackers."

"I certainly won't, Miss Glertish. I did notice, actually, that her fellow Rivinni had a bit of cotton-wool in his ear. Did she play that trick on him too?"

"Of course. It wore what helped to make him go stupid, like it did my dad."

Soft-soapingly: "I do hope that she didn't play the same trick on you."

"You hopes right. It wore something she only does to blokes."

With my back to Miss Glertish, I was at the sideboard at this point. I was nervously helping myself to a little more brandy. (I had told her the truth about my heart.)

"You keep off that stuff," she ordered. "Tip it back in the jar and put the stopper back in."

I nearly disobeyed, but the Gladstone bag had by now become so huge – in my feverish eyes – that it looked huge enough to contain the biggest prize pig on record. The sight reduced me to meek compliance. I cravenly tottered back to the sofa. I was instantly alarmed to see that she was getting up to leave. She was lighting a cigarette in doing so.

"Please," I begged her, "do stay a little longer. I'm still rather befuddled. Just one or two little things need to be made clearer. You may smoke if you wish to."

She subsided unwillingly, but official permission to smoke seemed to give her sulky satisfaction (as I rather knew it would. I can be very subtle, let me tell you). She said: "You just watch your mouth, sir."

I re-started with what I hoped would be a harmlessly oblique question. "How did your step-mother meet that fellow Rivinni?"

"He calls, at that bungalow-place, about two year ago – just after she moves in. He thinks he wore on a cushy number. Just doing the garden, he thinks. She takes him on and gives him hell. Simple as that."

"And how did you, Miss Glertish, come to make his acquaintance?"

"In your town-market. The old witch had my dad running a market-stall the minute they wore married. She wore brainy at it, I give her that. So I reckons she would have some other bloke doing the same. I wore right. I goes to lots of different towns. I gets wind of her eventual. I tracks her down real neat."

"Actually, what was her name? She never revealed it to me."

"And I ain't telling you neither."

"Why not, for heaven's sake!"

"All you needs to know is the name she takes up for Dackley. Mabel Smith." ("Smiff.")

"How many names did she use?"

"Different names at different times. Jones, Robinson, Williams. Anything ordinary like."

"How, then were you able to trace her?"

"She makes the mistake of thinking me stupid. I only had to ask around for her pet-name what I knowed she would keep to."

"I still can't see why you can't tell me her real name."

"Because you might start blabbing it if something goes wrong. Then it would get in all the papers. She wore on the run from a very posh family when she met my dad. He wore pulling petrol. She stopped for a fill-up. They wore married real quick."

"Miss Glertish," I said, in some annoyance, "I am not in the habit of blabbing. Not, at any rate, when it comes to confidential matters. I would not spill any beans."

"No? Not even to that Miss Holland?"

To my great embarrassment, I felt myself blushing like a lovesick teenager. Clumsily, I changed the subject slightly. "What was your objective in tracking down your step-mother?"

"Hobjective? What do you mean?" ("warrior mane?")

"Your intention, Miss Glertish. What was it?"

"Revenge, Mr Crackery. Hasn't you never heard of that nice word? Revenge."

Even more clumsily, even brutally, I asked: "Were you, perhaps, planning to kill your step-mother yourself?"

Miss Glertish had already stubbed out her cigarette (on the sole of her trainer-boot). She threw the stub into the fender and began to shiver and shudder as if having a dose of electro-shock therapy. All her arms and legs were twitching. She all but screamed: "Blimey, no. You think I want to go to hell when I die? To be chased around by that old witch? With her cane? For all time?"

"At the very least," I said, again as clumsily, "were you planning to rob her of her money?"

"Blimey, no," she howled. "Hasn't I already told yer? I ain't no criminal. Besides, you sees for yourself what she wore like. Who would dare to rob an old witch like that? Not me, thank you very much – not me," and she gave herself the self-prod with her forefinger, blazingly vigorous this time.

"Then what," I said, becoming bluntly exasperated, "was the nature of the revenge you were planning?"

She whimpered for a moment, then, suddenly, calmed down. She lit another cigarette. She had a new-looking lighter, I noticed. (Fancy buying just a new lighter and not some nice new clothes!)

She announced: "I wore planning to kidnap Ronnie."

It was now my turn to howl. "Ronnie? Who the blue devil is Ronnie?"

"My dad's dog. He loves Ronnie. I loves him too, what little I sees of him after having to live at Ma Tridwell's. He wore a lovely pup when my dad takes him in. More like a teddy-bear than a dog."

"Oh, dear." I groaned. "Are we talking about Masher?"

"We is," drawled Miss Glertish, in her hardest one yet. "But that old witch doesn't just change Ronnie's name. She changes his nature. Did it with a chunk of raw meat in one hand and her cane in the other."

Feeling dreadfully guilty about my part in the dog's fate, I said: "Miss Glertish, I like dogs myself. We could have a dog here, but my wife doesn't like dogs. We therefore can only have a cat. I can only tell you that I really do regret having done what I did to Masher – to Ronnie, I mean."

"You doesn't have to regret no more, Mr Crackery. Ronnie would have tore your throat out after you kills the old witch. There wore no saving him. The minute you kills my step-mum, she turns herself into Ronnie – body and soul. That's what a real witch can do."

My relationship with Miss Glertish might have gone a little better if, at this point, I had taken her advice and stopped asking more questions. But I simply couldn't refrain. Greed and curiosity were gripping my mind in just about equal measure. I did at least manage to make my next question fairly innocuous – or so I thought.

"Are you saying, madam, that Masher – Ronnie, I mean – was beyond rehabilitation?"

A snarl: "Too far gorn, yeah."

"Then what was your purpose in planning the kidnap?"

"To leave that old witch heart-broke, like she did my dad. She wore never going to know why Ronnie clears off, nor where-to neither."

"Where, in fact, were you planning to take him?"

"To a vet – to have him put to sleep. It wore all laid on in another town."

"And that fellow Rivinni was willing to help you?"

"You bet he wore. He hates Ronnie."

"You were planning to entice Ronnie into the van, I presume?"

"You presumes right."

"Wouldn't that have been a rather risky procedure? What if your step-mother had twigged what was going on?"

A shudder from Miss Glertish, gulpingly overcome. "I takes that into account, sir. I gives Leo some choc-lax powder to put in her coffee-tin. To keep her on the toilet at the time we sets."

"From what I could gather – during my interview with your step-mother – you succeeded in making her very uncomfortable, but it didn't completely inconvenience her."

"That ain't no surprise. Her intestines wore made of leather. But it wore a good plan – a plan you mucked up by killing Leo."

By now, I was not just itching but craving to know how Miss Glertish could possibly claim to have seen me wrestling with Mabel Smith.

I hesitated. I felt as if I were walking on thin ice over particularly dark and nasty depths, the more so when she added: "You got any more stupid questions?"

I decided to ask another oblique but intelligent question. "Actually, I can't quite understand why that fellow Rivinni was willing to help you. I exchanged a good few words with that stepmother of yours. I tell you frankly. She suspected a conspiracy. Once she found the dog to be missing, surely the Leo chappie would be the first to be accused? He knew that, surely?"

"Not only that, Mr Crackers. She would have got the truth out of him. He would have been unable to stop hisself telling on me. That's why he wore going to make off to Liverpool after Ronnie wore done in."

"Liverpool, eh?"

"Has a granny there, see?"

"I do see, yes. And when did you hope to put this plan into operation? Was it to be on that same day as my accidental involvement?"

"Of course not. Saturday wore to be a dummy-run. A practice. I has to get all sorts of things fixed up. I even has to show that fool how to open a bank-account."

"You have a bank-account yourself?"

"Of course I has a bank-account."

"Even though you can't read or write? How times are changing! But what I still don't quite understand is this: why didn't that fellow simply clear off if he found his situation to be so untenable?"

Miss Glertish stood up. In a more wearily resigned tone than she had ever used before, she said: "Pardon me as says it, sir, but you is real thick. As thick as two mattresses. Has I not already told yer?

My step-mum wore a witch. She puts Leo under a spell. Without help from me, he couldn't never have got away to Liverpool nor nowheres else."

"Oh, come now," I foolishly said, "isn't that a little too far-fetched?"

"Listen," she said, pretty much through clenched teeth, "I bet you all the money I got in that van. She wore a real witch."

"You surely can't believe such utter rot in this day and age?"

"No? When she had my dad under a spell just like the spell you would be under if you hadn't killed her?"

I began to feel jolly uncomfortable and mumbled: "Whatever are you saying?"

"Just you tell me this, Mr Crackery. What did she turn into the minute she comes out on that terrace? The minute you sees her?" ("der mini cher seizure?")

"I do have to admit it, Miss Glertish. She did look very much like a lovely old aunt of mine. A quite staggering likeness."

"Had you total fooled, didn't she?"

"Well, yes, I suppose that's true …"

"Then don't hargue with me no more. I loves a posh voice like yourn. In a man, of course – not in a woman like my step-mum. But I can't be doing with no more of your stupid brain. I be off to London. I shall put a phone-number into yer envelope if I needs more words with yer. You can then ring it if I sends you the envelope."

And with that, to my dismay, this strangest of all step-daughters picked up the treasure-trove bag – and walked out.

In following her, I was in a whirling state of despair. I thought she was making straight for the van. All my visions of paying off my debts so grandly were now vanishing. But, to my grovelling relief, she turned sharp left and pulled open the doors to my garage. Disappearing inside, she was out after a few seconds – without the precious bag. (She had stowed it with unerring commonsense under my work-bench.) Shutting the doors, she said: "Keep these here doors locked until you thinks up a more clever hiding-place. And don't you go splashing out too much and too soon."

Having issued these orders, Miss Asti Glertish went down to the garden-gate so swiftly that I was left standing – no doubt looking like a grinning village idiot. She was over the road – to the van on the far verge under the trees – before I could move. My admiration for her, I have to say, became hectic. I ran to her like a film-fan mobbing a film-star. I yanked open her driver-door, foolishly determined to extract the information she had not wanted to give.

"Miss Glertish," I panted, "I really do have to know. How can you possibly claim to have seen me at that frightful bungalow?"

"Go away, Mr Crackery," she snapped, starting the engine, "and let go of my door."

Being by now in a crazily facetious mood, I uttered the most tactless words you could possibly imagine. (A red rag to a bull, by comparison, could be classified as far more tactful.)

"If you won't give me a logical answer, Miss Glertish, I shall be forced to make the obvious assumption – namely, that you too are a witch, just like your step-mother."

Miss Glertish switched off the engine. Calmly, she said: "How dares you say a thing like that ..."

"I'm only joking, of course. But look at it logically. You could not have been present in that room unless you have the power to render yourself invisible. So what's the explanation?"

"Very well," she said, after a pause which I must admit I thought a bit frightening, "come round and get in the van – beside me. I shall tell you what you won't like to hear. But don't blame me for your bad dreams."

Without knowing why, I started tittering. Scampering around to the other side of the van, I jumped into it as if into the coach of a great lady. Still tittering, I said: "Prove to me you're not a witch."

Miss Glertish replied gravely, but not with any apparent emotion. "As soon as I sees you has killed that Leo, I has to change my plans. Understand me so far, does yer?"

"Yes, madam. I do."

Unzipping her shoulder-bag, she took out a small jar and unscrewed the lid. "Can you tell me what this is?"

Since the jar was labelled 'honey' and the substance within was thickened honey, I said (with a silly grin): "Honey, of course."

"Dead right, Mr Crackers. Honey." She dipped her finger in it and licked it off. "I likes honey myself. But not so much as Ronnie as likes it. He would go mad for honey. Can you understand that too?"

"Yes, madam, I can. Animals can have quite passionate tastes. Our cat, for instance, goes mad about beetroot."

"I ain't talking about beetroot. Honey I be talking about." She screwed the lid back on, but continued to hold the jar – weighing it in her hand like a philosopher. "Ronnie goes and eats almost anything if it has honey spread on it. Like a cushion. Spread honey on a cushion, just for a joke, and you has to stop him chewing his whole way through."

I was suddenly beginning to feel serious, apprehensively so, I said: "Wasn't that a rather unkind joke to play on a dog?"

"Me and my dad never lets a joke like that go too far, Mr Crackers. But what that means, sir, is that me and Leo could trick Ronnie into the van. Honey on a raw chicken-leg could do it easy. Get that, do yer?"

"I get that, madam," I said, beginning to feel quite ill. "But how could you have lured the dog into this van without being seen – if not by your step-mother then by one of the neighbours?"

"Easy, sir. There's a service-lane what goes behind all them big gardens. It's where they has the dustbins and the back doors for deliveries. You being a shopkeeper, doesn't you know about that service-lane?"

Remembering my encounter with the good-looking housekeeper, I said: "I vaguely know of it, yes …"

"But you ain't never been down it?"

"No. I do one or two deliveries myself – informally, by car – but we've never done any trade with Orchard Ash Road."

"That doesn't say much for your shop, does it? People from a posh road like that ought to be going to a shop like yourn. I begins to understand that Miss Holland. No wonder she wore so cross with you." ("sow crauze widger.")

Blushing again, I hotly said: "Don't ramble. Stick to the point."

"All right, Mr Crackers. I wore going to drive down that lane – with the body of the bloke you killed – and I wore going to pull up close to that back-entry."

I couldn't stop myself from glancing over my shoulder into the van's interior. Despite Miss Holland's frequent complaint that I lacked imagination, I can swear to you that I could see that fellow's ghost. He was in a sideways heap in the back of that ghastly van. Miss Glertish was saying: "Use your brains, sir. What does you think I wore going to do after I pulls up at that there back-entrance?"

"Just tell me, damn you!"

"All right, sir. Don't excite. I wore going to open the door with Leo's keys and dump his body just inside – on the path what leads up to the kitchen. Why does I plan to do that, sir? See if you can work it out yourself."

"I don't want to work it out," I cried. "Just give me the truth."

Without claiming to be clairvoyant or any rot like that, I want to tell you that I seemed to know what this woman was going to say. I knew it exactly. She was not taunting me, I hasten to add. She was simply stating facts but with only a slight (and possibly justified) degree of scorn.

Waggling the little jar of honey in front of my face, she said: "Can you at least work out what I wore going to do with what's in this jar?"

"No," I firmly said, my heart thumping.

"Well, sir, I wore going to smear it all over Leo's bare throat." ("beer froat.")

"Oh my God." I moaned. "Ugh!"

"Then, you see, I wore going to clear off with the van – back to London. In no time at all, I can tell yer, Ronnie would have found

Leo. Ronnie would have chawed right through to the back of Leo's neck."

Miss Glertish put the little jar of honey back in her shoulder-bag. She added: "It would have been a real heart-broke shock for that old witch. Not that I was expecting her to find Leo herself. Like Leo tells me, she hardly ever sticks her nose outdoors. But them delivery-blokes as comes with the market-goods would have found him for sure. The police would then make her have Ronnie put to sleep."

"Miss Glertish," I said, feeling sick, "I can't believe you would have done what you say. I refuse, in fact, to believe it of you."

"Why else, sir, does I think to leave that back-entry unlocked? That whole plan, I tells you, could have worked real good. Smooth as silk. But what happens to this new plan of mine? You, sir – you mucks it up."

"Are you expecting me to apologise, you ghastly female?"

"No need for that, sir. Things have worked out all right. Just go back to your cottage and don't do anything daft. Out you get, sir."

"Not until you've told me everything!"

"You ain't just too thick to be told. You is too sick to be told – too bad a heart. I can't be doing with another dead body," she said, but whether this was said as a joke or out of medical concern I couldn't quite tell. "Get off with yer, get out of it." ("giddah divitte.")

"Madam, I demand a full explanation."

She started the engine, but I refused to budge. With all the calm and skill of a born driver, she promptly backed out between the trees. Once on the road, she actually drove down it as far as the little bridge before stopping.

"All right, Mr Nosy Parker," she said, and she pulled up expertly on the verge. "You is going to wish I never told yer. And I shall keep you in this van until you learns the worst. It won't take long. But don't never blame me for your bad dreams from now on."

Unzipping her shoulder-bag, she again took out the honey jar. Unscrewing it, she had another finger-licking dip. I shuddered and she said: "There you are, you see – still upset. You is now going to feel real sick."

She put the jar away and asked: "When I has Leo in the back of this van, what do you think I sees first when I gets to that posh road?"

Feeling helplessly nervous: "No idea."

"I sees your empty Honda Civic sitting there – a bit further on from the front gate to that old witch's house. So what's that telling me?"

Tactfully correcting her misuse of the past tense, I said: "It told you, I can only suppose, that I had called at that insanitary bungalow."

"It tells me more than that, Mr Crackery. It tells me that you goes and buys yourself a new lock-bar. That wore more brainy of yer."

Feeling (heaven knows why) in need of even further praise, I said: "I faked it fairly well, did I not? No one would think it was not the old lock-bar, would they?"

"Huh," she disparagingly grunted. "I gets out and I looks in your car. You needs to rub more dirt over some of them scratches. Your brainy Miss Holland wouldn't be fooled if she sees that lock-bar. But what else did your parked-up motor-car tell me? It tells me, Mr Crackers, that you total ignores the message I leaves yer."

"Madam, as I've already tried to say, your so-called message was not clearly expressed."

"Which means, sir, that I has to change my plans yet again. So what does that mean I has to do? Have a think."

Miss Glertish lit a cigarette while I had a think.

"I'm sorry," I had to say, "but my mind has gone completely blank."

"It means I still has to drive down that service-lane. But for a very special look-see."

"Ah," I agitatedly mumbled, "I know what you mean," and I quoted: "Time spent in reconnaissance is never wasted."

Speaking with the cigarette bobbing between her lips – one of the root-causes (according to my father) of working-class mispronunciation – Miss Glertish said: "Yeah. That's about right. But what is I to do with the dead body in the back of this van? What is I to decide?"

Managing to restrain an uneasy look over my shoulder, I had another think. I said: "I can only suppose you decided not to dump it in that garden until you had reconnoitred."

"You is right, Mr Crackers. Well done. But what does I see when I unlocks that back garden-door in the wall and creeps in?"

"Very difficult to see anything in that neglected garden, I would say. I've been in it myself, although not through a back door. Chased by that confounded dog. I've never known a garden like it. Very remiss of your step-mother to let a once-lovely garden go to rack and ruin."

"It wore like that when she buys the place. Leo tells me she wouldn't let him hardly do no gardening at all. But good for me, wunnitt? Gives me cover, dunnitt?"

I was beginning to babble because I was beginning to dread the approaching horror of something I knew she would tell me – and which, weirdly, I had become frantic to know.

"Oh, yes – cover," I babbled. "Cover is vital to reconnaissance."

"But what does I see through all them bushes and stuff? That's what I be asking yer."

I babbled evasively until she cut in and said: "I sees you and that witch on that window-terrace having a nice cosy talk."

"I would hardly describe it as cosy, damn you."

"Mr Crackery," she primly reproved me, "don't swear. It's common. Also, it brings bad luck. That old witch used to swear real bad. Look what it done for her. I doesn't like swearwords. Look what they does for Leo too."

Brow-clutching apology: "I do beg your pardon …"

"You goes indoors with her quite meek and mild. Under her spell, complete and total."

I became a little indignant. "And it didn't occur to you to intervene?"

She chucked her cigarette-end out of her window and screeched: "Blimey, no."

"In other words," I pathetically said, "you simply left me to my fate."

She recovered instantly. "It wore more that old witch being left to her fate – not you."

"You surely don't mean that you were hoping for yet another tragic accident?"

"I wore hoping you would kill her, yeah."

"Oh, what a terrible thing to say! Tragedy could have been avoided – on both occasions – if you had made an effort to intervene."

"And how rich would that have made you?" She lit a fresh cigarette. "You killed them two people and that's that."

Fastidiously worried: "I wish you wouldn't keep using the word killed."

"But that's what happened, sir."

"You could at least say accidentally killed. That would be a more accurate way of putting it."

"Believe me, sir, the cops won't be calling them two killings accidental if you be daft enough to blab. Too much of a coincidence to be accidental. That's why they'll say," and Miss Glertish added an old-fashioned expression I hadn't heard since my childhood. "You mark my words. And you best 'ope you doesn't has to."

"Have you ever been in trouble with the police yourself?"

"No, sir. Never."

"Nor me, Miss Gertlish. But I heed what you say."

"You should, sir. And bear this in mind as well. I shall always be in the clear if there be any trouble. You'll be all on your own if that Miss Holland turns detective. It ain't the police you has to worry about. It's her. The cops will only trouble yer if she sticks her oar in."

A separate thought disturbed me. "Are you by any chance hoping that I'll kill Miss Holland too?"

"Well, sir, it wouldn't be a bad idea if she gets too nosy. Give her a good push down them stairs in the shop. If that don't break her neck, you can easy go down after and finish her off."

"What an utterly disgraceful suggestion!"

Without a smile: "Only a joke, sir."

"A very poor joke, if I may say so."

"No part of what I wore having to clear up wore much of a joke, I tells you that. Sit still, Mr Nosy Parker. You ain't yet heard the worst."

I became crazily contrite. "I'm sorry, Miss Glertish. I can't help feeling a bit upset. All this is not only new to me but very worrying."

"Just don't swear and don't go on the booze. Both them things will knock the shine off your star. Once I let you out of this van, mister, you just remember that."

I was now assuming that killing Miss Holland was the horror I had been dreading to hear. (After all, it was a fairly drastic suggestion.) I tried to get out of the van, but she gripped me by the wrist.

"Let me out of this bloody van," I cried. "I am no longer interested in how you came to witness that second accident. Let go of me!"

"Sit still. I ain't finished widger. And you has gone on to use a very bad word."

"It's not considered all that bad a word these days," and I tried to point out the recent use of it by the Duke of Edinburgh (as gleefully reported in the Press).

She interrupted: "That's for Her Majesty to deal with – not me. I'm going to let go of your wrist," and she did so. "Now behave yourself. Ask me a question. Try to make it hintelligent."

"How can you possibly claim to have seen the accidental death of that awful woman?"

"By looking in at the window, sir."

The simplicity of this answer (rather like the doing-a-wee answer in my office) took my breath away.

"The window? That latticed window," I managed to gasp. "You mean you were standing outside that window?"

"If you was to use your brain, sir, you would know I couldn't be standing nowhere's else."

"But all those latticed panes were grimy with dirt – as well as being partly covered in heaven knows what type of creeper!"

"Have a think, sir. Ask yerself what I has to do to see through the glass."

I had a fairly considerable think and said: "You mean you rubbed a bit of dirt off and made yourself a peep-hole?"

"Well done, sir," said more drily than ever before.

"But weren't you afraid of being discovered?"

"At first, yes. I wore afraid she might sees me blocking the light. But I finds some sort of Christmas tree close to the window. It wore blocking the light anyways. I only has to squeeze myself between that bushy thing and the window."

"Were you able to hear what was said?"

"Mostly, yeah. Puts me ear to the peep-hole now and again."

"And did you see my unpleasant struggle with that stepmother of yours?"

"I did, sir. I see you fall bang on top of her. You be a heavy bloke all right. It did the trick. Knocked the life out of her."

"There was no trick about it, I assure you. It was an accidental death."

"What I means, sir, is that I sees she wore killed stone dead. I could see that much through my peep-hole."

"How could you tell? Do you have medical experience?"

"No, sir, but I could see by the way you wore upsetting yourself. I wore expecting you to give her what's called the kiss of life. I can only say I be glad you didn't. It might have worked."

"Why couldn't you have tapped on the window or something after you saw she was dead?"

"Well sir, I did think of that, but I wore scared you might go even more mad and call the police. I has to be ready to run away. I has a dead body in this van to think about."

"Why did you let me kill that dog?"

"Because, like I has told yer, the old witch takes Ronnie over – body and soul, sir. You wore just about brainy enough to find a gun, but whether it would ackle or not I couldn't be sure."

"It did ackle, as you call it, as you must have seen. Why did you not then tap on the window or in some other way make yourself known?"

"Because I still doesn't know how barmy you wore. I near as anything runs back to this here van. I didn't, so what does you think I does next," and she lit a fresh cigarette.

Trying hard not to sound and feel too annoyed with her, I said: "Please just tell me."

"I stays out of sight in that garden. I needs to see if you wore to go even more daft. Also, I needs to work out another plan. Talk about chop and change." ("chaw purn chynge.")

A shade cynically: "Also, of course, you were no doubt beginning to think of her money. Am I at least right about that?"

With unaffected candour: "Yeah. And I wunt yet certain as to wanting to share it."

"But you knew she had lots of money and you knew where to find it?"

"You bet I does. That fool Leo doesn't, but I does because I knows she would use the same place she uses at home – under the floor-boards. Her favourite-hiding-place."

"How very peculiar! From what she told me, she quite clearly had a bank-account."

"Of course she has a bank-account. She gets real rich after her dad dies. Only child. Gets near the lot – even a real castle-like."

"A castle? Good heavens! Why on earth did she have to run a market-stall if she were so wealthy?"

"Because she wore a witch, Mr Crackers. It wore a disguise. Witches doesn't like being found out."

I was beginning to feel dazed again. Both step-mother and step-daughter, it seemed to me, were as mad as each other. But I was also beginning to wonder if I were as mad myself – as part of a trio, so to speak. I stared through the windscreen at the road. It was so empty and deserted-looking that birds were hopping around on it. I felt as if I were now on a different level of existence.

"Besides," Miss Glertish added, "she likes having money in the house and likes hiding it. Mean about it, too. Never pays out except where she can't avoid."

"A bit of a miser, eh?"

"You can say that again. She wouldn't even give money to my dad. She lets his motor-mend business go right down the sink."

This was an exchange of fairly ordinary words, as I'm sure you would agree. But that earlier feeling of slowly impending horror (which I had mistakenly thought had passed) was now returning. Again I seemed to know, in advance, the very words which Miss Glertish now began to utter.

She lit another cigarette after chucking the stub of the other one out of her driver-door window.

"Mr Crackery, did you ever go back to look for your hat?"

Faltering: "I don't quite know what you mean …"

"Oh yes you does. I sees it all. I sees you lock yourself out – after killing the old witch. You remembers yer 'at. You tries to get back inside. You fails. You goes real barmy. You clears off before I can think to stop yer. So I repeats my question. Does you come back or doesn't you?" ("or duzzenchar.")

Recovering my wits a little, I said: "I did return, yes. But may I ask a question of my own? How did you know that I was so concerned about my hat?"

"Because I has already sees you wearing it so proud-like. Just like my dad. He had a hat like yourn. He too would go barmy if he forgets it and leaves it behind. You be very like him, sir. Not so good-looking, of course, but very like."

Making an effort to take better charge of my relationship with Miss Glertish, I said: "So that's why I found the front door open! You were expecting me to return?"

"Yes, Mr Crackers. I needs help. So what takes you so long? I has to do everything myself. I has to carry the old witch down the path to this van. I then has to get a blanket off her bed to wrap what's left of the dog in. And then the wiping-up to do."

"How long did all that take you?"

"Well over an hour, and still you doesn't come back. I gets everything done, of course. I'm special good at getting things done. I repeats my question, Mr Crackery. What stupid things takes you so long as to stop you getting back to the bungalow?"

"I'd rather not say, Miss Glertish. It's too silly a thing."

Again she gripped me by the wrist, this time giving it a shake like an angry nursery-maid. (I once had such a type looking after me.)

"You has been asking me questions, mister. So I'm asking you now. Tell me what kept yer."

"Miss Glertish, please let go of me. I really think I'd better push off."

I tried to open the door of the van, but she shook me again (by the wrist). I decided to give in and reply. (The shake was too reminiscent.)

"I'm sorry to say, Miss Glertish, that it took me rather a long time to find my hack-saw. I eventually found it in the loft."

"Hack-saw? What does you want that for?"

"To get in through the pantry window."

"Why do that when you only has to come back and walk in through the front door? Pardon me as says it, but you is a real mad nut. No other way of describing yer."

Miss Glertish was being provocatively nonsensical, it seemed to me, in much the same way as Miss Holland often was. Horribly very odd. As with Miss Holland, I declined to argue. Instead, I resorted to pomposity (always a mistake with any lady of spirit).

"Madam, why did you leave the front door open after you so expeditiously quitted the premises? Wasn't that rather careless?"

"I wore sick of waiting for you, sir, but I wants you to see what I done. I thinks it might stop you from going even more daft and going back to the police-station."

"I see what you mean. Nevertheless, anyone could have gone in and poked around."

With an air of constrained impatience (also familiar to me in Miss Holland), Miss Glertish said: "After almost two hours, I knows you would be back fair soon and because of your 'at. But I personal couldn't wait no more. Not with this van-load of dead bodies."

I didn't just feel neatly skewered by this reply. I had an eye-bulging difficulty in stopping myself from glancing over my shoulder. If I did so, I was sure, I would now see two apparitional corpses in the back – plus the remains of a dead dog. I had to force myself to keep staring through the windscreen.

Falteringly, I croaked: "Might I ask what you did about the problem you had on board? How and where did you dispose of the – er – the er-rer evidence?"

"Never you mind." ("nivia moind.")

"Madam, I need to know!"

"All you needs to know, Mr Crackers, is them's you kills will rot down to nothing. Wunt be heard of ever again. It will be a real mystery." ("a rill mistry.")

"Madam, does it at least earn me your approval that I shut the door which you left open? What if I had left it open myself?"

"Oh, I knows you would shut it! I can read you like a book, Mr Crackers."

"Coming from someone who is virtually illiterate, madam, that's an inappropriate claim."

This remark was a cheap insult. I admit it frankly. I was almost in pieces. I snatched at her arm. I said: "At least reassure me about my brief-case. Have you handed it in?"

"Not me personal, no. But I gets the landlady at my stay-place to do it. Takes it in just after tea-time yesterday." ("yesser-die.")

"Oh, good – splendid," I babbled. "Thank you so much. Was she suitably circumspect?"

"There wore no one in the place, if that's what you means. She just leaves it on the counter and clears off. Go home now, sir, and pull yerself together. Ring the police to enquire natural-like."

I actually got out of the van, but I found myself holding the door open and asking a final question. I knew I would ask it. I knew, too, that it was a question I didn't want to ask but had been leading up to.

"Miss Glertish, what about my former lock-bar? What have you done with it?"

With a readiness that seemed calculated, she said: "I uses it to smash up the head of that old witch. Satisfied, Mr Crackery? What's more, I smashes her face in and all. You wouldn't even want to see that lock-bar now. You has no need for it no more, so just forget it."

I could hardly speak, but I managed to gasp: "You can't possibly mean what you say."

"It wore a bit of a last-minute thing," she said, in an impassive but informative tone and without anger. "I does it just after I dumps her. I had a pet-tortoise, see? The witch smashes it up with a hammer, see? One day, I tells myself, I'll smash your own shell and see 'ow you like it."

I found myself saying: "I can't believe you did any such thing … it's too nasty."

"Believe what you like, sir. Good morning to yer. Oh, but one thing more. I had a look in your garden-shed. Yours is as untidy as my dad's. I hates a mess like that. Mister, you needs to tidy up your shed."

I felt too weak to shut the van-door, but Miss Glertish shut it ("clunk!") with a neat twist of her steering-wheel after re-starting. She was gone in a flash. Heaven alone knows how an almost illiterate person could make her way through our country lanes, but I was in no doubt that she had her methods.

At first, I could hardly manage the short walk uphill to the garden gate. We had no near neighbours but I felt isolated for the first time in my life. (Is alienated the better word?)

"She must have been pulling my leg," I decided, and this thought renewed my strength.

As did the thought of that whacking big bag of money in the garage. My pace quickened to a run. Within moments, in the company of my much-loved Honda Civic, I was delving in the bag. Oh, how wonderfully heavy it was! (I could hardly drag it out from under the bench.)

In handling the contents, I was amazed to find myself gurgling with joy – much like the gurgling of our cat when guzzling fish … or, for that matter, beetroot.

FIVE

Hoping to Hoodwink Miss Holland

Having got up early the next morning, Wednesday and at five o'clock, it was damn near nine when I finished in the garage – counting all that money. I don't think I should tell you how much it all was. It would sound like boasting. Besides, it could annoy you if you're as hard up as I had been. But I should, I think, just tell you that I took possession of it as a duck takes to water. Once my joyful gurgling had died down, having a lot of money seemed to me to be my natural-born state. After all, I did have ancestors who were reasonably well off. It was only at my own particular birth that my entire family seemed to fall upon hard times. (Strange, eh?)

I thought no more of the dreadful talks with Miss Asti Glertish. They had gone from my mind like a bad dream.

It did, however, dawn upon me to heed her advice about my brief-case. Clearing all the little piles of money off my work-bench and back into the Gladstone bag, I shoved the bag under the bench and locked the garage. Grinning like Mr Punch, I strolled indoors and phoned the police-station.

"Good morning to you, officer. Any chance of my lost brief-case being handed in? I popped in on Saturday to report the loss. I do hope you remember me. I'm Crackery."

After some incompetent shuffling-noises, the desk-officer admitted to remembering me, and yes – the brief-case had been handed in.

"Splendid! And may I have the name and address of the finder? I wish to bestow thanks."

No, not possible; the finder was unknown, had simply left the brief-case on the counter during an unmanned moment.

"Oh, how self-effacing and honest some people are! Thank you, officer. I'll send my assistant to collect it. Holland is the name. Miss Holland. That all right? Good. Splendid."

I rang off feeling mightily pleased with myself. Although I now realised more fully that I was in love with Miss Holland, I no longer felt frightened of her. I felt I could deal with her as a man of the world. Coming into money, it would seem, does wonders for self-confidence in all human departments.

Also, it would seem, it stimulates the human brain. Immediately after putting the phone down, I went up into the loft (by way of the proper loft-ladder, not the chair as used by the athletical Asti Glertish). Still grinning like Mr Punch, I unearthed a simply ghastly oil-painting and took it down to the bottom of the garden.

"Ha," I said, sploshing paraffin over it and applying a match.

It was, I can assure you, an utterly worthless painting of one of my military forbears – a great-great grandfather in an unrecognisable uniform and sitting on a horse. It was so badly painted as to be absurd in representing an equestrian statue. No one in the family liked it. It had always been hidden away, I being the last to have it in my care. (My young and pretty wife had screamed at the sight of it when I once tried putting it up in the lounge.)

After making sure it was burnt to a frazzle, I went back indoors and phoned the shop.

"Miss Holland, I do apologise for my unexplained absence this morning and indeed yesterday. But I have two bits of good news.

First, my brief-case has been found and handed in. Secondly, I have taken to heart your wise words."

I paused, allowing her to reply wittily: "What wise words, James? There have been so many you've always ignored."

"Your wise words, madam, about our need for additional capital. I have raised no less than four thousand pounds."

I enjoyed the moment of stunned silence which followed. The relatively low sum I had announced (relatively low, I mean, against the vastly higher amount in the garage) was quite impressive for those days. Any local business in the Recession would have been glad of it.

Airily, I broke the stunned silence: "I want to invest almost all of it in the shop. I'm putting you in total charge of the outlay. All I ask for myself is five hundred pounds for my personal domestic use."

"Some form of gross self-indulgence? Is that what you mean, James?"

"One such use is for one of the ceilings. As you know, I greatly feared an imminent collapse. My fears were well-founded. The ceiling in our bedroom has partly collapsed and fallen all over my bed. Happened yesterday morning. Luckily, I had just got up and was having a shave. Quite a hunk of plaster could have given me a very nasty whack."

This bare-faced lie fully deserved the unsympathetic mirth which Miss Holland again had obvious difficulty in suppressing. (As before, she suppressed it, I knew, because she didn't want me to discern even the slightest loss of her self-control.) This time, she managed to recover more quickly. She sternly said: "I take it, then, that you're phoning me from home?"

"I am indeed."

"And when can I expect you at the shop?"

"I'm having to wait in, of course, for the builder's man. But I hope to be at the shop by this afternoon."

"And what has happened to Mrs Tridwell after you dragged her out of the shop?"

This question rather annoyed me. "I never dragged her out of the shop!"

"James, I saw you doing it."

"You saw nothing of the sort. I had persuaded her to take a little nourishment. I was inviting her to a pub-lunch, that's all. She had a very sad story to tell."

"Is she with you now?"

"Of course she isn't. Why on earth would you think she would be here?"

"Then where is she?"

"I've no idea. After that lunch on Monday, we went our separate ways."

"In other words, you abandoned her."

"Nothing of the sort, madam."

"A typical lack of consideration, this time for someone in distress. I could have helped that girl. In what form is the money you claim to have raised?"

"Madam, are you beginning to doubt me?"

"I am beginning to feel a shade sceptical, James, I must admit. Who could be so stupid as to lend you four thousand pounds?"

In a well-feigned tone of wounded dignity, I said: "You have misunderstood. The sum you question was not a loan. It was the result of an effective business-transaction. However, if you feel unable to handle the outlay, I shall attend to it myself. Please return to your duties. Good morning."

"All right," Miss Holland instantly and imperially said, "I apologise. But explain more clearly – and without rambling. How did you come by so large a sum? Have you held up a stage-coach on the Santa Fe trail?"

"The opportunity arose, madam, yesterday morning. Early. I had just finished my solitary breakfast. There came a knock at the door. I soon found myself in conversation with a total stranger."

"Oh my God," Miss Holland muttered.

"He was a bit on the rough side, I daresay, but he turned out to be a genuine example of a working-class trader. A dealer in antiques."

"A knocker, you mean?"

Although I knew of the term, I waggishly said: "A knocker? Whatever's that?"

"A knocker, James, is a dealer who calls at the homes of unsophisticated people who have little or no knowledge of antiques. He buys anything of antique-value, but at well below a fair price. What, James, did you sell him?"

"An old oil-painting, that's all – from up in the loft. A simply ghastly thing."

A sharp intake of breath from Miss Holland, excited but grim. "Wait, James. No customers yet in, but I have something to say which I don't want interrupted. I'll just shut the shop," and I heard her lay down the receiver and then bolt the shop-door. Resuming crisply: "No other items? You sold just the one picture?"

"Well, yes," I said, as innocently as a boy-scout. "It was all he seemed to want."

"I haven't been too frequent a visitor to your cottage, James, but I don't recall seeing a picture of any great apparent value."

"That's because it was a crude painting of an equestrian statue – in other words, a chap on a horse. One of my ancestors. I could never put it on show. Too frightening for Stephanie and our two girls. I can't think why."

Even more crisply: "Perhaps they could see too strong a likeness to you, James."

"Actually, madam, I've always thought he looked quite an nice old buffer. But I took it up to London once – to be valued by a famous auction-house. They said it was just unsigned rubbish, and by an obvious amateur. He probably copied it from illustrations in Dickens or possibly Thackeray. Nevertheless, to have sold it for four thousand pounds is surely a notable achievement on my part?"

"Not at all, James. You've been foolish to a simply unbelievable degree. The knocker to whom you fell victim probably saw it was a bad painting on top of a long-lost masterpiece. Probably worth millions."

"I can assure you, madam, that I was no push-over. He only offered five hundred pounds to begin with. I kept demurring. He was more the victim, I would say. He paid in cash. High-denomination notes. I shall pay them into the bank myself this very morning. Meanwhile, since you cannot bring yourself to congratulate me, kindly resume your duties," and I rang off.

Whooping like a schoolboy on the last day of term, I dashed out into the garden. I forked the ashes of the worthless painting into the soil with energy I didn't know I could summon up.

"I've put one over on Miss Holland," I cried, not caring if the birds and the bees heard every word. "And I've got her where I want her. Ha!"

In case you are wondering, please remember at this point: worthless really does mean worthless. I was actually being truthful in saying I had taken the painting up to London. (Did so years before: Bond Street.) That painting is not going to turn out to have been hiding a genuine old master. No such irony. The genuine irony about this latest and wonderful whopper – and which I'm inviting you to admire – is my sheer cunning. Miss Holland's contempt for my intellect had been my triumph. I had played upon her contempt like Paganini upon his violin. By pretending to be more stupid than I really am, I had made her believe me. Ha!

Although I was now passionately in love with her, did I have any moral qualms about the lies I was telling her?

None whatsoever.

I found this to be quite a surprise. I was revelling in my new-found ability to be so wickedly inventive. (I had only ever been a fairly normal liar before my adventure.) But I did promise myself that I would be as decently truthful as I could (to everyone) after things had settled down. But not about the source of my improved fortune. That, of course, was to be my life-long secret.

Am I dwelling too long upon my feelings here? Bad form, I know. But I think you need to know a little about my feelings because of the way they affected my decisions. These decisions drastically affected all subsequent situations.

For example, after forking-in the ashes of that undistinguished ancestor, I strolled back up the garden to the kitchen-door. I was intending to make a triumphant cup of coffee. I had no other plan in mind.

I heard the phone ringing in the hall.

It was Stephanie, the young and pretty wife. She ecstatically cried: "You clever old stick! Miss Holland has just phoned. Was she right? Four thousand quid?"

Feeling abashed at being in love with Miss Holland, I could only feel dismay rather than annoyance. Weakly, I said: "She shouldn't have phoned you. I was partly intending the matter to be something of a surprise."

"Actually, Jay, darling, it wasn't me she spoke to. It was your sister she was phoning. She wanted details of the painting you sold. She seems to think it could have fetched a lot more money."

"Oh no," I groaned.

"Your sister seems very upset about it all, darling, but I think you're marvellous."

"Thank you, sweetie-pie," I gloomily said. "I'd better speak to her. Put her on."

"I can't do that, darling. She's just rushed off to join the kids in the paddock with the donkeys." Although Stephanie was obviously alone, she dropped her voice to add: "I'm sorry, darling, to have to tell you this. She's gone bonkers again. Worse than ever before, I'd say. She's claiming that you owe her half the money. Can that be true?"

"Of course not ..."

"She's saying the painting was a whatsisname – an heirloom. She's saying your daddy only left it to you for safe keeping. She's saying you had no right to sell it behind her back. It was a sacred trust."

"Utter rubbish. Sweetie-pie," I sternly said, "refrain from any further discussion of this matter. Phone for a taxi. Return home with the children immediately. That's an order," and I rang off and strode out of the cottage.

I was fond of the old trout, I suppose, but what a nerve! I had been the only one to have actually saved the ghastly painting. My sainted sister, let me tell you, had been the one who wanted to burn it – and within two days of Daddy's funeral. Like everyone else except my father and me, she had always despised the painting. This neurotic claim of hers made me really indignant. I could hardly concentrate on the new falsehood I needed to fulfil.

"What a nerve," I couldn't stop myself from roaring, as I got the Honda out of the garage. "WHAT A NERVE!"

My sister, I knew, would now revert to being her same childish snoop. Having her own keys to the cottage (for baby-sitting comings and goings), she would soon be snuffling out that Gladstone bag. Older than me, she still claimed a senior right to go through my things as and when she fancied. The hiding-place in the garage was no longer safe. She could arrive within the hour, in the same taxi as my little family. Hence this new little plan of mine.

I was soon on my way into town with the Gladstone in the boot. No longer so fastidious about Willow Tree Lane, I parked there rather than face the Abominable Peasant (the entry-clerk in the multi-storey). Also, I felt in need of a nice healthy walk alongside the town-river. I knew it would calm me down. I had with me, of course, Stephanie's shopping-trolley. I could never have lugged so heavy a bag all that way, and worse, allowed the bag to be seen by potential witnesses. It fitted into the trolley's upright container, on-ended but very conveniently. With the lid buckled down the trolley was the perfect method of innocent transport. Another lovely day. I soon ceased my indignant mutterings. ("Half-share, be blowed! Never!")

I was once more grinning like Mr Punch by the time I reached the Bank.

"Just thought I'd pop in," I began by saying, "to stoke up my business-account," and I paid in the three thousand and five hundred pounds (the deficit mentioned to Miss Holland).

The clerk and I exchanged the usual local pleasantries. He was about ten years older than I, and I had known him from my youth when I used to accompany my father to this very counter. He didn't bat an eyelid. I knew he wouldn't. Although I had been running an overdraft, I was among those well-dressed and well-spoken people who are readily trusted if they suddenly pay out. Extra resources are assumed to have been respectably acquired. (Had I been wearing a grimy cloth cap and spoken in the idiom of Miss Asti Glertish, I was reflecting, I would not get away with what I needed to say next.)

"My wife and I are thinking," I said, "of going away for a couple of weeks. I'm a bit worried about our family papers. Nothing valuable but fairly precious to us. Can I leave them with you? In the vault?"

"Oh, certainly sir!"

I was instantly ushered past the raised counter-flap and into the hallowed regions of security. A white-haired porter in a black apron appeared out of nowhere. He lifted that heavy bag out of the trolley with no great difficulty (rather to my chagrin) and went off with it down the stone steps. This was someone else I remembered from my youth. My father had always deposited a battered old tin trunk every time we went away on holiday. It contained what he called his valuables – mostly his unpublished translations into Esperanto of very lengthy works of Socialist literature. He had undertaken this task on behalf of mankind, mostly assiduously. (My sister had burnt them all, just as assiduously, within days of his death.) But a new anxiety began to cloud this memory of my father.

"Excuse me," I said to the clerk, as he showed me back past the counter-flap. "Don't I get a receipt?"

The clerk chortled. "This isn't a left-luggage cloakroom, sir," and I had to join in the chortle, having realised I had made something of a gaffe. Strange as you may think it today (and what I had forgotten), my father had never been given a receipt for his tin trunk. It's what country banks were like in those days.

Another anxiety afflicted me as I trundled off with the trolley along King William Street.

What if there were mice in the vault? What if they nibbled at the label I had tied to the handle of the Gladstone? How would I be able to claim the bag as being mine? Would I be made to identify the contents?

Not wishing to leave you in suspense over this simple choice of hiding-place, let me tell you here and now: no one was ever to think I had all that money in that vault. The bag was as safe as the Crown Jewels in the Tower of London. My anxieties of ownership were to be a complete waste of my mental faculties. But I, not enjoying your privileged knowledge, was soon to have this anxiety increased by yet another – and just as massive.

Struck by a relatively innocent thought, I stopped in the street and exclaimed aloud: "By God, I forgot to tell Miss Holland to collect the brief-case. I must get it myself."

Trundling the shopping-trolley behind me all the way to Providence Square, I bounded into the empty enquiry-room at the police-station.

What did I discover from that same lethargic police-officer? Miss Holland had called in – and had taken away the wretched brief-case.

"You did give authorisation, sir," the officer explained, pointing in his ledger, "but now that you're here, would you very much mind waiting?"

"Wait? Me? What on earth for?"

"We have a new tec-super, sir, transferred from London for his own safety. He's a real hot-shot. Finds life a bit dull here, but he's keen to get his teeth into something worth his while. He'd like a word with you."

"With me? What about?"

"He was going to come to your shop, sir, but, since you're here, it will save his time of you waits just a few moments. I'll go and tell him. He's upstairs."

I smote the counter with the flat of my hand. "Officer, what can he possibly want to know about the loss of a mere brief-case?"

"It's nothing to do with that, sir."

"Then what, dammit?"

"Your Miss Holland called in to make a report. It's about a knocker in your area, sir – a bloke going around and taking advantage of feeble-minded old folk. Our new tec-super was very interested in what she had to say. You just wait there and I'll go and fetch him."

I sank down on the designated bench in horror, but soon recovered. Called in to make a report? What a nerve! Fuming, I cleared off with the trolley after being kept waiting for five whole minutes. ("I've a business to run," I yelled over my shoulder.)

At the shop, I found Miss Holland showing a lady-customer out but otherwise alone. I barked: "What the devil have you been up to? I never told you to collect my brief-case. Where is the damn thing?"

"Up in your office, James."

"You have grossly exceeded your authority."

"Why the trolley," she had the nerve to ask.

I stowed it behind the counter and said: "If you must know, I am planning to buy a few presents for Stephanie. She needs a new tumble-dryer, for instance, and one or two pots and pans."

"How very exciting for her. Have you paid the money into your long-suffering bank?"

"I have indeed."

"Did the clerks all fall off their stools when you paid the money in?"

"No, Miss Holland. Why should they?"

"I just wondered. Did you cancel the money-meeting you and I were to have with the manager?"

"I forgot all about that," I truthfully said.

"Then I suggest you phone and cancel. This fortunate but strange injection of capital has altered the situation. A further meeting might not even be necessary. Quite a pleasing thought."

A pleasing thought indeed. I didn't want the manager in such a meeting saying something like: "Mr Crackery, we can now give you the receipt you were so worried about." (In a lady like Miss Holland, intuition is like the instinct of a ferret.) I was so relieved that I burst out: "Miss Holland, I totally withdraw the accusation I have made. You were in no way exceeding your authority. At any rate," I was unwise enough to add, "not about the brief-case. But to report the knocker was a step too far."

Sharply: "Neither did I exceed my authority, James, in reporting the knocker who so clearly exploited your crass ignorance."

Two ladies entered the shop at this point. Miss Holland turned to greet them. I at once sloped off up the stairs to my office. There it was – the brief-case, standing on the carpet and beside my desk. It had slight scuff-marks on the leather, but, after phoning my bank as Miss Holland had helpfully suggested, I rubbed over the entire brief-case with a nice soft cloth. It looked as good as new.

I then found that it had nothing inside.

Going downstairs with it, I found the two customers had gone. Miss Holland was once more alone, in front of the counter and tidying stock.

"Madam," I said, "was nothing found in this brief-case at the police-station?"

Aloof reply: "What, James, did you have in it when you stupidly lost it?"

"Nothing much more than your excellent financial report," I said, feeling like a guilty small boy. "But I'm surprised to find it gone. I can't imagine why it should be of any interest to an illiterate person."

Sharply: "What illiterate person, James?"

My heart (already in a flutter at the sight of Miss Holland in her beautiful blouse and her close-fitting skirt) beat faster. I gabbled: "That wheel-clamper, I can only assume. That Rivinni fellow. He might well have been the person to find the brief-case ..."

Miss Holland continued to tidy the stock in her graceful manner but interrupted in the same sharp tone. "James, my report was still in the brief-case. There was nothing else."

"Then why," I said, feeling humbly puzzled, "is the report still missing from this brief-case?"

"In the light of the extra bit of money you've injected, the report is no longer relevant. Apart from one page being ripped out, it was intact but needs a complete re-write."

"You're saying, then, that you've destroyed that lovely-looking report of yours?"

"I'm not saying that, James. I'm saying that I've put it under lock and key."

My heart beat even faster. "What on earth for?"

"Because the entire file is covered with oily finger-marks. These could amount to forensic evidence if, as I suspect, there's a link to a possible crime."

A dry-throated question: "Might I just ask what kind of crime you envisage?"

It was at this moment – of all others – that a nicely dressed man in a trilby entered the open door of the shop. He took off his hat and gave Miss Holland an amicable nod. To me, he pleasantly said: "Is this a convenient time, Mr Crackery?"

Before I could even draw breath to reply, Miss Holland answered for me (and with a radiant smile for the man): "Of course it is."

Briskly, she shut and bolted the shop-door after a uniformed sergeant had also entered. Full of happy charm, she lightly added:

"Like other shops in this reactionary backwater, we always shut at lunch-time. So let's all go up to Mr Crackery's office, shall we? This way, Superintendent Brockadill."

We all followed her obediently up the stairs. Brockadill! Never before had I ever known anyone of that name. But he seemed a very nice chap. (A shame to deceive him.) He was right behind Miss Holland and seemed pleased to be in that position. The sergeant, however, who was behind me, seemed worried. He whispered to me: "This is almost our new tec-super's first day, sir. He's settled the hash of real top criminals in London, sir."

He had whispered as if anxious that I might not show his superior officer sufficient respect. I whispered back glumly: "I'm glad to hear of his success, I do assure you."

Miss Holland seemed to be in something of an euphoric mood. I had never before seen her in such a mood. She instantly sat down at my very own desk and began holding court from behind it, rather like a newly-elected American president in the Oval Office.

"Superintendent," she said. in tones of high gaiety if not mischief, "would you like to ask my employer what he's done?"

The superintendent, sitting beside his sergeant on my little sofa, was now becoming entranced with Miss Holland. (What man wouldn't be?) Turning his good-humoured eyes upon me, he said: "Mr Crackery, could you give me a description?"

Consigned as I was to a hard-back chair, I suddenly went totally empty-headed. The fatalistic brief-case was on my lap. It seemed to be shouting its significance.

"Speak up," commanded Miss Holland, "and don't mumble."

"Do you mean," I managed to say to this chap Brockadill, "a description of the wheel-clamper?"

"No, sir," he politely said. "We sympathise with you but have no interest in his doings."

"Thank goodness for that," I nearly said but managed to turn the words into a cough.

"It's the knocker I'd like to know more about," he went on. "I tracked down a London gang of art-thieves fairly recently. But I didn't get all of them. I'm wondering if one of them might be operating in and around this area as a knocker."

Miss Holland stuck her oar in to brightly say: "Superintendent, is this what the police traditionally call a hunch?"

"I personally don't use that word," he said, "but yes – I suppose it could be called a hunch."

Shakily recovering my wits, I said: "I'm hoping it wasn't a crime to sell a ghastly painting for so high a sum. How can I possibly be entitled to more money? In fact, I'm the one who is beginning to feel guilty."

"Mr Crackery," said Brockadill, and in the kindliest of voices, "I'm sure you have nothing to reproach yourself for."

"I am still of the opinion," I loudly said, "that what I sold was worthless. I do know a little about works of art. It can't possibly be worth four thousand pounds. It begins to look as if I'm the one who is the con-man."

"Not at all," said the jolly decent Brockadill. "Nothing can be done if, as Miss Holland believes, a lost master-work exists beneath the painting on top. You sold it and that's that. But what I'm hoping for is this – a link to a deeper crime."

"A link, eh?" (The very word used by Miss Holland.) "What sort of link?"

"That, sir, remains to be seen. It's what could be called my hunch."

Again Miss Holland stuck her oar in.

"James, just give the officer what he had asked you for – a description of the knocker."

I pretended to ponder and cleverly gave (or what I thought was cleverly) a nondescript description. The sergeant wrote it down in his note-book. To my terrified astonishment, Brockadill became excited. He said: "This is good! This is the EXACT description of a villain I couldn't collar! Thank you so much, sir."

Again Miss Holland stuck her oar in, smiling delightedly. "James, have you any of the money upon your person, which this obvious criminal gave you?"

Unnerved and unguardedly, I let slip a true detail. "Well, yes … in my inside-pocket."

"How much?"

"Ten fifty-pounds notes. In other words, the five hundred pounds which, as I told you, is for personal expenditure."

"Hand them over to the superintendent. They could be counterfeit."

"But they're genuine," I genuinely protested. "You think I don't know a forgery when I see one? I'm in trade. I'm experienced."

Brockadill produced surgical-looking gloves. Putting them on, he eagerly said: "Do please let me have a look at the notes, sir."

He pronounced them all genuine after checking each one, whereupon Miss Holland said: "What about fingerprints? Can you get fingerprints off bank-notes?"

"Thank you, Miss Holland," he said, "that's a most helpful suggestion. It's a bit difficult, but it can be done. You won't mind, Mr Crackery, if we take charge of these for a short while?"

"He won't mind," said Miss Holland.

I could only shrug in helpless agreement. (This, may I remind you, was a woman I was in love with.) I also shrugged in helpless agreement after she added: "And what about his bank, Superintendent? It can't be too late, surely, to get hold of the notes he has deposited? Just one fingerprint might lead you straight to the villain you're seeking. Or possibly," she was pleased to add, "a different villain entirely."

"That," said the kindly Brockadill, "is indeed possible, especially if the notes given to Mr Crackery were in wrappers. Were they in any kind of wrapper, Mr Crackery?"

"I'm afraid not," I had enough presence of mind to say. (And I gave myself a good pinch on my arm – to remind myself to burn the plastic bags which had contained the notes. I had merely thrown them into the waste-box under the bench in the garage.)

Brockadill looked so disappointed that I made a feeble but false effort to seem helpful. I said: "The money the fellow handed over was all in notes – no coins. Does that help you?"

"Not really sir – no."

Again Miss Holland stuck her oar in. She said: "James, whether the notes you received were in wrappers or not, they must have been carried in some sort of bag. What sort of bag was it, James?"

Instantly and idiotically, I replied: "A Gladstone bag."

Why on earth did I let slip this true and dangerous clue? Was it because I yearned to share the secrets of my soul with a woman I now loved more desperately than ever? A liar in love, it would seem, is perhaps always to be at risk from a lapse of this sort, especially if the beloved is a dominating presence in the same room. My only comfort (an uneasy one) was that Brockadill gave me a most grateful smile.

"A useful detail," he said. "Other people in your area might well remember seeing the same man with the same bag."

"Just as important," said Miss Holland, "is surely the vehicle he was using? Well, James? What sort of vehicle was it?"

She couldn't catch me out again. I was able to say (although somewhat croakily): "I didn't notice what he was driving ..."

"He couldn't have been on foot, James. Was it a van he had? A lorry? Surely you saw him leave in some sort of vehicle?"

"Madam," I said, (in some annoyance, but annoyance with myself rather than with her), "I was too overjoyed to stand and wave the fellow goodbye. I am not here to be gagged. We have a business to run," and I stood up in the hope of diverting (if not terminating) the course of this dire conversation.

Brockadill and his sergeant also stood up. Unknowingly, Brockadill now politely subjected me to even more mental torment.

"Mr Crackery, I've no real grounds for making this request. I'm fairly sure your sale of the painting was a perfectly legal one in every way. The purchaser might not be the man I'm looking for. But would you mind coming with us to your bank?"

I tried being haughty. "Brockadill, is this really necessary?"

"Well, sir, we don't want the bank jumping to any wrong conclusions about you. That's why it would be best if you accompany us – or, to put it another way, why we accompany you. It can be your suggestion that we inspect the money you deposited."

Miss Holland stuck her oar in yet again to say, brightly: "Or you could say it's at my suggestion – which it was!"

"Well, yes," said Brockadill. "But don't worry, Mr Crackery. We will be giving you a receipt for any money we'd like to check – including the money from your inside-pocket which you've already handed over."

It was again the word "receipt" which, this time, was like a thumbscrew soon to be applied. I could now hear the bank-manager saying (in the presence of the courteous tec-super): "Oh, by the way Mr Crackery. Set your mind at rest. We have made you a out a receipt for the Gladstone bag."

"Gladstone bag?" I could hear Brockadill asking this future question in the sharpest of voices. (I could even hear the clink of future hand-cuffs.) I had only two small comforts. First, in leading the way down the stairs and out of the shop, Miss Holland announced she wouldn't be coming with us.

"I'm staying behind," she said, and she opened the shop-door. "I'll be re-opening after my sandwich-lunch. Call in if you need more help."

It was a relief to know that she wouldn't be breathing down my neck at the bank, but she immediately petrified me by adding: "Oh, by the way, Superintendent. My financial report was in the brief-case which I retrieved from the police-station. Some of the pages have oily fingerprints on them. Would you like to have those pages?"

Brockadill was daft enough to decline them, thank God. (My second only comfort.) He happily said: "Thank you, but no. It's not the wheel-clamper we're interested in. It's the knocker."

"Very well," and she shut the door on us.

"A very nice woman," he said, as we halted at the traffic-lights during the short bank-journey. "Very nice indeed. Very attractive."

Thinking it best to maintain a degree of frostiness, I said: "Are you a married man, Brockadill?"

"I am," and he sighed wistfully.

I knew exactly what he was thinking. Despite my electrified stomach and my fear of detection, I was wistfully sighing in much the same way. Why on earth had I so hastily married that merry roly-poly when, amid and among all the assistants I had ever employed, I might have captured the heart of Miss Holland? Fond as I was of my young and pretty wife, and lovely as our two children were, I knew I had made a mistake.

"The worst one can make in life," poor old Brockadill murmured, like a mind-reader.

I pretended not to hear him. This instant rapport with a man who could put me in prison – and for life – was most uncanny.

As the bank hove in sight, he softly and sadly quoted from the 1607 poem: "I did but see her passing by, and yet I love her till I die." (One of my favourite poems.)

As we pulled up in front of the bank itself, he leaned forward and tapped the sergeant on the shoulder. Frowning through his blushes, he said: "What do YOU think, sergeant?"

The sergeant switched off the engine and stared ahead. His reply was like that of a tactful butler. "I have been attached to you, sir, in a uniformed capacity and on a temporary basis. It's not my place to comment upon your feelings."

"I am referring," said Brockadill, a shade more tersely, "to what Miss Holland called my hunch. As a local man showing me the ropes, do you think my so-called hunch is feasible?"

"Well, sir, it could be too much of a long-shot. That's what did occur to me, sir. The knocker could have been a knocker and nothing more. We do get a spate now and then."

"I see. Thank you, sergeant. Please drive on – back to the station," and to me, Brockadill said: "May we invite you to lunch in our canteen? It's the least we can do after causing you this inconvenience."

Not wishing to endure the task of having to deceive this nice man any further (to say nothing of the risk of doing so), I said: "Thank you so much. Jolly nice of you. But I'd rather not at the present time. Could you very kindly drop me off at the Silver Tureen? It's where I usually have my lunch. Unlike Miss Holland, I can't stand sandwiches."

The still very wistful Brockadill said: "Sergeant, do you know the Silver Tureen?"

"I do, sir. Too posh a place for me though."

"Pull up there, please, and we'll drop Mr Crackery off."

To drop me off meant a turn-back to Ambleside Lane, a cut-through from High Street – scarcely a minute walk from my shop. Both these wonderful officers got out to see me into the restaurant. I shook hands with them.

"Mr Crackery," said Brockadill, still wistful and a bit red-faced, "I'm hoping we shall meet again under less professional circumstances."

In a jokingly conspiratorial whisper, I said: "Brockadill, my dear chap, I hope that too. But may I just mention something to you of no little importance?"

"What! What is it?"

"Might I just have my money back? The five hundred pounds?"

"Of course, of course," and he hurriedly handed me back the illicit notes, apologising frantically.

Strolling into that neat and tinkling restaurant, I could hear Asti Glertish saying in my ear: "Don't you forget what I told yer. Don't start splashing the money around. And stop showing off, you silly old fool. You has just been lucky. Don't push it."

It was impossible for me to heed this warning. I was too much in need of celebration after the labours and trials of the day so far. Also, as I've mentioned before, I seemed to possess a natural criminal instinct. It was this instinct which told me to make the most of being in favour with the police. My solicitous arrival by police-car, at the restaurant, would soon be known to all the town-centre worthies. What better influence could there be in preventing any rumours against me? I would be the last to be suspected of anything untoward.

"You, Jay," I reassuringly told myself, "are back in charge …"

I strolled back to my shop feeling spreadingly well-fed. I had in my mouth the last inch or two of the cigar presented to me, free of charge, by the highly impressed restaurant-owner. I felt supremely self-confident. Even the agonies of unrequited love were lulled by my feelings of good fortune.

The object of my unrequited love was behind the counter as I entered. She was showing table place-mats to a woman whose back was all I could see of her.

The object of my unrequited love saw me coming in and focussed her gaze upon me. It was this which made the woman-customer turn and look.

"My God," this customer cried, "it's him – the very man! It's the prowler. I'd know him anywhere! Call the police."

SIX

Miss Holland Turns Detective

In the presence of two or three other customers – all goggling in fascination – she began to conduct the second of her meddlesome investigations.

"This," she said of me to my accuser, "is Mr Crackery – the proprietor of this shop. Nothing you can tell me will ever surprise me. What type of prowling has he been up to?"

My accuser was so excited she could hardly get her words out. "He was loitering in Orchard Ash Road with a hacksaw. I thought nothing much of it at the time, but, as I later reported to Lady Bannerfield-Frishley, this man was obviously up to no good. He was very shifty-looking. Very shifty indeed."

I now recognised this woman. She was the next-door housekeeper who had asked me to open a gate on her behalf. She had charitably mistaken me for a tramp and had promised me bread and cheese (and half a tomato). For a moment, I felt stumped. This was a jolly awkward matter to explain. But I had already been through the mill that day, to say nothing of my experiences with Asti Glertish and her step-mother. For me, to concoct an explanation about a mere hacksaw should be child's play.

"Madam," I began by saying, taking off my hat to her, "set your mind at rest. But you, first of all, need to explain something which has left me bewildered. Why half a tomato and not a whole one?"

Miss Holland: "James, stick to the point. Why were you prowling around with a hacksaw?"

"It was wrapped in newspaper," the housekeeper eagerly added, "and it fell at my feet. Nearly hit my toes. Quite a heavy object. He never explained. He just picked up the hacksaw and walked off in a guilty manner. Hunched up and shifty."

"You too would have been hunched up and shifty," I politely told her, "if you had just been bitten by a savage dog and chased up a tree. Ladies and gentlemen," I said to the shop at large, "I beg for your sympathy. I had been wheel-clamped that morning in Willow Tree Lane."

Cries of surprise: "Wheel-clamped? In Dackley?"

"I was forced to pay thirty pounds before the fellow would agree to removing the clamp."

More cries of surprise: "Thirty pounds? What's the world coming to?"

"My reaction, ladies and gentlemen, was the same as yours," I went on. "It was little short of blackmail. But I paid up. It was only after I had re-parked in that awful multi-storey that I decided to take action. We, the people of England, will not stand for this sort of thing."

Cries of "Hear hear!"

"After returning to this shop of mine and working out the fellow's name and address, I went back to my motor-car. I was determined to call upon this dubious firm – and with my big hacksaw. I intended to warn this new breed of criminals that I would use the hacksaw to remove the clamp myself if they dared to repeat their offence. I would then take the pieces to the police-station and lay charges."

"And I should think so too," someone said, and with enthusiasm. (I think it was the weedy husband of a stoutish lady.)

"But was I," I continued, "given any chance to deliver this warning? I was not. I was almost immediately set upon by the savage dog. I was hardly in sight of the front door. I was bitten and I was chased. I had to climb a tree. I was up it for some considerable time."

Miss Holland (sharply): "And what happened to the hacksaw? Did you take that with you up the tree?"

"No, Miss Holland. I dropped it as I fled. I was only able to retrieve it after the dog went away from the base of the tree. It was after this," I said to the dawningly contrite housekeeper, "that I considered calling upon the next-door neighbour for advice and assistance. That's when you saw me hesitating – at the gate to that property."

"Oh, Mr Crackery," she moaned. "Please forgive me. I misunderstood the situation. We know all about that dog and those common people next door. And their untidy dustbins in the service-lane. I should have known. I'm sorry."

She came near to kissing me. I had to console her by saying: "You've nothing to blame yourself for, madam. You made a perfectly natural mistake. It's a pleasure to see someone from Orchard Ash Road shopping here. I hope we shall see you again."

"Oh you will, sir," she said. "Lady Bannerfield-Frishley asked me to find table-mats – and these are very good quality. She will be very pleased."

Splendid," I sang out, heartily. "And now, if you'll excuse me, I have to go up to my office. I'm a very busy man."

Everyone in the shop (except Miss Holland) clapped as I mounted the stairs. Ha! There is nothing like the pleasure of being applauded, even by the smallest of audiences. I was beginning to feel what it must be like to be a successful actor. But I got ticked off, as it were, as soon as I was preening myself in my mirror (the one over the office-fireplace).

"Pardon me as says it, mister, but you is being carried away-like. Too clever by 'arf. I can only warn you again. That Miss Holland will do yer."

"Nonsense," I told my reflection in the mirror. "I've got her where I want her – under control. I am her employer and therefore her superior officer. She's beginning to know it."

This huge degree of self-assertion suddenly resulted in my complete exhaustion. (After all, I had been up since five o'clock counting all that money.) I awoke on my little sofa at closing-up time to find Miss Holland prodding me with a pencil.

"James, it's time you left the premises and went home. I'm locking up. It's been a long day for those of us who work."

I scrambled to my feet and went into my wash-room to splash water in my face. She had the nerve to follow me in. She said: "James, I gather that Master Brockadill ignored my advice. Investigated no fingerprints or run of the numbers. I shall have to deal with him a lot more firmly. Just drops you off at the Silver Tureen! Most unsatisfactory."

"Miss Holland," I said, as I got into my hat and coat, "you should have awoken me sooner. I have to get home to Stephanie and the girls. Please excuse me."

Following me down the stairs, she said: "You won't find your wife and children at home."

I stopped in alarm. "Why ever not?"

"Because, James, you've done nothing about the hole in the bedroom ceiling. Stephanie fears that spiders will come down through the hole at night. She rang up about it, but you were snoring like a pig. So she's gone back with your sister and the two little girls to Swerton. You need to exercise more foresight."

Standing in the centre of the shop, I spoke in a reasonable voice. "Miss Holland, may I please ask you not to interfere in matters concerning my private life."

"James," she sharply said, "what are you hiding?"

"Nothing, madam."

"If you've done anything wrong, James, now is the time to tell me. Last chance, James."

"I honestly don't know what you're talking about. Furthermore, madam, I can't understand why you let me sleep on and why you're still at the shop. I'm surprised to find you so mentally confused. Closing-time should be as prompt as opening-time. Do I scent a budding romance in the air? Is that it? Waiting for Brockadill, are you? To come and pick you up?"

I don't know if you've ever received what might be called a withering look of utter contempt, but that's what I now received from Miss Holland.

"That man," she said, "is a very fine man. It's always a treat to talk with a man of real intelligence and physical attraction."

"So I'm right," I said, grinning fatuously.

"But I," she finishingly added, "have other fish to fry."

The phone in her office rang after the very last of those words – or rather, in what she called her office (the part of the ground-floor stock-room she had annexed).

And guess what?

She looked at her watch before going into her office to answer. I had always been a bit unworldly. But not a total greenhorn. An eligible woman who looks at her watch before answering a phone is a woman checking the time of a pre-arranged call – from a lover.

I left her to it. I did remember to take the empty shopping-trolley from behind the counter (where I had stowed it). I feared she would make a disdainful fuss of I forgot. But I was very dazed indeed as I walked with the trolley to Willow Tree Lane (to my motor-car). The daffodils along the river on that early evening were still glorious, but achingly so. How was it possible that I had never before noticed that special radiance of hers? It was only too natural that such a woman would, at some time or other, have a lover. But for me never to have twigged! Are all men just as blind about a woman they suddenly find they adore?

"I doubt it, you silly old fool," I told myself. "Only you could be so uniquely stupid."

I had a feeling, though, that poor old Brockadill was in the same boat as poor old me.

In the next few days, may I tell you, I behaved myself dutifully. It had never been true (as you might have wrongly been led to suppose) that I never assisted Miss Holland with her counter-duties. Hoping for a crumb or two of praise (which I never got), I stood right beside her hour after hour – serving and smiling. Ironically, trade was beginning to pick up. Amazing! Really busy. But, all the time, a part of my mind was remembering all the other times when Miss Holland looked at her watch – looked at it in a special sort of way, I mean, before going into her office and answering the phone.

And one of those times? Recall it, can you?

It was, of course, when I had been cautiously escorting Miss Asti Glertish out of the shop ("dragging her out," as Miss Holland had exaggeratedly put it).

It was exactly on the next Monday morning (following that scene on the Monday before), that I bravely made an overture during a pause in serving. I was worrying about the exaggeration. I thought Miss Holland might report me for kidnapping or something of that sort. (She was being very tough on me, I don't mind telling you. I felt sent to Coventry.)

Hoping to dismantle her exaggeration, I thought it best to begin obliquely. I said: "I have made my peace with Stephanie. I have had the ceiling in the bedroom satisfactorily repaired. All is well in the Crackery household."

"That," said Miss Holland, breaking one of her elegantly disdainful silences, "I rather doubt. Stephanie should never have succumbed to your blandishments. She needs to extricate herself from your ogre-like grip."

I rather stammeringly said: "Are your sort of suggesting that she should leave me?"

"Certainly not. But she will never develop her potential if she fails to understand herself."

The phone in Miss Holland's office rang. She pulled back her sleeve to look at her watch, then, off-handedly, said to me: "Just answer that, will you?"

Obviously not the right time for lover-boy. All of her smile was for some old bat approaching the counter. Spurned and scowling,

I went to the school-mistressy desk in the so-called office and answered.

A titteringly apologetic woman's voice said: "Oh, Mr Crackery! Is that you?"

"The very man. How can I help you, madam?"

"Mr Crackery, we have sort of met. I am housekeeper to Sir Henry Bannerfield-Frishley. I was in your very nice shop last Wednesday. I was buying some table place-mats. You surely do remember me, Mr Crackery?"

"Somehow, madam, I rather think I do. Are the table-mats satisfactory?"

"Oh, yes, Lady Frishley is delighted with them. But that's not why I'm phoning. Sir Henry is very interested in your troubles with those nasty people next door. He would like a few words with you. Please hold and I will connect him."

Despite the old-buffer act, which I often adopted for amusing Stephanie, I was only sort of middle-aged; and Sir Henry, when he came breathily on the line, was obviously very much my senior. I knew at once that he was a genuine old buffer of a type I had always admired.

"Young man," he said, "I hear you've been chased up a tree by that dog."

"Er, yes, Sir Henry." (What a shame to deceive such a nice old boy!)

"You have a wife, young man?"

"I do indeed, Sir Henry," I said, so pleased at having something truthful to say that I spoke with ringing enthusiasm.

"It's always nice to know when younger people are happily settled. Rare thing these days. Young and pretty, is she?"

"Yes indeed, Sir Henry."

"Then would you and your young and pretty wife like to join us at luncheon some time this week? Or perhaps next?"

In a whirl of mixed feelings, I said: "That would be very pleasant, Sir Henry. Thank you very much."

"I have a feeling, Mr Crackery, that we need to join forces in seeking redress. Those two people next door need to be dealt with once and for all."

"I've already done that for you," I felt like ingratiatingly saying; instead, of course, I ingratiatingly mumbled: "Been a bit of a nuisance, have they?"

"More than a bit, young man. Can you imagine the state of their dustbins? Ever been down our service-lane?"

"No, Sir Henry."

"I shall show you those dustbins. Speak to our housekeeper again, Mr Crackery. Nice girl. I'll put her back on. She'll arrange the luncheon-date."

After grandly agreeing a date with the now very titteringly compliant housekeeper, I re-joined Miss Holland at the counter. I was bursting to reply crushingly to any meddlesome questioning. But she irritated me by saying nothing, not even during our coffee-break. Eventually, close on one o'clock, I sought to force a response.

"That call," I said, "was from Sir Henry Whatsisname. I've been invited to lunch the day after tomorrow – Wednesday."

No reply. She coolly continued to tidy the till. A shade sarcastically, I tried saying: "I do hope that won't be inconvenient to you. I won't be coming in. I'll be away all day."

"There's nothing new in that, James," she at last deigned to remark. "And it will certainly be no inconvenience. It's the very day I suggested to Nancy myself."

"Nancy? Who the devil is Nancy?"

"The housekeeper who bought the table place-mats. And with whom you've recently spoken."

A new anxiety began to afflict me. "Are you, Miss Holland, by any chance saying that you've been invited too?"

"Yes, James. I've been invited. But, as I say, it's no inconvenience. Wednesday, may I remind you, is our early-closing day. One of us, at least, will be able to put in a morning's work," and she coolly closed the till drawer.

"I suppose," I called after her, as she went off into her office, "you'll be expecting me to give you a lift?"

"No, James, I am not expecting that."

"Since you don't drive, madam, just how do you expect to get there? Are they sending a car for you? Is that it?"

"No, James. Brockadill will be picking me up – from here. It's his afternoon off too."

"You mean that chap Brockadill will be coming with you to Sir Henry Whatsisname's?"

I had followed her into her office. I was trembling all over. "What's going on? What do you hope to gain by wangling your way into a purely private luncheon-party? And wangling an invitation for that besotted policeman?"

"James," she dismissively said, "there's nothing I'd like more than to see Sir Henry's dustbins. The prospect fascinates me. I am always agog for new experiences."

And in that last-word way of hers, she added: "But the nature of Sir Henry's dustbin-vendetta is perhaps what stimulates me most. I have this feeling that it might contain a clue to a mystery that needs solving."

Ominous words, wouldn't you say?

After hearing them so deliberately enunciated, I did tend to brood upon them both day and night (prior to the luncheon-party). But here's a motto of mine. (You might one day find it useful yourself.)

"Never allow even your worst troubles to ruin your digestion or your sleep."

I was far too excited by the thought of the invitation even to be worried by imagined reproaches from Miss Asti Glertish. ("I warned yer not to make things worse for yerself. You just can't keep yer marff shut, can yer?")

Foolish as you too may think it, I was actually licking my lips as I drove down that impeccable drive with Stephanie. (I was envisaging a lunch superior to the Silver Tureen.)

"By God," I jubilantly said to her, "this is the life we need to be leading."

Giggles from Stephanie. "Oh, sweetie-pie, you clever old stick! What a lovely big garden! Are these people real aristocrats?"

"They are indeed, madam. Make sure you don't disgrace me."

"As long as they don't get me on the Asti Spumante I'll be quite all right."

"Just choose water," I growled, frowning over that haunting name for her favourite tipple.

More giggles from Stephanie. "That's what Miss Holland said. She still thinks she can boss me about."

"The only person who can boss you about," I further growled, "is old Crackers himself. You will keep off the Asti because that is what old Crackers is telling you to do."

All around were far-reaching lawns. Beyond cedars and other dignified trees and their dreamy shadows I could see a gleaming lake – not huge, but certainly jolly impressive.

"Blimey," giggled Stephanie, as we got to the villa itself, "I never knew a place like this existed – not in Dackley."

"And do try," I pleaded, "not to giggle."

The villa, for me, was like a magical vision. It was at an entrancing distance down the sweeping curve of the drive. In a sense, I couldn't quite believe what I was seeing. There was no hint whatsoever of any proximity to that insanitary bungalow on the neighbouring estate.

The front door (the one forbidden to tramps, if you remember) was noble in the extreme. I simply stood there just looking at it. But only for a few seconds. It opened and Nancy, the housekeeper, darted out and gushingly greeted us as if were old friends.

"Come in," she cried. "This is Stephanie, is it?"

"It is," I said, more than a trifle heavily. (I was ungallantly wishing I hadn't brought her.)

After ushering us through a well-appointed hall and into a spacious cloakroom, Nancy the housekeeper said: "Just push the bell-button when you're ready and come out into the hall. I'll then take you in to see Sir Henry. He wants to have a private word with you in particular, Mr Crackery, before luncheon."

Nodding and smilingly, she closed the door on us. What a civilised set-up! Two splendidly separated wash-rooms (within the cloak-room) for ladies and gentlemen!

"Oh, look," said Stephanie, still in giggles, "Miss Holland must have already arrived! There's her nice new coat. You did say she would be here, didn't you?"

"I did, yes," I said, only too aware of feelings I couldn't possibly describe. (Just the sight of her coat did this to me.) "But I also thought she might not. I've been thinking that she might only have been pulling my leg – in her usual high-flown way."

I managed a chortle, adding: "At least one thing's for sure. She wouldn't be allowed to bring her tame policeman with her. She must have come in a taxi."

"Crackers, old boy," said Stephanie, "I sometimes think you're under her thumb as much as me. More so, I sometimes think."

"Nonsense," I said, and I distractedly looked for the bell-button (on the wall in the outer part of the cloakroom).

I found the button but paused at the sight of a framed photograph hanging above it. It was an elongated group-photograph which, given my own background, I assumed to be a school-photograph like the one in my office (of my final year at Beagley).

"My God," I cried, after putting on my glasses and looking more closely.

It was a police-college photograph, as were all the others adorning the walls. In a premier position, another photograph showed Sir Henry Bannerfield-Frishley shaking hands with Her Majesty the Queen. Our host was nothing less, the caption told me, than the long-retired chief constable. I had never heard of him, but, for me, even a retired chief constable was surely still as dangerous as a retired old lion. Even an old lion can have a few teeth.

"James," I told myself, as I pressed the bell-button, "you have probably just trodden on the worst cow-pat of your career. As Miss Glertish would say, you have only yourself to blame."

"What's that, darling?" Stephanie was so awed by the royal photograph that she had become absent-mindedly solemn. She hadn't really heard me and wasn't really enquiring, but I was alarmed that I had muttered aloud.

In the hall, we were promptly split up. Stephanie was taken away by some lesser domestic minion to join the other arrivals (for sherry, as it turned out). I, meanwhile, was led off by the senior minion (the housekeeper) for the "private word" with Sir Henry.

"How good of you, Crackery, to come and see me!"

He had risen from a cosy chair in a book-lined study, which had its own veranda – and a breathtaking view, through the open French window, of his estate. (I had no idea that chief constables could be rolling in money to this extent.)

"It's very nice of you," I rather mumbled, "to have invited us."

Although he wasn't intimidating, I was nevertheless intimidated. Handing me a sherry, he jovially said: "This is much better than the stuff the others are drinking. But that's not the reason for this private word. I need to warn you, Crackery."

"Warn me?" I quavered.

"Before we join the others. My wife is a lovely girl and so is my daughter. But they both regard my dustbin-campaign as an obsession. I am not permitted to mention it at table. I am only permitted to introduce the subject – to any guest who might be interested – in a private word beforehand. You, Crackery, strike me as the very man I've been looking for. I can fill you in on the details later if you can agree, in principle, to help."

Feeling uneasily reassured, I said: "I can only do my best, Sir Henry."

"That's wonderful of you, young man – wonderful!"

He patted me on the shoulder and took my glass away, saying: "We now join the others," but, to my renewed terror, he added:

"You see, Crackery, it's not just about dustbins. I have what's sometimes called a hunch."

Where had I heard that word before? Do I need to tell you?

"I have this intuitive feeling," he said, piloting me through the hall, "that something very seriously criminal is going on next door. But Ralphie won't do a thing. Ralphie says it's a civil matter through and through."

I weakly asked: "Who is Ralphie?"

"My son-in-law. He's now the assistant chief-constable – in charge of the detective-part. He's with the others," and in a whisper, Sir Henry added: "Get him to one side, if you possibly can, and make him see sense."

In taking me down an enticing passageway beside the staircase (this was no bungalow), Sir Henry was for some reason walking on tip-toe. I did the same. I wanted to be loyal to him, yet, at the same time, I was feeling horribly guilty. Who would willingly deceive such a lovely old chap? In having been appointed on the strength of past colonial experience (as I later found out), he was certainly an old-fashioned example of a former chief-constable. But he was no fool. Do please get that right. His excited grip on my arm could just as easily be an arresting grip.

I copied his urgent whisper. "Where are we going, Sir Henry?"

"To the drawing-room," he whispered back. "And I don't mind betting that Ralphie is telling everyone I'm off my chump. Let's see if we can overhear what he's saying …"

Releasing his grip on my arm and opening the door a crack, he softly ordered: "You just put your ear to that, young man."

I put my ear to the crack, but it wasn't a male voice I heard.

It was Miss Holland's. She was calmly saying: "To murder Sir Henry in that particular way, in my opinion, is ridiculous. The easier and better way for doing away with him, I would suggest, is to – "

I burst into the room, interrupting her in a shout. "Just what the hell are you involved in, Miss Holland? What's going on?"

She and the other guests were standing in an aperitif group at a convivial but discreet-looking bar. She was startled enough almost to spill her drink (and others did so), but she, of course, was quick to recover.

"Don't be absurd, James. We are discussing that story about the Hound of the Baskervilles. To murder Sir Henry Baskerville by way of a phosphorescent dog is, as I say, ridiculous. The story is vastly over-rated."

She had obviously been enjoying herself in being the centre of attention. Even in dabbing themselves down, the six ladies and gentlemen I had startled were still far more interested in her than in me. They hung on her every sacrilegious word.

She lightly and charmingly prattled on: "I have, of course, seen two or three story-adaptations on television. Total rubbish. But it's only recently that I've begun reading the actual books. My employer has two volumes of the stories in his office bookcase. I've been reading through them in my lunch-hour – while he, of course, has been stuffing himself at the Silver Tureen. I can't fathom why men are so devoted to Sherlock Holmes. It must be, I can only suppose, because they've never outgrown their boyhood."

All the wives present – including Sir Henry's lovely old lady of a wife – were chortling in a knowing sort of manner. (My own wife was merely giggling again.) Not one person present leapt to the defence of the great detective. Neither the assistant chief-constable in the shape of Ralphie, nor even the handsome Brockadill did anything other than grin feebly. As for Sir Henry himself, he was only too eager to lead Miss Holland in to luncheon when it was announced by the housekeeper. (I freely confess that I remained as meek as the two police-officers.)

I found myself seated between their two wholesome wives. Bad form as it is to say so, I was thankful for the obscurity of this position. "From now on," I could imagine Miss Glertish saying from behind my chair, "button your mouth." ("burton yer marff.")

The dining-room itself, it need hardly be said, abounded in good taste (and not least, may I add, for the table-mats from my shop). And the food was beautifully served by the housekeeper and her assistant. But the food itself! Frankly, it was among the worst meals of my life. I had eaten very little breakfast in anticipation of this lunch. I don't exaggerate. I would honestly have preferred the bread and cheese (and half a tomato) on offer to passing tramps.

"Coffee, sir?"

Again, I don't exaggerate. It tasted like luke-warm black ink.

Yet here's the mystery. Miss Holland, who was sitting at Sir Henry's right hand, appeared to be relishing this ghastly coffee – as, indeed, she had delicately relished the whole ghastly meal. She had her head very close to Sir Henry's, conversing with him quietly and intently.

What plot was she hatching?

While that nice old chap was himself talking to her – in the same close and quiet way – I saw her give that lucky devil Brockadill a look-away glance. From it, I knew – and from the look-away glance he returned – that a previous intimacy had been shared. (As I've said before, I'm no greenhorn.) It might, of course, have been just a kiss. But it might just as easily have been a lot more. (I was remembering how she had said to me: "I am always agog for new experiences.")

Out of torment and curiosity, I raised my coffee-cup and gave the black ink a second chance to redeem itself.

"Ugh," I couldn't help loudly exclaiming.

No one took a blind bit of notice. As an object of interest, I remained forgotten. Man or woman, everyone in the room was too subjugated by the presence of Miss Holland. Even the well-and-correctly dressed assistant chief-constable, although obviously intending to stay married to his wholesome wife, was staring at Miss Holland more than a little admiringly.

I don't know if anyone else noticed, but I distinctly noticed

Miss Holland prompting Sir Henry. She did so by quickly touching his forearm. Instantly, he got to his feet.

"Would anyone here" he asked, "like to come and see those dirty filthy dustbins?"

Lady Whatsit, his sweetly old but still very feminine wife, gaily protested. "Oh, Woffles darling! Don't start being silly. We have yet to get back to the drawing-room. We have yet to try the nice chocolates Ralphie brought us. Tell him, Ralphie."

"Those dustbins," intoned the good son-in-law, "are a civil matter – not a police matter."

Sir Henry addressed the new tec-super. "How about you, Brockadill? You're new here. You've yet to see those notorious dustbins."

In his well-cut suit, Brockadill looked handsome but unhappy. "Well, er, I – "

Sir Henry breezed on: "We only have to go through the kitchen-garden to the tradesmen's entrance, then along the service-lane. Far more than a civil matter! Mr Crackery has been attacked by that savage dog and chased up a tree."

Nobody even looked at me, except Stephanie who was giggling her head off. (Against my orders, she had naughtily asked after Asti Spumante. To her joy, she had been given it. She was now as tight as a tick.) The two off-duty police-officers, one each side of her, didn't move; and the ladies certainly had no intention of doing so, but Brockadill (it seemed to me) looked as if he were merely following the example set by his senior.

"Very well," Sir Henry blithely said, "I and Miss Holland will inspect the dustbins on our own. With young Crackery, of course."

Miss Holland stood up and the poor old Brockadill chappie would have changed his mind if she had allowed it. He half rose, but she swiftly stopped him by saying: "No, please. You stay and look after Stephanie. She'll be legless very soon. It will take the two of you to get her to the cloakroom, let alone the drawing-room. She will soon need to vomit."

Poor old Brockadill sank back on his chair. I felt as sorry for him as I was for myself.

"Look here," I complained to Miss Holland as soon as we were in the open air, "why did you say Stephanie would need to vomit? She never needs to vomit when she's tight."

"It's a possibility, James."

"Only a remote one, surely?"

"Remote or not, James, we don't want those two police-officers with us. Do we, Sir Henry?"

"We sure don't," he chuckled. "Come along, young Crackery. Don't hang about. Hop in."

We had emerged through the noble front door and into the roundel where, earlier, I had parked – along with the other arrivals. What I had not noticed, at the time, was that toy-like conveyance known as a buggy. It was this which Sir Henry had invited me to hop into. He, with Miss Holland, occupied the two front seats. Behind them was a box-like structure containing his walking-stick and a hoe; it was this I had to "hop" into and stand half-crouchingly.

"It's all I'm allowed to drive these days," he said, still chuckling. "But I am no back number. It's time Ralphie and that new bloke Brockadill appreciated the fact. Hop out again, young Crackery, and open my gate."

We had arrived at his carriage-gate. I did as requested, and Miss Holland's expression was inscrutable. I cautiously asked Sir Henry: "Shall I leave the gate open?"

"No, boy – shut it after we've gone through. We don't want that lot knowing where we go," and he burst into more chuckles. "Strictly speaking, I'm not allowed to drive this beyond the gate."

"Excuse me, Sir Henry," I said, as we crawled slowly along Orchard Ash Road, "may I ask you a question? Why don't you want those two police-officers to see the dustbins?"

It was Miss Holland who answered for him.

"Because, James, it's not just the bins we're going to look at," and she, although not chuckling, was certainly beginning to look happily bright-eyed.

Sir Henry stopped at the carriage-gate to the insanitary bungalow. He said: Hop out again, boy, and open up. We're going in."

"Sir Henry," I bleated, "I really must advise against what you seem to be about to do. A savage dog is loose. Besides, this gate is padlock-chained. Look!"

To my heart-thudding amazement, Sir Henry presented me with a bunch of keys – the padlock-key selected between his finger and thumb. He said: "This used to be poor Mary's place. I've had the spare keys to it ever since she died. Ralphie doesn't know that. Neither does my wife. But our children used to play here – before it was left empty and to rot for years and years. Just open the damn gate, Crackery, and let us through."

His voice had suddenly taken on a quite menacing tone which, as they say about such a tone, filled me with foreboding. After hastily complying and handing back the whole time-worn bunch of keys, I followed on foot as he drove on up that unkempt drive.

We reached the beech tree. Remember it? (The tree with that horribly daubed "4" on its trunk.) It was here that Sir Henry suddenly halted his eccentric vehicle. Pleasantly but strongly, Miss Holland said: "Sir Henry, why have you stopped?"

"I'm having second thoughts," he mumbled, to my hopeful relief. "Legally, I suppose, we're trespassing."

"Nonsense," she gaily told him. "You are simply exercising a neighbourly concern. Drive on, Sir Henry."

He drove on but remained subdued. At the front door, he stayed huddled in his seat. He buried his face in his hands for a moment and then brokenly said: "I haven't come in here for two years at least – not since that awful woman moved in. I can't bear to see the place in this state. Miss Holland, we shouldn't be doing this. I think we should go back."

"Don't be silly, Sir Henry," she smartly said. "Let's get out and go in. Come on!"

She got out of the buggy; he did so too but hung back, saying: "Ralphie isn't going to approve – nor will that new chap from the Met."

"Never mind them," she airily said. "You have legitimate suspicions to follow up. You told me you questioned the postman."

"I did, yes."

"Thoroughly?"

"Fairly thoroughly, yes."

"And he told you the place seems deserted. No dog, phosphorescent or otherwise. And no yellow van parked in the service lane outside the trade-entrance. Your own staff have told you that. So give me the keys, Sir Henry. You have a neighbourly duty. I and my employer are happy to assist you. Isn't that so, James?"

"Well, yes," I said, feeling (as I so often did in Miss Holland's presence) like a small boy.

Without needing Sir Henry's guidance, Miss Holland quickly selected the right key from the bunch. She was inside the bungalow in the boldest of seconds. Horrifyingly efficient, she went straight to the half-dark warehouse-cum-office – that former dining-room – and switched on the chandelier-light. Sir Henry, I then noticed, had tears in his eyes.

"This change of use is so dreadful," he said to me; and, having his walking-stick with him, he gave one of the boxes on the floor an almighty thwack. "And I hope that one has got eggs in it."

For my part, I must say I was to some extent feeling relieved at being granted a certain forensic opportunity. I had been worrying no end about the fingerprints I had left behind. I was now busily fingering everything to negate any future police-investigation. But, of course, Miss Holland spotted my surreptitious behaviour.

"For heaven's sake, James. This is a crime scene. Put your hands in your pockets. Keep them there."

Although without her coat and hat, she was wearing natty outdoor-gloves and was expertly going through plenty of stuff herself. Sir Henry, meanwhile, was thwacking a few more boxes. He was getting quite savage.

"I've never set eyes on the woman who took this place over," he said. "But I've had reports from people who have. A real nasty piece of work! I've tried to be neighbourly. I've written letters. She ignores them. I've tried phoning her about those dustbins. She puts the phone down when she hears my voice. I could kill her for what she's done to Mary's old home. I could smash her head in – smash it to a pulp. D'you hear Me? A pulp."

This declaration frightened me, I have to say, but Miss Holland simply said: "Stop being so silly, Sir Henry. Stay on track. Your instincts were right. This is obviously the nerve-centre of a criminal operation. Hugo has been telling me about criminal gangs in London. There could be a link."

Hugo, did she say? She did. How lucky for that handsome Brockadill to have been given such a masculine name! Why couldn't my parents have called me Hugo instead of James?

These sad reflections of mine were dispelled in the very next instant by a bit of real drama.

I had seen Miss Holland open a cupboard – and then shut it quickly after looking inside.

It was the cupboard I had looked into myself (when trapped in this same room by old Masher). The main eye-level shelf had contained toy-tomahawks and dozens of tubes of unbranded toothpaste. These items, as I now could see, were in a heap on the floor.

She said: "Sir Henry, come and look at what I've found," and she re-opened the cupboard door.

And on the shelf previously occupied by the tomahawks and toothpaste? A gigantic mass of miniature Swiss-rolls.

Swiss-rolls, I mean, formed by rolled-up bank notes – each held in shape by a rubber-band.

Sir Henry lumbered over to this hoard, his hand on his stick wobbling in excitement.

"By golly," he cried, "we can bet Ralphie's best boots no tax has ever been paid on this little lot!"

SEVEN

Oh Dear, is She Starting to Suspect Me?

At first, I was as astonished as Sir Henry himself, which was perhaps just as well. It helped me, in Miss Holland's eyes, to appear innocent of any connection. But, even as Sir Henry was still clucking and goggling, I was starting to remember some exact words spoken by Miss Asti Glertish.

After bringing the Gladstone bag to the cottage, she had said: "The place wore stuffed with money under them boards. Plenty to divide up real clever."

I was also remembering how I had returned to the bungalow with the hacksaw. I had entered this very room and seen how she had cleared it of all evidence. I was even remembering how I had seen the tomahawks and toothpaste-tubes dumped on the floor – but was too dumbfounded to regard the sight as significant. I had not even thought of looking in the cupboard.

Would I have pinched any of the money, at that time, if I had opened the cupboard?

Undoubtedly. (As I've said before, I am trying to be accurate in these memoirs.) And I began to shudder at the thought of being found out by Miss Glertish. I couldn't quite imagine my fate, but I knew it would have resembled a whole ton of bricks. ("I could HATE you for this. Mucking up my plans YET AGAIN.")

Faintly, I heard Miss Holland say: "James, have you too had too much to drink?"

I found I had swooned like a village maiden. I had slumped down on a dining-room chair. (You perhaps remember the one I mean.)

Like Miss Glertish, Miss Holland had no patience even with my genuine ailments. "Pay attention, James. We need to work out why all this money is in this cupboard."

I could have told her at once. I knew it in a flash.

"Why not go real stupid, Mr Crackers, and tell her?" (I seemed to hear the grating voice of Asti Glertish, tempting me into this imbecility.) "Go on! Tell her! Tell why I stuffs a nice lot of them dregs in the cupboard. Tell her I done it for the police to find when they final gets around to searching for them two. Tell her so it's to stop the police using a bit of brain – and realising you and me has got the main lot. You has been so stupid so far. Why not go complete mad? Just one more step and you'll be over the edge, just like my dad."

This strange impulse of mine, I could only imagine, was due to my being in the same room where that dreadful old woman had hit me over the head – as well as having screamed down my ear. An after-effect of delayed shock? (I leave you to be the judge.)

Even if I had wanted to obey this impulse, I would not have been able to do so. Miss Holland was already holding forth in her own mad way. I struggled up off the chair (with poor old Sir Henry helping me) to hear her saying: "Sir Henry, please answer my question. Are you, like James, a life-long admirer of Sherlock Holmes?"

"Yes, indeed," he said with rosy-faced enthusiasm.

"Then please listen to what I've just been telling you both. Are you both familiar with the story about the resident hypochondriac – a man called Blessington?"

"Ah, yes," cried Sir Henry, in delight. "Story number twenty, you mean – the Resident Patient. One of my favourites. Brilliant story."

"Mine too," I supportively said. "It's an absolutely brilliant depiction of Holmes at his deductive best."

"You are mistaken, gentlemen," said Miss Holland. "The story is as nonsensical as the Hound of the Baskervilles."

"Madam," said Sir Henry, more than a shade coldly, "I don't think I quite follow you."

"Me neither," I cried.

Miss Holland chivvied us closer to the cupboard and waved at the money on the shelf.

"Bad as the story is," she went on, "it does at least suggest a clue to the reason for this large sum of money. Think, gentlemen – think."

"Miss Holland," said Sir Henry, "what I think is this. You should not be naming that story as bad. Retract that word immediately."

"Oh, for heaven's sake," she impatiently said. "Would common criminals really have the talent to impersonate a Russian nobleman and all the rest of it? Would they, in addition, have had sufficient medical training to be conversant with catalepsy? But, for the moment, forget my criticisms."

"We shall certainly do that," said the now rather huffy Sir Henry, "with no great difficulty."

"Indeed we shall," I said, again supporting Sir Henry (but this time very nervously. I was scared stiff that she had picked up a clue pointing directly to Miss Glertish).

"The clue I'm referring to," Miss Holland blandly continued, "relates to the fact that Blessington was a man in hiding. His former associates, whom he had betrayed, were planning to break into his bedroom and murder him. But they planned to make the murder look like suicide. Are you with me so far, Sir Henry?"

Much to my disappointment, he was already beginning to restore Miss Holland to favour. "My dear girl, I think I begin to see what you mean …"

"Can you see the parallel? The old woman you've been talking about was like Blessington – if, that is, what you've been telling me is accurate."

"Oh, it's accurate all right – as far as I'm able to ascertain. Common as muck. And living with that hooligan from off the council-estate. What could be a more revolting situation?"

"Common as muck she may have been, Sir Henry, but, having gone through her computer and her desk, I would say she had brains. But not clever enough to avoid being murdered."

Sir Henry was instantly fired up with approval and excitement. "Murdered, you think?"

"Like Blessington, you see, she had been living under an assumed name. Of that, I think, we can be pretty sure."

Sir Henry turned to me to say: "Agree with that, young Crackery? Blessington, as it turned out, was a chap called Sutton. I've long suspected that Mabel Smith's name to be bogus too. Bogus!"

Not waiting for my reply, he turned back to Miss Holland with every appearance of professional satisfaction. "Has that Mabel Smith, do you think, been murdered in this bungalow?"

"I would say so, yes. Everything points to it. And very possibly murdered in the same way as Blessington."

"Strung up, you mean? Hanged, eh?"

"And made to look as if she did it herself – in other words, made to look like suicide. As was done with Blessington."

"Somewhere in the bungalow?"

"Either indoors or somewhere on the estate," said Miss Holland, with unbecoming relish. "As in the Blessington case, as described by Dr Watson, it will no doubt be a most unpleasant sight."

Smiling all over his face, Sir Henry rapped his stick on the floor and said: "Then let's get going. I know this place inside-out. Follow me."

"One moment, Sir Henry," Miss Holland calmly said. "My employer is far too squeamish a man for an expedition of this sort. I suggest you send him back to join the ladies. It's no good suggesting it myself. He ignores my advice – even when it's in his own best interest. Make it an order, Sir Henry. We don't want him having another fainting-fit, do we?"

To me, Sir Henry cheerfully said: "Not squeamish are you? Is she right?"

Miss Holland was of course right. I was squeamish. Still am. I loathe modern crime stories which revel in post-mortems. As for the story about the resident patient, I had falsely concurred in praising it. I had always detested Dr Watson's nasty description of the hanging body. But, knowing that no similar hanging had taken place at the bungalow, I felt free to be pompous.

"Sir Henry," was my instant reply, "my insubordinate shop-assistant is far from right. Quite apart from her unfounded deductions, she is encouraging you to trespass. I suggest we should all return to your home, Sir Henry, before she gets you into serious trouble."

"Miss Holland," said Sir Henry, getting a bit rattled, "are you really sure about the death of this awful old woman?"

Still calm: "In broad terms, yes."

"And what about the hooligan who lives with her? Her live-in lover?"

Firmly: "Equally dead."

"Hanged in the same way, you mean?"

"I would doubt that. He might, of course, turn out to have been part of the conspiracy."

"Like the page-boy in Dr Watson's account? The page-boy who let the murderers in after dark?"

"A possibility, Sir Henry. But a remote one, I think. We know the van hasn't been seen in the service-lane for quite a few days. That points to it being stolen by the murderers if, as is possible, they exacted their revenge in some other method of execution."

"Such as smashing her skull to a pulp?"

"Well, yes, Sir Henry. Or shooting her. The dog, too. And then carting away all the sundry remains – including the body of the live-in lover – in the yellow van. They probably killed him, of course, to make use of the van. Variations are always possible."

"But you feel certain?"

"It's just a feeling. But yes, I feel certain. It's a hunch."

Sir Henry (more comforted): "Ah, a hunch! Well, young Crackery," he added, turning to me rather heavily, "are you with us or not?"

Daringly stern, I said: "I most certainly am not. Miss Holland has chosen to denigrate Sherlock Holmes. But, as he himself could tell us, she is over-indulging her lurid imagination. Odd things do happen in Dackley. But not to this lurid extent."

"Then how," said Miss Holland, " does James account for all this money being left in this cupboard?"

"James," I said, "can only say the same as Sherlock Holmes would say. The owner of this property is entitled to keep his or her money where they please. It's none of Miss Holland's business – nor ours, either."

"Where the money is kept is not the point," said Miss Holland, adopting her nursery-governess tone. "What we need to consider is the parallel between this amount of money and the money in Blessington's strong-box."

"Ah, yes," exclaimed Sir Henry, in ecstasy, "the strong-box mentioned in the story!"

"The strong-box," she added, "which the resident hypochondriac kept at the bottom of his bed – and which the police thought he had jumped off in order to hang himself."

"I've got it," cried Sir Henry, firing up with renewed energy. "Can't you now see what she means, Crackery? The criminals who murdered Blessington – by hanging him in his own bedroom – didn't make off with all his money. Can't you see why?"

"No," I firmly said, trying hard to bring all this dangerous speculation to an end.

"Crackery," Sir Henry admonished me, "You need to read that story with more attention. I would agree that Dr Watson doesn't emphasise the point. Nor does Holmes. It's a point easy to miss. But Miss Holland here has spotted it. The murderers couldn't take the money away because, if they did, it would tell the police that Blessington hadn't committed suicide. Have I followed your reasoning, Miss Holland?"

"Perfectly," she graciously told him.

"See what she means, Crackery? The people who murdered this awful old woman will have tried to make it look like suicide. That's why they couldn't take her money away. It's been left where they found it for one reason only – to divert suspicion of murder."

"But Miss Holland has no grounds," I tried to insist, "for assuming that a murder has been committed."

"Superficially, Crackery, perhaps not. But she has a hunch, you see. A hunch. I'm no back number, you know. I too am becoming very conscious of the same hunch. Follow me. We must search this property immediately. Prepare yourself for a possibly very unpleasant sight if, that is, you wish to accompany us."

I took the liberty of placing my hand on Sir Henry's shoulder, as if making a citizen-arrest.

"Sir Henry," I said, as sternly as I could, " the only action you need to take immediately is to leave this property and return to your home. Miss Holland is exceeding her authority. She could land you in a lot of trouble. The owner or owners of this property could return at any moment – and find us trespassing. I urge you to consider my words very seriously."

Sir Henry glowered at me, for the first time showing the anger he was capable of in a hard-breathing silence.

It was in this silence that solitary footsteps could be heard approaching in the hall.

The effect on both Miss Holland and Sir Henry was most interesting. I was staggered myself, yes; but they were both staggered to a degree I would call shock. (It's not often that anything I say is so dramatically backed up.)

Sir Henry obviously imagined it was the nasty old woman he thought dead and was not expecting to meet. But Miss Holland's shock was more akin to tight-lipped exasperation.

It was, of course, poor old Brockadill who appeared in the open doorway.

"Sir Henry," he hesitantly said, as would anyone sent on an awkward errand, "do please excuse me. I've been sent to see if you're all right."

"Of course I'm all right," said Sir Henry, breezy again. "And I'm jolly glad to see you! You're an early doer, unlike that Ralphie. He's going to wish he listened. We've discovered a murder. Follow me – and prepare for a ghastly sight."

For someone of Sir Henry's advancing years, Sir Henry was incredibly energetic now that he had his glorious objective. He led us in and out of every room – including the unspeakable bathroom – and each time, before entering, he would shout: "Prepare yourselves for a ghastly sight."

He was in no way put out by the lack of a ghastly sight. Off he took us to the ruined old outbuildings. It was only in an old vinery, inside the large and neglected conservatory, that he began to fail. (I think it was the sight of the dead vine, trailing overhead, which depressed him.) I was faithfully at his elbow, but Brockadill was lagging behind – in the conservatory entrance – with Miss Holland. She wheeled round on him to say, in a low but intense voice: "Are you absolutely determined to embarrass me?"

"You know I'm not," I heard him miserably say.

Leaving her standing in the entrance to that once-magnificent conservatory, Brockadill joined Sir Henry and myself. Brockadill looked so fed up and remote that I was hoping (I fully admit it) that his agonies would block any further hunches. Trying rather desperately to be waggish, he said to Sir Henry: "I've already spent far too much time in trying to find you, sir. Please come back to the house. Your wife is very worried. She'll be sending out a search-party for us all if we don't get back soon."

Sir Henry had become morose. He said: "Look at this vine. Nothing but a few raisins clinging on. How did you know where to find me?"

"First, sir, I went down to see the dustbins. I then went back to go along to the bungalow. Your wife had said you might have called. I saw your buggy outside. I saw the open front door."

A very annoyed Sir Henry: "Damn it all, our visit was intended to be top secret."

"Your wife, sir, suspects you of having retained the spare keys to the bungalow."

"Oh, hell! How did she find that out, I wonder? But you're right. We'd better get back."

He marched out of the conservatory, but, at the entrance, Miss Holland stopped him and said: "Sir Henry, I would like to see the dustbins. It's a treat you promised me. Are you going to break that promise?"

"Certainly not," yelled Sir Henry, and all his energies were instantly renewed. Off he went, steaming ahead of us down the untidy path to the tradesmen's entrance. "I'm no back number!"

In his wake, poor old Brockadill said to Miss Holland: "I really do need to get those keys off Sir Henry. Can you please help?"

She disregarded him, rather than ignored him. (There is a difference. I had been enduring it for days.) Walking on, she halted after a few yards and picked something up.

I recognised it at once.

It was a slipper. I had last seen it worn by the old woman I had killed. (My auntie lookalike.) Blue velvet, the same colour as the dining-room curtains in the room Miss Holland had been brainily dominating.

"Sir Henry," she called out. "Come and examine this …"

He came steaming eagerly back. "Found a clue, have you? Has it passed me by?"

"A slipper," she declaimed, "of undoubted quality. See the lining? Silk. Still fairly new, I'd say. This slipper probably dropped off the murder-victim's foot when she was being carried, dead or drugged, down this very path."

Sir Henry (joyfully): "To that horrible yellow van, you mean?"

"The van, in other words, which has not been seen in the service-lane for quite a time."

"This," said Sir Henry to Brockadill, "is a major clue. Don't you think so?"

"It could be suggestive in some ways," said Brockadill, speaking unhappily but carefully. "At present, however, I am under an instruction. I have to fulfil it. Sir, you seem to have admitted to having spare keys to the bungalow. Both your wife and your son-in-law have instructed me to take charge of them."

"What a nerve," cried Sir Henry, using the very expression I so often use myself (and which comforted my heart very considerably). "What you can jolly well take charge of, Brockadill, is this piece of evidence. Let's look for more."

He strode off down the path and Miss Holland, politely but without a word, presented the slipper to Brockadill. Henceforth, I have to say, Brockadill went into something of a trance. I too went into a bit of a trance myself. I could actually see that dead woman. I could see her being carried in the arms of her surely very peculiar step-daughter. I could see that slipper dropping off a dangling foot.

Ugh!

Sir Henry and Miss Holland had reached the door to the service-lane, a door in a massively high garden-wall. Like most of the properties, I suppose, it had been built in Edwardian or perhaps earlier Victorian times. It was so topped with half-dead creeper that Sir Henry had to push aside the droopings to get at the lock.

"By God," he turned to bawl as Brockadill and I joined him, "this door has been left not only unlocked but unbolted. Note that, Brockadill. It's another clue."

I don't know about Brockadill's trance, but mine, once we were through and into the service-lane, was transformed into a state of unreal wonder. It was like being taken back-stage after a pantomime in a theatre. The lane was narrow but enchanting. It was obviously very long and bendy (in running behind all these illustrious estates). On the side opposite to the massive wall were fields and woods like the pastures of heaven. And to think that I, as a fairly local sort of fellow, had never known of this lane and its landscape!

"This," Sir Henry was bawling, waving his stick, "is where that lout always parks his van. Next to the dustbins he can't be bothered to properly maintain. He allows rubbish to spill right across the tarmac."

Being in my state of unreal wonderment, I was genuinely puzzled. The three dustbins he was brandishing his stick at seemed to me to be wholly inoffensive. They were under their own little roof at the base of the wall. They were clean-looking and no rubbish was spilling from them.

"Sir Henry," I said, "I can't quite see what you're complaining about."

He looked a bit angry for a moment, then began to chortle. "Young Crackery, you're as splendidly obtuse as Dr Watson. It's a pleasure to have met you. But I have to get our man Simpson to keep these bins in order."

"Your butler?"

Even more chortles. "Good Lord, no. We don't have butlers. Not that posh. Simpson is our gardener-handyman. Not here today, but he could tell you how bad these dustbins have been. They are a very sore point."

"Far more than a sore point," Miss Holland called out. She had removed one of the lids and was holding it in her gloved hand. "It's obvious that we have here another vital clue."

My mind remained blank but my heart began to quicken. I said: "What, then, have you found?"

"Come and have a look, James."

I looked into the dustbin. "But it's empty!"

"That, James, is the clue." She replaced the lid daintily. "They're all empty. Nothing has been put in these bins since they were last emptied. It's little things like this, James, which will enable us to pin-point the time of the murder."

And again Sir Henry said: "Note that, Brockadill. It's another clue."

Sir Henry, it was clear to me, was oblivious of what was going on between Miss Holland and the new tec-super. But may I make one detail even clearer? Miss Holland was not in any way taunting old Brockadill. As I've said before, I'm no greenhorn. For private reasons of their own both he and she were probably trying to disentangle their hearts as quietly as they could. Only the slightest tension was visible between them and only at moments. I was the one being taunted. Could I blame her? I could not. I greatly feared she would have burst into tears if she hadn't someone like me to whack. (I can't bear seeing women in tears. No gentleman can, surely?)

All the same, I must admit I was beginning to feel a bit sour at being her whipping-boy.

"Sir Henry," she called out, "come and look at this …"

She had walked up the lane a little. Given that she had been disparaging Sherlock Holmes, she was behaving in a manner remarkably like his.

"All she needs," I heard myself mutter to Brockadill, who was standing beside me, "is his deer-stalker hat and his magnifying-glass."

Brockadill was still holding the velvet slipper. He gave me a weary, despairing look and didn't move. Sir Henry, on the other hand, showed amazing alacrity. He left off staring at the dustbins and joined Miss Holland in practically one leap.

She was peering into the drainage-ditch (almost a stream) which ran alongside the lane with the massively silent bean-field beyond. I began to panic. What had she found? Had Miss Glertish dumped the two dead bodies – or perhaps the remains of Masher – in that ditch?

"Brockadill," Sir Henry called out, "come and look at this. It's another clue. A big one. Come and note it."

I followed Brockadill. I found myself looking down at the wheel-clamps, which I had last seen – on that Saturday when I was wheel-clamped – in the back of Rivinni's van.

Miss Holland spoke steadily to Brockadill: "These are wheel-clamps, are they not?"

"They are," he replied, equally steadily.

"And dumped," yelled Sir Henry, excitedly, "by the murderers who stole the van – to make room for the bodies!"

"Perhaps so," said Brockadill. "Sir Henry, we really must return to your home after we secure the bungalow. Please hand over the keys."

Sir Henry looked mutinous but gave in as soon as Miss Holland said: "I agree, Sir Henry. We must return to your home immediately. There's just one last thing I want to check, but we can check it by going back through the bungalow-estate. I want to see the tree which my employer says he was forced to climb."

"Miss Holland," I complainingly said, as we went back through the wilderness, "are you by any chance doubting my word?"

Her reply: "We need to pin-point both the time and the positions of all the relevant physical actions. Where is this tree?"

In the same way as she had annoyed me over those wretched pots (remember them?), she began annoying me by satirising the search for the mythical tree.

"Is it this one," she demanded, gesturing at a mere sapling no higher than herself. "Or is it this," gesturing at a stunted rhododendron.

"Madam," I all but snarled, "I was in a state of well-justified panic at the time. How can I be expected to remember which tree I was chased up?"

"James, you have stated that you were up it for a long time. That, James, would have given you enough time to familiarise yourself both with its species and its location. I ask you again. Where is this tree?"

I knew I couldn't choose just any old tree. As quickly as Sherlock Holmes himself, she would have deduced that any such tree had not been climbed. I knew I was on the brink of being caught out. Not a nice feeling. It was like having a winged avenger at my back.

Fortunately, Sir Henry (bless his heart) came to my rescue. "It must be one of those in the copse between the tennis-court and the old kitchen-garden. I know the way. Follow me!"

Both Miss Holland and the love-stricken Brockadill followed him before they were to realise I had been left in the rear.

I seized upon this guilt-laden but precious moment. The pergola-walk was nearby. Remember it, do you? I dashed along it until I came to the hole in the trellis – made by Masher when chasing me. I ducked through this splintered hole and at once came upon a highly eligible cedar.

Like a lamplighter, I sprang up by way of a suitably low bough. I was able, in doing so, to fake the necessary signs of a previous ascent. But I had not climbed a tree for many years. I was absolutely puffed out. I had to stay put.

"I'm up here," I sang out, as my three companions came looking for me. "This is the one – without any doubt at all."

"Good man," Sir Henry yelled up at me.

Did Miss Holland believe I had climbed this tree to escape the dog? I can only say she began making her way back to the bungalow, alone, before I had finished getting down. She left Brockadill to accompany Sir Henry and me. Her mood was now impossible for me to judge.

She was already seated in the buggy when we got to the bungalow ourselves. She spoke not a word. Brockadill quickly checked the interior of the bungalow (the front door had been left ajar during our excursion) while I helped Sir Henry to get behind the buggy-wheel.

Sir Henry waited until Brockadill emerged, then said: "Well? Is there a murder to investigate or isn't there?"

Brockadill carefully said: "A degree of investigation is certainly worth considering."

"A degree? Is that all? Bah!"

Sir Henry drove off, slowly but scowlingly. Brockadill and I followed behind, like two mutes at a Dickensian funeral.

I pass over what happened at the villa after our arrival. It was a bit of family-fuss which isn't really relevant. All I need say is that I heard poor old Sir Henry getting it in the neck. (Ralphie: "You seem to think, sir, that you have residual powers, like a field-marshal. You have no such powers.") Tactfully withdrawing with Stephanie to the cloakroom, I found that Miss Holland had already withdrawn to it herself.

She was already in her coat and in a headscarf which made her look tenderly soft and appealing. She was sitting on one of the chairs. She stood up as we came in and said, as cool as you could imagine: "James, I want a lift home."

Confused at being granted this royal favour, I stupidly stammered: "Didn't you come with the Brockadills? Won't they be expecting to take you back?"

"I didn't come with the Brockadills. It was arranged, yes, but I changed my mind. I thought it best to come by taxi."

Stephanie paused in putting on her coat and innocently squealed: "Ow, yes! Jay said you was coming in a taxi."

"And I don't want a taxi back," said Miss Holland. "Am I in some way not making myself clear, James? Are you going to give me a lift or are you not?"

"Glad to, glad to," I hurriedly muttered.

With the distant sounds of dispute still in our ears, we saw ourselves out into the parking roundel. Miss Holland declined to sit with me in the front and ordered Stephanie to sit beside me. ("Sit with your husband, Stephanie.") She herself got in the back, which meant, in my type of two-door Honda, tipping my driver-seat forward to let her get in. Another awkwardness was my new but well-faked lock-bar. I had left it on the back seat, unused because of our being in a safe location. Miss Holland promptly seized it and said: "Is this the thing you call a lock-bar? Am I supposed to sit on it?"

"I beg your pardon," I gabbled. "Just bung it under Stephanie – under her seat, I mean."

But Miss Holland was examining it. "Is this a new lock-bar?"

"A new one? Of course not." I got behind the wheel and again said: "Just bung it under the seat."

"It seems to me," she said, "to be a lighter shade of green than it was before."

"Madam," I said, getting really testy, "it's exactly the same lock-bar which you've seen on the occasions when I've had the privilege of acting as your chauffeur. Had it for years."

We set off, but not without my remembering Miss Glertish saying that Miss Holland wouldn't be fooled by the new lock-bar. Fancy being able to detect a lighter shade of green – and on a lock-bar she had hardly ever glanced at before!

She remained silent throughout the simple and shortish journey to her flat while Stephanie, thank goodness, stopped giggling. Me, I had another worrying thought. Why on earth had Miss Holland virtually demanded a lift? Frugal as she was in her habits, she was well able to afford another taxi for her return-journey.

I was soon to find out after I pulled up in front of the line of terraced houses where she had the ground-floor flat (and its garden, so Stephanie had told me). I had never myself ever been in her flat. Never invited in. Only Stephanie had been allowed in – and that rarely.

Miss Holland stayed silent until after I had helped her out of back of the Honda. I was regretting my outburst. She was looking calm but certainly not cordial. Opening her handbag to take her keys out, she said: "James, I've something to tell you. I won't be at the shop tomorrow. You'll have to cope on your own. I'm going to London."

"London, eh?" I tried a little joke. "Calling in at Scotland Yard by any chance?"

"No, James. But I'll be back first thing the day after – which, in case you can't work it out, is Friday. I expect you to be punctual. I want to see you at nine o'clock sharp. I shall have something even more important to tell you."

She turned, unlatched her front gate and walked up the short path to her front door. I just stood there, washing my hands with invisible soap and water (complete with sickly grin). I was hoping she might turn and thank me for the lift.

But no, she unlocked her door and went in with ne'er a backward glance.

EIGHT

Left in the Lurch

I was so determined not to be late for work (on the designated Friday) that I arrived at the shop well before Miss Holland.

Ha!

After re-locking the shop-door behind me, I bounded up the stairs to my office. ("Always go for the highest ground in any kind of forthcoming battle" – Uncle Rufus.) I wanted, in other words, to be well-entrenched behind my desk before I received her.

I won't bore you with my thoughts as I sat waiting, except to say that it was silly of me to be so absorbed in them that I never heard her arrive. (I had left my office-door ajar.)

Without knocking (simply pushing my door wider), she entered in her hat and coat and plonked an oblong envelope in front of me.

Although I nearly jumped out of my skin, I managed to utter a witticism. (Not one of my best.) I said: "What's this? Your last will and testament?"

Her reply: "In a sense, yes. It certainly brings an era to an end. It's my month's notice of resignation," and she turned and went back down to the shop.

I followed her down with the stark missive in my hand. I was more upset than I can possibly put on record.

"How long," I gasped, "have you been planning to leave me in the lurch?"

"Oh," she casually said, "for some six months or so. But my intentions began to consolidate long before that."

She went into her so-called office (the back room) to take off her hat and coat. I followed her in to say: "Don't you realise that you'll upset Stephanie no end? She admires you enormously."

"Your wife, James, is more resilient than you think. You've never had any real idea of her potential."

"And where the devil were you yesterday? I'm still your boss. Your employer. I've a right to know."

"As I told you in advance, James, I went to London."

"To do what?"

"To go to the airport, James, to meet someone – and see him into his hotel. He lives and works in Canada."

She sat down at her desk to add: "He is, in fact, Canadian."

My knees weakened. "And who is this man?"

"The man I've decided to marry."

She looked up at me with that steady look many women tend to use on me. Her arm was outstretched on top of her desk, palm uppermost. She now turned her hand over, slowly – and I saw the engagement-ring.

Blimey, I thought, what a rock …

I all but collapsed into her visitor-chair. Automatically, I said: "My dear Miss Holland, may I wish you every happiness?"

"You may, James, and thank you."

"Will I be permitted to meet this man?"

"Of course. He's in London for a few days on business, but he'll be down in Dackley very soon."

"Has he ever been here before?"

"Many times. He's even been in the shop. It's how I met him. He happened to come in one day," and she dreamily began to inspect her engagement-ring from a variety of happy angles.

And she added, in a faraway voice: "There really is nothing like the experience of being swept off one's feet by exactly the right man."

Mournfully: "Miss Holland, couldn't you have given me just a little more notice of your impending departure?"

Briskly: "A month is as much as you deserve – and certainly enough for me to start clearing up one or two other matters."

Thinking of Brockadill, I said: "Other matters?"

Ignoring this question, she got up and went out into the shop. I followed meekly. Opening the shop-door, she fastened it back. She said: "Opening-time – and time for you, James, to get back behind the counter for a change. I've a lot of phoning to do," and she went back into her office and shut the door.

"What a nerve," I said, but it took me a good few minutes before I had the courage to open her door and stick my head around it.

"Madam, I was behind the counter all day yesterday. Kindly bear that in mind."

She was on the phone, but she covered the mouthpiece and said: "What is it you want, James?"

"Are you on the phone to Stephanie?"

"I am not, James."

"I don't want to be the one who has to tell her you're leaving us in the lurch."

"Tell her tonight, James, but you can soften the blow by telling her I'm going to buy her a nice new evening-gown. Tell her it's for the engagement-party I'm planning. Both of you are invited. It will be at the Royal George Hotel in Dackley, which is where my fiancé has often stayed. I want Stephanie to enjoy herself. I want her to get some glimpse of what it's like to have a soul of her own. Meanwhile, James, get back behind the counter."

Wickedly, I said: "Are you by any chance inviting Brockadill to this party of yours?"

"James," said Miss Holland, and in a crushingly sweet voice, "the Superintendent will only have one reason for putting in an appearance. It will be to arrest you on suspicion of having murdered two people."

May I, at this point, offer some advice to my fellow men? Never try to have the last word with a woman of Miss Holland's calibre. You'll only end up feeling you've just been socked under the jaw. For me, this feeling lasted for the next ten days or so – right up to the day of the party.

To a certain extent, despite this sock under the jaw, I began to feel nervously relieved during those ten days. One advantage, for example, was the constant absence of Miss Holland. Even when she did appear at the shop, she was in and out in a jiffy – mostly without a word. This (although I felt like an awful cad) enabled me to go through her desk – in search of the desecrated financial report. I never found it and it wasn't in the safe, but I was soon telling myself: "Don't worry, old sport. Even if she's given it to old Brockadill, any Asti Glertish fingermarks will get him nowhere. She has no criminal record. Ha! From now on, my boy, everything is plain sailing."

However, when I came to be driving Stephanie to the engagement-party, I was beginning to realise that "plain sailing" was not going to be the best description for the evening ahead.

"I wonder," said Stephanie, looking so innocently pretty in her new gown, "why the police seem so busy tonight?"

She was referring to the rise and fall of the police-car sirens, all sounding distantly engaged but sinister. They did die down a bit as I made for the town-centre (by way of the esplanade road along by the river), but a police-constable flagged me down in a location ominously close to Willow Tree Lane.

"Yes, officer?"

"Excuse me. sir, but have you ever been wheel-clamped in Willow Tree Lane by this man?"

He shoved a bad photo-copy of Rivinni under my nose. I recognised it instantly and had no alternative but to say: "I think it must be the very chap. I've been in conversation about him – with the former Chief Constable. What's going on, officer?"

"Just checking for people, sir, who might have made his acquaintance in that particular way."

He looked impressed, perhaps because I had mentioned the Chief Constable and perhaps because I was in evening-dress. (I always look impressive in evening-dress. I merely state a fact. Evening-dress has always suited me. Some men, no matter how good-looking, it simply doesn't.) But my heart was in my mouth. It took so little to arouse my fear for all that money in the bank-vault.

"Going anywhere nice, sir?"

"Engagement-party," I snapped. "The Royal George Hotel."

"Thank you kindly, sir," and he waved me on, but, in my mirror, I could see him jotting in a black notebook.

Stephanie was giggling her head off. "You done anything naughty, Crackers old boy?"

"And have you, madam, been drinking?"

"Only a tiddle – to get me in the mood."

"Miss Holland won't be pleased. I warn you advisedly. She's highly conventional."

Stephanie had taken the news of Miss Holland's resignation with none of the alarm I had feared. She had excitedly said: "We'll probably go bankrupt, of course, because she's got the brains and you ain't. But it's lovely she's getting married. I'm over the moon about it."

And, as we neared the hotel, she added a post-script to this earlier statement. She cheerfully said: "But she needn't think she can get me to go back in the shop! I've two kids a well as a silly old fool to look after."

Stephanie was already excited enough, but the closer sight of the Royal George excited her almost to delirium. Overlooking the town river at its widest and looking both historic and magical, that delicately-illuminated hotel (the most swagger in Dackley) should have excited me just as romantically.

It did not.

I parked in the choc-a-bloc car-park (the former stabling-yard) feeling conscious of an impending ambush. Detectives, I was becoming convinced, were lurking in every shadow. My young and pretty wife sweetly took my arm and we went in by the side entry-door. The hall was respectfully quiet. We mounted the main staircase (a bit of grandeur added in 1811, like the ballroom itself). Once in the crowded Regency ante-room with its hauntingly beautiful mirrors, I found that Miss Holland had for some reason deceived me.

But why? To what end?

No gentleman present, other than I, was in white tie and tails. A few were in black ties and dinner-jackets, but most men were in all sorts of convivial get-ups.

"She definitely told me," I began to complain to Stephanie, "that it was to be a ballroom-party. Formal dress essential."

But Stephanie wriggled away from me as swiftly as an eel. Deserted, I found myself in the company of a chap who had the face of a scholarly ambassador. He was dressed in a stripey and jolly blazer so similar to the one in my office-cupboard that I thought he must have pinched it.

"Pardon my mentioning this, sir," I said to him, "but wasn't this supposed to a formal bash? What have you been told?"

"Nothing specific," he said, glass in hand. "I only know that I can't wear evening-dress. I always end up looking like a sack of potatoes. So my fiancée told me to wear what I liked."

He had spoken with an attractively mellow Canadian accent, and I realised this was the lucky groom-to-be. I had been left to stumble across him, as it were; no formal presentation whatsoever. I even had to crane my neck to observe the future bride. She was on the far side of the room and in the loveliest of low-cut gowns. She was murmuringly chatting to a temporarily privileged group of grinning admirers. Need I say she was more beautiful than I had ever seen her? I'll only mention her shoulders. I had never before seen them so magnificently visible.

Suddenly, for me, the huge room-mirrors were more crowded than the room itself. The glass in my hand, which I could not remember receiving, almost began to spill. I was having one of my funny turns. But who is going to be interested in that? No one.

"Excuse me a moment," I could see her lips murmuring, and she graciously threaded her way towards me.

"Darling," she said to the lucky Canadian, "do please go and look after Stephanie. You know the problem. Stay with her a little. Tell her about our wedding-plans. She's dying to know."

He vanished like a puff of smoke after saying to me: "Very nice to have met you, James."

In all honesty, I must put on record that he was in no way as handsome as the hapless Brockadill. He was shall we say oldish – or at least well-seasoned. But what secretly unrequited lovers of any woman can ever hope to understand her ultimate choice of man? He was no hob-goblin, of course. I'd say he seemed a jolly nice chap.

"He's a dentist," she said, as if this were an answer to everything that puzzled me.

"A dentist, eh?"

"In Toronto, James. He doesn't do much yanking out nowadays. He owns and runs a whole string of surgeries. He's been in London for an international conference. Forensic dentistry."

"Forensic, eh? Miss Holland, I have to say that I'm amazed and disappointed."

"Someone, James, has to do these things."

"I am referring, Miss Holland, to the way you've organised this party of yours. You told me it was to be formal. You said evening-dress was obligatory. And you said it was to be a ballroom-party – which, as a matter of etiquette, means white tie and tails."

"The best-laid plans, James, often have to be changed. Especially," she dreamily added, "if one is marrying such a wonderful man."

"You could have let me know of the change."

"Oh, but it's so nice to have an assortment. More picturesque. Besides, I have always wanted to see you in full fig. You look very striking, James. Just look at yourself in the mirrors."

I looked at myself in the mirrors and at her – and could recognise neither of us. Could this really be me? And could this really be Miss Holland? I was also beginning to see the fortune in diamonds which she was wearing.

"And it's still a ballroom-party," she said, and with the lightest of touches from her gloved fingers, she led me into the ballroom.

It was like a dreamland grotto with the well-appointed tables, its soft lighting and all the floral stuff. (Cupid's innermost bower?)

"And I'm in full fig myself, James," she said, "and we have a lovely little jazz-band who know how to play the smoochiest of standards."

"Miss Holland, are you hinting that you might consider a dance – with me?"

"A stately dance with you, James, is a good possibility – always assuming Brockadill won't burst in and clap you in irons."

"Is he likely to? Is that why I was stopped on our way to this binge?"

"I've no idea," she said. "Stopped by whom?"

"A police-constable on the esplanade road."

"My goodness me," she said, becoming aloof again, "that sounds like a most promising development. But I do hope my party won't be disturbed by too much intrusion. Excuse me."

She dissolvingly vanished, leaving me to find my own table-place amid other guests finding theirs. I was not offended by her change back to her more customary tone. I was rather glad of it. My unprecedented glimpse into her softer feelings (as I saw them) had aroused in me the weirdest form of fear. It was a fear separate from the fear I had of being arrested – or, for that matter, any fear of having all that lovely money being found and taken away from me. It was a fear I couldn't understand – nor wanted to.

The long table where I found myself sitting had no one seated on the opposite side, presumably to avoid blocking a forthcoming floor-show. The jazz band had struck up but was playing in the most winning of ways. Everyone was settling down and happily awaiting the grub.

"Who the devil," I asked myself, "are all these people? Where have they all come from?"

I was unable to recognise anyone. I felt worse than estranged. I felt starkly isolated. I couldn't even see Stephanie. Except for an empty guest-place to my right – ticketed by a guest-card saying "reserved" – I was at the end of the table nearest to the door of the ante-room. The young buck to my left who was wearing some sort of yachting-tunic only gave me the briefest of nods. (He was too busy flirting with his lady-neighbour.)

"Will I get a stiff neck," I was worryingly asking myself, "if there's a draught from this open door?"

My father was always worrying about the dangers of draughts. (He used to light matches to detect any leak through the excluders. The slightest flicker of the flame would drive him mad.) I had inherited the same sort of anxiety. I fully admit it.

This anxiety was as nothing to the anxiety I felt when the bride-to-be abruptly returned. She sat down beside me and uttered not a word – well, not at first. She waved a hand to the head-waiter to signal her readiness for attention, but didn't actually speak until we were between the first course and the second.

I can't remember the first course, but I do jolly well remember the second.

There was plenty of surrounding chatter and euphoria, by this time, to conceal any individual confidences; perhaps this was why she had chosen this moment.

"James, I've just been called to the phone. Sir Henry rang to wish us good luck."

I stupidly said: "Us?"

"My fiancé and I."

"Of course," I blushingly said. "Did you invite that lovely old couple?"

"I did, yes. But Sir Henry is not too well. He has had to rest, you see."

"Oh, poor old fellow ..."

"He became, you see, rather over-excited and his wife is too concerned to be able to leave him."

Miss Holland, I knew, wanted me to ask the question I now asked. (She was designing the conversation in much the same way as she had designed the party.) So, of course, I asked: "Over-excited, eh? By anything in particular?"

"By the discovery, James, of two dead bodies and the remains of a fairly large dog."

I was not expecting this reply, although I had known she was leading up to something dramatic. I put down my knife and fork. We were half-way through *Selle de Pre-sale Rotie* which, lest you don't know, was lamb fattened on the aromatic pastures of Brittany. (I didn't know this myself until I saw it on the menu.) It was, may I just say, vastly superior to the grub at Sir Henry's, but, instantly, it became just as tasteless. And the more so, I will just add, because of the details about Rivinni's state of decay which Miss Holland began reciting.

"Madam," I said, "I am only interested in the intellectual aspects of the mysterious disappearance of those two people. Begin, please, by telling me where the bodies were found."

Elegantly continuing to eat, she said: "You're not going to pretend you don't know?"

Seething with anxiety over this fresh and inexplicable surprise, I quietly but hotly said: "Will this satisfy you? I swear on the lives of my wife and children that I damn well do not know."

Miss Holland, I'm glad to tell you, made a mistake at this point in her machinations.

She could have asked: "And do you also swear on their lives that you know nothing at all of these two deaths?"

Had she asked this question, I would have been done for. Finished. I couldn't possibly lie upon something so sacred as the children's lives – or Stephanie's life, for that matter. I was still her husband. I was still a father. But Miss Holland did not ask this question. I therefore didn't scruple to let her mistakenly assume that I had sworn to my total innocence. (Her assumption, of course, was not all that complimentary.)

"To be blunt with you, James, I can't imagine you'd have the guts to kill even the most unpleasant sort of person. And to murder an old woman by smashing in her skull so savagely doesn't match your squeamishly weak spirit. You could have a psychotic tendency which made you lash out, I suppose. On the whole, perhaps, I think it best to keep an open mind."

"Thank you," I managed to say without being too sarcastic. "Might I ask you again to tell me where the bodies were found?"

Calmly and sedately, she continued to eat for a few moments before speaking, and then to say: "And that's another thing ..."

"Another thing what?"

"The fact, James, that the bodies were so cleverly dumped. You, in my opinion, would not have had the intelligence to choose so clever a location. Another few hours, James, and those remains would all have disappeared for ever. Even the bones, Sir Henry tells me, would have sunk down in the mud and been leached away."

Having finished eating, she centred her knife and fork and took a sip from her wine-glass of pure spring water. Through fairly clenched teeth, I said: "Where were the damn bodies found? How many more times do I need to ask?"

"Willow Tree Lane," and she took another sip of water before signalling the waiter.

He took both our plates away (including my abandoned left-overs). She continued: "They were discovered in the marshy undergrowth around the edges of the harder ground – the hard-standing where people like you park their motor-cars. Discovered at four o'clock this afternoon. You say you were stopped by a police-officer. Didn't he tell you anything?"

"He did not. I've not been told a thing by anyone," and I finished my glass (wine, in my case) as the only sustenance I could stomach. Our shadowy waiter had set a dessert before us (*Crème Renversée au Caramel*). I gazed down at it in pure horror.

What vision could I see in that dessert? It made me feel like an old crone in a tent at a garden-party – with her crystal-ball. I could see Miss Glertish driving off from Willow Tree Lane. I could see the body of that Rivinni fellow in the back, amid his unused wheel-clamps. I could see her returning with the additional body of her awful step-mother and the dog. No wheels-clamps now. Those she had dumped in the service-lane ditch. Oh, it was all so vivid! What on earth was happening to me?

The worst part of the vision was the sight of Miss Glertish going to-and-fro and dumping these remains, each time at a cleverly opportune moment. Her expression was terrifyingly blank.

"The dead woman," said Miss Holland, eating her dessert with the greatest delicacy, "was beyond recognition. Her face and indeed her entire head had been smashed into quite a mess. Or so I've been told. Can you imagine it, James?"

I didn't dare try to imagine that much. All I was able to imagine was the sight of Miss Asti Glertish returning to the van and about to drive off. I could then see her having her wicked afterthought. I could see her taking my lock-bar and going back in the bushes ...

But had she left the lock-bar at the same spot? Would it incriminate me? This I couldn't see. Surely she had not been so careless as to do a thing like that? She who had been so clever? In my panicky doubt, I nearly gave myself away to the equally clever Miss Holland.

Hardly able to breathe, I bleatingly whispered: "Do please tell me. What else did you learn from Sir Henry when he phoned?"

Very coolly: "About what, James?"

"What sort of weapon had been used?"

"On the dog, do you mean? The police think the dog was shot. They have a forensic vet working on that."

"A forensic vet? Not a forensic dentist?"

"No, James. A vet," and she calmly added: "If you're referring to the woman's injuries, they were caused by an undiscovered blunt instrument. It could be a brick or a stone – or possibly a monkey-wrench. Do you have a monkey-wrench in your garage, James?"

I had difficulty in concealing my relief on thus learning that my lock-bar had not been found. I managed to say haughtily: "Madam, what are you implying?"

"James, I am only implying what the police will imply when they question you. Be sensible. You cannot expect to be disregarded as a suspect. The prime suspect, very possibly."

"So they are coming to arrest me, are they? Is that what you're definitely saying?"

"Whether or not you will be arrested, James, will probably depend upon your level of co-operation. It's only for the sake of your wife and children that I'm urging you to behave."

She looked at her watch. "Brockadill will be arriving here very shortly. Please go quietly. Don't launch into a we-the-people-of-England speech. I don't want my party ruined by the sight of Stephanie in hysterics."

Somewhat resentfully, I said: "As a matter of slight interest, who was it who suggested a search of the waste-ground in Willow Tree Lane? Was it you, Miss Holland?"

"As a matter of fact," was her smooth reply, "it was. I suggested it to Sir Henry and he passed the suggestion to Ralphie. He, in turn, suggested it to Brockadill – who acted promptly."

"And what, might I ask, led you to make this public-spirited suggestion?"

"Your copy, James, of the Hound of the Baskervilles. I was inspired by Dr Watson's description of the Grimpen Mire on Dartmoor. Where, I wondered, might there be a similar swampy morass in Dackley? That's when I thought of the soggy fringe in Willow Tree Lane – surrounding where I know you often park."

I managed to restrain a pitiful moan.

She went on: "I've sometimes walked with you to and from that little spot. You've very kindly given me a lift home from there. And it just came to me think: what a clever place to hide a body!"

"Well thank you, Miss Marple," I snarled, really sarcastically.

Instantly and sharply, like a female fencing-champion pinking her opponent, she said: "Surely, James you would want the killer to be caught if you're innocent?"

"Well, yes," I hastily and cravenly mumbled. "I would welcome that outcome. It's the only decent attitude to take."

"Then why the sarcasm?"

"It's just that I'm beginning to feel sort of hemmed in. I could find myself wrongly accused."

"You needn't worry about that," she loftily told me, "if you're innocent. I happen to have got to know Brockadill fairly well. He's a brilliant but honest detective. He will soon clear you of any wrongful suspicion. He had an instinct for his true quarry. That's why he had to leave London. His talents were endangering his life – and the lives of his wife and family."

Having long since finished her dessert, she stood up. I stood up too, but feeling very shattered. I desperately whispered: "Tell me, does Sir Henry think me innocent?"

"He does, yes. A lovely sweet man. He's quite a fan of yours. So is his wife. I'm at a loss to understand it. Both are getting rather woolly, of course. That might account for it. Sit down, James. Finish your dessert."

I sat down but didn't tackle the dessert. Miss Holland drifted off to join – or re-join – some other table. A floor-show was in the offing. According to the programme-card, it was to be given by a troupe of talented teenagers. I was destined never to see this particular nuptial. A waiter bent low to my left ear.

"Excuse me, sir. You have a visitor who wishes to see you in the ante-room – alone."

I turned my head and squinted through the door into the ante-room. My visitor was Brockadill. He was standing at the far end of the ante-room, having just come up the wide stairs. Hat in hand by his side, he was looking sadly serious in a simply magnificent Raglan overcoat. ("By God," I thought, "I'd like a coat like that!") But he wasn't my only visitor. He was only one of a little gaggle which included the uniformed sergeant. I stood up and strode out to confront this gaggle. My exit from the ballroom, may I add, went unnoticed. Stephanie was giggling her head off at something the Toronto dentist was telling her; as for Miss Holland, I couldn't see her anywhere.

"Well, gentlemen? What is it?"

I spoke briskly but with no plan in my mind other than a dictum of my rather unpleasant old uncle. ("War is war. Knock the enemy off balance before he knows what's hit him.")

Before Brockadill had time to reply, I therefore said: "Why have you intruded upon Miss Holland's engagement-party in this unseemly fashion?"

The poor devil blushed but was looking past me. I then realised that Miss Holland was behind me in the doorway. He moved towards her in some confusion and murmured: "Do I gather good wishes are in order?"

"You gather correctly," she said, firmly but pleasantly. "Please don't disturb my other guests."

"Isn't this all rather sudden," he said, and in real agony.

"It's long been planned. The invitations went out months ago. Goodbye, Superintendent."

He hurriedly said: "Actually, madam, I'd like to ask you for those pages you found in Mr Crackery's brief-case."

"You mean the pages with those oily fingermarks all over them? They've been disposed of, I'm afraid. I've been burning up a lot of stuff one acquires in life," and with that she went back to her party.

I tut-tutted reproachfully and said to Brockadill: "My managing-assistant has done her best to help you. You should not have spurned her."

I hated saying this to him. It was like wounding a much-loved younger brother I should imagine. (I had always longed for brothers. Only ever had that terrible sister of mine.)

Brockadill coldly said (but with remnants of the blush still on his cheekbones): "Sir, I am in charge of a double murder-enquiry."

I was quick to say: "You mean about those two dead bodies found in Willow Tree Lane?"

Startled and angry, he said: "How did you know about the location? It's not released."

He wheeled round on his goggle-eyed gaggle of fellow-officers. "Who's been talking?"

"Dunno, sir," said one of them.

I have to say some of them were grinning slightly. (Anyone in a position of authority should never think his or her goings-on will always pass unremarked by junior staff.) The poor chap was now close to rage. But I couldn't let up. This was a man who could have me put away for life. He was the enemy.

"Mr Crackery," he chokingly said, "I need to question you officially."

I decided to adopt the stern army-officer voice my father had taught me.

"What," I barked, "does that mean?"

"It means," he said, rising to the bait, "that I have to interview you under caution."

"I demand an instant interview with your superior officer," I said, and, to the sergeant, I barked: "Sergeant! Did you come here in a police-car? If so, where is it parked?"

"Outside, sir, at the entrance. Two cars."

I stalked off out of the ante-room and down the stairs. I collected my top-hat and my white scarf from the cloakroom-lady. (I had not worn the top-hat on my way in, but I was determined to wear it on the way out.)

Fortunately, there were few guests and staff in the hall and foyer to see my bad behaviour. (It was not my tactic to make the police look or feel ridiculous. I was trying to make the police regard ME as not only ridiculous but stupid. They would then, I hoped, be more likely to start making useful mistakes.)

"Hurry it up," I said to the gaggle which had followed me out, and I opened the rear door of the leading car and got in. "I shall expect to be brought back here within a reasonable time. I am an important guest."

Sitting there with the top-hat on my lap, I was asked by the sergeant: "May we please have your keys, sir? The keys to your car?"

More outraged incredulity: "Whatever for?"

"We need to have your car looked at, sir."

"Looked at? What the devil do you mean?"

"Well, sir, yours seems to be the only car wheel-clamped as far as we know. So we need to nave it looked at forensically. We need it to be taken to the station."

"Sergeant, you will not lay one single finger on my Honda Civic."

"Please, sir, we'll be real careful with it. Please co-operate. Our new tec-super has had an awful bad afternoon. He's got a cold coming on. Ought to be at home and in bed."

Brockadill intervened, looking white-faced. "It's all right, sergeant. We'll get the keys off him when he's searched. Arrest him."

I was arrested and cautioned, there and then, in the car and to the strains of "Stranger on the Shore" from the ballroom balcony-windows.

"I am arresting you for unlawfully killing two persons as yet not fully identified," was how the sergeant put it, plus other blatherings.

He was behind the wheel and had to twist around in his seat to administer the arrest. Brockadill was slumped beside him and looked back at the hotel as we drove off.

"Unlike Miss Holland," I said, rubbing it in, "I have little or no knowledge of the law. I only know that I've never been arrested before and that I suspect this arrest to be highly irregular. I shall wish to phone Miss Holland as soon as we reach your police-station. Take your hands off me."

This last remark was directed at the young fellow beside me – a mere common inspector – who was gripping me by the forearm. I barked it out so loudly that he shrank from me as if old Masher himself had just bitten him.

The second police-car was following us as closely as a fox-hound. Reaching the police-station in Providence Square, we went in by way of some back yard or other. As we all got out of the cars, it seemed to me that Brockadill was beginning to regret having been so impetuous. He had certainly shown his hand too soon and looked exhausted. In the half-light of the building's entrance-lobby, his face was the colour of uncooked pastry. I decided to repeat the pain-inducing name of Miss Holland.

"I need to phone Miss Holland, my managing-assistant. Take me to a phone, please."

"Mr Crackery," said Brockadill, turning on me frigidly, "it's your solicitor you're going to need, believe me."

I had put my top-hat on and he was glaring at it as if he wanted to knock it off.

He muttered savagely: "Who does he think he is? Fred Astaire?"

NINE

A Further Spot of Bother

By eleven o'clock that same night, Brockadill was looking at me as if he had always hated me.

"Mr Crackery," he said, for the umpteenth time, "did at any time ever meet or converse with the woman whose body we also found in Willow Tree Lane?"

Tom Grantiscombe, my solicitor, was present in the white-tiled interview-room.

"Crackery," he said to me his severest tones, "it is perfectly all right for you to answer these questions."

Tom was a member of the family-firm who had been my father's solicitors. I'd known him all my life, but he was six years older than me and had been Head Boy at Beagley. He always addressed me by my surname when (even as an adult) I earned his disapproval.

Primly, I said to him: "I refuse to answer any questions under duress. How many more times do I need to say so?"

"You are not under duress, Crackery. You are simply under caution – a form of legal protection for both yourself and the police. I'll soon chip in if I think there's a question I judge you shouldn't answer."

He was speaking as if I had just been caught walking in at the front door at School – a privilege reserved for prefects and subprefects, any transgression being rewarded with D.T. (detention on Saturday afternoon).

"It's all very well for you, Tom old boy, but I'm not just under duress. This police-officer has had me arrested and threatened."

Brockadill: "Mr Crackery, at no time have you been threatened. You're being absurd."

Ignoring Brockadill, I said to Tom: "You will please inform this officer that he must withdraw the threat if we are to converse as gentlemen. How can we possibly converse as civilised human beings with a threat hanging over me like the sword of Damocles?"

"Mr Crackery," Brockadill all but yelled, "you are not under threat," and he hit the table with his fist. "You're no longer under arrest. The arrest has been withdrawn. I've admitted I ordered the arrest in haste. I've conceded that to your solicitor. What more do you expect me to do? Grovel on the floor?"

Again ignoring the poor chap, I said to Tom: "All this officer needs to do, if we are to converse, is to withdraw the threat openly made in what he calls a caution. I am being threatened with having anything I might say being used as evidence against me. That's a pretty sneaky intention, Tom. You shouldn't condone it."

Brockadill's nice old uniformed sergeant was also in the white-tiled room. He made a worried-looking effort to intervene.

"All we're asking of you, sir," he said to me, "is a bit of co-operation."

"Tom," I said, even more primly, "please inform these officers that co-operation, as a form of discourse, can only be a two-way process. No threat can be a part of it on either side."

It was Tom that sighed the most in the brief silence that followed.

No relative of mine, as far as I knew, had ever been in the Intelligence Corps (make no jokes about this, please) and none had ever been members of Colonel Buckmaster's spy-team. But some had been prisoners-of-war and had spoken of what are called counter-interrogation techniques. I had learnt from their table-talk that questions from an enemy can be informative. ("Just make the Kraut angry.")

It was not, therefore, Brockadill alone whom I was manipulating. I was manipulating Tom, my very own solicitor. I wanted him to show sympathy for poor old Brockadill, enough to lure Brockadill into asking "informative" questions. All I really wanted to know was what (if anything) Miss Holland might have said about Mrs Tridwell.

"Crackery," said Tom, as obligingly as if I had prodded him, "I think we've all had enough of your behaviour. I'm advising you to answer the investigating officer's perfectly reasonable questions."

Brockadill tried again, looking grateful.

"Mr Crackery, could it be the case that you never sold a painting to a so-called knocker? Could it be, in fact, that you sold the painting to Rivinni – the market-stall dealer whose body we also found? We know he bought and sold antiques as well as other stuff."

These were new questions and a new tack which, although fanciful, showed me that Brockadill could be as dangerously intuitive as Miss Holland. All Brockadill's previous questions had been of threadbare significance; these last ones were the sort I was angling for, although I pretended to ignore them.

"Answer the officer," the former Head Boy impatiently tried to command me.

I stayed silent and folded my arms.

Brockadill sat forward hopefully and almost pleadingly. I felt terribly sorry for him. (He really did look ill.) He said: "Mr Crackery, could it be that the four-thousand pounds you received came from the cupboard in the dead woman's bungalow? Is it possible you were mistaken about the knocker? Was he Leo Rivinni? In some sort of disguise?"

Brockadill was becoming worse than frantic. He was becoming wild. He jumped up and added: "Just tell us that, Mr Crackery, and we'll call it a day. It's very late. You want to go home, don't you? Or back to the party – if it's still going on?"

His voice broke on those last words and he rushed from the room. His uniformed sergeant bustled faithfully after him. Tom and I were left with two somewhat open-mouthed and touchingly youthful policemen.

"Your behaviour," Tom said to me, "can only be described in one word – despicable. He's already had one nervous breakdown. Are you deliberately trying to give him another?"

"No," I could have triumphantly told him. "I've been trying to extract information. I've succeeded. Miss Holland has told him nothing about the so-called Mrs Tridwell. Neither Miss Holland nor Brockadill have twigged that a lot of money is missing from that bungalow – and that I've got a good chunk of it! Ha!"

Instead, of course, I put on an air of injured innocence just as I used to at School. Tom didn't actually say, as he did in those days: "Crackery, you're letting down the School right left and centre," but I'm sure he would have done.

He was stopped, I still think, by Brockadill storming back into the room.

"Mr Crackery," he all but screamed, "I haven't been wrong about an arrest for many years. I have an instinct which tells me you've something to hide. I don't need any help from you in finding evidence against you. I'll have it within days, damn you. Arrest him again," he said to the sergeant, who had come panting in behind him. "Charge him and bung him in God's Waiting-Room. Let him stew."

The puzzling reference to God's Waiting-Room was soon explained to me by the sergeant. After ceremoniously charging me, he led me to an ancient-looking door – wooden but iron-bound. He unlocked it with quite a heavy key.

"In here, sir, if you please."

I peered in and hesitated. "Sergeant, this is no cell. It's more like a dungeon."

"That's right, sir." He personally plumped up what appeared to be a floor-level palliasse. "It's part of the old jail-house. Very historic. Important visitors to Dackley often ask to see it. It used to be a sort of holding-cell for some poor devil or other – before being hanged in Providence Square."

"And why," I asked, feeling rather anxious, "are you showing it to me?"

"Oh, sir, I'm not showing it to you. It's where you're going to spend the night. Although we don't use it much, it's still an official part of our accommodation. Come inside, sir. I'm going to lock you up."

I won't describe the other furnishings, but, although still in my dress-suit, I managed to settle down as comfortably as I could. It was really only the harshly modern electric light which really upset me. To shield my eyes, I had to cover my face with my top-hat but the top-hat kept falling off and rolling away as if it had a life of its own.

The next day, being a Sunday, meant a sparse hearing in front of shocked magistrates. All of them were known to me and I hoped this irregularity (surely an irregularity?) would help to grant me bail. It did not.

I have to say that my very own solicitor, also, didn't exactly exert himself. He was still very cross with me. But he had at least brought me a hold-all with a change of clothes and other necessaries.

"Crackery, you've only yourself to blame for the mess you're in. I can't believe you're guilty of anything too terrible, but perhaps there are things which have yet to come to light. Even if nothing comes to light, however, let us hope that a spell on remand will bring you to your senses."

He had spoken in the same way as the old Buzzard of Beagley!

"Some people," I very nearly said to him, "Never seem to outgrow their schooldays."

I decided to say nothing and to clamber into the prison-van as a country-gentleman should. (I was now in my favourite tweed-suit and tweed-cap. I'm sure I very much looked the part I had decided to play.) Tom took away my dress-suit which, I'm happy to tell you, didn't suffer the ordeal in God's Waiting-Room as badly as I had feared. Just a bit crumpled, that's all.

I'm also happy to tell you that I had the prison-van to myself and, in fact, sat with driver after we got out of town. Just like my boarding-school, East Wildering Prison was at a sequestering distance from my home. The "sat-nav" was not yet in vogue and my driver got lost. (I had to do the map-reading.) Despite my inglorious fuss of the night before, I felt in no way threatened on this journey. I was thinking of the official apology I would soon receive – perhaps from the incumbent Chief Constable (with Brockadill in meek attendance).

"Don't mention it, my dear sir," I was planning to say. "Anyone can make a mistake."

Who was the first to visit me? Who was it who brought me horribly down to earth?

Surely you can guess?

Dressed in the best of taste, she looked superb. No other word for it. Many eyes were drawn to our drab little table in the visiting-hall. She had travelled, if you please, not by train and bus but all the way from Dackley in a taxi (put down as expenses). What a nerve!

"I mustn't keep the man waiting for too long," she said, drawing off her gloves. "But I have one or two things for you to sign," and she began sorting out papers from a smart-looking document-case. "I must say," she broke off to add, "things seem a bit lax around here. I'm beginning to think I should complain to the governor. Hardened criminals like you shouldn't be molly-coddled to this degree."

"It's nice to see you of course," was my riposte, "but I was rather hoping to be visited by my wife. I can't even get her on the phone – which I have to line up for. May I ask you to point that out to her?"

Miss Holland now delivered the first of several shocks. This one was relatively mild but nevertheless amazing.

"Stephanie," she said, "is far too busy with the shop to visit you at present."

"Busy with the shop? What on earth do you mean?"

"James, it's a most interesting change of personality. After her hysterical reaction to the news of your arrest, she suddenly calmed down. She became eager to return to the shop. Now that we are all free from your shallow-minded ineptitude, she's been coming up with all sorts of bright ideas."

"But she always said she never wanted to serve in the shop ever again!"

"For instance, she's planning to turn your office into a bridal-wear department."

"Oh she is, is she? And what about our two little girls?"

"Don't worry, James. They are happy with the donkeys over at Swerton. It's all temporary, of course. It's only until I can find someone of disciplinary talent to replace me."

"Might I ask," I said, more than a little acidly, "If you'll be leaving poor old England and living in Canada? If so, how soon?"

"Yes, I'm off to Canada within weeks. The wedding is in Toronto. I can't entirely be rid of my property in England, but, obviously, I have a lot to do."

"Property? What property?"

"The house where I have my flat. I own it. I bought the entire house as an investment. You surely don't think I was surviving on the meagre salary I got from you? I could, perhaps, pop back for your trial. I'm not quite sure."

"Surely you'll be wanted as a witness?"

"Apparently not, James. I seem to be regarded as a dubious asset by the police."

"By God," I muttered, "how little I know you …"

"James, you've never spoken a truer word. Now, please, sign here and sign here. It's just the usual routine-stuff."

"Which," I sourly said, "could just as easily have been done by post."

"Of course, James. But I wanted to see you. After all, it's been a long six years. I've never been in love with you," she added, watching as I scribbled my signatures, "but one feeling I will admit to. I was often oddly comforted by the knowledge of your presence upstairs. I'd already had one bad love-affair in London. I didn't want another in Dackley. But, as I say, I did find your presence a comfort. For that reason, and for the sake of your wife and children, I'm hoping you are not a murderer and won't be convicted."

I didn't know how to respond to this statement. I could only mutter: "Thank you, madam," and then I added: "I say, though, wouldn't you wish to testify as a character-witness or whatever they call it?"

"That, James, would be most inadvisable. I would be obliged to tell the truth."

She unzipped another section of her document-case. "I have here a copy of my most recent financial-report. We're doing remarkably well, thanks in part to your notoriety. Local interest in the shop is as great as if you are to be hanged in Providence Square."

I began looking through the report with real interest until she said: "Did you ever hear from the mysterious Mrs Tridwell?"

"Who?" (For the moment, I had forgotten the name Asti Glertish had made use of.)

"I now suspect that name to have been false. I also doubt that she was married. No wedding-ring. A married woman of that class wouldn't be without a ring."

"I didn't look for that," I truthfully said.

"No, James, you wouldn't. But did you ever see her again after you dragged her out of the shop?"

"No," I untruthfully said. "And what's more," I added, in a bit of truthful anger, "I never dragged her out of the shop."

"Forgive me, James," she blandly said. "I only ever exaggerated that occasion as a way of trying to get you to confide in me."

"Miss Holland, I told you the truth. What more do you expect of me?"

"Nothing, James. I only ask this next question out of mere curiosity – and in the vaguest hope of an accurate answer. Did she ever tell you where she hailed from?"

"All I know, madam, is that she was from the local council-estate where, frankly, I have never set foot. Probably born and bred there. I could tell that from her accent."

"Her accent was not local, James. In my opinion, she was from London – probably south of the river. I know London quite well."

"Thank you, Professor Higgins," I said, anxious to change this tack. "Will that be all?"

"And she didn't make those pots, James. As I later found out, she bought the pots from the charity-shop further down the street."

In well-simulated amazement: "Good Lord! Is that a fact? What have you done with them?"

"They've gone in the dustbin, James."

"Perhaps you should have kept them," I daringly said, "to check her fingerprints. She could be an out-and-out criminal."

"That, James, I very much doubt. To my mind, she was a simpleton. But a gifted simpleton. You, too, are a simpleton. But not, in your case, a gifted one. You, James, are only a privileged simpleton. You're like so many of the men running this country. The only difference between you and them is that you, fortunately, lack power and position. But that girl had real potential. I could sense it. I could have done a lot to help her."

"Perhaps," I even more daringly said, "you should try to trace her."

"I've tried, James. There's no trace of her locally and I've drawn a blank in London. I've had to give up."

"That's a pity, Miss Holland, I'm sure. But at least," I said, borrowing the tones of a patiently pious vicar, "you tried your best."

I was now in the strange position of longing for Miss Holland to stay but fearing, if she did, that our conversation would take even more dangerous turns. I tried to get up. I found I couldn't. Although my voice was firm enough, my knees were not.

"It only remains for me to thank you for calling," I said, managing a slight rise (and then subsiding. My eyes were on her diamond ring).

She sat very still, hands well in sight.

"And it only remains for me, James, to thank you for all you've done."

I blinked a bit and said: "Is this a genuine compliment, Miss Holland?"

"Of course it is. Although without knowing it, you have helped me to change my life. I couldn't be happier than I am now."

"I see," I said, with a bit of a sigh.

"Working for you, James, I can only suppose has been a much-needed form of purgatory. I had to go through it to discover my truest love. As I've told you, I used to find your presence to be a comfort. Only for a year or two. I then began to find you exasperating. Impossible, in fact."

She stood up smiling, smiling nicely. I managed to stand up too. She added: "All in all, James, I really do thank you," and we shook hands before she put her on her gloves.

Always the gentleman, I rather dazedly muttered: "I'm sorry you had to come so far. I can't imagine why I wasn't kept in Dackley."

"Oh, there's no mystery about it. It's all due to Sir Henry. He pulled a few strings. He wanted you to be somewhere pleasant. This, apparently, was all he could wangle."

"Oh, how very nice of him!"

"What about your cell? For company, have you managed to tame the usual rat or cockroach?"

"Not yet, no. Actually, this place is vastly superior to Beagley. I can wear my own clothes, I can even have food sent in. Not that I need to – they do a jolly good cheese-rice here. Delicious scrunchy bits. I'm trying to obtain the recipe. Certainly better food than we ever got at Beagley. I must write and thank the old boy."

"Yes, James. You should. But do try not to upset him. He's already upset by the news about your garden-shed."

"What on earth do you mean? What news? Has it fallen down or something?"

Miss Holland moved closer to me, almost as if she were about to kiss my cheek. But it was my ear she was going for. She breathed into it: "The police, James, have searched your garden-shed. They were looking for the gun which they think you might have used for shooting the dog. Did you shoot the dog, James?"

Not wanting to continue lying to so elegant a woman, I avoided the answer by saying: "Is that what they're saying about me? That I've shot a dog?"

"That's what they think, James. But they found no gun."

"Nor would they," I said, remembering how I'd chucked the gun in the old reservoir. "I could have told them if they'd had the courtesy to ask me. Poking around in my shed? What a waste of police-time!"

"Oh, no," said Miss Holland, in the most delicate of whispers. "For them, it was no waste of time. They were, in fact, delighted. What they found instead, James, was your lock-bar – the one they are calling the murder-weapon."

I was too shocked by this news to stagger. I really did feel rooted to the spot. Still whispering (and smiling, smiling nicely), she went on: "James, I do rather think this rather looks like the end. Sir Henry has shown me a colour-photo of the lock-bar they found. It exhibits some fairly nasty encrustations. But even I could see that it was your lock-bar."

"And what did you say to the old boy?"

"Nothing. I've made no comment to anyone. But why, James, did you hide it in your shed?"

"I did no such thing," I feebly growled.

"Typically stupid absent-mindedness, I suppose. You go out and buy a second lock-bar but forget about the one you've hidden up! James, I saw that second lock-bar myself. I saw it when you gave me that lift from the luncheon-party. I could swear it wasn't the same lock-bar I had seen at other times."

"And is that what you're going to do?"

"James, If I'm asked to testify, I shall have to. May I urge you to be frank when you next see your long-suffering solicitor?"

"Miss Holland, do you believe I killed that woman with a lock-bar?"

Aloofly: "As I think I've told you before, James, I'm keeping an open mind."

"An open mind, madam, is an empty mind and not to be recommended at all. Even at its best, it represents non-commitment at its most complacent."

I was quoting my father (a quote I had not really understood), but I knew the quote would impress Miss Holland. She actually sat down again in her surprise. "My goodness me, James. I never realised you could be capable of such profundity. Might I ask an intellectual favour of you?"

I sat down again myself. Somewhat gloomily, I said: "Madam, I am hardly in a position to grant favours of any sort to anyone."

"I'm simply asking you to refrain from revealing your source of information about this latest clue. It would get Sir Henry into trouble with Ralphie – his son-in-law."

"Then why have you told me of this clue?"

"I made no promise to Sir Henry, Ralphie or Brockadill. I have therefore broken no promise. Legally, you are still my employer. I believe it my duty to warn you of the ambush that's obviously being planned at high level."

"This is very good of you, Miss Holland. Thank you. But it's still a bit of a shock …"

"You've only yourself to blame for virtually goading Brockadill into arresting you. But you deserve a sporting chance – if, by any chance, you happen to be innocent. Goodbye, James."

She got up and walked out, never looking back but smiling regally at the warders. (One of them asked her if she would like a cup of tea, which she graciously declined.)

Back in my cell, I paced the floor in absolute bewilderment and said: "This really is most inconsiderate. What on earth could have possessed the wretched Glertish? Fancy leaving the damn thing in my shed …"

I was recollecting only too clearly how I'd found her loitering in the garden (when I was burning up that ghastly oil-painting).

"That's when she did it," I said, pounding my fist on my little table. "But to what end? What purpose?"

I racked my brains. All I could first think was that she had expected me to tidy up the shed and find the lock-bar – which, for some eccentric reason, she wanted me to dispose of in the same way as the pistol and other bits.

"Mister," I remembered her telling me, "you needs to tidy up your shed …"

"She had no right," I finally exploded, "even to look in my shed!"

I was still standing and pounding the table when my allotted warder came into the cell.

"Mr Crackery," he said, "I've got the recipe you wanted – the one for the cheese-rice."

He handed me a slip of paper, which I thanked him for and placed in my wallet. I was still shaking.

He kindly asked: "Bad news, Mr Crackery?"

"The worst possible," and I more-or-less collapsed in sitting down at the table.

Yes, Miss Glertish had rudely told me I needed to tidy up my shed. Her final words. But why couldn't she have given me a stronger hint before driving off? Surely it would have been in her own best interests to make sure I got rid of such incriminating evidence? Damn it all, she knew I'd bought a new lock-bar. She surely didn't think I'd still want the old one?

My kindly warder said: "Don't tell me too much, Mr Crackery. I would have to report anything indiscreet. But is there any way I can help you?"

I was on the brink of confiding in him more than I should. He seemed so very much like the old station-master at Swerton railway-station, at the village in my childhood (a line long since torn up by the destructive Dr Beeching). But he again repeated: "Don't tell me too much, sir," and he added: "Just tell me enough to enable me to help you. I've been in this job a long time. So was my dad and my grandpa."

"Officer," I said, "I have just discovered that I've been framed. No other word for it. Framed. A deliberate attempt to implicate me in the most disgusting way possible. Framed."

The kindly warder sighed. "Well, sir, that's a word I have to say I've often heard before. But it can turn out to be true. It was even true in the days when they hanged you for murder. Warders often knew more than lawyers and judges in them days. They still do."

"I can't understand the motivation," I hotly said. "I've done nothing to upset anyone."

"Any idea, sir, as to who's framed you?"

I hesitated. I was as reluctant to lie to this excellent fellow as I was to everyone else. But it had to be done. (War is war.)

"Officer, I have only the vaguest idea of her identity."

"So it's a she, is it?"

"Not necessarily, no," I hastily said, cursing myself for this idiotic slip.

"Is it that nice lady who came to see you today, sir?"

"Good God no. Miss Holland isn't as bad as all that. To some extent, I'd like to blame her if I could. I admit that. She's been a bit nasty. But no, it could easily be someone I would never suspect of harbouring a grudge."

"And they've planted evidence?"

I got up to pace the room. "That's about the size of it, yes."

"Evidence you can't refute?"

"Very difficult to refute. The police are calling it the murder-weapon. It's been found in my garden-shed."

"And someone put it there, sir? Is that what you're saying?"

"Well, yes – obviously…"

The kindly old warder sighed in his nice old way and said: "Not a very good defence, sir, if you don't mind me saying."

"Then what the devil am I to do?" I sat down again feeling pretty stumped.

"I could make a suggestion, sir, but you might not like it."

"I'm willing to consider any suggestion other than confessing to something I've not done. Fire away, officer."

"First of all, sir, don't let your own lawyers talk you into having a paper committal."

"A paper what?"

"A way of by-passing the magistrates, sir. Your lawyers might think it best to go straight to Crown Court. Take my tip, sir. Insist on a proper committal-hearing in front of the beaks."

"Why is that an advantage?"

"Well, sir, magistrates are more down to earth than lawyers and judges. Magistrates are ordinary people. Lawyers and judges prefer law to facts. Beaks is opposite. They have the power to throw out the evidence on the facts – if the facts are just plain daft."

"You mean they have the power to find me not guilty?"

"No, sir. I don't mean that. A committal-hearing ain't a trial. It's a hearing, sir. And you can be re-arrested if the police find more sensible evidence. Is that likely, sir?"

My heart began to thud. (I was fearing again for that Gladstone-bag of money in the vault.) I almost shouted: "All they've got against me is that piece of false evidence planted in my garden-shed!"

"If that is so, sir, then the facts will set you free. It could be a different matter if your lawyers ask for trial. You could be in jug for months while they split just one hair."

"How soon could I be out of this place?"

"In a month or two, possibly. It varies."

"And how often does a committal-hearing throw out a murder-charge?"

Another kindly sigh from the kindly warden: "Not very often, I do have to say."

"I quite like this suggestion of yours, officer. Why did you say I might not?"

"Well, sir, it does mean keeping your mouth shut as much as possible. You have a lovely voice, sir, if you don't mind me saying so. But keep it in reserve-like. Just sit there in your nice tweed suit, like a nice country-gentleman, and let the lawyers do the talking. For you, sir, least said soonest mended."

"Actually, officer, I was rather thinking I should conduct the case myself."

"Blimey, no," he cried, as if in pain. "That would never do!"

I bristled a little. "Why on earth not? I am a subject of Her Majesty the Queen. I am entitled to my point of view in her courts."

"If you're unlucky enough to be sent to trial, sir, then yes. Perhaps. But not at the committal-hearing."

"Frankly, I don't understand that."

"Well, sir, it's because of the barristers. Magistrates don't much like them – especially when they chuck their weight about. But judges have been barristers theirselves. Judges therefore tolerise barristers. They makes more allowances for them. For you, sir, nothing would be better – at the committal-hearing – than to have a real snotty bugger as the prosecution-barrister."

"Someone who would insult me up hill and down dale? Is that what you mean?"

"Congratulations, sir," said the warder, beaming with pleasure on my behalf. "You're getting the idea. It's called tactics. Without tactics, you'll be done for."

I jumped up again and paced the room in excited enthusiasm. The scent of battle was in my nostrils.

"So let's run through what I need to do. I sit in the dock. I maintain a polite silence. But what if the prosecutor is just as polite himself? How do I stir him up?"

"You won't need to, sir. He's certain to be cocky. He will be jumping at the chance to go in hard. It's the future trial he's thinking of. He can't influence the jury in advance, but he knows he can influence local witnesses. Even they as ain't at the hearing will be just as influenced."

"How does the slanderous fiend manage that?"

"Because everything he says at the hearing will be all round your town if he wins the hearing. Them's his tactics, see? And you has to meet tactics with tactics, see?"

"Yes, but what tactics?"

"It's all very simple, sir. Beforehand, research yourself. Note down every detail of the events what led up to your arrest. Time and place. Be accurate. Have every detail on the tip of your tongue. And then, sir, listen real careful to what he's saying. Sooner or later, he's going to make a great big mistake."

"I get it," I cried. "That's when I go in for the knock-out blow!"

"That's right, sir. Congratulations."

"In other words, I deliver a master-stroke."

"A good name for it, sir."

"In what way do I deliver it? Any tips on that?"

"Just sit in the dock, sir. Keep your mouth buttoned. Let your own barrister handle the master-stroke. Advise him by way of a short but clear note. Get the usher to deliver it."

"Him?" I was really getting into the spirit of all this. "Might it not be better to have a lady-barrister? A young and pretty one?"

"A good idea, sir. With any luck, the chairman will be a nice but sad old bloke. A young and pretty barrister speaking for you would cheer him up. To your benefit, sir."

"By God," I said, slapping the kindly warder on the back, "I'm beginning to look forward to all this. Thank you, officer. Leave me now, will you? I must map out my campaign," and I sat down at my table to unscrew my father's favourite fountain-pen. (A wine-coloured Onoto, genuinely gold-nibbed.)

TEN

Just a Little Local Difficulty

I

The day of the hearing dawned just over three months later, but, for me, it seemed no time at all. Amazing. And I do mean dawned.

I had to get up at six in the morning for the journey back to Dackley. My kindly warder had lent me an alarm-clock and personally saw me off in the much-delayed van, but I had it all to myself, together with my belongings in a sack.

Despite this privileged treatment (as Miss Holland would have described it), I was having misgivings about the magistrates. I had a feeling they might not have the charitable commonsense, which the kindly warder had predicted.

Only the day before I had lined up for the telephone (abortively, I might add). I had exchanged a few words with a new arrival – a new boy, as it were – who was in front of me. He was a frightened-looking young man who had a wife and two baby-children.

"My goodness me," I said, on hearing his sentence, "the magistrates surely haven't put you in prison for that?"

His offence? Not buying a television-licence. He started blubbing. To cheer him up, I said: "Why didn't you stick to reading free library-books?"

"Can't read, sir."

Another illiterate in this day and age! But what a difference in spirit from Miss Glertish, eh?

I was thinking about her all the way to Dackley. I was still cross with her. Who wouldn't be? Yet (though I was tempted) I refused to contemplate blaming her for the pickle I was in. It wasn't just the thought of losing all that money which deterred me. I really did feel an urge to protect her (but disbelieve me if you like, Miss Holland).

Fancy having had one's pet-tortoise smashed up with a hammer! Could any childhood memory be more shocking?

II

I was troubled by more immediate misgivings after arriving at the car-park behind the court.

Their Worships' court, I must tell you, was in the same ramshackle complex as the police-station in Providence Square. I was escorted from the van by a policeman (who popped up out of nowhere) and taken straight to a tiny basement-room to meet my defence-team.

It consisted of just two people – poor old Tom and a man whom he introduced by saying: "This is your counsel, James."

Although I hadn't blindly accepted everything my kindly warder had told me, his advice about arrogant barristers very regrettably applied to the very barrister Tom had briefed.

Not only was he not in wig and gown (which confused me) but neither did he get up from the little table or make any move to shake hands. Only Tom showed me this courtesy (rather pensively, I have to admit). Also, this was a far cry from the young lady-barrister who had featured in my day-dreams. He was very old.

Briefed, as a word, was not a misnomer for this barrister. He had so "brief" an acquaintance with my case that he couldn't even remember my name. He began by addressing me as "Mr Whoever You Are" after crustily consulting his watch.

"You're late, Mr Whoever You Are. Do you think I like sitting here with the stink of disinfectant in my nostrils? And where's my junior? I've got to have my junior."

"Perhaps," suggested Tom, in his pacific way, "she's been held up in traffic."

My dismay was slightly eased on hearing the word "she". Could this be the young and pretty lady-barrister my imagination had painted? This pathetic hope was dashed in the next second by this terrible old man.

He positively shrieked: "Where is the stupid old bitch? I've said it before and I'll say it again. It's time she was pensioned off. As it is, she's already got one foot in the grave."

Like many ordinary people, I daresay, I had thought the term "junior" – when Tom had mentioned the expensive necessity in his one and only letter – referred to someone young. Because of this disillusion, perhaps, I was sitting at that table feeling more and more indignant.

The following words were the last straw. He uttered them in fierce contempt.

"Mr Whoever You Are, your solicitor says you want to fight this open-and-shut case in the lower court. You're a fool. You should take his advice and reserve your defence. Magistrates are amateurs – amateur judges. Shop-lifting and television-licences they can cope with. But not the ins and outs of a double-murder charge. Hearings like this ought to be done away with. All you'll be doing, Mr Whoever You Are, is to provide the prosecution with rehearsal-time. Get yourself in front of a proper judge and jury, you utter idiot."

It was at this final insult that I lost my temper completely.

Leaning forward across the inadequate interview-table, I said: "You, sir, are the person with one foot in the grave. I suggest you put your other foot in with it. I'd sooner conduct this case myself than have a senile old fool like you mucking it up."

He didn't die, thank goodness, but he did suffer what turned out to be a fairly serious heart-attack. Clutching at his chest, he yelled: "I forgot to take my pills this morning. Where are my pills?"

He crashed forward on to the inadequate table, upsetting it and then sliding off it on to the floor. This led to several moments of chaos. Case-papers and police-photographs were scattered, but he was taken away, literally within minutes, on a sort of chair-stretcher.

At the time, of course, I didn't know what to make of what I'd done. (I only later heard that he recovered in hospital and retired.) But Tom was very tough with me as soon as we were alone. I had never known him to be so furious.

"Crackery, that was no way to speak to a well-known QC. I'm totally ashamed of you. How many more deaths do you want on your soul?"

"Grantiscombe," I reprovingly said, "that's not very nice of you. A bit too steep, I'd say."

"Furthermore, Crackery, what he said made sense. Yes, he was a little tetchy. But he's been a brilliant man in his time. We were lucky he was available. If hanging were still on the statute-book, he was the man to have got you off. He was the man to enter a plea of mitigation which, as in all his manslaughter cases, would have been respected."

"Tom," I said, reverting to our usual form of address, "might I ask, in friendship, whether or not you intend to stick to my instructions?"

"James," he said, getting frantic, "don't you even realise why this hearing has been brought on with such expedite care? It's because it's going to be a walk-over!"

"If that's what the enemy thinks, I said (outwardly confident but inwardly all of a tremble), "then that's all to the good. It means the enemy will tend to be careless. I will then pounce on the one big blunder the enemy is bound to make. I shall pounce like a tiger."

Tom sighed and sat down again at the restored interview-table.

He put his head in his hands and said: "Is this what you meant in your reply to my letter? Your battle-plan?"

"It is indeed my battle-plan."

"James, it would be helpful to me if you were to explain your battle-plan in more detail. You're like a kid who's been caught scrumping apples. To deny you have anything to do with the apples in your pockets is not a good defence. I beg you, James. Be frank about what really happened. Were these deaths somehow accidental?"

"Ive already been frank damn it all, as frank as an innocent man can possibly be. Your trouble, Tom, is that you lack faith."

He sprang up despairingly.

"James, I'm going to make one last appeal to your intelligence. I know you of old. You're bluffing. You have no battle-plan. You're simply refusing to face reality. Stupidly, you're just hoping for the best in a hearing which can have but one result. You will be sent on to Crown Court. You will be tried for two murders. As yet, you have no defence."

As with Brockadill, Tom was a man I would very much liked to have had as a brother. I had no brothers. All I had was a disgruntled sister. So can you imagine what happened next?

Before I could reply to Tom's perfectly fair assessment of my fate, I was interrupted by the breathless arrival of the old trout herself – my vinegar-like sister.

Well, not really my sister but so similar as to be indentical. A depressing development. How many more shocks like this could I endure?

Chokingly, she said to Tom: "Sorry I'm late, Mr Grantiscombe. I got here just in time to find my cousin being worked on in the ambulance. They've taken him off now, but he could die. I was brought up with him – my favourite cousin."

"I'm dreadfully sorry," said Tom, "Do please sit down."

"No time," she snapped. "I must withdraw. He could die. I must get to the hospital."

"I quite understand," said Tom.

Giving me one of my sister's nastiest looks, she said to me: "I am obliged to ask you this. Will you accept a devil?"

Not knowing what she meant, I felt confused. I said: "A devil, madam? What for?"

"To represent you at this hearing."

I rather feebly said: "I'd prefer an angel, quite frankly. I'm beginning to think I need one."

"Don't be facetious. It ill becomes you at a time like this." Snappily re-addressing Tom, she said: "We must have continuity, of course. I'll take over, therefore, at the subsequent trial. That I can promise. Does your client meanwhile agree to the devil?"

Before I could re-open my mouth to make any kind of protest, Tom hastily said: "My client agrees."

This sisterly replica plunged out of the half-open door. I heard her say to someone obviously waiting outside: "You go on in, my dear. You'll be all right. It's an elementary procedure. I must fly."

To put it simply, a young lady entered.

I don't know what Tom thought of her. Dimly, I heard him say: "I must phone your chambers and, of course, have a quick word with the clerk here. I won't be long. The court has adjourned for lunch. We have a good forty minutes. James, have yourself a snack. I've brought you a hamper."

He disappeared. The stout policeman on sentry-duty outside the room came in and stood on guard as gravely as if I were Jack the Ripper.

The young lady sat down at the inadequate table. I did, too. Ignoring the hamper, I was already having a sort of delusion. I was imagining myself to be in a fashionable restaurant with this young lady sitting opposite. My heart was on wings. I was imagining soft lights and beguiling music. The policeman, of course, was turning into a courteous waiter – standing there while we browsed the wine-list.

My heart stayed on wings even after (in a voice like thistledown) she said to the waiter: "It's all right, constable. Thank you, but I'm sure I can cope with this old gentleman on my own."

Old? I was in the pink and still forty-seven.

"Very good, miss," he said, obeying her grudgingly, "but you seem very young. I'll be within call if you need me."

Alone with me, she said: "It's true. But I'm not only young, I'm broke. I'd get more cash working at the check-out in a supermarket. Could this be my big chance, I wonder?"

It's always rude to stare at a woman, but I couldn't altogether help myself. It wasn't that she was pretty. She was more than pretty. It wasn't that she was beautiful. She was more than beautiful.

She was, in a word, perfect. Never in my life had I ever seen a young woman looking so perfectly herself. And, of course, unattainable. I was in no way hoping for a dalliance. Damn it all, I was old enough to be her father. But not her grandfather. Get that straight, please. Not that I'm making any objections to men who marry ladies young enough to be their daughters. My own father, for instance. Like many military men, he married late in life. (He had been just about old enough to have fathered my mother.)

"Madam," I said, suddenly getting worried about something more important, "are you sure you've chosen the right sort of profession? I have two lovely little girls. I'd be most unhappy to think of them going in for criminal law. I'm fairly harmless, of course. Ask Miss Holland. But some of the types I've come across in East Wildering are a bit on the nasty side."

"Please don't worry about me, Mr Crackery. I'm sure I'll be all right."

"I can't agree with you. Wouldn't it have been just a bit better to have gone in for a nicer branch of the law?"

"Mr Crackers," she started to say, but I interrupted sharply.

"I've heard that joke before, madam. Do not repeat it."

"All right," she said, smiling patiently, "I will not crack it again. I promise."

"Also, madam, I want you to promise not to moan about your troubles to poor old Tom – my solicitor. He's worried enough as it is."

"I promise that too," she said, this time becoming firmly urgent in tone. "Mr Crackery, don't you think you need to be intelligently concerned about your own predicament? I've been shown the brief. That nice old biddy who brought me here to sit in, she says you're in really big trouble. You appear to have been less than candid with your solicitor. That's the delicate way he put it to her."

"In other words, you mean my case is hopeless?"

"Well, yes," she said, and with a smile I could have died for. "I've tried to be informal and put you at ease, but you need to be realistic."

Tom re-entered at this beautiful moment. He looked more worried than ever. Standing still, he announced: "I have some simply terrible news."

Blimey, I instantly wondered, have the cops found my pot of gold? All that lovely money in the bank-vault? Have I become a liar for nothing?

But he only added: "I've just been spoken to by Prosecuting Counsel. He's a simply awful fellow known as the Greasy Slob. I've heard of him but never seen him in action. He's a nastily ambitious lawyer of the worst possible type. He'll make mincemeat of us."

It was hard for me to conceal my relief, indeed my delight. An absolute bounder was the very advantage my kindly warder had mentioned. Slapping Tom on the back, I said: "Never mind all that. We are going to win. Victory will be ours."

What I did not explain, of course, was that I had just discovered the age-old cure for love. Romantic love, I mean. As I should have known, it's simply a matter of falling in love with someone else. But, for me, my love for this re-consigned counsel (or "devil") was greater than for Miss Holland. Fear was no part of it, nothing of that sort. It was all sheer ecstasy, a sublime form of love, which, of course, would always remain unspoken. And (again which I chose not to explain), it would be this love which I knew would inspire my success.

It didn't, of course, render me infallible. In fact, I very nearly came a cropper in the next few moments. (Lying to someone you're in love with must always be difficult enough; on this sublime level, it was almost impossible.)

With her dark hair flowing (but flowing respectably), this lovely-looking mite of a girl happened to pick up a police-photograph. It was a grisly picture of my lock-bar – the one found in my garden-shed. She said: "In effect, Mr Crackery, your solicitor is talking about incontrovertible evidence. In other words, evidence like this. Today, the magistrates only need to be shown that it's valid. Please look at this photograph, Mr Crackery."

"Thank you, madam, but no. I don't like looking at stuff like that – ugh! In any case, it's not my lock-bar."

"Not your lock-bar, you say?"

"I have only ever had one lock-bar, madam, and that's the one for my Honda Civic."

"You never bought a second lock-bar?"

"Never, madam."

"The police, as I understand it from these disclosures, are still looking for the place where you bought the second lock-bar."

"They won't find it, madam. Having already got a lock-bar, I didn't need another."

"And you didn't hide the first one in your garden-shed?"

"Why on earth would I?"

"Can you explain why it's so similar to the other lock-bar? The one listed here? In this police-inventory of your Honda Civic?"

"That's not for me to explain, madam. That is for the police to explain. They are the people making these false accusations."

"And can you explain why this particular lock-bar – in this photograph – bears unmistakable signs of a blood-letting?"

What a delightfully quaint way she had of expressing herself! My admiration for her inspired me to utter a hugely bold denial.

"Madam, I do not go around bashing in people's faces with a lock-bar. Any lock-bar the police say they found in my shed can't be mine. I have but one lock-bar – for my Honda."

It was at this point that I went on to make a silly slip – just as I had with the nice old warder. I would describe it as an involuntary mutter. The words of it were: "I still can't really believe she would do any such thing."

I was of course thinking of Miss Asti Glertish and her pet-tortoise. For some time, I had been unable to believe that anyone would avenge a pet-tortoise in the way Miss Glertish had claimed. Too awful a thing to believe! I had vaguely supposed that she had wanted to shock me before finally departing. But now, ever since Miss Holland had imparted the news about my garden-shed, I had angrily but reluctantly accepted that Miss Glertish HAD made ugly use of my lock-bar. Yet I still wanted to protect her. I was, indeed, wishing that I could have her at my elbow – invisibly giving me common-sense advice in her ghastly voice.

I emerged from this split-second reverie to find my more official advisers gazing at me with gleaming interest.

Tom left it to my spiritual sweetheart (if I may so describe her) to ask: "Mr Crackery, who is she? Who is the she you're referring to?"

I was only stumped for another split-second. Rather to my own amazement, I found myself glibly saying: "Isn't it obvious? I was referring to the woman whose body was found in the undergrowth at Willow Tree Lane. I still can't believe she would have done any such thing."

"A thing like what, Mr Crackery?"

"I never set eyes on the woman myself, but, according to Sir Henry, she was increasingly a recluse. Virtually a hermit. From all accounts, she never even went into the garden. Although I'm not Sherlock Holmes," I modestly asserted, "I can't believe she would have gone anywhere near Willow Tree Lane."

Tom frowningly said: "But the police are of the opinion that she was killed in Willow Tree Lane."

Daringly making use of a true fact, I retorted: "The police, my dear Watson, are wrong. The woman was obviously killed in her bungalow. The police need to consult with Sir Henry more closely. He would share my view, I'm sure."

Still frowning, Tom said: "It's certainly true that Sir Henry is being regarded as a bit of a nuisance by the police …"

Loftily: "I should have thought that chap Brockadill, at least, would have more sense."

"Brockadill, James, is not completely his own master. But I must warn you. The prosecution-barrister has been quick to pin his ambitions to Brockadill's coat-tails. Together, they will turn you into mincemeat."

"Tom," I had to complain, "this is the second time you've mentioned mincemeat. It's not a nice word to use. Please desist."

"Mincemeat," he defiantly cried; and, to our lovely barrister he said (and very much through clenched teeth): "Our client must never himself give evidence at any stage in future proceedings."

This being exactly what I wanted (being too squeamish to lie on oath), I pretended to throw in the towel philosophically. I patted him on the shoulder and said: "It's all right, Tom. I agree. Anything to avoid upsetting you, but let's leave mincemeat out of it."

Our young lady-barrister was looking a little wide-eyed after these exchanges, but, on the whole, she was maintaining an air of calm neutrality. She looked at her watch and began gathering up the documents.

"Mr Crackery," she said, "it's nearly time for the hearing. Have you any final instructions?"

"Yes, madam. I shall occasionally send you a note from my command-post."

"Command-post?"

"In other words, the dock. I've already stood there, of course. It was at many a disgracefully biased bail-hearing. This time, however, people are going to be surprised. You and I, madam, will be turning the tables upon the enemy. So do heed my little notes."

"I will receive them by way of the usher. I presume?"

"You will indeed, madam. And the result will be a big feather in your cap."

Her protective policeman quietly entered. Propitiously good timing, I would say, but it made Tom look even gloomier. This policeman said (whisperingly, but in high reverential tones): "They're back from their lunch, sir."

I was taken out by the policeman and down the passage to the stone steps leading up to the dock. The spiritual sweetheart was of course left with Tom to go a more dignified route. And I heard him say to her: "See what I mean?"

I heard her reply: "Well I do rather."

Striding up those steps, I had with me my folder of notes (not compiled in code but written in a deliberately impenetrable scribble), and my father's fountain-pen and a nice new writing-pad from the East Wildering tuck-shop.

May I also mention that I was wearing my best Irish thornproof tweed?

III

Taking possession of the fixed seat in the dock – within the confines of the quite majestic brass rail – I could see no sign of Miss Holland. No sign of Stephanie either, but plenty of other people were settling down in the public pews.

The barrister whom Tom and called the Greasy Slob was quick to open fire for the enemy – the Prosecution, I should say.

"May it please Your Worships, the prisoner has exercised his legal right to silence. He has refused to help the police in any way whatsoever. I make no comment upon his silence, except to say that it has left gaps in the evidence against him. These gaps mostly concern the second of his two murders – that of Mr Leo Rivinni of Orchard Ash Road. However, the major item of evidence is, as we lawyers say, incontrovertible. It relates directly to the prisoner's lock-bar, used in the killing of Miss Mabel Smith, also of Orchard Ash Road. On that evidence alone, Your Worships, I shall very soon be submitting that you send the prisoner to trial."

He paused to make what sounded like a well-practised legal cough.

"Your Worships have heard formal evidence of arrest. I intend to call only one witness for testimony to that major item of incrimination. It should never be the wish of any counsel to waste the valuable time of those who nobly serve the community as magistrates."

He paused to make another legal cough. His compliment was only cautiously accepted by the three magistrates – two nice-looking middle-aged ladies, one each side of the much older chairman. None of them had been the beak who had repeatedly denied me bail. All were total strangers; being a local man, I was amazed by this. They could have come from Mars.

"My one witness," Mr Greasy Slob went on, "is a forensic scientist of the highest repute. But, before I call for his testimony, I think I should briefly outline the background to these two horrendous murders. And, incidentally, the cruel killing of a faithful household dog. Shocking as all human murders are, I have always regarded cruelty to animals as being utterly beyond the pale."

Murmurs of agreement from the magistrates and quite a few from the audience. And from me, as a matter of fact. I was really very impressed by his attack. He knew his stuff. And, of course, I was still feeling guilty about shooting old Masher. After all, a dog is a dog. But my enemy had already made one big general mistake.

He had revealed his strategy.

"Let him ramble on," I wrote in a note to my spiritual sweetheart. "He will soon be making a slip of the tongue. It will destroy the evidence he is relying upon. Await my next note."

The spiritual sweetheart unfolded the note (taken to her after my signal to the usher) and showed it to poor old Tom. She herself remained calm, but Tom shrugged in despair, a sight that pleased the enemy and his cohorts.

Had I any idea what the slip of the tongue might be?

None whatsoever. I'm not that brainy. But I did know a slip would be forthcoming. Instinct. I'd made enough slips of the tongue myself. I would know it when I heard it, possibly because – as Miss Holland might have said – I had something in common with all greasy slobs. (She would have had a point. I can be very smooth.)

This particular greasy slob went on to demolish my character far more effectively than Miss Holland could have done.

"Until very recently, Your Worships, the prisoner has been very heavily in debt. His shop in Dackley has for years been just limping along. But, riddled with vanity as well as greed, he has always pretended to be a prosperous businessman. In reality, his well-cut suits were secretly purchased from a local charity-shop run by the Quakers."

I was admiring this performance, but I did think he went a little too far in places. Where, I wondered, had he got that last true titbit? It would not have been Miss Holland. (She was in no way as nasty as all that.) Going through my folder, I soon uncovered the likely source. Among various letters which I had received in prison was one from my sister which, unwisely, I hadn't bothered to read.

It said: "Unless you pay me my fair share of the heirloom you sold, namely that painting, I shall soon take such steps as may well surprise you. Also, you took Daddy's pen. It's mine."

I emerged from this distraction to find the Greasy Slob in full flood.

"It was this vanity and greed, Your Worships, which impelled the prisoner to do murder."

He paused dramatically. The phrase "to do murder" was murmuringly repeated all round the court. That old barrister I had all but finished off had been right, hadn't he? This hearing was blatantly a rehearsal for a later trial.

"Your Worships, we still don't yet know where and when the prisoner became acquainted with his two victims. We also don't yet know how he induced them to meet him on that fatal piece of waste-ground. But meet him they did."

Another dramatic pause. One of the two lady-magistrates broke it by piping up: "What for?"

"What for indeed, Marm," said Mr Greasy Slob, as if addressing the Queen. "The full facts, we can be sure, will be elicited by the police by the time the prisoner stands trial. For now, we only need to know that he was secretly negotiating the sale of a valuable family heirloom. His story of having been wheel-clamped was a fabrication from start to finish. As was his additional story – that of having sold the heirloom, a valuable painting – to a passing knocker. He sold that painting to his two victims."

The other lady-magistrate piped up. Eagerly and brightly, she asked: "Are we able to see this painting? Has it been recovered?"

"No, Marm," (this second lady also being addressed as if she were the Queen). "The two victims were professional dealers in a whole variety of both modern and antique goods. The painting was already sold on – possibly to dealers abroad – by the time the prisoner tried to extract more money for it. Not content with the sum he haggled for, he became enraged when he found the painting to be worth far more than he, in his ignorance, had thought. Enraged, Your Worships."

The Chairman: "Enraged? How do you know?"

"From the nature of the terrible injuries inflicted upon the old lady."

Both lady-magistrates shuddered. One said to the Greasy Slob: "And how do you know the painting had been sold on?"

"Because, Your Worship, no trace of it was found at the address of the two murder-victims."

The other lady-magistrate: "And how do you know the painting was so valuable?"

"Because, Your Worship, the two dealers who were murdered paid the prisoner no less than £4000 for it," and this sum was loudly repeated to ensure more audience-murmurings.

"And what was the painting actually of?"

"The true painting, Your Worship, had been painted over, but we can have no idea of its subject or its merit. By now, we can only guess that it's been restored by some secret collector with the money to pay for such venal trophies. In years to come, perhaps, it may well see the light of day. We just don't know. What we do know is that murder was done on account of it."

This preposterous distortion of the facts was fascinating to me but not fruitful. No part of it held the slip of the tongue I was looking out for. Then, like so many surprises in life, the slip came unexpectedly and as the result of a diversion.

The word "murder" was being repeated all round the court, but its dramatic effect was suddenly reduced by another intervention by the Chairman. (As the warder had said, he might be a nice but sad chap – and he was.)

Frowning, he sat back to say: "I need to address Counsel for the Defence. Does she not wish to object to anything that's been said? In my experience of them in this court, barristers are not usually so reticent."

How on earth, I wondered, could she explain? Would she say "I have to obey the dotty instructions given to me by my dotty client" or something of that kind?

Rising politely and calmly, she gave a little gem of a reply. "Sir, I am content to leave all control of my learned friend's fertile imagination to the supervision of the court. Thank you, sir," and she just as politely and calmly sat down.

This reply earned her a perfunctory but pleasant chairman's nod. She had just thrilled me to bits. What a lass, eh? But the Greasy Slob was unabashed. Neither the Chairman nor she had affected his performance. He hadn't even bothered to sit down while she was delivering her gem. He just stood there akimbo, like Henry the Eighth. His back was to me, so I couldn't see his face, but I could guess the look on it. The Chairman, in having a more direct view of the look, seemed inclined to take issue.

"My next remarks," he more drily said, "are for Counsel for the Prosecution. We've had different types of barrister in what they sometimes call this lower court. I've often felt on such occasions that I'm like a wallflower of a girl at a dinner-party. She finds herself being talked across during the whole meal. She is left puzzled by the conversation passing to and fro across her lonely dinner-plate. To save my having to elaborate, will Counsel for the Prosecution tell me whether or not he understands my criticism?"

Still unabashed, the Greasy Slob said: "Your Worship, I have only been trying to outline the background as simply as I can."

"For whose benefit?"

"For yourself, Your Worship, and your companion-justices. Who else?"

"That's what I've been wondering. In future, in this lower court of ours, please stop taking facts for granted – particularly those facts which are unsupported suppositions and little more. You may continue."

"Thank you, Your Worship," said the Greasy Slob, his condescension gigantically unabated – indeed, enhanced.

It was at this point, in the whole of our spinning universe, that he made the slip of the tongue which I knew would set me free.

Here are his exact words. Every one of them was the truth. No unsupported suppositions. (The slip was in just one of the sentences.)

"Your Worships, the lock-bar in question is known as a Kraube and Mendel lock-bar. It belongs to the prisoner. His fingerprints and his alone are on that same lock-bar. That is a fact, Your Worships. I call my witness."

Although I had been awaiting this slip of the tongue, I nearly swooned when I heard it. I felt a thrill at the back of my neck which sped up and down my whole spine. I suppose it must be very like the thrill of discovery enjoyed by people of accomplishment – poets and explorers, people like that. (I had something a bit like it when I scored three runs at cricket. Almost a boundary.) But let me tell you, this wasn't entirely a thrill of triumph. It also included the emphatic realisation that I would have been cooked if I hadn't heard this slip. In a full and later trial at the Crown Court, most if not all the unsupported suppositions would be ingeniously consolidated. (Instinct told me so.)

Everything now depended upon just one sentence which the Greasy Slob might never have uttered. Here it is (if you didn't twig):

"His fingerprints and his alone are on that same lock-bar."

I was unable to grasp the implication of this sentence with any clarity, but I did understand its importance – and not least because I was imagining Miss Glertish whispering encouragingly in my ear. ("Don't worry, sir, if you dunno what them words real signify. Give it time and the penny will drop. Meanwhile, you just write another note to that nice girl. She'll do the rest. She's a lot brighter than you, sir. Pardon me as says it.")

Shakily, I wrote the note and signalled to the usher. I had written: "The enemy has now made the slip which will destroy him. But do not ask for an adjournment to discuss it. Let him run on. Await my next note."

Being up front in facing the three more highly-mounted magistrates, my little defence-team had their backs to me. For one ghastly moment after unfolding the note, my heaven-sent saviour (as I now saw her) tried to show the note to Tom. Had she succeeded, he would have requested an adjournment and demanded that I should explain fully. That would have been the end. I couldn't have explained fully. I was still feeling my way. Fortunately, Tom's head was bowed and turned aside. His eyes appeared to be screwed shut in some sort of agony. He was probably mumbling the word "mincemeat!" several times over.

The heaven-sent saviour turned in her pew to look at me in the dock behind her. Her face was expressionless and somewhat clinical I would have to say. But she gave me an almost imperceptible nod. I'm sure no one else saw this nod. They were all too busily anticipating my surrender.

Although I was unable to grasp the full meaning of the slip which the Greasy Slob had made, I paid the keenest attention to his witness.

He looked impossibly young, rather like a brainy choir-boy. He recited his qualifications modestly, but they were horribly impressive. At this point, I must admit, I did suffer a more than a few qualms.

This recital over, he was asked by the Greasy Slob: "What was the first call made upon your time and skill following the prisoner's arrest?"

"I arrived in Dackley solely to examine the prisoner's old but well-conditioned Honda Civic."

"What was the reason for the examination?"

"At the behest of the police, I was ascertaining if any of the tools or other articles in the vehicle might have been used as a murder-weapon."

"How, sir, would you summarise the overall condition of the prisoner's vehicle?"

"As forensically negative."

"I have here, sir, your conscientious inventory of the vehicle's contents. Again, how would you describe their forensic significance?"

"Again, in the same terms. I found all and every item to be of no forensic significance. And that includes the steering-wheel lock-bar."

The Greasy Slob looked up at the ceiling to ask (as if only casually interested): "How many other lock-bars were you asked to examine?"

The answer came pat: "Just one other – a second lock-bar. Ostensibly, it was identical and was found in the prisoner's garden-shed. Hidden."

"And what is this," asked Mr Greasy Slob, magically producing a police-photograph of my poor old garden-shed.

The usher handed the photograph to the choir-boy, who confirmed: "It's the shed where I later conducted a further examination," and he rattled off date, time and place. (These extra details were made as metrically exact as possible, I could only presume, to make his examination sound not only scientific but endorsed by God.)

Openly oozing with self-confidence, the Greasy Slob actually snapped his fingers.

A uniformed constable stood up and opened an enormous steel security-box on a side-table. From it, he took out an elongated object. It was inside a transparent plastic sleeve. What was it? Need I tell you?

My lock-bar.

"And far from forensically negative," said the Greasy Slob. "We can see that without even having to take it from its sleeve, Your Worships. This, Your Worships, is the only exhibit you need for this hearing. You can inspect it for yourselves in a moment," and to his witness he said: "Please take it from the constable and identify it."

With the magistrates still passing my garden-shed from hand to hand (and it looked very nice with the creeper all over the roof and now in bloom), the witness began his slick identification of the lock-bar almost before the constable had put it into his hands.

"It is a vehicle lock-bar, like the other, manufactured in Germany by Kraube and Mendel and imported through Antwerp."

"And what," said the Greasy Slob, again coyly addressing the ceiling, "is its normal and legitimate purpose?"

"Security, like all lock-bars. This particular type enforces a deterrent rigidity to the steering-wheel, but it's becoming old-fashioned. Automotive technology always moves on. Only a belt-and-braces mentality would cling to this outmoded form of car-security."

Frankly, I had never known the name of the manufacturer or anything else about the wretched thing; and the details, so eagerly rattled off, even seemed to tire the Greasy Slob himself. (Or perhaps he feared being upstaged?) He waved down the details and asked: "Who was in overall charge of the laboratory-analysis?"

"Our team-leader, basically, but with the deputised attendance of myself and other experts. Our areas of expertise all overlap."

"And are you in a high enough position of authority to speak for your entire team?"

"For the purposes of this hearing in this lower court I am indeed. I am senior deputy. We're a very busy team. Each of our experts only need to attend in person at the proper trial. This is in no way an attempt to short-cut the proper presentation of forensic evidence. Have I made that quite clear?"

What a pompous ass! He was looking in the direction of my spiritual sweetheart as he uttered those words. Since I could only see the back of her head, I couldn't see how she reacted to them. The Chairman, however, reacted to them by sitting bolt upright. He was very riled.

He said: "And have I, too, made something quite clear? I quite thought I had. This is certainly a preliminary court for this afternoon's order of business. It is not a lower court in the pejorative sense which Prosecution Counsel and this witness infer from their tone of voice."

"I apologise unreservedly," said the Greasy Slob, blandly and without repentance.

"Also," added the Chairman. "I think I speak for my colleagues when I say that we've been Worshipped quite enough. We are not here to be mocked. I remind you both. This is a court of law. We can cite for contempt."

"I understand and respect your wishes," said the Greasy Slob, even more blandly.

"As indeed do I," said his witness, "but may I just explain, Your Worship? I was trying to be helpful by dropping a hint to Defence Counsel. Pedantic objections waste a lot of time."

Ignoring this explanation, the Chairman said to the Greasy Slob: "Have you any further questions for your witness? If so, continue."

One of the ladies seemed to whisper approval to the Chairman (possibly the words "needs to be said") and I, naturally, was hoping all this baiting of the magistrates would work in my favour.

"I only need to be brief," declared the unchastened counsel and re-addressed the choir-boy in the witness-box. "What is the technical function of the transparent wrapper in which the lock-bar is enclosed?"

"To preserve, as scientifically as possible, the dried-out encrustations which, for a future jury, will indicate the ferocity of the blows repeatedly struck."

"Struck upon what?"

"Mostly upon the face of the deceased female-victim. You have the medical reports."

"Was the exhibit you are holding found to belong to any particular person?"

"It was, sir. And easily verifiable. Clear fingerprints were found upon the outer shaft which, in turn, were found to belong to the prisoner."

"Is there any doubt?"

"In the opinion of our print-experts, none. You have their report. It is logical to assume, therefore, that ownership of this lock-bar can be directly ascribed to the prisoner."

"Fingerprints come in for a bit of criticism these days. Is there any room for hair-splitting concerning these particular prints?"

To everyone's surprise (including me), it was my spiritual sweetheart's turn to rise and interrupt. Politely and clearly, she said: "We the defence accept the fingerprints. We also accept that lock-bar as property of the defendant."

In the space of just one second, I feared she was letting me down. Why had she chosen to ignore what I had clearly told her? Not my lock-bar, I had said. Did she, perhaps, have some lawyer's trick up her sleeve? I decided to remain content with this answer. (You could, I suppose, say that I had no other option.)

At the end of that fleeting second – and it is in such a second that empires can be lost or won – that she gave me a backward glance before sitting down. No one, I'm sure, saw her give me that glance. No one, I'm also sure, saw her give me that almost imperceptible nod which she had given me before. (It was a nod to treasure for the rest of my life.)

I began writing her a final note (with Daddy's fountain-pen) for dispatch by way of the usher.

"Question this witness about the two lock-bars," I wrote, "and then demand a side-by-side comparison in open court."

Where did I get the inspiration and the strength to write this note? It was partly from the mutual glance we had shared and partly from the thought of Miss Asti Glertish. (I could still feel her hovering presence.)

Meanwhile, and in the following vital moments, everyone (including the Chairman) thought my spiritual sweetheart was ready to throw in the towel on my behalf. The Greasy Slob and his cohorts watched the usher's delivery of the note with complacent delight. After it was unfolded, the Chairman quite tenderly said to its recipient: "Are you ready for us to rule on a submission?"

She rose to say politely: "No, sir. First, I shall wish to cross-examine this witness."

She sat down again and even Tom, who was coming back to life, caught at her arm in puzzled surprise. As for the Greasy Slob, he behaved with cheerful satisfaction. Still on his feet, he re-addressed his witness. Unwisely, I would say, he chose to rub in one last detail.

"You mentioned an identical lock-bar. Remind us, please. Where did you find it?"

"On board the prisoner's Honda Civic in the police impound-yard."

"And what did you conclude when, later, you were asked to inspect the murderous lock-bar you are now holding?"

"As soon as I saw this lock-bar in the shed where the police had discovered it, my conclusion was immediate. That other lock-bar had been bought as a replacement."

"Thank you," said the Greasy Slob. "Please return that murderous lock-bar to the exhibits-officer. Unless, of course, Their Worships would like to have a closer look at it?"

"Their Worships," said the Chairman, more than a little heavily, "would not. It can go back into the security-box."

The usher returned the exhibit to the exhibits-officer, but it didn't go back into the box. It was left to repose on the lid – as if on a public plinth. Several members of the audience started to crane their necks to look, but the Chairman sharply said: "Order, please. This is not the local repertory theatre. Has Prosecuting Counsel finished with this witness?"

"I feel I have very little to add, sir, and I doubt if anyone else has."

The great man sat down.

The Chairman quietly and invitingly said: "Defence Counsel?"

IV

It was only a few seconds later, but, to me, it seemed like a century before my defence-counsel – as I suppose I should now mundanely call her – began her calm and efficient cross-examination.

Her voice was still like thistledown.

"Sir, are you familiar with every type of lock-bar?"

"Not personally," said the Expert, "but, as an expert, I have information-access to all known vehicular types."

"Is the lock-bar we see on open display of good quality?"

"Excellent quality, madam, but no longer manufactured. As I've already said, technology moves on."

"Nevertheless, how easy is it to buy a Kraube and Mendel lock-bar?"

"Not easy, madam, but your client was obviously able to buy a replacement not only successfully but quickly."

"If anyone were to use a lock-bar as a murder-weapon, would that result in much damage to the lock-bar itself?"

"Possibly, madam, but not in this case. The only appreciable damage to be seen would be to the shaft-paintwork – if, that is, we were to wash off the delicate encrustations of blood and mud. The entire lock-bar is made from best quality steel. Very strong."

"So you don't actually know how much damage has been done to the paintwork?"

"It isn't necessary to know. The paint, although of good quality, has signs of wear and tear. This is not a forensic factor."

"And what of the lock-bar you examined in the police impound-yard? Did it, too, show any signs of wear and tear?"

"It did, yes."

"And what did that suggest to you?"

"At the time, it simply suggested a normal usage of the lock-bar."

"After you were subsequently called upon to examine the lock-bar we see on show, what conclusion did you draw from the lock-bar you examined first?"

"As I've already said, madam, I concluded it to be an obvious replacement."

"Despite the fact that it showed normal signs of wear and tear?"

"Madam, have you never heard of emery-paper? It would have been easy for your client," this all-too-knowing witness proclaimed (with perfect truth), "to abrade the paintwork."

"He faked the appearance of wear and tear? Is that what you're saying?"

"I am, yes."

"Have you been able to prove what you're saying?"

"Not yet, no. Until now, the matter hasn't arisen as a forensic factor. But it will be a simple omission to remedy in time for the trial, I do assure you!"

The witness was getting a bit ratty over what he seemed to think was an emerging criticism. He quite glowered at Mr Greasy Slob, who, without bothering to stand, reassuringly said: "Your Worships, the Prosecution doesn't regard this matter as an omission. We only need the police to discover where the second lock-bar was bought. But I thank my young learned friend for helping us to clarify this minor legality."

In no way put out by the interruption, the young learned friend addressed the witness even more pleasantly. She said: "I don't myself drive a car," and I thought: "Oh, the poor girl! Obviously can't afford it. I'll buy her one, damn it."

"I therefore don't know much," she went on, "about Kraube and Mendel products. As an expert, sir, will you help me out? You spoke, earlier, of the two lock-bars being ostensibly the same. What exactly did you mean by the word ostensibly?"

"The word simply means that both lock-bars appear to be the same but are not – not, that is, to the eye of the trained observer."

"What is the main difference between the two lock-bars in question?"

"For one thing, the key."

"So the lock-bar has a key, does it?"

"Of course it has a key! How else could it be securely fixed to the steering-wheel? A key to a lock-bar of this type is exclusive. It won't fit any lock-bar other than the one it's designed for."

"Thank you, sir," and she looked briefly at a document in her hand. "Why isn't the key to the so-called murder-weapon listed among the exhibits?"

"Because," he said, getting rather testy again, "it hasn't been found."

"And why is that?"

"Because your client must have disposed of it too cleverly for the police to find."

For a moment, my defence-counsel seemed to be a bit stumped – or was pretending to be. As for me, I knew damn well the fellow was dead right. I had chucked the key out of the open casement at the multi-storey. (I'm not expecting you to remember this detail, but I remembered it only too well – and was wishing I'd been as clever as this fellow seemed to think. The key could easily have been found and handed in. The town-river would have been a better choice.)

No sooner did I have this thought than this wretched witness sourly added: "He very probably threw the key in the river which I understand runs through this town. But the absence of the key in no way lessens the weight of the evidence. You will gain no advantage for your client by harping on about it."

Rather like the sound of a woodpecker, the Chairman rapped on his rostrum. He sternly said: "Witness will confine himself to answering Counsel's questions."

My defence-counsel politely sat down at this intervention and Mr Greasy Slob stood up. He said: "I apologise, Your Worship, for my witness. But he is only trying to help this obviously inexperienced and very young recruit to my arduous profession. Her questions are very much beside the point."

"I note your objection. I don't agree it," said the Chairman. "Your witness will heed my warning and defence-counsel will continue."

Still grandly unrepentant, Mr Greasy Slob sat down and my defence-counsel stood up to continue calmly and politely.

"Sir, what has happened to the second key?"

"What second key? What are you talking about?"

"I am referring, sir, to the separate lock-bar which you, sir, have described as a replacement lock-bar. Surely there's a key to that separate lock-bar?"

"Of course there is!"

"Then why have you not listed it on the inventory you made of my client's motor-car?"

With renewed exasperation: "Because, madam, the car and its contents were found, by me, to be forensically negative. We do not waste time and money on reporting upon items of no forensic value."

"When you were called upon to inspect the forensically negative motor-car, was the so-called replacement lock-bar in its proper place?"

"What proper place?"

"In other words, was the lock-bar attached to the steering-wheel and locked in position?"

"No it was not. The police had taken the lock-bar off – at the hotel where your client was arrested. They then drove the car to the impound-yard."

"And why didn't the police re-attach the lock-bar when they impounded the car?"

"Because, madam, there was no need. The impound-yard is a perfectly secure location. I left the lock-bar where I found it – on the back seat."

"But was the key to it available to you?"

"Of course – along with the rest of your client's car-keys. It was on a key-ring with the ignition-key and the key to your client's garage. The ignition-key, however, was on a separate slip-ring – to facilitate its convenient removal for starting the car."

"And the key to this so-called replacement lock-bar? Did you check that it fitted the so-called replacement lock-bar?"

"Of course I did. At the risk of being reprimanded yet again, may I make clear that no possible confusion can exist between these two lock-bars. May I also add that my inspections are always thoroughly motorological."

That's what he said – thoroughly motorological. I tried repeating these two words to myself, in the dock, but I failed. The two lady-magistrates, I noticed, were trying out the same tongue-twister. Like me, they failed. But the Chairman was becoming as stern-looking as my old headmaster. I began shuffling through my folder of notes, feeling as guilty as a schoolboy in chapel with an ill-concealed copy of the Beano.

My defence-counsel changed tack, slightly but tellingly.

"Sir," she said to the undeflated witness, "I have here your report upon the lock-bar we see on public display. Why does the lock-bar have a mixture of both blood and mud upon it?"

"Until your client reveals what actually happened, madam, we can only make an educated guess in accounting for the mud. Delicate as the accretions are, we can only surmise that he dropped the lock-bar in the murder-location. Or possibly he laid it down while attending to the task of covering the bodies – including the body of the dog – with old ferns and fallen branches. We just don't know. But of one thing we can be certain. He took that lock-bar with him when he fled the scene. Possibly in his Honda Civic. Possibly not."

"Sir, did you find any trace of related residues in my client's Honda Civic?"

"No," he snapped. "I did not. He would no doubt have cleaned the car. Even an expert can be deceived by superficial cleaning. But I promise you this: the Prosecution shall be notified. If requested, I shall re-inspect the Honda Civic. If there are residues, I shall find them. Do you hear me? I shall find them!"

My defence-counsel was hotting up this witness very effectively, it seemed to me; and Mr Greasy Slob, although still sprawling in his pew, at last seemed to sense a hint of danger to his case. Without rising, he said: "We the Prosecution will undoubtedly request a re-inspection of the Honda Civic. Once again I must thank my young learned friend for helping to clarify this particular matter."

It was at this point that I stupidly dropped my folder. All my private papers wafted about all over the floor of the dock. The policeman guarding me picked them up for me.

"Order, please," said the Chairman, giving me a cold stare. In no way was I becoming his favourite, but I could see that he was looking with favour upon my counsel.

"Do please continue," he told her.

Without trading upon the approval she was getting from the Bench, she calmly continued the hotting-up.

"Sir, wouldn't it have been easy for my client to clean the lock-bar if he had used it as a murder-weapon?"

"Superficially, yes. Very easy. The dried-out encrustations are fragile. He could have rubbed them away with his pocket-handkerchief."

"And he could have gone on using the lock-bar for normal reasons?"

"Of course, madam."

"Then why, sir, would he choose to hide it in his garden-shed and throw away the key – and then go off and buy a new lock-bar, which, according to your testimony, is hard to come by?"

"Madam, I am not a forensic psychiatrist. But I can tell you this much. People who do murder are often in a state of panic. They can often hide a weapon – such as a bloodstained knife – and forget all about it in a fit of guilty absent-mindedness. I have read the draft of the psychological profile of your client. I suggest you study it once you have the final copy."

"Thank you for your advice, sir. You're being very helpful," and my defence-counsel may have given this chap a slightly alluring smile. (I still couldn't see much of her face, but he seemed to relax a little – not knowing, perhaps, that an alluring smile means exactly that. He was probably being lured. As I've said before, I am not a complete greenhorn. Even the most angelic women are women.)

She now went on to fulfil my written instruction ("demand a side-by-side comparison in open court") but very much in her own way.

"Sir, why is the so-called replacement lock-bar not on show?"

"Not on show? Whatever do you mean?"

"Why hasn't it been included in the list of exhibits – and why hasn't it been presented at this hearing?"

"Madam," said the re-stiffening witness, "I am not the prosecuting authority. I decide neither the order of exhibits nor their priority."

"Nevertheless, sir, you have testified – under oath – that my client bought a replacement lock-bar. This assumption is now a part of the Prosecution's case. Don't you agree, therefore, that any such replacement should be presented at this hearing?"

Mr Greasy Slob suddenly became angry. He leapt to his feet to say: "Your Worships, my young learned friend is badgering this witness. I strongly object to her uncouth behaviour. Her questions are becoming more and more futile – a time-wasting tactic which should no longer be tolerated."

His previous baiting of the magistrates now began to yield fruit – for me.

"On the contrary," said the Chairman, "I think defence-counsel has made a valid legal point. What does our learned clerk say?"

Our learned clerk was an oldish cove sitting at a humble table below (and in front of) the magnificently higher Bench. He had been scribbling away all through the goings-on – not with a quill pen, to be sure, but certainly a dipping-pen. His table actually had an inkpot-hole in one corner, just like the schoolroom-desk of my earlier childhood. (This little detail comforted me no end.)

He looked over the top of his glasses at Mr Greasy Slob and said: "It may seem to be an immaterial formality, but no evidence should ever be taken for granted. It's rather careless to assume that evidence can be deposed in this court but not presented – irrespective of whether it is to be presented at Crown Court or not. The other lock-bar is part of the accusation. It should have been brought in."

"I stand corrected," said Mr Greasy Slob, and he sat down with a magnanimous wave. From his sitting-position, he added: "What do we do now? Waste more time by having an adjournment? I for one have an extremely busy schedule."

"Unlike we more idle legal officials," said the Chairman. Even more caustically but with a vague gaze all round his court, he added: "Are we able to avoid an adjournment? We have to save this gentleman's valuable time – and I don't entirely refer to Prosecuting-Counsel. The gentleman in the dock, it seems to me, should also not be kept waiting too long for our decision."

What a nice thing to say! But I was still in too much of a nervy state to be pleased. All army-commanders know how easily a battle can be lost (and I don't just mean Napoleon). I still didn't know what instinct was guiding me. I was still "feeling my way" or, as Miss Holland would have put it, "muddling through." I hadn't the slightest idea of what would happen next.

What did happen next was, for me, another little surprise.

"Sir," said a voice (as if out of nowhere), "I rise to make an informal suggestion. May I continue?"

It was Brockadill, of all people; he had been sitting unobtrusively in the rear pews, so unobtrusively that I hadn't noticed him. He was, in fact, within spitting distance of the dock.

The Chairman: "Are you that new detective-superintendent from London? Brockadill, is it?"

"Yes, sir. I am the officer in charge of the investigation. Although I've not testified today, my sergeant has – in giving evidence of arrest – and he is still therefore under oath. Might I suggest that he and the exhibits-officer go to the impound-yard and fetch the second lock-bar? The impound-yard is all part of these premises. There is absolutely no need for these difficulties," and he sat down looking fairly tight-lipped (and not giving me so much as a glance).

His sergeant was sitting beside him but I hadn't noticed him either (not even when he gave evidence of arrest), possibly because he was not in uniform and seemed so different.

A sweet little palaver followed. The exhibits-officer objected to being ordered to go with the sergeant.

"Beg pardon, sir," he said to the Chairman, "but I can't leave this security-box unattended."

"No one is going to run off with it," said the Chairman. "So do as the court orders. Put that revolting object back inside the box, close the box and go with the sergeant. Fetch the second lock-bar with no more delay."

"And bring the car-keys," said the clerk, "to avoid any possibility of further muddle."

The de-uniformed sergeant and the uniformed exhibits-officer went out together, both looking very serious. The clerk had a question for Mr Greasy Slob and made it sound like a reproof.

"Will the Prosecution wish the court to attest the car-keys and the other lock-bar? As official exhibits?"

"Oh, certainly," cried Mr Greasy Slob, all joviality again, and again not even bothering to rise. "Once more I must thank my young learned friend for assisting us. Where would we be without the younger generation?"

His joviality earned him a sterner reproof from the Chairman. "Prosecuting-Counsel please note. This matter is not a matter for jokes. Two people are dead and a man's life-long liberty is at stake."

"I apologise unreservedly, Your Worship."

"And so you should. Does defence-counsel wish to continue questioning this witness while we wait?"

"Thank you, sir, yes," said my defence-counsel, and she rose to re-address the witness who, by now, had adopted an air of patience. "Tell me, please. What other dissimilarities are there between two or more Kraube and Mendel lock-bars?"

To everyone's surprise (even Mr Greasy Slob), the po-faced witness succumbed to a fit of laughter. He could hardly get his words out.

"Apart from slight differences in the shade of paint – depending on the batch-system of manufacture – each Kraube and Mendel lock-bar has its own serial number."

It was the two words "serial number" which really had him doubled up. He had to wipe away tears of mirth with his handkerchief and while gasping for breath.

In the quite stunned silence of everyone else, this highly reputable forensic scientist managed to get control of himself. As for me, I was only too clearly remembering how Miss Holland had noticed the slight difference in colour of the new lock-bar. (It was when I gave her that lift in the Honda back to her flat, after that notorious luncheon-party.) And the existence of a serial number was a new worry for me. How would my defence-counsel cope with this possibly fatal detail?

She was the first to recover from the performance. Leafing neatly through all of her papers, she said: "Sir, there is no mention, in this list of yours, of a serial number for the so-called murder-weapon. Why is that?"

Still verging upon more mirth, he managed to say: "Because, madam, differentiation between the two numbers was not a relevant factor at the time of my first examination."

"But the serial number is surely a relevant factor now?"

"Now we know we have two separate lock-bars to identify, then yes. It's not, of course, a number that any ordinary motorist or driver would notice. It's not only small but very much occluded by the paint-dip process."

"But easy to see, surely, if you apply a little solution of paint-remover?"

In a shocked tone, he said: "Good heavens, madam, we wouldn't use paint-remover! We have special equipment for detecting occluded numbers which, in fact, are quite common in car-crimes. But it all adds to the expense, of course, an expense we try to avoid if, as I have said, any such matter is irrelevant – or seems so."

"Are you telling me, sir, that you ignored the serial number on the so-called murder-weapon?"

"I am not telling you that I ignored it. I am telling you, madam, that I didn't need to look for it – and, furthermore, it was not only occluded by the paint-dip process but occluded by encrustation of blood and mud. Those dried-out substances are very fragile. To have exposed them to paint-removers and the like would have severely damaged their evidential impact."

His professional indignation seemed to have completely overcome his tendency to splutter. But no, the splutter was still there – ready to be re-awakened by the next question.

"So you don't know the serial number which you say is to be found on the so-called murder-weapon?"

"No, madam. But I do know the serial number on the replacement lock-bar!"

Loudly, he spluttered into laughter again, positively choking with it. He was actually holding his sides like a laughing washerwoman. Some laughter, as we all know, is infectious. This was not. He was entirely on his own with it.

"I beg the court's pardon," he said, again managing to control himself a little, "but it really is too funny for words."

Everyone else being stunned afresh, except my defence-counsel, she alone had the presence of mind to seize the initiative and move on.

"What, sir, is too funny for words?"

"For the reasons I've explained, I didn't officially record the serial number of your client's second lock-bar. But," and he began to titter, "I do happen to remember its serial number. It was relatively easy to discern through my strongest glass. As you will be able to see when those two officers get back, it's a most amusing number to remember," and he was almost overcome with mirth yet again.

Calmly patient: "What is it, sir, that so amused you about the second lock-bar's serial number?"

"It's a most humorous coincidence, madam. I'm very interested, you see, in Egyptology. A hobby of mine. It's a bit irrelevant to this hearing, but would you like me to explain?"

"Please do, sir."

"The figures of the serial-number are followed on this make of lock-bar by two batch-letters. These happen to be B and C. This makes the whole serial-number look like 2141BC, which, as you may know, is the datum-date for the Great Pyramid at Giza. The very idea of the Pharaoh Khufu driving around in a Honda Civic – and with a lock-bar of that date – is something I find amusingly incongruous. Quite a joke."

Never before had I seen such dumbfounded blankness as I saw on the faces of those three magistrates. Everyone else in the courtroom, including my young defence-counsel, looked much the same. None of even my own worst jokes had ever fallen this flat.

After a few seconds, one of the two lady-magistrates said to the Chairman: "What's a datum-date? What does it mean?"

The Chairman was about to reply but was diverted by the return of Brockadill's sergeant and the Exhibits Officer. Both were looking deeply worried.

"Beg pardon, sir," said the Exhibits Officer from the doorway, "we has the car-keys for the right vehicle," and he held them up, giving them a little tinkly shake, "but we hasn't got the lock-bar. It wasn't where it was supposed to be – on the back seat. It were gone, sir."

Giving way to irritation for the first time, the Chairman said: "Then where the devil is it?"

It was my very own defence-counsel who brought the court to order by saying to the Chairman: "I suggest, sir, that we look for it in the security-box."

"Young lady," he said, "you're getting confused. There's only one lock-bar in that security-box – the murder weapon."

"Exactly, sir, or, as I would describe it, the so-called murder-weapon. I suggest this witness re-inspects it – and under oath, let him remember."

This was a development which I, for one, was only dimly able to comprehend. It was like being present at one of those incredible stage-illusions. Everyone was open-mouthed, including me. The only one who wasn't was my clever conjurer of a counsel.

She prevailed. The box was opened and the lock-bar was put back into the hands of the brainy choir-boy.

"In what section of the lock-bar," she asked him, "is the serial-number?"

Pointing it out: "Here, madam, adjacent to the specialised locking-mechanism."

"Why is the dried-out encrustation particularly thick at that section?"

"Presumably," he snootily said, "because it's where the heavy end of the lock-bar impacted upon the victim's face."

"With hindsight, don't you think it would have been wise to uncover a little bit of the encrustation? Enough to reveal the serial-number?"

"What are you implying? That I smeared occlusive matter over the serial-number?"

"I'm not implying that you, sir, did any such thing. With the court's permission, I suggest you use your handkerchief and wipe away enough to enable you to check the serial-number. Better late than never, eh?"

He rubbed away with a handkerchief already well-dampened with his previous tears of mirth. I shut my eyes. For me, this was an unbearable moment. What if my vague instincts had failed me?

I opened my eyes to see the witness looking a lot more worried than me.

"It's not possible," he wailed. "It's the same date as the other lock-bar – serial-number, I mean. How can this be possible?"

"In other words," said my wonderfully calm and brilliant defender, "it's 2141BC – the same as a date famous in Egyptology. Do you confirm that or not?"

He croaked: "I've no alternative, have I?"

"And that so-called murder-weapon you're holding," she magnificently said, "is no such thing. It's simply my client's one and only lock-bar. But tampered with! Yes?"

There was no "sensation in court" as the phrase has it – just a pin-drop silence. Icily, the Chairman said: "Does the Prosecuting Counsel have any explanation to offer us?"

Mr Greasy Slob leapt to his feet, seething with fury.

"My young learned friend is making a totally outrageous accusation. Is she suggesting deliberate fabrication? By the Prosecution? In collusion with the police? The lock-bar that should have been in the Honda Civic, up in the impound yard, has been temporarily mislaid. That's all there is to it. There can be no other explanation. This prisoner must be sent for trial in the proper court. I demand it."

When one reads in the Daily Telegraph of a prosecution-case "collapsing", there can be no better word for describing this particular case. Mr Greasy Slob literally collapsed. Head in hands, he was wildly clawing at his hair. I could understand him. I, too, was trying to reconcile the facts (as known to me privately).

It was only now that I fully began to realise why Miss Glertish could NOT have left my abandoned lock-bar in my garden-shed.

"Probably chucked it in the river," I was thinking. "Dare I also think that she never, in fact, bashed in her step-mother's face? But why the devil would she say she had done such a revolting thing? I'd like to think she didn't, but how can I ever be sure?"

My head was aching with the strain of trying to keep this self-questioning within bounds. Like Mr Greasy Slob, I was in no fit state to follow the last part of the hearing. Feeling as if I were on another plane of existence, I was just about conscious of my young defender saying: "Let us apply one final test. To quote the Prosecution's own witness, the key to every Kraube and Mendel lock-bar is exclusive. One key to such a lock-bar won't fit another. Bring forward, please, my client's car-keys …"

Needless to say, the lock-bar key nestling amid my other car-keys fitted the lock-bar. For me, what a relief! (Only a bit of puffing and blowing away of particles, out of the key-hole, delayed this denouement.) The witness had no option. He had to say: "There is but one lock-bar to this case. It is this lock-bar, the very one I first examined. I found it to be forensically negative. I now find it to have been cunningly tampered with."

Like my old headmaster in Assembly, the Chairman grimly addressed the back of the courtroom: "Is that senior police-officer still present?"

Brockadill stood up, quietly but white-faced with anger. "I am, sir, and I shall insist on an enquiry at the highest level. I shall say no more at present, except to request that Mr Cracker's lock-bar be kept in forensic custody. Mr Crackery, I mean."

I was just about ready to keel over in a faint when, distantly, I heard my lovely young defender say to the Chairman: "Sir, I now submit that my client has no case to answer."

"And as far as I'm concerned," declared the wonderfully British Chairman, "Mr Crackery leaves this courtroom without a stain on his character."

Knowing this to be not quite the truth, I staggered down the steps into the bowels of the building (to the holding-cell) to collect my sack of belongings. The dock-officer (or whatever he was called) had to assist me.

"Someone's for the high-jump over this," he said, grinning happily. "By the way, sir," and he gave me an unopened letter, "this was something we missed when we was picking up all them papers you spilt. Only just seen it."

"Thank you, officer," I said, hardly bothering to look at the envelope, "it's just another of my sister's letters."

I shoved it in my jacket-pocket. It was, like her other letter, addressed to me at the cottage but sent on by Stephanie (with other letters) in a big brown envelope. In prison, I had not even bothered to open it because, even there, I really did think it was from my sister. All letters (even to unconvicted prisoners) were supposed to be opened by the authorities, but the occasional one did get overlooked. This, I simply thought, was just an unwelcome example.

I was far more interested in getting out of that building with the hamper poor old Tom had brought me. Although I'd had an excellent breakfast on the way from East Wildering Prison, I was now suddenly and ravenously hungry.

Also, I have to admit, I wanted to get away before my young lady-counsel had time to question me further. I feared her skills. Having seen her in action, I feared she would have the truth out of me in a jiffy. Ungallant as it may seem, I wanted to put as much mileage between us as I possibly could – until I had recovered at least some of my wicked abilities.

I was too exhausted to get any further than the public open space in Providence Square. But I felt reasonably safe there. Sunny and quiet.

Sinking down on one of the empty cast-iron seats, I was soon chewing on a cold but scrumptious roast-chicken leg.

"Ha," I said, as soon as I had the energy to say it – my usual expression of triumph.

Frankly, I'd like to finish my account of that exhausting day with that expression of triumph; but I must add an embarrassing epilogue.

ELEVEN

Closing Ranks

I had unscrewed the Thermos and was having coffee when, for no apparent reason at all, I thought of the unopened letter in my jacket-pocket.

"I wonder," I said aloud, and rather nastily, "what else the old trout had to say? Daddy wanted ME to have his fountain-pen."

Only when I looked more closely at the envelope did I realise the truth. This letter was not from my sister. I had been misled by the fact that my handwriting is fairly similar to my sister's. Also, we both used Royal Blue ink (as had our nice old dad).

I don't know if you will remember that far back, but this was the envelope I had written – in my little office – at the request of Miss Asti Glertish. (She had even made me put the stamp on.)

"By God," I cried, ripping open the envelope (and nearly upsetting the coffee all over my gentlemanly tweed-trousers).

Inside, I found just a small and grubby postcard in black-and-white of a London scene. Although looking old, it was unused except for two words written in the message-space. I recognised them as the fist of Miss Glertish – two words in clumsy capitals.

"NOT ME."

For a few moments, I could only think of how she used to say "Not me!" when emphasising a denial. She would stab at her own chest with a cocked thumb – sometimes quite savagely – as an accompaniment to those two words. This was an overbearingly ripe memory (although there were worse).

"James," I heard myself croaking aloud, "let this be a lesson to you. When in jail, open all of your mail."

But, although I realised these two words had been intended as some sort of message, I simply couldn't think what. My brain had suddenly become, in substance, little better than mashed potato. How often, I was just about able to wonder, do others find themselves victorious but in a state of perplexity? Did it happen to Wellington after Waterloo? Or Field Marshal Montgomery after 1945?

I was helplessly pondering upon these great soldiers when, all of a sudden, a voice in front of me said: "Excuse me, Mr Crackery. Would you like to come over to the car?"

I was being addressed by a man in a bowler-hat (very like my own bowler-hat but, of course, which I was not wearing at this time. I was in my matching tweed cap.) He also had a nicely-rolled umbrella. I took him to be a lawyer from the Prosecutor's office.

"Oh, definitely," I cried, jumping up.

I thought he had come to hand me back my impounded Honda Civic. I followed him across the public grass to where several motor-cars were parked alongside the adjoining pavement. I completely forgot my belongings. I left them on the seat in my eagerness to be re-united. Tom's hamper, too, was left open to the sky.

"Hang on a sec," I said, "this isn't my Honda Civic!"

I had been led towards an extremely swagger saloon – all black and glossy. Was this the Mafia? A uniformed chauffeur – in field-grey, no less – got out. He opened the rear door. He said nothing, but a voice from within the back said: "Get in with me and look slippy."

I took my cap off and got in. I found myself sitting next to the only occupant – a woman I didn't recognise. The chauffeur closed the door but didn't return to his seat; instead, he joined the lawyer chap on the pavement and stood with him at a distance.

I said: "Where are you taking me?"

"Nowhere," said this woman. "I just want a word with you, that's all. Not me means not me. Didn't you get my letter? Why did you have to go and make such a muck of things?"

"Good God," I said, staring at her like Buttercup Joe, "you're Miss Glertish."

"Who else would I be? Still as thick as two mattresses, are you? Let's make it four, shall we? As thick as four mattresses. Either that or you're just plain mad."

Although sometimes reverting, her voice and pronunciation had improved. Her appearance more so. Her hair was no longer like a clump of post-office string. It was smoothly parted in the middle, as in a picture of Miss Charlotte Bronte; and she was as demurely dressed.

She was wearing white cotton gloves. She pulled one off and said: "Like to see my nails? Better, are they not?"

They were still in the process of repair, I would say, but they certainly were no longer the nails of a former tyre-fitter.

"Very much better," I uneasily confirmed, and she severely pulled the glove back on.

Weakly trying to make a little joke, I said: "Who is that fellow outside and why is he wearing my bowler-hat?"

Sternly crushing this little joke, she said: "It's not your hat. It belongs to the bloke wearing it. He's a lawyer."

At least I'd got that bit right, but, naturally, I asked: "Whose lawyer?"

She astounded me by saying: "One of mine, of course. Whose else would it be?"

"You have more than one lawyer?"

"They come with the properties. But he's the one I chose for keeping an eye on yer. I've come to pick him up. He's been in the court, on watch-like. He's been telling me what happened."

Dimly, I began to remember something Tom had muttered before that chap had his heart-attack.

"Well, yes," I said, "I think I remember my solicitor did say a lawyer for the relatives would be attending. It's what they call a watching-brief, I think Tom called it."

"Well, Mr Crackery, you surely didn't expect me to come and watch personally the muck you'd made of things? I have better and more important matters to attend to."

"I'm sure you have," I gabbled. "Am I also right to assume you're among the relatives?"

"I am not among the relatives. I'm the only relative there is."

"You mean you've inherited everything?"

"Every little thing," she harshly whispered.

"But," I tried to persist, "my solicitor did refer to relatives – in the plural."

"That's just the way lawyers talk and that's the way I like it. I don't want no big thing made of all this. I don't want no other people knowing what you knows about me. Got it?"

To be in the back of a luxurious motor-car after being in East Wildering (may I just say) is a contrast most bewildering.

"No I don't get it," I blundered on. "How did you come to inherit everything?"

"Because, although I didn't know it, the old witch adopted me. Her lawyers found the papers under her bed."

"Do you get a title? Are you some sort of marquess or something?"

"Adopted kids can't inherit titles. I wouldn't want it anyway, so don't talk about it. Probate's put in for and that's that."

"She left a will?"

"Also under her bed, yeah," and Miss Glertish uttered a weird kind of sob. "She left everything to me and no one's else. I don't know why, but she did. Like I tells yer, I want total clamp-down on all this. Don't you never forget that." (Some distinct reversions here, eh?)

"How much does that lawyer-fellow of your know?"

"Only as much as was found under her bed – and what he heard in that there trial."

"It wasn't a trial," I was pedantically able to point out. "Only a hearing."

"Whatever it was," she impatiently said, "he tells me you was lucky to escape being stuck away for life."

"And no thanks to you, madam, if I may say so." (I felt a bit miffed all of a sudden.)

She responded fiercely: "Oh, so I'm to blame for your stupidity? I knowed, of course, you'd do something daft the minute I takes me eye off yer. It's why I phoned that landlady who had that stay-place I went to. I phoned her before I went to Brazil. Phoned from London."

"Brazil, you say? Where the nuts come from?"

Crushingly ignoring this little joke (as she had the joke about my bowler-hat), she said: "Brazil is where the old witch had other properties. Pay attention, Mr Crackery. That landlady at the stay-place told me what was all over the town – that you was arrested for murder. I did my best to help yer. I sends you a message in that very envelope of yourn."

"Just two words," I complained. "Why couldn't you have been a bit more explicit?"

"Not me," she almost yelled, "means not me. Anyone with half a brain could understand it. Why, therefore, couldn't you? Or don't you even have half a brain?"

"Actually," I felt I had to say, "I didn't open the envelope until relatively later. Just after the hearing, as a matter of fact. Are you by any chance going to live in Brazil from now on?"

"Never you mind what I do in Brazil. How long did it take you to work out that I didn't hide that lock-bar in your shed?"

Hoping to impress her (and God knows why I wanted to impress her), I said: "Frankly, I made a rather clever deduction. The prosecuting barrister, you see, made a point of proclaiming that my fingerprints – and mine alone – were on the so-called murder-weapon."

"And that told you what, Mr Crackers?"

"I admit, of course, that it took me quite a bit of time to understand the implication."

"It would, yeah."

"Nevertheless, I intuitively knew I was on the right track."

"Because you knew, you mean, that I would not have been wearing gloves?"

"Well, yes," I said, feeling annoyingly deflated.

"Which would have meant," she impatiently said, "that my fingermarks plus yourn would have been on that same lock-bar. If, that is, I had so much as touched it. Which I never did."

"Thank you, madam," I stiffly said, "for scoffing at the way I'm expounding my deduction. Let me finish. Miss Holland, of course, had handled my second lock-bar. It was during a journey to a luncheon-party engagement. But she had been wearing gloves. My fingerprints and mine alone, therefore, meant that lock-bar was not the lock-bar YOU handled. Now please tell me. What did you do with my original lock-bar?"

"Chucked it in the river, of course! Where else?"

"In the river, eh? Good thinking. That, at least, is one more worry resolved. But there are still outstanding considerations. They are already casting, it seems to me, a long and sinister shadow. Someone, Miss Glertish, very definitely smashed your stepmother's face in."

"That's rubbish," she said.

"I beg your pardon?"

"No one smashed her face in – least of all me. You got my message. Not me didn't must mean I didn't hide the lock-bar in yer shed. It meant I didn't bash her face in with it neither."

"But madam," I bleated, "you told me you DID bash her face in. As I understand it, you did so on behalf of your pet-tortoise."

"It's still true about my tortoise. The old witch did smash him up with a hammer. And I did think of doing the same to her. But I couldn't bring myself to do it. I backed off."

"But I've been shown the awful photographs! I didn't study them closely, but I must say they did look as if you'd made use of the lock-bar."

"All I did was to dump her in that mud-pool in them bushes and chuck some dead branches over her. Then I dumps lover-boy and then Ronnie."

"Who is Ronnie? Remind me, please."

"The dog," she cried, and burst into tears. "I did what I did," she moaned, "and she goes and leaves me everything. Will she ever forgive me, do you think?"

She seized me by the wrist and gave me a shake. Most embarrassingly, I then found myself uttering words I couldn't recognise as mine.

"The dead forgive everything. How, otherwise, could they ever hope to rest in peace?"

These words sounded like tosh to me and I didn't know where they came from. But they worked. I can't stand seeing women and children in tears. She left off blubbing fairly quickly, thank God.

But can you believe what happened next?

I could hardly believe it myself. I suddenly found my teeth chattering. I felt horribly cold all over and within myself. Was it some sort of late-summer chill or something? Or some form of delayed after-shock? After all, these had been quite nasty events for everyone.

"Why," I managed to say, with my teeth chattering non-stop, "did you say you'd smashed her face in, when, as you now claim, you did not?"

"You was putting too much blame on yourself. You was feeling too guilty. I was fraid you'd go and blurt everything out to that Miss Holland. I wanted you to think of me as the guilty one."

"Very considerate of you, madam. God, it's cold in this car. More like a refrigerator. What happened to the van you pinched?"

"Oh, that's been dead and gone a long time."

"And is this car yours?"

"It's one of what they call a fleet. Belongs to a haulage-firm the old witch owned. Yes, I suppose it is mine. I've come down from London in it. But let's stick to the point, shall we?"

"Madam, I'm awfully cold. Have you a rug or something I could put round me?"

Ignoring this request, she said: "I got the lawyers to get a private autopsy done." (She pronounced this word "ow-topsy".) "It's been sent in. It turns the case against you inside-out."

"Oh," I shivered, "if only that were true!"

"You needs to see the report. Them first experts was wrong. It was the acid mud-stuff what made the face look squashy and bashed in. That and the branches maybe, but the old witch dies natural. Unfamiliar and sudden exertion."

"What the hell are you talking about?"

"Don't swear, Mr Crackery. I've told you about that before. I won't have no swearing."

"I beg your pardon, madam. Died natural, did you say? What does that actually mean?"

"It means she dies of old age. Probably dies while you was wrestling with her. She was a lot older than she looked. Ninety-six."

"Good God! Really? But what about the dog? Who do they now think shot old Masher?"

"That will all be blamed on Leo. They'll wrap it up nice. You can stop worrying."

I managed to control my shivering, but I still felt horribly cold. I felt I wanted to get in front of a nice log fire as soon as possible. Yet this was still summer!

"Miss Glertish," I said, having completely lost my nerve, "I think you'd better have that money back – the money I've got in the vault at my father's bank. My bank, I mean."

"Don't be daft," she primly said. "What I give, I give. Take it as compensation."

"Compensation for what?"

"For the way you was treated when you called at the bungalow. You was chased by a dog. You was bitten by a dog. I'll get City lawyers to write you a nice posh letter. That will cover you for what you've hidden. Smuggle it into your proper account, but don't rush it. Goodbye, Mr Crackers. I've got to go."

Feeble again: "Got to go, you say? Go where? Back to London? To Brazil?"

"I just need to go and look at the bungalow. I'm having it done up."

Even more feebly: "Are you thinking of living there? Staying there?"

"Blimey, no. I've got a right lush place in Brazil. But my chief finance-lady ought to have a proper home when she's over on our England business. She's a widow, but she's got kids. I don't like the thought of any kids being away from their mum – not even short-time."

She paused a moment, looked closely into my face and added: "Still got a mum, have yer?"

I almost yelped. I said: "What on earth has that got to do with all this?"

"I dunno. I'm just asking if you still has a mother. Is she still alive?"

"I've no idea. She was a lot younger than my father. She left us. Never saw her again. Went off, as I understand it, with a former sweetheart. To Hong Kong, I think it was. It is no longer a matter of any great concern to me or my sister."

"Then what's you looking so worried about?"

"I'm simply wondering, thank you, who it could be who hid my new lock-bar in my garden-shed. And, what's more, tampered with it."

"The answer to that, Mr Crackers, ought to be clear enough even to a brain like yourn."

"Well it's not," I feebly growled.

"The cops, Mr Crackers – the cops. It could only be they."

"That, madam, I refuse to believe. Not of Dackley police. As a child, I once got lost in Dackley. A policeman found me and brought me all the way home on his bicycle. He sat me on the cross-bar, sideways. I was so small, you see."

"Mr Crackers," said Miss Charlotte Bronte, more than a shade impatiently, "find yer mother. Find her before it's too late. Goodbye and for ever. Personally, I don't want to see you again. Can't stand real stupidity. Gets me down."

Miss Bronte must have signalled or waved to her chauffeur. Instantly, he came striding back along the pavement to usher me out, curtly but silently, from the car. The lawyer-chap was close on his heels. Both were equally po-faced. Both, too, had that same look of anxious loyalty for their employer which that nice sergeant had for Brockadill. I almost said, sarcastically: "It's all right. I've shown her every respect," but something made me want to have the last word in another way.

Before I quite got out, I said to this magnificently wealthy illiterate: "Talking of being worried, aren't you worried about Miss Holland? Being in Dackley, you could easily find yourself crossing her path."

The calm reply: "Not a problem. I checked. She's in Toronto. I don't reckon she wants to bother with me. She's going to have twins."

Staggering a bit, I gasped: "How on earth did you find that out? And why have I been left in the dark about this news?"

Both these questions were aloofly unanswered and were destined to be the last-ever words to pass between us. The lawyer (giving me a most suspicious glance) took the seat I had vacated and the chauffeur closed the door. As the car pulled away, another similar car (which I hadn't noticed) followed it; this car, I could only presume, contained more of the entourage (presumably faithful Brazilians).

"Blimey," I mumbled to myself, "I wonder what poor old Sir Henry thinks of all this?"

I was pretending not to be concerned, but, frankly, I had a sort of snapped-off feeling after this female had gone. I have to admit it. I knew I was going to miss Miss Glertish. Yet I also knew that I greatly feared any further confrontation with her. My shivers returned.

Can you believe it? After all I had been through, only two matters suddenly gripped me.

First, I was worried by the fact that I had abandoned old Tom's picnic-hamper. What if someone pinched it? What would Tom say to me then?

Secondly, I was worried that I might be fined £1000 for the relatively new offence of littering. (This was the maximum penalty; before I had gone to prison, everyone had been talking about it. Nowadays, of course, the offence is mostly neglected. Litter everywhere.)

I dashed back between the flower-beds and between the trees. There was public bustle at the periphery, but, in the centre where they once burned witches and hanged felons, all was as I had left it. I tidied up the hamper. I snatched up all my lunch-litter. I bunged every last scrap in the nearest litter-cage, even litter which wasn't mine but which I feared I might be blamed for.

"Oh, so there you are!"

These words, spoken in those thistledown tones, drifted into my mind rather than into my ears. They seemed to come homing down from the blue sky above.

I turned round. Two persons were crossing the grass towards me. With bulging brief-cases.

One person was Tom Grantiscombe. But the other?

The other was my victorious saviour.

She was smiling in a way that went far beyond being merely pleased with herself. It was an outward smile of glowing achievement. It melted all my heart instantly. My cold shivering vanished in a flash.

She added: "Mr Crackery, we've been looking for you everywhere."

I couldn't immediately reply. It was Tom who spoke. And he, I have to tell you, was not smiling in any way at all.

"How DARE you simply walk off," he railed at me, "without even a word of thanks to your counsel! Have you lost all sense of common decency? Have you any IDEA of the sheer chaos you've left behind you?"

I hardly heard him. Never in my life had I felt so serenely stunned by a woman's smile. I actually found myself sinking down on the seat in the presence of this lady – and without so much as politely raising my tweed-cap.

With my eyes still upon her, I heard myself replying to Tom: "But surely, old boy, it's winning that matters most?"

"Winning," he roared. "You call it winning when you begin by giving a head of chambers a heart attack? When you reduce a senior police-officer of Brockadill's character to the depths of depression? When you drive his loyal sergeant into falsifying the main item of evidence?"

"Oh, dear," I said. "It surely wasn't that nice sergeant? I do hope he doesn't get into too much trouble."

"He's already confessed," said Tom quite savagely. "He's under arrest. But don't you worry, Crackery. He'll probably go on the sick-list and be pensioned off. All you've done is to disgrace an honest man. No great harm done."

Despite my concern for the sergeant, I began to feel indignantly puzzled. With my eyes still upon my victorious saviour, I said: "Tom, I can't quite see that I'm to blame for all of these things."

"People like you," he said, bending down almost nose-to-nose, "never do. You were like it at School. You're like it now. Why couldn't you have told us, right from the start, that you knew your lock-bar had been tampered with? Why all the ducking and weaving? I'll tell you why, shall I? You have an inborn desire to create chaos. You goaded Brockadill into arresting you. You goaded his sergeant into a misguided form of support."

Feeling a bit shifty, I uneasily said: "Look here, Tom. Just tell me. Am I finally in the clear or not?"

"Oh, you're in the clear all right! But don't you even remotely understand how your irresponsible behaviour nearly got you prison for life? Don't you yet understand why the hearing kept being delayed? It was because the sergeant was desperately seeking high and low for another lock-bar. You were lucky. He even went to Antwerp. He simply couldn't find one which would match the one he had taken from your Honda Civic."

"Tom, I really do hope they won't be too hard on him. What more can I say?"

Addressing me as if I were still in the Lower Third and he in the Sixth, he said: "There is nothing you can possibly say, you miserable little tick, which can justify the way you've behaved. Had the sergeant found a lock-bar identical to yours, what would have been the result? I'll tell you, shall I? Your counsel would have been made to look a complete fool."

He broke off from this tirade (how else can it be described?) and quite wildly added: "And give me back my picnic-hamper."

He seized it back as if I had stolen it and moved away a few steps, clutching it in addition to his bulgy old brief-case.

My victorious saviour, it seemed to me, was unaffected by Tom's tirade. She was smiling at me (tolerantly, I'd say).

She said: "Mr Crackery, I was only a little confused by your initial instructions. I soon realised your lock-bar had been tampered with."

She sat down beside me in a well-poised way as if we were on a settee in Sir Henry's drawing-room. Her back was sweetly straight and she was half-turned towards me. She looked like the happiest lady in the world.

"Mr Crackery," she added, "I have only one question I'm dying to ask you."

As a result of Tom's perfectly deserved tirade, I instantly decided to do the only gentlemanly thing possible. I would answer her question truthfully, no matter what the consequences. This decision made me a lot prouder of myself. It also gave me a feeling of wonderfully fatalistic serenity.

"Madam," I said, (and yes, I did put my hand on my heart), "it would be an honour for me to answer any question you care to put."

Before she could put any such question, Tom butted in with renewed vigour. (I had hoped he would walk off and leave us together.)

"Quiet," he ordered. "Look at that! Let's get a bit closer and see what's going on."

We followed him over to a tangled flower-bed on the perimeter. With him, we peered through hollyhocks and whatnot at whatever he had seen.

Still encumbered with hamper and brief-case, he said: "I thought so! Not wasted much time, have they?"

Several top-brass police-officers, in full uniform, were coming down the steps from the police-station. They all got into two executive police-cars waiting at the kerb. They drove off. All I really noticed about them was their new-looking leather gloves, but Tom rounded on me as if I were fully accountable.

"Well, Crackery? Do you know where they're going?"

"No idea, old chap."

"They are off to Sir Henry's place for afternoon tea with the relatives. Are you trying to pretend you know nothing about this cover-up?"

"Afternoon tea, did you say?"

"To follow an inspection of the refurbished bungalow. Are you telling me you didn't know the old lady owned half Dackley? She even owned that chunk of land in Willow Tree Lane!"

He was so chokingly angry that I feared he might go the same way as the head of chambers.

"For heaven's sake," I told him, "do simmer down. I can honestly say I know very little of what's been going on. I've been in prison, you see."

He sat down on another of the seats, still clutching hamper and brief-case. He said: "Not in all my professional life have I known the police to re-attach criminal facts to a completely new theory at so great a speed. It takes my breath away. You are at least aware, I suppose, that a new report had been commissioned by the relatives? That it was handed to the Coroner's Officer only this morning?"

I laid my hand on his shoulder, but, before I could say anything soothing, he said: "I can accept that Brazilian experts probably know more about nameless insects than we British. But it's all a little too pat. A nameless insect is now thought to be responsible for Rivinni's death."

"Good Lord," I said. "A nameless insect?"

"He was stung, it is now thought."

"Do they know when?"

"No," snarled Tom. "But it took effect, it would now seem, when he was dumping the old lady's body in Willow Tree Lane. He collapsed and died on top of both the old lady's body and that of the dead dog."

I was genuinely amazed by what Tom was saying. I sat down beside him on the seat, but the victorious saviour seemed to be taking all this in her stride. She seemed happy enough to stand and listen – her head intently angled.

"Am I to understand," I said to Tom, "that Rivinni is now being blamed for that old lady's death?"

"Indirectly, yes …"

"Indirectly or not, old boy, isn't that a bit unsporting? After all, he's in no position to defend himself against your accusations."

"They are not my accusations. They've been cobbled together, in record time, to absolve the police from mistakes made about your rotten lock-bar."

"All the same," I said, feeling genuinely pious about this injustice, "it's unfair to put all the blame on Rivinni. He was a bit on the rough side, I suppose, but I'm fairly sure he wouldn't countenance a death."

"Oh, don't worry yourself," said Tom, more than a little scornfully. "The inheriting relatives have been very generous to his memory. Apart from having him decently disposed of, they have compensated his grandmother for her loss. She resides, it would seem, in Liverpool."

"Good Lord! That's jolly decent, I'd say."

"And I for one," said Tom, "fervently hope their spirit of generosity will never extend to compensating your own utterly unworthy self."

My victorious saviour came to my aid with a cheerfully impartial smile. How lovely! She said to Tom: "But our client was bitten by the dog and chased up a tree. And then put in prison. I think he has a strong case for compensation from more than one source."

I began to mutter something about not wishing to cause any more trouble, but Tom leapt to his feet with his encumbrances.

"You," he told my saviour, "simply don't know this man! He doesn't deserve a penny in compensation! D'you hear me? Not a penny!"

I got up and patted Tom on the back sadly. "Tom, old chap, there's no need to upset yourself. I respect your views. I'm a changed man. I soon will be, I mean. Where's that prison-sack of mine? I may well need it."

I had left it on the other public seat. Feeling like Sydney Carton, I went over to retrieve it and I returned to my advisers.

"James," said Tom suspiciously, "what new game are you playing now?"

"No game, Tom, I said, feeling sadly but greatly ennobled, "and you will soon become aware of my true measure. Madam," I said to my young lady-saviour, "what is the question you were dying to ask me?"

But she was looking preoccupied and began fishing around in her new-looking brief-case for some document or other. Addressing Tom, she said: "Tell me, Mr Grantiscombe. Who do the police now think shot the dog? I missed that bit."

Tom's cynical reply: "Very conveniently, the police are saying Rivinni shot the dog."

"And why, Mr Grantiscombe, do they think Rivinni shot the dog?"

"It's rather embarrassing," said Tom (more of a gentleman than I). "It's only a supposition, of course. That's why it will no doubt be glossed over when the inquest resumes."

Rather crisply said: "Mr Grantiscombe, I am not a Dresden figurine. What's the full theory?"

"That the old lady died," said Tom awkwardly, "as the result of physical activity of a kind I won't describe. That result, however, is thought to have frightened Rivinni. He thought he would be blamed for her death. So he decided to dump the body in Willow Tree Lane."

"And how does this relate to the dog?"

"They say the dog probably attacked him as he went down the garden to the service-lane. He must have had a pistol with him while carrying the body. It's presumed that he shot the dog and put it in the back of the van – along with the old lady."

"And how does this theory correspond with the movements of our client on that day?"

"Oh," said Tom, airily cynical by now, "you needn't worry about that. This old school chum will be well able," and he glowered at me, "to match his every single movement to the new theory."

Actually, Tom was absolutely right. I could see, in a flash, how to re-jig every one of the lies I had told. You can't go through what I had gone through (including my sessions with Miss Holland) without acquiring maturity of skill. But I was now determined to rise above all that. I became, as it were, eager for the guillotine.

"Madam," I said, for the second time, "what is the question you are dying to ask me?"

Perusing a document from her brief-case, she was still more preoccupied with Tom than with me.

"Here," she said to him, "is the evidence that Rivinni hated the dog. He told his mates so. He told them that he would like to see it put down. Have the police been able to trace the van yet?"

"Of course not," snapped Tom. "Nor will they ever bother to continue trying," and he looked at his watch. "You have time to catch the next train. Would you like a lift?"

"Thank you," she said, brightly and swiftly returning the document to her newish brief-case.

"Madam," I said again, "what is the question you are dying to ask me? I am prepared to answer it truthfully, I do assure you. It's a far, far better thing that I – "

She interrupted me before I had even got into that famous sentence from that famous story.

"Oh, my goodness! How could I have forgotten such an important question?"

She re-opened her brief-case but hesitatingly thrust her hand inside. She added: "Mr Crackery, I'm hoping you'll allow me to keep the little notes you sent me. May I please keep them?"

She withdrew them from the brief-case and waved them at me so appealingly that I was happily reminded of how young she was.

"Of course, madam," I instantly said.

"I shall always treasure them as a memento of this successful day. But I particularly want to show them to my mother. I would have liked her to have been in court, but I had no idea I would be taking over."

She returned the notes not to her brief-case but to her shoulder hand-bag.

"And please tell your mother," I said, "that I'm very grateful for the way you put my instructions into such brilliant legal shape."

"Oh, I will! Thank you, Mr Crackers – Mr Crackery, I mean."

Tom frowningly intervened to say: "We need to get to the car to be in time for the next train."

He hurried us over the grass, with me carrying my prison-sack like Father Christmas. We reached his car on the far side of the square. He opened the door for my victorious saviour and she said to me: "Goodbye, Mr Crackery. I'm sure we'll meet again soon."

She was wrong about that and I knew it. But I had no feeling of loss. How can anyone have a feeling of loss when they have just realised they no longer have any fear of love?

"One moment, madam," I said. "Is your mother a good cook?"

A little surprised (but only a little), she replied: "I believe her to be a good cook, yes."

I put down my sack and took my wallet from my inside-pocket. "I have here a recipe for a jolly good cheese-rice. Delicious scrunchy bits. Please give it to your mother with my compliments."

"Thank you, Mr Crackery."

Tom saw her into the front seat of the car.

Before getting behind the wheel, he grumpily said to me: "I'm not taking YOU home if that's what you think. Have you money for a taxi?"

"No, Tom. Totally broke."

He thrust a five-pound note upon me and said: "I want that back first thing Monday – no matter how hard up you are. Is that clearly understood?"

"Yes, Tom. Thank you, Tom."

The beautiful barrister lowered her window as he was getting in. She gave me a farewell smile. I smiled back. I heard her say to Tom as he pulled from the kerb: "Was that a quarrel between you? I didn't quite understand it."

"Me neither," was his terse reply.

I stood and gazed after them. Although I was never to see that beautiful barrister again, I did hear from Tom, later, that she getting briefs by the bucketload.

Meanwhile, I was soon hailing a passing taxi.

"Take me home," I ordered.

"Where would that be, sir?"

"Kind Maiden Green, you idiot. Where else?"

I sat in the rear seat with my arm around my sack as if I were with an old sweetheart. Any more thoughts of Sydney Carton? None whatsoever.

At the cottage, the two children were the first to come running down to the gate to greet me.

THE STORY ENDS

Other Books by D.V.Haines

THE SOCIETY FOR BETTER BREAD
and other scripts

These "microphone-exercises" were written for the audio magazines of the sixties and early seventies as well as for the drama-recording groups of the period.

The Society for Better Bread has been performed on stage at various "fringe" venues, beginning with the Royal Court Theatre in 1975, but, technically, it was an experiment with theatrical stereo. Although recording on magnetic tape has long been abandoned, this was a delightful time of many pioneering experiments and is worth remembering.

Also included: some examples of Aural Mime (the telling of stories through sound-effects alone) which were first published in 1967 in *Dramatape Miscellany*.

Publication date to be announced.

ENJOYABLE MOTORING –
A guide to freedom from accident

Have you ever passed your driving-test? If so, how long ago – and do you enjoy your driving as much as you should?

This book unveils the author's many years of private research into the so-called "born" drivers he has met.

How are they able (so magically!) to avoid having accidents? How are they able to concentrate so enjoyably and without any apparent strain whatsoever?

Essentially, this book is about the differences between motor-sport and motoring and how a proper knowledge of the difference can reduce accidents on public roads.

Unfortunatly, the juvenile glorification of fast driving is too insidious for this knowledge to be of interest other than to a minority. We can only hope this minority is in a position to influence others – particularly the young.

Available in print and as an e-book.

TRESSELL AND THE LATE KATHLEEN

As a political agnostic living in Hastings, Mr Haines writes of his personal involvement in the Tressell legend as well his efforts to salvage the Tressell Mural (now in the Hastings Museum). Illustrations (including film and audio recordings) will be posted on a dedicated website in due course.

Publication-date to be announced.

THE STRANGE CASE OF JAMES HADLEY CHASE

A critical and appreciative biography about the highly succesfull writer whose formative years were spent in Hastings (in the town of Robert Tressell). Graham Greene once wrote to him: "You are the greatest living writer walking the earth."
Other fellow-writers were not so kind.

Publication-date to be announced.